MIDTERM REPORT

MIDTERM REPORT

The Class of '65: Chronicles of an American Generation

DAVID WALLECHINSKY

VIKING

VIKING
Viking Penguin Inc., 40 West 23rd Street,
New York, New York 10010, U.S.A.
Penguin Books Ltd, Harmondsworth,
Middlesex, England
Penguin Books Australia Ltd., Ringwood,
Victoria, Australia
Penguin Books Canada Limited, 2801 John Street,
Markham, Ontario, Canada L3R 1B4
Penguin Books (N.Z.) Ltd., 182–190 Wairau Road,
Auckland 10, New Zealand

First published in 1986 by Viking Penguin Inc.
Published simultaneously in Canada

LIBRARY OF CONGRESS CATALOGING IN PUBLICATION DATA
Wallechinsky, David, 1948–
Midterm report.
1. United States—Social conditions—1960–
Case studies.   2. Baby boom generation—United States—
Case studies.   I. Title.
HN59.W26   1986   306'.0973   85-40800
ISBN 0-670-80428-2

Printed in the United States of America by
Haddon Craftsman, Scranton, Pennsylvania
Set in Times Roman

For Aaron,
Class of 2004

Acknowledgments

It would be impossible for me to list all the people who were kind enough to help me while I was working on this book. I would like to express my thanks in particular to the following: Emmit Acterman, Sylvia Anderson, Margaret Bird, Roberta Bleiweiss, Betty Castillo, Al Chan, Kathy and Alan Chapman, Barbara Collins, Barbara Decker, Karen Ehrnman, Winston Evans, Walter Farmer, Joel Franklin, Helen Ginsburg, Pat Gray, Cecily Green, Steve Griffiths, Ada L. Hannibal, Cheryl Herbert, Jane Hill, Jerry Hirata, Nancy Johannes, Linda Johnsen, Carolyn Jonas, Terry and Bill Kerry, Abe Kestenbaum, Connie Leshin, Antonietta Lopez, Josef Marc, Frances Marquez, Ann McColaugh, Michael Medved, Jan Miller, Richard Percy, Kathy Perez, Alice Pistasio, Helen Pollicove, Linda Rader, Judith Regan, Alan Robbins, Sgt. Gerald W. Rogers, Wally Rosenblum, Rita Rush, Joanna Sand, Carol Saturansky, Judy and Darrell Schmidt, Major Keith Schneider, Robert Schwartz, Sally Schwarz, Tony Serra, Ellen Shelley, Lt. Col. J. R. Shields, Kay Simmons, Sherri Spector, Jason Squire, Margaret Traudt, Charles Verrill, Ed Victor, Tony Walker, Amy Wallace, Irving Wallace, Sylvia Wallace, Flora Chavez Wallechinsky, Tim Wernette, Ceal Williams, Marjory Wolfe and, especially, to Patricia Begalla and Sandy Ryan, without whose help the manuscript could never have been completed. And a final debt of gratitude for the hospitality provided to me by the Normal *Community* High School Class of 1965.

CONTENTS

MIDTERM REPORT

THE CLASS OF '65

It was a special time to be alive. The war was over. The fear and the killing were no more. The healing and rebuilding could begin.

In Europe, World War II had left behind such devastation that it would be another five years before the populace felt settled enough to devote itself to serious baby-making. But in those countries that had not become battlegrounds, such as the United States, Canada, Australia, and New Zealand, there was an immediate baby boom.

Loss of life had been great, but Americans came out of the war not only as winners but with a worldwide reputation as liberators, as a people who had combined strength and intelligence to further the cause of freedom.

It was a time to be proud. It was a time to feel good about the future. It was a time to settle down and raise a family. The high-school class of 1965, most of whose members were born in 1947, was conceived in this spirit of celebration and optimism. Americans were so confident, so hopeful, so determined to make up for lost time, that the birth rate in 1947 was higher than at any time since the post–World War I baby boom of 1921. The 1947 rate of 26.6 births per 1000 has not been approached since then.

Although all the stories in this book are told by people who graduated from high school in 1965, in spirit it describes the generation of the early baby boomers, graduates of 1964 to about 1970, who were born between 1946 and 1952. It was these young people who graduated into an era of conscription, war, and social change.

Every generation is shaped by the period in which it comes of age. For example, when the class of *1955* entered the adult world, there was no war, the economy was booming, jobs were relatively plentiful. Life proceeded in a normal fashion.

The class of *1935,* on the other hand, grew up in the midst of a worldwide depression, which was followed by the deadliest and most far-reaching war the world had ever seen. After fifteen years of uncertainty, the prosperity that followed that war was greatly appreciated— like a dream come true.

Despite all the talk of a "generation gap," the class of *1965*, 3.8 million strong, has more in common with their parents' generation than with the generations in between. Like that of the '30s, the generation of the '60s came of age in a world filled with turmoil and change. It was the first generation to grow up with the threat of nuclear war, the first to grow up with television, the first to grow up with space flights, rock-and-roll, oral contraceptives, and LSD.

In 1976, when Michael Medved and I wrote *What Really Happened to the Class of '65?*, a study of our own high-school class ten years after graduation, we used as our point of departure the January 29, 1965, cover story from *Time* magazine, entitled "Today's Teenagers: On the Fringe of a Golden Era." The article hailed the good fortune of the high-school class of 1965, benefactors of an explosion of support for teachers and schools and for education. *Time* predicted a glorious future filled with exciting careers. It also announced, "The classic conflict between parents and children is letting up." *Time* turned out to be a bit off the mark. The classic conflict between parents and children would heat up almost immediately.

Within a month of graduation the first U.S. combat offensive was launched in Vietnam. One month later draft calls were doubled. Two weeks after that came the Watts Uprising—rioting in a black section of Los Angeles. Before the year was out there were antiwar rallies and draft-card burnings. The next five years in particular were characterized by a questioning of established authority in all aspects of life.

Ten more years having passed since the publication of *What Really Happened to the Class of '65?*, I have decided to study the generation once again. This time, instead of limiting myself to one high school, I have traveled all over the country and talked with and interviewed men and women from a very wide range of backgrounds. I listened to career military officers and draft resisters, fundamentalist preachers and human-rights activists, farmers, lawyers, factory workers, office workers, housewives, entrepreneurs, unemployed auto workers, and many others. Some people were members of graduating classes as large as 1800. Others came from classes as small as eight. Only a small percentage of the people I spoke with tell their stories in this book.

The United States is a vast country of enormous diversity. During one twenty-four-hour period I woke up on the floor at a commune, flew to New York City, rode to the top of the World Trade Center, and sat down with a multimillionaire.

For all their differences, there is one thing that all the people in this book have in common: I liked them. Readers looking for biting criticisms of individual lives or acid-tongued remarks will have to look elsewhere. I enjoyed visiting with each man and woman in this book and would gladly socialize with them again. This is not to say that I agreed with everything they said. Indeed, I had some healthy arguments with a number of people, particularly about politics. But I would rather spend an evening with someone who has put a lot of thought into forming an opinion which opposes mine than with someone who follows the beaten path or who just doesn't care.

I have not tried to produce a scientific study based on a statistically accurate sampling of the population. In fact, this is not even an objective study. I am a very subjective person. Although I have attempted to restrain myself from bludgeoning the reader with my opinions, I also have not hesitated to express them.

I would like to make clear that I do not find the generation of the '60s to be better or worse than any other generation. I do believe it is an intriguing generation, which found itself on the cutting edge of a period of confrontation, questioning, and transformation.

I learned early on that members of the generation fall into three categories. There is a sizable minority who were virtually unaffected by the events and social movements of the '60s, another sizable minority whose lives were radically and permanently altered by those events and movements, and a plurality who were touched by it all and moved but who went on to "normal" lives, although they would never forget what they saw and heard and felt. I have made a point of ensuring that each of these categories is properly represented.

I have chosen the title *Midterm Report* because the class of '65 has now reached the halfway point in its journey through life. It is an appropriate time not only to reflect on the sometimes frantic years that have gone by but to look ahead to the even richer years that are to come.

Contrary to the expectations of others, I did not find a generation of hippies turned yuppies and I did not find a generation of self-indulgent acquirers. What I did find was far more complex and far more provocative, as I believe the stories that follow well illustrate.

THE PROM QUEEN:
Susan Mason

As I began my journey among the members of the class of '65, I knew that I would encounter an enormous number of people whose lives were shaped by the diverse and explosive events of the '60s and early '70s and whose experiences would have been completely different had they been born only a few years earlier or later. It seemed to me proper to gain some early perspective by meeting class of '65 graduates whose lives were basically unaffected by the turmoil of the era, people whose experiences would be easily recognized by Americans of all generations. Put simply, I wanted to talk with "normal" people.

I first heard about Normal High School from a bookstore clerk in Minneapolis, who told me somewhat sheepishly, but with much good humor, about the mixed blessings of growing up in a town called "Normal." He found it particularly tedious to have to sit through endless "normal" jokes whenever professional comedians came to town.

I was sufficiently intrigued to follow up by contacting several members of the class-reunion committee of the Normal High School class of '65. Right at the start they made it very clear to me that the proper name was Normal Community High School, and that it wasn't just comedians who made "normal" jokes. Even visiting rock singers and musicians could not resist taking the microphone and blurting out a few "normal" one-liners.

And yet, in talking with these fine people, there was no question that Normal really was outstandingly normal. There was very little evidence of the sex, drugs, rock-and-roll, and radical politics that swept through other parts of the country.

4

As I learned more and more about the 268 graduates, I kept hearing over and over again about Sue Pearcy. She was beautiful, intelligent, well liked—clearly one of the most popular girls in the class. Sue Pearcy, now Susan Mason, seemed the right person for me to start with.

We met in Louisville, Kentucky, where Susan had been living for more than fifteen years. She was still beautiful, still bright, still gregarious. As it developed, her life was a reminder that even "Normal" people, basically untouched by the tumult of the times, are sometimes confronted with unexpected obstacles that are far, far from being normal.

My father was a college student in Galesburg, Illinois, when I was born. When I was two years old he graduated from college and became a sales representative for the Kentucky Lithography Company. That's when we moved to Normal. We were not wealthy, but we were very well off for that community. I mean, we belonged to the country club. I always wanted to go to the public pool because that's where most of my friends were. The country club was in Bloomington, so I had my Bloomington friends and my high-school friends.

I have fond memories of high school. I had lots of dates, lots of friends. It was a pretty wholesome time. There was no drinking, no drugs. If there was drinking, I think the guys sometimes would drink beer, but never with the girls. It was a really good time, and my parents were very, very involved in my life and my sisters' and my brother's lives. I was the oldest of four.

I remember going on dates before I could drive or my dates could drive. Then when we turned sixteen—that car sure makes a difference! A lot more freedom, a lot more responsibility. I could always have my boyfriends over to the house. My mother used to say, "Please don't park out in the country; park in the driveway and I'll leave the lights out." She was so afraid that something horrible would happen to me out in the country, but she said the driveway was long enough that we could park at the end. They were really super parents and still are.

I had a really good, healthy attitude about sex, but I was determined I was going to be a virgin when I got married. I remember my mother saying to me, "The feelings that you have are wonderful and they're normal and don't feel guilty because you *want* to. But just keep in mind that there goes along with it some responsibility. You're dealing with another human, and you could get pregnant. Then there would be a third human being."

I was always nominated for the homecoming queen and prom queen. There seemed to be about five or six of us that were always the same ones nominated. I was prom queen, junior year. I remember standing up there on that stage. They walk behind you. And I thought, this isn't really going to happen, and sure enough, I was chosen. My parents were there. My mother was a fashion designer and she taught me how to sew and from the sixth grade I made most of my clothes, and I always made my prom dresses. Well, the dress I made that year was yellow satin and it had no back in it at all. It was funny because the guys would go to dance with me and they didn't know where to put their hands. After that, when I was crowned prom queen, it was kind of a fairy-tale feeling, kind of magic fun.

The next year I had to go back and crown the next prom queen—and I didn't have a date. My mother said, "You are *going*. You can't not show up! If your dad has to take you, you'll go." I was getting pretty desperate, so I said, Gee, I've got to do something. I got an old boyfriend to take me. He said he wouldn't because he was mad at me, but then he did take me.

Graduation was kind of a bittersweet thing. There was a sadness there about it being all over, kind of nostalgic. Every time I hear "Pomp and Circumstance," I just start crying—still. It's very sentimental, I'm sure, to a lot of people. But I was really excited about college and I was glad to be moving on.

I was a good student, but it wasn't too hard for me. I really didn't study much at all. I thought it would be really neat to go to college in California. My dad said, "You can go anywhere you want, but if you go someplace like California, we'll only see you in the summer. I can't fly you back for Thanksgiving and Christmas." That made my decision right there, because I knew I could not stand to be away from my family that long. So I chose Southern Illinois University in Carbondale. My aunt, my mother's sister, had gone there and I am very impressed with her, and I had been down there and visited the campus. Academically, Southern was a good school, but it was also known as a party school, a lot of fun. I was glad to go away to school, but maybe because I knew I could get home very easily. All I had to do was get on the Illinois Central Railroad and straight up to Champaign, and my dad or mom would pick me up.

My major was interior design. Actually, I have a degree in home economics with a specialization in interior design. I really didn't know much about it until I got into it, but I did like it. My aunt had been a member of Sigma Kappa sorority and I became a Sigma Kappa. It was really a very, very neat experience. Lots of good, good friends. To go beyond being a pledge and actually become a bona fide member of the sorority, you had to make a certain grade average, which I think is good. The first quarter I pledged I didn't make grades, so I had to try again, and I did it. I made my grades. Then, the third quarter, I made a four-point—straight A's. I can remember I had come back from my last test and I walked out and thought, I did it. You know how you just know when you've done well. Then I was facing coming back to the sorority house and gathering my stuff up and catching the train, to go home. And as I walked around the corner, my mother's car was sitting in front of the sorority house. I can remember like a kid jumping up in the air and screaming and running in there. It was just a really neat time. I'll never forget that.

I dated a lot the first couple years at Southern. I worked at the information desk at the University Center. It was the best job on campus. I saw everybody and everybody saw me. That's the way I met my husband. The way he tells it, he saw me there and he told a friend of his that he was going to marry me. I remember him coming up (I didn't really know who he was) and acting kind of cocky and abrasive. He threw his change on the counter and I said, "Don't you ever do that again." I was mad at him for being cocky. He was on the baseball team at SIU. He had already signed his professional contract. One of the pledges in my sorority was dating a friend of his on the baseball team and he told her that he wanted to take me out. I was heavy into this other fellow that was singing to me and reading and writing poetry, so I said, "No, I'm not interested."

Then I broke up with the other fellow and I said, "Well, you know, I'd like to go out." I don't know if I was on the rebound or what, but we went out all the time. We dated constantly, saw each other every day. I met him in January of '68 and we were engaged in February. Isn't that crazy? I was very sensible and very logical and very level-headed, very mature. I think that I was so sensible and level-headed and mature that I thought I was boring. I really did. And the man I married, he's the opposite end of the scale. Very fun-loving. You know, a likable personality, always kidding around. And I think that's what attracted me to him.

That summer he played baseball in Winston-Salem, North Carolina, for the Boston Red Sox's Class-A farm team. He left for spring training in April; I saw him one weekend in May and ten days before the wedding in September. It's incredible! It's so funny; I talk to my friends and so many of them did the same thing. You know some people say, "If I had to do it over again, I'd do exactly the same thing." I *know* I would not do what I did. I was still a virgin when I got married. So my first sexual experience was on my wedding night. It was not spontaneous and it was really not pleasant. It was like, Okay, now we really know we have to do it. It was not fun.

I finished my senior year at SIU and graduated. I was really down about my college years being over. I think in terms of my fun college years being over after my junior year, when I got married. I didn't get to fulfill everything I wanted. I missed a lot that senior year. I have, to this day—and it still happens to me—a recurring dream, I call it a nightmare, that it's the last day of my senior year in college and I don't want it to be over. It was really special, and yet I wouldn't want to go back.

The first year my husband and I were married, he played in Pittsfield, Massachusetts, which was Double-A ball, and the next year he moved up to Triple-A ball and we spent four years here in Louisville. Coincidentally, my parents had moved to Louisville just before I got married, because my dad became president of Kentucky Lithography. As we were growing up, he had bought stock in the company.

I didn't work until we moved to Louisville. That's when I contacted a friend who got me a job at a local department store. I started working in the silver department of the store and moved into training in the drapery department, then into the design department, and was there for a couple of years. Then I became pregnant with my son. That was back in the days when at six months you had to quit. In fact I got special permission to work an extra month. I think I had to sign something that if anything happened, I wouldn't sue the store. Really crazy.

When Shad was ten months old, the man who owned the team here in Louisville sold it to a fellow in Pawtucket, Rhode Island, a little industrial town. So we moved out there and that was a very, very hard time. At least half the time the players are on a road trip, and, like, for two weeks at a time. I just about lost my mind. If I had been in a familiar place with my friends and family, it would have been fine. But out east the people I ran into were not terribly friendly. It was very hard to get to know people. So that was a tough time and I was very isolated. I loved being a mother and loved having a baby, but he couldn't talk. I would call my parents and say, "I'm just calling to see if I can carry on a conversation with another adult."

After that year in Pawtucket, we came back to Louisville, and of course I didn't have a job and my husband decided he was going to try and find a job in Louisville and maybe something more permanent than major-league baseball. It was really rough. He tried insurance for a while, but didn't like that, and then started training with a bank and ended up in the leasing department.

Then I went to work for one of the designers from the department store who had gone off on his own and opened up a shop in a quaint little shopping center. I worked for him a couple of days a week, which was really nice. It was enough to make my car payment so we could have our second car, and pay the babysitter. It was great. Then I left him and went with E. B. Schilling, a wonderful woman, and her design firm.

When Shad was about five years old, I became pregnant again. Looking back on when Shad was born, it was so frightening because I didn't know what was going on. I also think that it's extremely cruel for the father to be sitting off somewhere by himself while his wife is in absolute pain. They had given me Demerol the first time, but Demerol doesn't take away the pain; it just renders you incapable of dealing with it. I had talked to some people who had had natural childbirth and I thought, well, if I draw my husband into it and he's an active participant . . . and he was. He was thrilled to death. My daughter, Kendall, was born in the hospital, but when people ask me who delivered my baby, I say, "We did."

That was a really special time in our lives, really special. I was really close to him and we did this thing together, but it wasn't too long after Kendall was born that I began to suspect my husband of having this affair with my best friend. It's funny: I don't like to look back and say I don't think we had a really good marriage. We had an okay marriage. We had a good life and I really think I loved him; I really do. I certainly don't now. But I really felt like he absolutely thought I was terrific . . . and that's a nice feeling.

Shad was very upset about the divorce. He was six at the time. But he was a very mature little boy and he coped pretty well; he really did. I had made up my mind I was going to try to be a stable person, and I was. Then after a period of time I began to realize that Shad probably thought I was totally unaffected by all this. I'd lost twenty-six pounds in two months. I'd become emaciated. I couldn't eat. But he didn't know any of that. So I talked to him and told him, "You need to know that I have hurt here, and I have suffered, but I didn't want you to see it." So as a result we got really close. It was a slow, gradual process. I just felt like the only way I was going to communicate with him was to let him know how I feel.

Meanwhile, it was strange being suddenly single. I've never felt so disoriented in my life. It was like being born in one generation and waking up in another one. Here I was a grown woman with two children, faced with dating. I had this horrible fear that I was going to shrivel away and die and become a boring spinster-type person. And that really scared me, because I think women, especially, are probably at the peak of their sexuality in their middle thirties to middle forties. So here I was at my peak. I mean, you realize that dating when you're thirty-two isn't what it was when you were in high school.

So that was very strange. But I decided that I was not going to feel strange for very long. I just made up my mind to do like I do everything else—forge ahead. So I called up all my friends and said, "I want you all to fix me up with everyone you can think of, because I'm going to get over this hurdle fast." One more thing I had to face was pregnancy. I knew I didn't want any more children, so I had my tubes tied. My dad took me to the hospital. I thought, I'm not going to keep this a secret from him. Since then I've had a few relationships with guys that have been really nice.

My husband and I were divorced in May of 1980 and he and the other gal got married in January of '81. I worked full-time for E. B. Schilling for a while, but I could not make ends meet. It was a great job, but I got paid by commission, and only when my customers paid their bills. I would go three months with nothing sometimes. My parents were having to help me out. So I got a job with Kentucky Lithography and I've been working there ever since. I was in sales for a while, customer service, a little bit of everything. Now I'm in the accounting department. I do accounts payable.

In August of '81, Shad was having what I thought were emotional problems. He was throwing up sporadically, and I kept a diary because I was trying to find some pattern to it. The pediatrician couldn't find a reason until finally . . . there's an instrument they can use to look into the base of the eye, and there's a round disk that should be very clear, very precise, and it was fuzzy with pressure—pressure building in his head causing this disk of his eye to not be precise and clear. So the doctor said, "There's a list a mile long that could make a kid throw up." He sent us to the neurologist. He checked him out and called me into his office and I said, "Do you want to see this diary, this history?"

And he said, "I don't need to see it. There's something wrong. His EEG is not normal." And I'll never forget, he sat there and looked at me and he just held my eyes—like he was giving a little bit at a time to see what my reaction was. And he said, "Do you understand what I'm saying to you?" He really handled it very well. Fortunately for me, I was dating someone at the time who was very supportive and took a week off from work. He was by my side every minute. Now I *will* have to say, he's kind of a caped-crusader type. Once the crisis was over, there wasn't a whole lot . . .

This was on a Monday. The neurologist said we want Shad to check in the hospital that night and he is to have a CAT scan the next morning. One o'clock, next day, Tuesday, we find that he has a tumor the size of an egg behind the stem of the brain, which is a very difficult spot to get to. Shad's father was really upset and we were both crying. It was really horrible. I went into the room where Shad was and said, "Shad, there's something in your head, that's growing in your head, that should not be there. And they are going to have to do an operation and take it out." Oh, we had conversations about death, what it's like to die. He was so mature. He kept asking a lot of questions.

He had surgery on Friday. The only time in my life that I have become physically ill without really being sick was the day before the surgery. I had such incredible stomach pains I could hardly walk. The operation was about five or six hours long. He did very well. I'll never forget, they let us see him and we walked into intensive care and my ex-husband said, "Do you know who's here?" And he said, "Mommy and Daddy," and we just lost it.

We used to ask him things like "What day is it?" Everything centered around the baseball All-Star game because the players had had a strike that year and it was late. So we'd say, "When is the All-Star game?" and he'd tell us. We used things like that to keep his mind working and functioning in reality. And he recovered very well from the surgery—except physically. For two weeks there was a lot of rage, disorientation, yelling, screaming. I just attribute it to the fact that they had to go through the stem of the brain to get to this tumor and every pathway from the brain to the body is there. That's where your rage centers are—everything. And I really think it just took a lot for those wires to get sorted out. We didn't realize it at the time. We were very concerned with this disorientation.

When he became more conscious he was talking normally, but he couldn't see very well. It became apparent that his whole right side was not working well at all. He was taking radiation, lost all his hair. He had to go through physical therapy. He had to learn how to crawl, walk, tie his shoes, all over again.

I didn't work for the whole time. My dad was still at the company, and they continued to pay me. I just really lived and breathed getting Shad back on his feet. It was really hard, but he finally got through the radiation and went back to school. He was going half days. He couldn't write with his right hand. He trained himself to write with his left hand. His penmanship was gorgeous, excellent student, just coped. The kids would carry his books. The kids were super.

He went on to play indoor soccer. His coach didn't even know he'd had a problem. Next summer he played baseball with a team that he had played with before. He was a superstar before. He had his dad's genes. That's probably why he compensated so beautifully and came back so well. He couldn't play very well, but the kids would pick up the slack for him. Other parents would tell me, they'd come home and say, "You know, Shad almost goofed today, but we took care of it." That's neat. And they won the championship that year, which was even more special.

The next year he had to move up to an older group, the eleven-, twelve-, thirteen-year-olds. More competitive. Nobody wanted Shad because they all wanted to win. But one coach said, "I will take any kid who wants to play baseball." And they won the championship that year too. That was in June, July. He was not looking as coordinated to me then, but I thought, Oh, well, he's going to be okay. Then, in August, almost two years to the day of the first operation, he had a recurrence in the middle of very, very aggressive chemotherapy. And he developed a tumor, a large one, on his right side, in the temporal lobe. Really big.

The surgeon told us he would need another operation. He would survive the surgery and we could do some preventive measures, but he told us then that Shad would not live. It was my theory that until we knew for *sure* that he was going to die, that he didn't need to be told. I mean, we're all going to die someday. That was my feeling.

So after the operation the doctor told us, "We got it all, but we will have to put a burr hole in his head with a little plastic bubble," that his hair would grow over. They put chemotherapy directly into his spinal fluid. That's where the cells are contained. And he developed a tumor right after that in his back and in between his shoulder blades. And he did radiation again and also another two types of chemotherapy. This kind, in his veins, made him throw up for six to eight hours. And I decided at that point we were going to need some help with this. So I contacted a wonderful psychologist my husband and I had gone to a couple times for marriage counseling. He saw Shad on a regular basis, and I would talk to the doctor, too, about coping.

The last year of his life, Shad was in and out of school. He couldn't walk. He had moved up to the middle school. It was a three-story school with stairs to climb. He did it. I don't know how he did it. It took a great deal of time, but he did it. This psychologist just worked with him, and then he worked with me, too. Then, in May, Shad was having behavioral problems and personality change, really bad. So we ended up in the psychologist's office, the three of us, Shad's father and I and Shad.

I said, "I don't know what's causing you to be this way, Shad, but you're pushing away everyone who loves you. I love you very much, but I don't understand what you're doing, or why you're doing it." Well, ultimately, it was because the tumors were back in places in his brain and altering his personality.

After this, they do a CAT scan and it's back, it's bad, it's everywhere, and he has a couple of months. We are in the doctor's office. At this point my husband told Shad the tumors were back.

Shad and I left and went straight over to the chemotherapy doctor's office. I had to get some medicine over there, and I wanted to see this one nurse we had become close to. And Shad was raging. Just in a rage in the lobby, and he said, "Why should I even bother to go to school if I'm going to die?" So from that point on we talked about dying, not him dying, but about death. And we had a lot of good communication, but at the same time, he was disoriented.

We had Hospice, which is a program where a nurse is assigned to the patient and the family. They have volunteers, and they help you work through a terminal illness. We had a wonderful, darling young nurse, and she walked in the door the first day, and Shad walked up and put his arms up and said, "I'll take you, any day." Really neat. He stayed at home. I told Shad's father that he and his wife could come anytime they wanted, and they did.

Two of Shad's buddies continued to come and visit him . . . this is going to break me up . . . this one friend of his was able to tell him how much he meant to him. I wasn't there that night. The mother was there.

She said, "You would not have believed it. It was really something. He said, 'I am glad you were my friend.' "

Kendall was six years old. She was very involved in Shad's care because he was at home. She helped him with his medicine. We told her that he was going to die. One day she walked in and he was in bed in the den where he died—he did not ever get up out of that bed again after about June—and she looked right at him and said, "God, Shad, you don't look like you're going to die." It was just amazing, the honesty.

We talked, two weeks before he died, about him dying. He had been disoriented. He didn't know where he was half the time. And he said, "Mom, am I dying?" And I said, "Yes, you are." And he said, "I don't want to do it." And I said, "You don't have to do anything. It'll just happen."

Then about a week later, he said, "Mom, would you please get me a knife?" And I said, "Why?" And he said, "I want to kill myself." And I said, "I don't believe in that. And the only thing I can tell you is that your mind is ready and your body's not. And until they come together, I'll make you as comfortable as I possibly can." He suffered a lot, but he handled it beautifully. He had problems, but he was very positive.

The nice thing about Hospice is the nurse came in and said, "He's going to die today." Okay, now we can get everything ready here. Kendall was going to go swimming. And I said, "Kendall, Shad is going to die today." She knew he was going to die at home. We talked and prepared a lot. I had told her what I felt death was.

I said, "Do you want to go swimming?" And she said, "Well . . ." She was very concerned with him being taken out of the house without her seeing him. I said, "Well, if he dies, I can get you home." That took care of it. She could go swimming, but she knew I'd get her home to see him before he left the house. She hadn't been gone twenty minutes and I had to call her back.

Shad's greatest gift to me was that he waited until we were alone before he died. I was alone with him, and I knew he was about to take his last breath, and I called my parents and a very dear friend who were in the next room. And it was very peaceful. A very peaceful end. Shad's father had gone out, and he came back shortly after, and he carried Kendall into the room. I took her in my arms, and I sat her down in front of Shad and I said, "Do you want to touch him?" She said, "No." And I said, "I want you to look at his chest." One night she had said, "Mom, you know he's still alive because his chest is moving up and down." So I said, "Look at his chest. The life has gone from his body, and right now I'm sure he's up there asking, 'Where do they keep the baseball bats and soccer balls?' "

She kind of buried her head in my shoulder and I walked her out of the room, and she said, "I wanna go back and go swimming," which is normal. Kids grieve in very short intervals. But she talks to me about him all the time. She misses him terribly. We talk a lot, usually at night when she's getting ready to go to bed. She talks about how she misses him. She thinks he's coming back. She doesn't really, but she wants to believe that, because kids believe in magic. You know, in TV cartoons a character's flat. Then he gets up and walks off.

When I was a kid, I imagined God was this man dressed up in a white suit, sitting on a white throne, and he had a kind of a mauvy-colored shirt on and white tie and wire-framed glasses, and he gave every kid Dentyne gum. Now I believe God is inside me, that God is there to help you get through the tough times. God is this strength inside of me that allows me to cope.

I walked in the first day at the funeral home, before visitation. I hadn't seen Shad since he died, and I was so scared. And I walked in and I looked at him—whew, what a relief! He was not there. That part of him that I loved was in some special place, and he was not there. I don't go out to the cemetery, because he's not there.

I believe that there is another dimension beyond this earth. I think we spend hell on earth, and when we die, I think we meet our Maker. I really think that everybody's "up there"; I mean here, everywhere. For example, two weeks before Shad died, this woman I'd worked for, E. B. Schilling—she had helped me a lot through my divorce—she died of cancer. And I imagined her there waiting for him, and I told her son, who's a good friend of mine, I said, "I'm so glad she went first because she had three boys and she knows how to take care of boys. I just feel like she's there. I think everybody that's ever died is there. I feel really close to Shad all the time—all the time. I talk to him all the time and I think Shad hears every word I say. I believe that he's going to somehow make some communication with me, in a dream or whatever, and I hope he does.

I truly believe that Shad will live forever, and that all of us will live forever. We will not ever truly die.

It was awkward at first after Shad died. You don't know how to act. My parents both had moved in with me and were incredibly supportive, and all these people. Then, all of a sudden, the funeral's over, everybody's gone, and it's just me and Kendall. Two weeks after Shad died, I said to her, "You know we can get in the car and go anywhere we want to." And she said, "We can? Well, let's go."

She's not doing too well in first grade. I mean, her brother died on the 15th of August, and the following week she goes to first grade. Her teacher was wonderful. She said, "Ah, leave her alone. She's a very smart little girl. She just can't concentrate long enough to finish an assignment." I certainly didn't do what I was supposed to do for the first three or four months after he died. I didn't clean my house. I went to parties. I boogied until four or five in the morning. It was like I had to do all these things, feel this freedom—and I thought, well, Kendall's got to feel the same way too.

Right now I choose not to make any really monumental changes. I'd just like a little boring, everyday life for a while. And a little calmness. I think I would like to be married again. I miss having the companionship of a male. However, I really enjoy my independence.

For me to have asked and received as much as I did from other people, I will never, ever, pay back what I've received. I hope I never know someone who needs that kind of support, but you can be sure if they do, I'm going to be there.

THE CLASS CLOWN:

John Higgins

One day, I was perusing a county-by-county breakdown of the vote totals of the four leading candidates in the 1980 presidential election when I thought it might prove interesting to determine which single county in the United States most closely approximated the results of the nation as a whole. After a couple hours of scanning and computing, I came up with the winner: Greene County, Ohio.

I spent my first two days in Greene County just driving around, stopping here and there to talk and listen. The basically rural, small-town Republican electorate of Greene County was spiced up by the inclusion of an air-force base, a couple of suburbs of Dayton, a black university, and, incongruously, Antioch College, a progressive institution considered positively communistic by some of the older citizens of the county.

Coincidentally, Greene County is represented in the U.S. Congress by a graduate of the class of '65, Michael DeWine. Mention of Mr. DeWine elicited a wide range of responses. As a Reaganite Republican, he was praised for his clean-cut, all-American, family-man image. Some Greene County voters were disturbed, however, by his voting record, and described him as "just to the right of Attila the Hun."

The county seat of Xenia is a classic American heartland small town, immortalized in Helen Santmyer's best-selling novel, . . . And Ladies of the Club. *I spoke with several members of Xenia High School's class of '65, and was assured that if I wanted a realistic, insightful view of what it was like to grow up in the '60s in a typical American town, I should get together with a fellow named John Higgins.*

I reached John by telephone, at his home in suburban Dayton, and he invited me to join him for dinner. When I explained that I was a vege-

17

tarian, and that I had been having a difficult time meeting my dietary needs while staying in a motel in Greene County, he offered to take me to a health-food store and allowed me to use his kitchen to prepare a much-needed home-cooked meal.

John watched with curiosity and skepticism as I boiled some brown rice and sautéed vegetables and tofu (soybean curd). While we waited, John played with his huge, blind Springer spaniel, Newport, and explained to me that I was not the first to be attracted to his part of the country by its "typicalness." In fact, every marketer of consumer goods in the nation seemed to descend on Dayton with new products before trying them out on the rest of us.

When dinner was ready, John politely ate his share, and then spent the rest of the evening mercilessly mocking me for eating "toe food." I finally got him to stop by turning on my tape recorder, shoving a microphone in his face, and asking him how long his family had lived in Xenia.

My family's been around Xenia for a long time. My great-grandfather on my father's side was a stonemason and a builder who helped design and build the old courthouse in the center of the city. His son, my grandfather, was postmaster for Greene County, and his brother was the editor of the newspaper in Xenia for sixty-two years. My mother's father was the founder of a local bank. He died before I was born, but I've read about him in books. He ran a bank for probably thirty years on a handshake and a man's word. In today's world it's not a very good way to make a living. It just doesn't work anymore. But I have always admired a man who could trust another man for his word on a handshake and still make a living.

My father was vice-president in charge of sales for a fairly large-volume cement company. He was the kind of guy that everybody knew—an affable type of guy. He was good with my older brother and me. He was not a drinker or a womanizer. He was home every night with us. So I have fond memories of my father. He died of a heart attack when I was ten years old. My mother never let us know that she was hurt by it. She never remarried. It just wasn't the thing to do in a small town. She is a remarkably strong woman and she was always mother and father to Tom and me. My disdain for giving up most certainly came from her. Through cancer, heart attacks, and numerous other problems, she always stood strong.

My older brother, Tom, whom I admire very much, still lives in Xenia, as does my mother. Tom has been married to the same woman since 1967, and he is a real family man. Our father was gone by the time we were active in sports, and although Mother attended our football games and baseball games, it's different than having your dad there. Maybe it's because of this that Tom very seldom, if ever, misses any activity either of his two sons are involved in. I think that's nice.

My mother taught school for thirty years and I think she saved every dime she ever saw. A few years ago I took her to the hospital and they wouldn't let her sign for her own financial responsibility because she was an unemployed sixty-five-year-old woman. So I had to sign a paper saying that if anything happened, I'd pay for it. My mother looked at me and just cracked up. She thought that was the funniest thing in the world.

High school was a time of experience, experiments, learning, fun, irresponsibility, friendships that you thought would last forever. I liked high school. I ran with the popular crowd and did all the fun things. I got away with more because I was one of the few kids that didn't have a father. I was also a letterman on the golf team, a soft spot for our principal, who was a total golf addict. Any trip to his office quickly turned to discussion about my game. I always used to take the blame for all the shit whenever we used to get into trouble, because I wouldn't get punished. My mother was a small woman, so what could she do? So anytime we had any major problems, it was always Higgins that did it. My mother always stuck up for me anyway. I could do no wrong.

I remember back in 1964, when Goldwater was running against Johnson, the high school came up with the idea that the student body should experience the democratic process as it actually takes place in a national election. Various students would act as state delegates and candidates. Conventions would be held, politics would be discussed, a presidential campaign would be carried out. So they were running us through this horseshit, and they had invited the local media to see what wonderful students Xenia High School had, what a grasp of the system they had, and how much a part of it they would grow up to be.

People were making speeches about why Goldwater should be president. People were making speeches why Johnson should be president. Well, we figured a fucking pumpkin should be president! I think it was David Janssen's idea. So we started our own party: the Great Pumpkin party. In the middle of this great campaign, with the newspapers there and the local television stations filming this wonderful student enactment of the actual campaign, we stormed into the room with our pumpkin, took the podium, and declared the pumpkin a candidate for president of the United States! He was going to be our man. We had him on a broomstick. It caused great embarrassment to the powers that be at the school. I think we got suspended for three days. But the pumpkin won! The pumpkin was very well accepted by the student body. It did much better than Goldwater and a hell of a lot better than Lyndon Johnson! I think it was the rural vote that pushed him over the top.

We used to have parties sanctioned by our parents. Your parents would take you to the party, and you'd go down in the basement and play music. Then the parents would leave you alone and you'd turn the lights off and you would make out. It was great. You didn't really know what was at the other end of that trip, but you had such a wonderful time searching. That was before we had cars. Cars opened up a whole new world. I'm still tied up with cars. With cars nobody knew you didn't really get laid. Some guy would go out on a date and come back and you'd say, "Well, did you fuck her or what?" The reply was always, "Well, you know." "Well, you know" covered a lot of territory. I'm pretty sure none of us were actually "doing it," but it was important to imply, without actually admitting anything.

Cars were a big deal. Anybody who had a car was cool. He was your friend whether you liked him or not. My mother always bought cars that we wouldn't like to drive. I remember leaving the house, driving two or three blocks, and taking all the hubcaps off the car and putting them in the trunk. If you had your own car you never had hubcaps on it, and it was very uncool to be driving your mother's car. And you'd take the air cleaner off because when you accelerated, it made a great, big, throaty noise. Then they knew that it was *definitely* not your mother's car. Of course, looking back, it was such a little town, obviously everybody knew whose goddamn car it was.

The social center for us once we got mobilized was the drive-in, where they had carhops and microphones where you called in your food. If some nice girls would ride by, you'd chase them in the car and try and talk to them. But you'd always end up back at the drive-in.

But cars opened up a whole new world. You could go other places. Xenia was fairly remote. If you ever wanted to go clear over to Dayton, it was a monumental task, probably fifteen miles away. Dayton was the real world. Dayton had more than one high school. There were girls that you might be able to conceivably do something with. You knew all the girls at home, and you'd already tried and couldn't. You could even go as far as Columbus. Shit, that was the other side of the earth. It's amazing the miles you could put on your parents' little car on a Friday or Saturday night and not have them even know it.

I remember when we discovered beer, how great that was. We thought that was very mature. They used to have dances at the YMCA after all the football and basketball games. I can remember six of us getting in a car and finding someone to buy us a six-pack, or maybe an eight-pack, of beer. This is for six people. We would ride around in the country in the car, talking about getting to the dance, getting this girl, getting that girl, drinking the beer. We didn't even like the beer, but it was very cool to drink beer, so you'd drink maybe half your beer and then try to throw it out the window. The beer can made a different noise if it was empty or still half full. I can remember great arguments we used to have as to whether that can that just went out the window still had beer in it.

"Sure that wasn't a full can?"

"No way, man. That was suds!"

When you got to the dance it was very, very cool in our minds to have beer on your breath. So if there was a girl that you wanted to impress, you'd immediately blow your breath all over her and let her know you had had many beers, when in fact you'd had maybe half a can. But you acted drunk, hoping that the girl would think, "This guy is very mature and I really like him."

These dances were great! We couldn't wait to slow-dance, but it was embarrassing to "get a chubby" from rubbing up against the girls.

I thought that graduation was something I should remember for the rest of my life, that it was very important. I remember how you try to capture every small moment, every friendship, the things you wanted to say to someone that were so important to remember. It was kind of sad. High school was your whole life; it was everything. And all of a sudden it was over. Of course we wore only underwear under our robes, but it was a hot day.

I thought I'd made it through twelve years of being forced to get up every morning to go to school and that's the last time in my life I ever have to do anything. We thought we were adults. We were sad, but we were also kind of glad it was over. You could relax now and you could choose what you wanted to do for the rest of your life.

By the time I graduated from high school, my friends thought I had been fucked about two hundred times. Really, I don't think I had ever even been close. I don't think I'd ever had my pecker out of my pants other than to take a pee.

Well, that summer we worked at Put-in Bay, which is a resort island in Lake Erie, about 180 miles north of Xenia. The father of a friend of mine was with the state Department of Natural Resources, and he got us all jobs on the island for the summer. I didn't last with the state parks very long because all I wanted to do was party and chase girls. So I ended up washing dishes and stuff at a restaurant in the marina there.

One day a boat came in from Cleveland, and there was this girl named Colette. Colette was an older woman, probably twenty-one years old, and very worldly. I had a fake ID, my brother's driver's license, saying I was nineteen, so I took Colette to this bar, this hangout called Stoiber's, for some big mugs of draft beer. I'm sitting on a chair in this bar, drinking beer with this girl who was very attractive, and I said to her, "Would you like to go up to my room?" She was pretty game. Colette had been down the road a couple of times.

There was a hotel on the island for kids who worked there. It was only men—no women allowed. I had a room that had a door that opened into my friend's room—Bill Smith, who was a cabdriver. I'd had a few beers and was pretty well fucked up. I was floating. So Colette and I went up the fire escape because you weren't allowed to have girls in your room.

We got into bed and we really got going. I was doing it all and I was having such a good time. It came to the point where I knew I was going to have to fuck her, and I had no idea exactly how to go about this. Well, Colette kind of pulled me over on top of her, and I found the right place—what I thought was the right place—and right in the middle of this great experience, my first sexual encounter, Colette fainted, just absolutely passed out.

Now I thought that I had done it wrong and she was dead. This is the God's truth. It scared me to death. Here I am in a hotel where you aren't allowed to have girls, my very first piece, and I've killed the girl! I've put it in the wrong place. She stopped breathing; something's wrong; she wouldn't wake up. I didn't know what to do. I was seventeen years old, I'm away from home, and I've killed my first piece of ass in a hotel where you are *not* allowed to have girls.

Finally I picked her up and carried her over to Bill Smith's room. I put her in his bed, put all her clothes in his bed, I locked the door between our rooms, and I split. I went back downstairs to the bar and had a beer and thought about what the fuck I was going to do with this dead girl. I was thinking about leaving the country. I was thinking about changing my name and moving away. I mean, I'd murdered my first piece!

Eventually I went back upstairs and got a wet washcloth and put it on her face—and she woke up! I felt like I'd received a reprieve, like the governor had called. She explained to me that sometimes when she drinks too much and has sex, she gets excited and faints. It's happened before. Well, that just changed my life. Now I'm thinking I'm so good that I make them faint! This is fantastic! I went from a murderer to the biggest stud in town, my first time out of the gate. I thought, Holy shit, look out! I'm probably the greatest lover that has ever walked the earth. When I fuck them, they faint! I'm definitely on the road to glory. Don Juan, look out! Of course, when I told Bill Smith what had happened, he was not too pleased that I had put a dead girl in his bed.

At first I went to college at Miami University in Ohio. I had had a trust fund my grandparents had left me, but it kind of got pissed away on fun things as we were growing up. So when it came time to go to college, I really didn't have the money, and I started working for the Chevrolet dealer in Xenia. I didn't do well at Miami, so I transferred to Central State University. It was academically easier, didn't require much study, and it was closer.

Central State was 90 percent black. They were glad to have me. I was pretty much a token honky up there. I played on the golf team for two years. There were not a lot of black kids in the ghetto playing golf. Actually, it was a real eye-opener to be the only white kid in a classroom. Some of the problems they discussed were totally foreign to me. The teachers were great. One of my instructors used to call me a "pink baby." I used to cut classes, and she would say, "Some people cut these classes and I don't miss them. But when one of my pink babies is missing, I know you're not there."

All the time that I was in college and working for the car dealer I was also actively fighting the draft. The Vietnam War divided the country drastically between those who would and those who wouldn't, those who cared and those who didn't. You were either an army guy or you weren't. I never was ashamed that I didn't go in the army, because it was goddamn hard not to go. It was easy to get in the army. You just walked down there and they took you. It was hard *not* going in. That was the task at hand.

I was very adamant that the war was wrong. People were dying.

There had been no formal declaration of war. It was something the French had handed us: "Here, there's a war going on. You guys want to handle it?" I had friends that had gone there and died. I did not want to be a part of it. I didn't even want to do alternate work. I did not want to contribute to the belief that that war was right.

I was all caught up in the antiwar movement. I grew long hair and a mustache and I felt a camaraderie with other people who were caught up in it. I stayed out of school one semester and I became draft eligible. I got invited to go down to Cincinnati to have a preinduction physical. I rode this bus down from Xenia with all these other guys. There were guys eating salt tablets to get their blood pressure high, guys acting like they're gay, guys on drugs—every trick in the book. We were thinking we had just thought this shit up, but, of course, they'd seen all these tricks. There was a guy who had taken six hits of LSD. He was so fucked up when we got down there, they probably took him right away and made him a general. They gave you an intelligence test that a moron could pass. A lot of guys failed it on purpose, and the army took them right away.

Barney Bloom was my draft-resistance adviser. He was a CO, a conscientious objector. At the time, there were a lot of loopholes in the draft laws, and one of the major loopholes was you could not be inducted into the armed forces as long as you had a legitimate appeal on file. Well, there were millions of appeals. You just filed them, they rejected them, and then you filed another one. And there were three levels of appeal—a local board, a state board, and a national board. It took forever to run the gauntlet for each one.

First you would appeal to the local board. You had to look in the faces of people that you knew, and they knew you were fucking them around, and you knew they were trying to put you in the army. They would tell you you were full of shit. Then you had thirty days to file an appeal with the state board, and they were fucking backlogged for years. The state board would tell you you're crazy and you couldn't do it. Then you would hit the federal board, and it was backed up for centuries. I must have been reclassified six times. I took four different army physicals in Cincinnati. I mean, I took so many physicals that I got to know the desk sergeant. His name was Rock. He was actually a nice enough guy.

I can remember going in and saying, "Rock! How you doing?"

"Higgins! Goddamn, are you back again?"

"Oh, these fucking people won't give me a break, Rock. They're hassling me to death."

I'd come home, and the next month I'd receive my induction notice to go in the fucking army, to be on that bus at 6 A.M. in Greene County, Ohio, and to report to Fort Knox for basic training. Then I'd file another appeal.

They eventually abolished that law, and you could be inducted while under appeal. That was real bad news if you got down to Fort Knox or someplace and they knew you had an appeal for conscientious objection or something. They'd probably kill you. It came down to the end, and I was running out of things to appeal for.

Well, my mother, like any mother, didn't want to see her son go to war. She also didn't want to see me go to jail for three years, or leave the country. My brother had gone in the army and she thought that was enough. So her doctor wrote a letter that my mother's heart was bad, which was true, and, since my brother was already in the army, it was important that I be at home to take care of her. Somehow we squeaked that through. I think they just got tired of trying to wear me down.

In later years I felt a little bit bad when I met people who had gone to Vietnam, after I had worked so hard to stay out. But I never felt any negative feelings towards Vietnam veterans. These were people who had heartfelt patriotic feelings and who were taught to fight for their country. When they got home they were treated awful. I personally can't imagine the feeling that a man must have if he had gone and killed someone and the only justification he had was that it was necessary for his country and for his family. Then to come home and find out it wasn't necessary after all.

On the other hand, I lose feelings for some of these guys that come home and spend the rest of their lives hiding behind being a Vietnam veteran. People look for a good excuse. You know, "If I had not been to Vietnam, I would be affluent and successful and happy and a neurosurgeon."

In early 1970 I graduated from Central State with a bachelor-of-arts degree in marketing. After that, four of us decided to drive across the country. It was John McCoy, Nelson King, and myself, and another guy who'd been in the air force with John. We took our 1958 Chevy bread-delivery truck and painted it all to hell—put flowers all over it and put CLEAN UP AMERICA: WASH A HIPPIE across the front of it. Then we left for the great land of California.

Some days we would only go two miles. We'd just drink beer and smoke pot and sit in the truck and laugh and listen to music. Nobody had to be anywhere. Nobody had to do anything. We lost track of time and of the days and of responsibility. Who gave a shit? It was irrelevant. We each had a few hundred dollars, and at that time eight hundred dollars was a million bucks. I can remember picking up every hitchhiker, sharing food and everything. It was all "beautiful, man." There was no such thing on the highway as an asshole or a robber or a thief. You'd just take them into the truck.

When we finally reached California, we drove around L.A. and then got out at the Beverly Hilton and pissed on the front yard. We thought that was a real social statement. Right around the corner was a famous nightclub that even we had heard of, and there was a group playing there that to us was a big deal, probably the Nitty Gritty Dirt Band or Vanilla Fudge or somebody that wasn't much by L.A. standards but would have been hot shit if they'd ever shown up in Xenia.

So we go in and we're sitting there, and we have definitely copped a serious buzzaroni. We'd been smoking and drinking all day. And these two girls come in, obviously L.A. They were beautiful. Dressed in the latest shit, makeup on, hair real nice. Nelson said, "We have to talk to these girls." I said, "We can't talk to these goddamn girls. They obviously just showed up in a limousine and we've been living in a bread truck." We're all dirty, haven't shaved. I said, "We're looking real rough here, Nelson."

But he insisted. He worked himself up to it, and finally, Nelson, who was wearing bib overalls, jumps up, goes over to them, and says, "Hi, I'm Nelson from Xenia!" Judging by the girls' reaction, I would say the equivalent today would be jumping up and saying, "Hi, I have AIDS and herpes. Would you kiss me?" I thought these girls were going to die. They must have thought Xenia was somewhere near Mars or Jupiter. Needless to say, they moved away quickly.

We hung around the beach for a while, and it was kind of a nice scene. Everybody was friends. There was no fear of new people, no recoiling from new relationships. Whatever you had, a beer or something, you shared it. Then we drove up to Northern California. A friend of ours was a promising young engineer with Bechtel. He had a fairly nice condo up there in Mill Valley, and we camped out in his parking lot for two or three weeks until the other people in the building decided that was bad news. I went on to Hawaii for a couple weeks, visiting Barney, who had become a philosophy instructor at the University of Hawaii. And then I returned to Xenia.

It was a great trip, a wonderful time. It didn't cost as much to have a good time in those days as it does now. I would do it again. But as you get older, it's harder and harder to find time to do that kind of thing. I think too many kids go through college and immediately start taking jobs and getting married and having kids. I think it's good to be irresponsible and crazy for a while, and travel and go places.

When I got back to Xenia, I was offered a job as the director of the Chamber of Commerce. They had had a succession of older, semiretired guys taking the job and just filling in the day with it, not really aggressively doing anything. My grandfather had founded the Chamber of Commerce, and because I was young—I was the youngest Chamber director in the state of Ohio—they thought I might revitalize things and maybe Xenia would become like Palm Springs or Greenwich, Connecticut, in about six or eight months.

I had a Fu Manchu mustache, wire-rimmed glasses, and long hair, which I had to cut. It was a minimal-pay job, but I thought it was pretty important. I started the first recycling center in Greene County. That was a really nice experience. A girl who was in charge of the center in Dayton helped me. She came in for the ribbon-cutting ceremonies. Here I am, dressed in a Brooks Brothers suit, with short hair, but fresh from being a goddamn hippie. This girl and I partied until four o'clock in the morning and then slept right through the opening ceremonies.

I did the Chamber of Commerce job for a year and then I got involved in cars. A family friend, who was a Ford dealer, sponsored me to go to driving school and become a race-car driver. For a while in there I also tried my hand at a couple different jobs. I traveled around the Midwest in a small airplane selling sales-incentive systems to automobile agencies. I also did part-time work helping a guy do a children's television show. I used to dress up like a dog and get paid seventy-five dollars a night to make public appearances. But by 1973 I had settled into the two things I have stuck with ever since: racing cars and selling them.

I started a business with a partner buying and selling used foreign cars. We went to New York and bought some used Mercedes and absolutely got reamed to death. The worst bunch of shit you've ever seen. Never made a dime on any of those cars, but it was a learning process. We started with two people in an old warehouse in a suburb of Dayton and it just grew and grew to a company that generates almost three million dollars a year. We've got fourteen employees and it is kind of getting out of hand.

We don't buy and sell any cars we wouldn't keep—mostly Mercedes-Benz, BMW, Jaguar, Ferrari, Maserati, Porsche, Lamborghini, and old cars. They're all cars that I really enjoy. At the same time, it's gotten to the point, after all these years, where it's not as much fun anymore. It used to be simple. I could close the door at four o'clock and go home and not have to worry about it. There was no responsibility. Now we have a big building, overhead, insurance policies, interest, computers, responsibility for employees and their families. Having your own business is almost like being married. After a while, you get real attached to it, and you hate to let it go.

Now we also have a leasing company that leases new cars and we have an auto-parts store and a service department. The automobile-service business is very difficult. People don't like to spend money to fix their cars. They're pissed off when they get there. It's very difficult to keep people happy. It's also hard to maintain a certain level of integrity in the motor trade. It's not rampant in the business. But I don't doctor up cars and sell them to people. And we don't misrepair automobiles or make up stories. It may not be industry standard, but at least I don't feel bad in the morning when I get up and look in the mirror. I feel no remorse about the way my business is run. I subsist on it. I have no visions of grandeur, and I am proud of our company's integrity.

My philosophy about money has always been, You either make just enough to live comfortably or you make so much that you couldn't piss it away. It's that gray part in the middle that makes people die young. I'm not a real good relaxer. I don't sit down very well. So anything I can do to lower the stress factor in my life is a positive point. I could make a lot more money, but I'm comfortable enough, and I'm satisfied to get up in the morning and have breakfast on my porch with the woods behind the house, and my old blind dog bumping around.

The other big part of my life has been racing. I started by working on the crew of Dick Lang, a Chevy dealer in Xenia who was a national champion racer. After I went to driving school and started racing myself, it took me to places I couldn't even imagine: Monaco, England, South America, all across Canada and Europe. It opened up a whole new world that I never would have known. I enjoy the camaraderie of racing. It's a friendship that supersedes economic background. In road racing you have guys that are mechanics in gas stations and guys like

Paul Newman sitting having breakfast together and talking. Once you're at the track, you're either a racer or you're not a racer; there is no in-between. And if you are a racer, it's like walking into a room and you have your own key and everybody in there has the same key, but nobody else does. I have had the same teammates, Chip Mead and James King, for almost ten years, and that doesn't happen often in motor sports.

While I'm driving, I don't worry. There is no time. It's one of the few places where you can't think about yourself. You can have all the worries in the world, but once you get into one of those cars and start to go, the concentration level erases them. It's almost like being in a vacuum tank. You get pumped up. It makes me feel good about myself. I feel like I've accomplished something in a five-hundred-mile race if I've driven two and a half hours and made no mistakes.

Things can happen, of course, but if you worry about it, you shouldn't be doing it. I've been in some near misses, but in a car race, what happened a second ago is a thousand years ago, because you can't reflect on any of that shit while you're doing it. At the speed you're moving, you can't take your mind off the future to think back. Maybe afterwards, after the race is over, and you're sitting back in the hotel or someplace and having a drink and talking about it, then you think, Jesus, that was pretty close.

The other day I was in a race at Riverside, California, and there was an incredible accident. I was the first car through. It's dirty, smoke and dust, you can't see. I just happened to be in the right place at the right time, and I got through. At the time, I never even gave it a second thought. But, watching it on television, it would have scared the shit out of you.

I have not had a great, illustrious career. I think probably people would say that I'm too careful. But I have a record of finishing over 95 percent of the races I've ever started, and almost always inside the top ten. In any endeavor, it's always important to be there when it's over. I've never had to spend time in a hospital. I've never been burned. I've also never been embarrassed about the way we run our program. The sponsors have gotten what they paid for. And, let me tell you, winning a race is only 20 percent of the job; 80 percent is making sure the sponsor gets something for his money and making his sales figures go up.

Unfortunately, I'm to the point now with racing where I'm not having as much fun anymore. It's a fairly large budget situation now. We've got six employees that travel with the car. You've got hotel rooms, airplane tickets, arrangements to make. You've got sponsorship responsibilities, trade shows. I think I'll keep driving maybe two years and that's enough. I'll probably always be involved as a car or team manager or something. I know what it takes to keep sponsors happy. It's the salesman in me.

In 1978, I met Sally. She was from Long Island, but she'd come to Dayton to visit her family. She was an incredibly intelligent lady. She was vibrant and very independent. She didn't need to be coddled and she didn't need to be reinforced constantly. She moved in and we lived together for about two and a half years and then we got married.

But there was an awful lot of conflict in our relationship, a lot of arguments. I didn't like going home and having to fight my way in the door because I'm twenty or thirty minutes late. All of a sudden our relationship lost its spontaneity. Each of us had to weigh things we were going to say to make sure it wasn't going to start an argument. I can't live like that. The "walking on eggs" syndrome. It just came to the point where I'd rather say nothing than to constantly think about being on your guard. It's stupid for people to live like that. So we just separated, and eventually divorced.

It was very hard for both of us. We both cried a lot and missed each other a lot. I don't place any blame for the failure of my marriage. It's just a situation where it just didn't work for us on a day-in, day-out basis. I probably still love my wife. She's a good friend. I still talk to her on the phone three or four times a week. We just can't be married to each other. I'm the first member of our family that's ever been divorced, and it was really hard for me to do. I've never been a quitter about anything. I hate being divorced. It was the first thing I ever really wanted to work that failed.

Of course, Sally had to put up with my occasionally odd behavior. One time we were invited to dinner at the Van Heckes' house up the street. I was tired and I just didn't want to go. I tried to get out of it, but it was, "No, you can't. We've been invited. You have to go." I said, "You go on up and I'll be there in a few minutes." After she left, I put on my pajamas and a robe and got into slippers and I went to these people's house for dinner. They were all wearing jackets and ties and I had dinner in my robe.

There are certain things I like to do to cause a little shockwave, without causing a real landslide. I sometimes think people think things are too important. There's certain places where people have cocktail parties and invite everybody that's important, and these people try to out-important each other. I think sometimes it's necessary to be the opposite—to create a little spoof of the establishment, a little jab at the structure.

Well, a few years back I was invited to a Halloween party and I was looking for a car salesman's uniform, because if you can't make light of yourself, what can you make light of? So I went to a Goodwill store and for two bucks I bought this dandy lime-green polyester leisure suit. Periodically since then, an occasion will arise where this suit should be worn.

About a year or two ago a friend of mine had a Christmas party and invited all these people that he thought were important, including a lot of judges. I waited until the party was in full swing and then I showed up at the door in the good old green leisure suit. The pants are too short; the white belt is about three inches wide and it's plastic. It's just the grossest thing you've ever seen in your life.

I walked into that party and it was like Moses parting the Red Sea. People were afraid to get close to it. It was as if the minute they touched it they'd turn into a Plymouth station wagon. I didn't know anybody there, and they didn't know me. I never acted like anything was out of the ordinary. I just introduced myself to people as one of Larry's best clients. I had more fun that night than I'd had in months. So did he.

I have a fair amount of woman friends, and, fortunately, women feel sorry for me for some reason. They always want to fix my food and do things for me. I'm such a son of a bitch for taking advantage of it, but what the hell. I'm still healing from the divorce, but I'm not having that awful of a time. I have the option of having the company of women and not having it, and there's no man that's going to tell you that that's not that bad of a deal! I'm not against marriage; it's just that I need time to regroup.

Essentially, the only thing I try to do is stay happy and maintain a group of friends. That's important to me. I think the thing I prize most is having my house full of people whose opinions I value. Sitting around the table with people I like, trying to be a little funnier than the next person, making jokes, laughing and having fun. I don't think I'll ever lose that.

THE TEXAN:
Rusty Rhodes

The assassination of President John F. Kennedy was an awful event that first made our generation aware of its shared identity. One factor that enforced this awareness was that almost every one of us, in every part of the nation, was doing the same thing when the terrible news was learned: We were going to school. Most people told me that they were sitting in a classroom when normal daily routine was interrupted by an unexpected message over the classroom intercom.

Few members of the class of '65 actually understood Kennedy's policies, but his image was one of youth, hope, and a positive future. When he was shot to death, it was as if a bubble had burst. Our unquestioning confidence that the American system worked smoothly was deeply shaken. Assassinations were supposed to be something that happened only in history books. Suddenly here was history being made before our very eyes, and, in the case of Jack Ruby killing Lee Harvey Oswald, live on television.

At first, blame for the assassination of President Kennedy was placed on Lee Harvey Oswald, who was portrayed as a Marxist who had once defected to the Soviet Union and was now a pro-Castro activist. He was said to have acted alone. A prestigious commission, headed by Supreme Court chief justice Earl Warren and including future president Gerald Ford, former CIA director Allen Dulles, and former World Bank president John McCloy, supported this version. The American public generally accepted the scenario, but in most of the rest of the world the conclusions of the Warren Commission were received with great skepticism.

Slowly, Americans became suspicious as well. It took a bit more time, but along with the general questioning of authority that accompa-

nied the late '60s came a growing willingness to accept that sometimes even U.S. presidents, chief justices, World Bank presidents, and CIA directors can make mistakes—or, worse, can cover up the truth. Early on, conspiracy theorists were considered weirdos or even subversives, but now a large majority of Americans believe that John F. Kennedy's death was the result of an unsolved conspiracy.

For some, the need to understand what really happened in Dallas on November 22, 1963, became a very personal matter.

It was very hot and very dry in Palm Desert, California, and Rusty Rhodes's car wasn't working. So I picked him up at his workplace and drove him across town to the trailer park where he lived. As the details of Rusty's odyssey unfolded, the trailer park seemed an increasingly incongruous locale for us to be having our discussion.

I was born George Wayne Rhodes, but it seems that anyone with the last name of Rhodes has the nickname of Dusty. My father was Dusty Rhodes, and people had an inkling to call me Little Dusty. When I was about six years old I decided I didn't want to be Little Dusty, and made it Rusty. It's very difficult to try to force a new name upon your family and friends when you're only six years old.

When I was born, my mother was sixteen years old and my father was twenty-two. He was working as an accountant for the Katy Railroad in Dallas during the day and pursuing his master's degree at night at SMU in marketing and merchandising. My mother's side of the family are passionate Creole people. My father was from a family that was very educated. They lost everything in the 1929 Wall Street crash, so they became dirt farmers in East Texas. My father had this tremendous desire to make it, to get it all back, and because of that my younger brother and younger sister and I rarely saw him when we were children, because he was always working. It wasn't as bad a situation as it might sound, because my grandfather, my mother's father, moved in to fill that role. He was a wonderful fellow—a woodsman, a true survivalist.

A large portion of Dallas is built on landfill because it was swampy creeks and marshes. I enjoyed being by myself a lot, and I had a swamp that I could disappear into and no one would come looking for me. I had a cave that I shored up with lumber from building sites. The trees formed a cathedral effect. Some of the best recollections of my life, to this very day, are poling through those green, frothy waters in a johnboat that I built.

My father became a salesman for the Ronson Corporation, the cigarette-lighter people. In 1962 he received a promotion to general sales manager, so we moved from Dallas to Los Angeles, where he ran the L.A. office. My mother, who had been a journalist, gave up her career when we moved. We leased a house in Santa Monica from Stan Laurel. The garage was full of all his mementos, and for six months he kept coming back every week to get things. We'd go out and help him dig through all this stuff, and he'd give us little things. His wife was a real slavedriver, always harping. But he was a nice man, and he would tell us stories for hours about what Hollywood was like in the twenties and thirties.

When I came out to Southern California, I felt all the guys were acting like idiots, fruitcakes. They all had long surfer hair and over-sized shirts, and none of them carried knives. I couldn't figure out how people got by. I was fifteen years old and my classmates in Dallas were already getting pregnant, dropping out of school, and dying in knife fights. When I was growing up in Dallas, the only avenues of upward mobility were to be an athlete or a hoodlum. I tried to be an athlete. I broke several bones in my back trying to play football. My nose was broken; my feet were broken. It took me a year to recover. Then I bought a black leather jacket with a lot of rabbit feet on it. Went out and got some black Levis and some black engineer boots and tried to be a hoodlum.

They had this cute little practice in Dallas called "curbing." Once you worked on somebody real bad, you opened their mouth, put it on a curb, and stomped on the back of their neck to break their teeth. I could never curb anybody. I guess I was generally a failure as a hoodlum.

When my parents moved to California, it was the best thing they ever did for me. I didn't know until then that it was okay to ask yourself questions about the universe and personal philosophy. The moment I got out there I noticed that there was this kind of force about the beach and the ocean and surfing. I could feel it in the way the kids would talk about it: There was something about the sea that drew them. I didn't understand it at first, but it wasn't very long before I was completely enamored as well. The beach, for me, was a tremendous liberating factor.

When we first went to the beach, I couldn't believe how proud people were of their bodies. In Texas, everybody always wore clothes, even on a 105-degree day. And here were girls walking around with bikinis. I thought, God, this is great! I was embarrassed by my body, but all of these people were walking around feeling so good about themselves, and it didn't take me long to pick up that attitude.

My parents were very strict. They were members of the Church of Christ, which is so strict they think the Baptists are liberal. I had to be home by ten o'clock. But surfing was a clean sport. For the first time in my life I could take off for weekends with no parental supervision. I would go sleep on the beach with friends and surf and watch the sun go down.

It was at school, ninth grade, that I met my best friend, Arnold. He was certainly the funniest-looking person in the class. He was about five foot four, he weighed 160 pounds, and he wore size 12½ double-E shoes. He had a short, parted haircut, but he had a cowlick right in front, so his hair would stick straight up in front. He wore bright Hawaiian shirts with cotton pants, and colors that usually didn't match. I couldn't believe anybody would go to school this way. Arnold looked like a funny person just walking down the street. The whole image really intrigued me. I decided I've got to know this person, because here's somebody that doesn't care about social statements. Here's someone who just kissed it all off. I really admired his fortitude. Then, when this funny, little person would open his mouth, I realized he was also one of the most intelligent people I've ever met.

Arnold's family was progressive Jewish, and my family was conservative Christian, but both of us had home lives that were not great, and we decided that we did have a lot in common. I don't know if we ever said this openly, but it was a quiet understanding that we needed each other's strength to get through life. When we started high school, Santa Monica High School, things had gotten a bit difficult at my house, so I moved in with Arnold's family.

We had a nice home, a charge account at the liquor store, and a pool in the backyard. We didn't date, because girls would come over. There weren't any other sixteen-year-olds around with such luxuries. Arnold and I kind of drank our way through school. We only went to school regularly on Fridays to take tests. We would ace our tests, get A's, and never do any homework. So we got C averages and it all worked out. Arnold's mother thought as long as we were reading Plato, and other classical philosophers, which we were, then it was all right. She was the type of lady that really built you up and made you feel very, very special.

So Arnold and I went through high school as best friends, and there were several tragedies that kind of reinforced the idea that he and I had to face the world together. Both of our mothers had drinking problems, his father had moved out, and my father was still gone a lot. Then, when we were in the eleventh grade, on the way to school, Arnold hit a woman in a crosswalk. She saw a friend of hers and darted across the street. Arnold struck her. As we were standing there with the ambulance and the police, a school bus came by, and kids stuck their heads out and screamed, "Murderer!" That really hurt Arnold bad. The woman died three weeks later. It made our own bond even tighter. Arnold lost his license for a year. He wasn't charged. But my buddy was broken, and you couldn't have punished him any worse than the thoughts in his own mind.

November 22, 1963, was a bright, sunny day in Santa Monica. We were about to take our noon break when the word came out over the PA system that the president had been shot and that Governor Connally of Texas had also been shot and that he was possibly dead.

I couldn't believe it. I had such tremendous feelings for John Kennedy that I couldn't deal with them. People would come up to me and ask me about Dallas. I told them, "The governor's a great guy. I talked to him. I'm really sorry that he stopped that bullet." I think I even said, "I don't care about the president." I didn't really feel that way, but if I was to say what was in my heart, I was afraid I would start crying and sobbing and not be able to control myself. I had to put my face on and appear calm to protect my image.

After lunch I went to history class, and since it was known that I was from Dallas, the teacher asked me if I was familiar with the motorcade route. I got up to the blackboard and made a little diagram of downtown Dallas and how the streets go. Then it came across that the president was dead. There was an athlete in the class, a great big guy. This fellow was sobbing. He completely lost control of himself and picked up his desk and threw it at me. He missed, but he made a big hole in the wall. The teacher hit a little button, and immediately the counselors and the assistant principal were up there. They sent me home for three days. People really wanted to hate Dallas and anything in it or from it.

I went to the beach to think about what all of this meant. In a panic, you don't think straight. I thought that because the president had been shot, Nixon was going to be president! I'm thinking, Oh, my God! I was really concerned about the country. I went back to my parents' home, and we learned about Lee Harvey Oswald. My family's so huge back in Dallas that it always seemed like we knew everybody in town. I think I asked my mother twenty times, "Does anybody in the family know this guy?" But nobody did.

On Sunday, we were all getting ready to go to church when it came on the TV that Jack Ruby had murdered Oswald. Jack Ruby—I knew who he was. I had a friend whose father owned a bar in East Dallas by the name of the Casbah Club, and his partner was one Jack Ruby. I had heard about Jack a lot because he was the "fixer." He got the liquor license and this, that, and the other. He could soothe it over with the cops. You could run girls because Jack could fix it with the cops. He was a cruel fixer who hated the world, tremendously self-centered, did what he did for himself or his own sense of self-importance. I couldn't envision the man being motivated by Caroline crying and Mrs. Kennedy having to come back for a trial. No, I couldn't see that side of the man. We're talking about a man who worked in Chicago as an enforcer for the Scrap Iron Handlers' Union and for Frank Nitty. So we're not talking about a "patriotic innkeeper" here. "Patriotic innkeeper"! When I heard that TV explanation, that was the first red flag.

I went to Dallas around December 14th, three weeks after the assassination. My grandfather Rhodes was ill, so we were going to make a family showing of it. My aunt, who was a Dallas socialite, and her husband, who was a very prominent attorney, had a cocktail party— basically the shaker-and-mover crowd. At that party I spoke with an old, old family friend, a surgeon who was usually the one who put the medical package together for the DAs on murders and such. He had reviewed all the notes the day of the president's death.

The doctor was aloof, didn't recognize me. He was extremely nervous and agitated. I had never seen him like that. His wife offered an explanation to my aunt that he had not been himself since he came back from Washington, where he had been interviewed by the FBI and other groups. He was under strict orders not to talk, as all Parkland Hospital doctors were, and he had not been right since his return. I knew this man very, very well. I couldn't imagine what kind of pressure or situation would have him react in such a way. This is an emergency-room surgeon, a fellow that sees everything. All of his personal notes on the case were seized, and he was treated roughly. This is someone who went to fine schools and was of a good family and had never been treated roughly in his life. That's when the second red flag went up.

At this point I became very interested in the president's death. I got the feeling that possibly something was wrong, and it deserved explanation. I heard, through a friend, of a newspaper editor in Midlothian, Texas, named Penn Jones, Jr., who was conducting his own work into the events of the assassination, to learn if the official explanation was just a cover-up and if there had in fact been a conspiracy. He came out and spoke at a conference at UCLA, and I started conducting some interviews for him in Southern California.

My senior year, my girlfriend got pregnant. She happened to work as an office helper for my dean at high school, so the dean promptly released me from school. The mother of the girl went down to the DA and had rape charges filed against me. I decided that the time was right to return to Dallas. I gave the girl a plane ticket and three hundred dollars and told her to meet me in Dallas and I would care for her until she had the baby. Instead, she went downtown to a hospital where pregnant women have babies and place them in adoption. The rape charge died on the vine when the girl refused to testify.

In Dallas I stocked shelves at night at an A&P market and worked for Penn during the day. At first it was mostly basic, light work: tracing people, mostly witnesses, through county records, credit sources, neighbors. Pretty much the basic investigative techniques that either a journalist or a homicide detective would use.

It was during this time that I met Officer Roger Craig, who was one of the more important witnesses of the shooting of the president. He was Policeman of the Year in 1962. He had been in Dealey Plaza all morning and afternoon to secure it, and had noted movement of spectators, cars, traffic, etc. At first Craig's statements about the case did not appear startling, but once you knew the case, they became very important. He talks about a light-green station wagon picking up Oswald, while the official version has him leaving by bus and cab. Because he insisted on talking to the media, and because he was a cop with very good credibility, Roger Craig was fired by the Dallas Police Department, and ostracized. After one attempt had been made on his life, I became a live-in with the Craig family. I stayed with the family off and on. Eighteen years old, revolver, three-piece suit. I was scared half to death but trying to look professional.

I returned to Los Angeles and expected my girlfriend to have had the baby. When I visited her, I discovered she was almost ten months pregnant. We went to the Downtown Hilton, and were having dinner there when her water broke. I didn't know a whole lot about women and babies, and I thought when the water broke, that's it, the baby comes immediately afterwards! So I fainted.

A waitress revived me with a cold towel and said, "You'd better get the hell to the hospital!" I drove about seventy-five miles an hour through the streets of downtown Los Angeles, with the police roaring behind me. Finally I let them catch me, and pointed and said, "Baby, baby." The chase ended up with a police motorcycle in front of the car, and they escorted me to the hospital. About twenty hours later, she had the baby. She named him Rusty.

As I understand it, an architect and his wife in Orange County adopted the child. I do wonder sometimes what it would be like for a twenty-year-old man to show up here one day.

Back in Dallas, I intensified my work for Penn Jones. There were approximately 150 primary witnesses to the shooting of President Kennedy. I probably interviewed 60 of them. I was young enough to go out and do this kind of foolhardy work. Because of my age, and because I was a local boy, I was not threatening to these people. Most of them were extremely private, God-fearing people who felt like something was wrong and that they ought to tell their story. They had witnessed an event and told the truth, and then a resulting press release by the police department or by the DA's office would say that they were mistaken or lying or seeking publicity.

Dallas had an official tour guide that would take people through Dealey Plaza and give them the official Warren Commission story. I would stand out there and catcall him. "What about this? What about that?" Eventually my side was much more interesting because I knew so much more than the other guy, and I'd win all the people over. After three days they sent a guy out there who told me they would get a writ to remove me unless I left on my own. I said, "These are public lands here." He said, "Don't give me this legal bullshit, boy." The man's an attorney from the DA's office—what are you going to say?

At that point I set up a pattern where I would work in Dallas for eight or nine months and then I would disappear to California for three or four months. I lived a completely schizophrenic existence. In Dallas I had a sidewall haircut, mohair, three-piece suits, and a big gun. I lived an extremely disciplined life. I never even smoked a joint.

Then I would go to San Francisco, wear diffraction jewels stuck on my forehead and a headband with feathers stuck in to try to cover up the short hair, and walk around being a freak. I guess I needed some avenue of self-expression that was completely different. I would take a tremendous amount of LSD and walk around Golden Gate Park every day. I stopped going to the Haight-Ashbury when Methedrine became the drug of the streets and all the good cheer evaporated into the woodwork.

Finally, I became tired of running around Dallas. Two witnesses that I knew well, and liked, met their demise, and I was upset. I was tired of the threats by the police, who were embarrassed by the assassination and wanted the subject to go away and die. I was becoming an individual that I didn't like. I was too hard. I decided there was a lot of bookwork for me to catch up on, some eighteen thousand pages of the Warren Commission Report which I had not familiarized myself with.

So I came back to California and did some serious studying for several months. I went back again in '67 and helped transport a witness to New Orleans for the Jim Garrison trial. Before the witness, Richard Randolph Carr, testified, he was stabbed in the stomach on the street when he went out to get something to eat. But he did live and testify. Garrison tried to prove a conspiracy to murder John F. Kennedy and to prove that Clay Shaw, a local New Orleans businessman, was involved. When the jury was questioned after they rendered a not-guilty verdict, they said that a conspiracy was proved but that Clay Shaw's involvement was not.

Back in California again, I started building files and meeting the other Warren Commission critics and started an exchange of information. I was doing a lot of odd jobs at the time, working on boats in the marina, but mostly I was living off the college trust fund that my grandparents had set up. I would get the class cards and send them to the attorney that ran the trust. He would send the check, and I would immediately withdraw from classes. It made it rough later when I really went to college.

My parents lived in a good neighborhood and were starting to feel a lot of police pressure, mostly cops coming by and asking my mother questions about my whereabouts. That's when my mother's drinking problem became paramount. She paid the price, in many ways, for what I was doing. Years later we would discover that it wasn't paranoia, that the FBI had told the Santa Monica Police that I was possibly dangerous and they wanted information. The local police department, wanting to look good to the feds, spent a lot of time on it. The harassment became very, very bad. You can't believe what happened to this little upper-middle-class family, who had always done things by the book, because their eldest was involved in something that was not fashionable.

The straw that broke the camel's back came one day when I had dropped by to see my mother. I laid down on the couch to rest and fell asleep. I woke up to hear my mother screaming. She was in her robe, and there were three men with suits in the house. Two of them had a hold on her. Ronson used to make these large, terrible-looking rosewood candles with butane in them. The first thing I did was grab one of these things and hit one of the men on the head as hard as I could. The guy went down like a sack of potatoes. We started fighting, and the guy I'd knocked down hit me on the head with a flashlight or a gun barrel. I started to get up—and there's three pistols pointed at me.

They said, "You're going to jail." And I said, "For what?" They said, "Assaulting an officer." So they brought me out to this unmarked squad car. My mother came running out, screaming, "Let him take his jacket! Let him take his jacket!" This one detective became so nervous about the way my mother was reacting that he turned around and backhanded her—knocked her to the ground. Blood was drawn. Our neighbors across the street saw it because they were out in front watering.

I was handcuffed in the back of the car, and I said, "You're going to pay for that. You drew blood on an unarmed civilian, a five-foot-tall woman that weighs ninety-five pounds." He did the only thing he could do: He put her under arrest to protect himself from a civil charge. They charged her with "interfering with an officer's duty."

When we got to the jail, my mother desperately needed her Librium. They held it in front of her cell and wouldn't give it to her. They tortured her—"Is this what you want?"—and they called her crazy.

My father got home that evening, and the neighbors told him what happened. He came running down there and they released my mother to him. Then he came back and got me. My father was really confused. He'd always lived by the book. He was used to donating Ronson lighters to the policemen's ball for door prizes. My mother had flipped out in the jail cell. She was home for a couple of days, sedated, then she went to the hospital for eight months, and we couldn't see her for four of those months. It was a real terrible event. When I finally got to talk with my mother, it turned out they had told her that I was with the Black Panthers and the Communist Party, and that I had these files dealing with a planned insurrection. It was absurd, but I did learn what mattered to them, and it came in handy later, when I got my induction notice.

When I took my draft physical, I brought with me all these doctors' letters. They knocked them all down. They ask you to fill out this white sheet of paper and on the back they ask if you have ever taken any drugs. So I wrote down that I had taken every drug known to man. They sent me to the psychiatrist and I described memory loss, and situations where I would come back to with blood on my hands. That was fine with them. I tried everything. So I was very scared, because the army let us know the FBI fellows were there for the people that refused, to immediately take you into custody.

When it became apparent to me that I was going to pass through everything, I noticed that most of the room was blacks. So I started talking very loud to the blacks nearby, something to the effect of, "You know what they're going to do? They're going to take my black brothers here and they're going to train them to be the most efficient killers on the face of the earth, and send them to Vietnam, and these white men are still going to be raping their mamas!" Half the place went "Right on!" with a resounding boom.

So I got on top of a trashcan and started really going to town with whatever I could come up with. Mind you, I was wearing nothing but my underwear and my Cuban zip boots with the stacked heels. I looked like a complete idiot. But the brothers were great: "Let the dude talk." A scuffle broke out between the authorities and the blacks, and I got hit in the side of the head with a club. I was thrown into a room and told, "Get your clothes on." Two minutes later the door opened and six marines grabbed me, walked me to the front door, threw me out, and told me never to come back again! That one worked.

In 1969 I started doing investigative work for various attorneys—mostly movement cases. By this time I was familiar with some pretty dirty stuff—body mikes, parabolic mikes, surveillances. I was hardened, and I knew what I was doing.

I also started going to Santa Monica College on a part-time basis. The following year I ran for office and was elected speaker of the assembly, which was like president of the student body. We established an experimental college with twenty-eight classes and we won several community-service awards for bringing people into the college, like little old ladies who came for the class on breeding roses.

Of course, we had a class on political assassinations. I got myself a good budget and I was able to bring in speakers from all over the country. The class started getting a lot of publicity and finally grew to about two hundred people every Tuesday night. After two years I was entrenched in a position of power, and the school, to get rid of me, awarded me a transferring scholarship to move on! So I did.

I was approached, and kind of sidetracked, by a group called the California Community College Student Government Association that represented all 104 community colleges within the state. With the eighteen-year-old vote having just become a reality, this represented a tremendous voting bloc. Because I had managed the budget so well at Santa Monica, I was brought up to Sacramento and offered the executive vice-presidency. I took the job and worked there for a year in the state government under Ronald Reagan.

It was an exhausting and maddening job, but I did learn that if you would take the time to learn the protocol, the system would respond. I started getting a good feeling about democracy, and I got the idea that eventually we would reopen the Kennedy case due to popular pressure.

I came back to Santa Monica and opened an investigative office, with another office in the Mission District in San Francisco. Then I teamed up with a man named Lake Hedley, who was the former chief of homicide in Clark County—Las Vegas. Our first case together was the investigation into the televised gunfight that killed the members of the SLA, the Symbionese Liberation Army, the people who kidnapped Patty Hearst. We were hired by the families of the deceased to tell these parents what had happened to their children from the time of the kidnapping up to the time they died in the shootout. It was quite a tall order. It was a one-year-long investigation. When we ran out of money, both of us used up all our own savings to continue, because we felt we were doing something that was pretty important.

The Los Angeles Police Department had said approximately 2000 rounds were fired in a hotly contested firefight. I went out into the area the day after the shooting occurred, with my camera and my tape recorder. Having been trained in ballistics analysis, we didn't find any evidence of a "hotly contested firefight." We didn't find evidence of more than 50 rounds being fired by the SLA, but we did find evidence of in excess of 6000 rounds being fired into the house by the L.A. Police Department. They said my figures were all wrong and that I was obviously a Marxist because a friend of mine was a Marxist. The L.A. *Times* went on for about a paragraph about my character. But in an

LAPD internal investigation booklet, which we got a copy of, they admitted to firing in excess of 6500 rounds. So we did our work well, and they were forced to eat their words.

We never did really resolve the entire matter. We did ultimately find out that the SLA had no political philosophy, that it was a confused operation with a megalomaniac escaped convict at the top. Donald David DeFreeze, aka Field Marshal Cinque, was not indeed a revolutionary. He was a cheap turnover punk for the LAPD. Here's a black man who'd been arrested nine times on weapon charges—armed robbery, forced rape, things like that—and the man's continually probated. He had been in Soledad Prison for two weeks when he was given a job on the outside servicing a power generator. This is a job that's reserved for men that've been in there for five years. DeFreeze walked away the next week.

As for Patty Hearst, if all of our information was correct, she was probably playing revolutionary. Not to the point of picking up a gun or anything like that. She just had a mild, rich-girl interest in the things around her. I certainly don't believe that she deserved what she got. She was another victim of that whole tragedy.

After the SLA case, Lake and I were broke and disgusted. We had been followed by helicopters several times. Once we were coming out of a restaurant in Hollywood with two journalists, and there's two men with crowbars trying to break into Lake's car. It turned out they were FBI, intent on getting his notes on the SLA. So there was a lot of repression and harassment. Lake and I did a few more cases together and then he decided to retire.

In 1975 I got into a little trouble in San Francisco. My office was in a gay neighborhood, and a guy came up to me and wanted to find his roommate because the roommate had taken his stereo. This guy had been a good street tip, so I asked all around, finally found out where the guy was, and gave the information to the fellow. It turned out that the guy hadn't stolen the stereo—he was a lover who'd rebuffed him and left. The street tip went over and murdered him.

I felt pretty rotten, and the San Francisco Homicide Department made sure that I felt rotten. They were going to lift my license and I'd be lucky if I didn't go to jail as an accessory. They didn't want me leaving town.

Two weeks later, I left my apartment to buy a pack of cigarettes at a bar on Market Street, and right as I left I saw a man struck by a vehicle traveling sixty miles an hour. I ran out to offer whatever aid I could.

He was still alive, had a pulse, so I cleared the breathing passages and kept him going until the ambulance got there. He died en route to the hospital. But a little German man saw the accident and ran after the car. The driver was drunk, and the car was so mangled he couldn't see through the broken glass. He drove three blocks, got out, and escaped on foot. But the German man found the car, wrote the license number down, and gave it to me.

The driver turned out to be a city official. So I went down to the police department, homicide, the guys who'd put me over the coals. I gave them the driver's name, and asked them what they were going to do about it. The man had not been charged. They started making every excuse in the world for him. I wouldn't let up. Finally they said, "Look, we'll make a deal. You'll never hear about yours if we never hear about this one." I said, "Okay."

I closed the office in San Francisco shortly thereafter and was only doing movement cases in L.A. I took a side job doing custom stereo installations and became manager of the store, but I couldn't see myself staying in retail sales, so I left.

Meanwhile I did a lecture on the John F. Kennedy assassination for the Legal Society of Loyola University, a small, liberal-arts college in Los Angeles. People really responded and they subsequently asked me back for three occasions. After my fourth appearance, I was approached by members of the political-science department and offered a salaried position as a staff consultant, as well as free tuition for undergraduate work. I accepted it, and spent a year there. I was able to do my Kennedy research in an academic setting and actually be paid for it. We started a citizens' drive to petition Congress to reopen the matter of John Kennedy's death.

I was contacted by Notre Dame and asked to come to Indiana to do my speech. It was a sold-out audience, so they asked me to come back and I did. During one lecture, one guy in back kept loudly yelling encouragement. I assumed it was some radical student, but when it was over, it turned out to be Digger Phelps, the basketball coach. I ended up staying there two weeks and did a week-long series of lectures for the history department.

During my stay at Notre Dame, I met the famous football coach Ara Parseghian. Remember, he did some Ford commercials. Well, this motorcade of Fords came to pick me up at the hotel. It was the linebacker coaches. They took me over to the athletic complex, and I did a private lecture for Ara Parseghian. It was like meeting the pope. At the end, Parseghian said, "Can you do me a favor?" I said, "I'll try." He said, "Find out why I was on Nixon's enemies list." I did try, but I never could find out. The closest we could come is that he once attended an event with Paul Newman on behalf of a halfway house for alcoholics. I don't think there was any particular logic to that list in the first place.

I was nominated for the senior fellowship by the senior class at Notre Dame, and after that I was contacted by Fordham. This is kind of the Catholic circuit. My lecture at Fordham really popped everything out in the open, because the old Robert Kennedy staff network showed up for the lecture. It became a very important moment in my life, because we were getting closer to power and to really doing something about it.

We had a press conference the next day at the Waldorf-Astoria and all seven New York City Congress members committed to vote to reopen the case. By this time I'd been in touch with Congressman Henry Gonzalez of San Antonio, Texas, who'd written House Resolution 204 calling for a reopening of the case. My associates, Delphia Arrowood and Greg Roebuck, and I began pinpointing those districts where swing votes were needed. We'd go to a town for free, we'd rent the local hall, do all the buildup with the radio and TV people, have the lecture, and then stay in town for several days afterwards. Then we would try to leave a small support structure that could continue after we were gone. We'd give them a copy of the Zapruder film of the assassination that shows Kennedy getting shot from both back and front. We'd supply them with fact sheets and an organizers' manual. It was a beautiful thing watching this direct democratic process work. We'd pick up votes by the week, just by targeting districts.

I was contacted by the American Program Bureau, the largest speakers' agency in the country, and I went to work speaking on college campuses. I averaged 4.3 lectures a week for two and a half years and traveled over 250,000 air miles. It took a terrible toll on me. Doing the same thing every evening, and all you see is a hotel room. It's difficult living that way.

When the resolution passed and the House committee was formed, I stopped lecturing and ended up on a farm in Illinois for three weeks, trying to figure who in the fuck I was. All I had done for two and a half years was get up in front of a podium and give the same introduction. Every time I spoke I got genuinely mad, and I'd get emotional every time I'd see that film of Kennedy getting shot. I knew I'd done a great job, and felt good about the work I'd done, but, boy, on a personal level it was the only time in my life really that I felt like I had no idea what my identity was.

I was slated to be one of the investigators on the committee. Then there was a power struggle, and Congressman Gonzalez, who had shown such tremendous bravery and resilience, was deposed as the chairman. In the mixup that followed, I was knocked out of my job as well.

The congressional investigation ended up being a terrible job. The scientific work was good, particularly the acoustic analysis, but the investigative techniques were very sloppy because there were no real investigators. Instead of hiring some good, hardboiled Miami and New Orleans organized-crime street detectives, with a few Kennedy researchers thrown in, they got a bunch of Harvard and Princeton law students and young attorneys. This was their first big assignment in public service, so the quality of people was not that good.

I'll give you one for-instance: One of the more interesting figures in the Kennedy assassination was George DeMorenschild, a White Russian who was arrested in 1943 while walking along Galveston Island drawing detailed pictures of the gunnery emplacements. He befriended Oswald in Dallas, became his mentor, paid his rent. DeMorenschild was visited at his home in Florida by an investigator for the House committee. The man knocked on the door, a servant answered, and he said, "I'm an investigator for the U.S. Congress. I'm here to talk to Mr. DeMorenschild." The servant said, "Mr. DeMorenschild is not here. Can you come back later?"

The investigator came back later and DeMorenschild was dead of what was later ruled a self-inflicted gunshot. Cardinal rule in investigations: You don't reveal your identity until you're talking to the person you want to talk to.

So I was disappointed by the investigation. It cost six million dollars, and we heard about that six million dollars for years. On the other hand, the committee did turn in reams of information on organized crime. You can't look into the assassination of John F. Kennedy without looking into organized crime. But that money was a big deal. Given the pragmatic nature of politics, to go searching for truth for truth's sake is just not a good explanation in Washington. The congressional card had been played, and it can never be played again.

After the House committee, I returned to Los Angeles. I was completely intrigued with a new instrument called the "psychological stress evaluator," PSE. It was a new type of polygraph that did not have to touch your body. It scanned your central nervous system. It could go right into the islands of Langerhans, where stress is born. I found this tremendously exciting. I also thought it was about the scariest thing I'd ever heard of. I had to have one. It was still within the realms of Army Intelligence and the CIA, but was just starting to come out. You had to be in a police department or a DA's office. A friend of mine in the CIA, who had used a PSE to analyze the Oswald tapes, wrote a letter for me on CIA stationery saying that I wished to purchase one and to attend a class in the instruction of such. They were having these classes in Los Angeles.

I went to those classes. I had long hair, I have to remind you, in a ponytail, and I'm in there with narcs and Drug Enforcement Administration guys. They thought I was really something. I wouldn't say who I was with. Everybody else, it was, "Oh, I'm from San Jose Narcotics"; "I'm from San Francisco Vice." They'd ask me, "Who are you with?" and I'd say, "That's not important." It was a four-week class and I graduated with flying colors. Former head of U.S. Army School of Counterintelligence, Colonel Charles McQuiston, one of the creators of the PSE and the class instructor, really liked me. He was associated with George L. Barnes and Associates, the highest-class private-investigations agency in L.A., and I was hired by them. Their offices were in a four-story home with a circular driveway, tennis courts, pool. They had twenty employees.

My immediate boss there was a former Green Beret, a gung-ho type who wore nice suits and had no feelings for me because I was never in the service and I wasn't gun-happy. About two months after I was hired, we were partners on a case together. The Chemical Workers' Union was striking against Lever Brothers, and somebody was going through the hierarchy of Lever Brothers and bombing their homes. It had happened twice, so we knew who was next on the list.

We moved the family into a hotel and we set up in their home. I had low-level-light video cameras at all the windows. We had cars on both sides of the house, and I was inside the house. We were looking for a yellow car. About four o'clock in the morning, a yellow Dodge Dart comes driving slowly down the street. Checkpoint A calls it in. I turn on all the video cameras and recording devices. The car comes up to the house and it stops. Somebody gets out and walks up the sidewalk. My boss, who was in a car covering the street, leaves his position, which he never should have done, and comes running into the house to be with me.

I was standing there looking through the window with the video monitor. I couldn't see very well, but I could hear the footsteps. All of a sudden we could see somebody throwing something. I looked over and my boss had drawn and cocked a .38 and was about to fire. I elbowed him as hard as I could and knocked him down. It was the paper boy! Can you believe that? The car was right and everything. He was going to shoot a fourteen-year-old boy. And this guy had been treating me like I was a piece of trash.

I was promoted to vice-president, and my first assignment as vice-president was to fire my boss. I worked for Barnes for a period of two and a half years, and I was paid very well. I wore shorts and Hawaiian shirts to work. I did my dictation next to my wireless phone out by the pool. I had my own private shower and bath and closets. My company car was a Mercedes 400—the big sedan. It was like being in a TV show—a very class operation.

Barnes' work was always big civil cases. He worked exclusively for the American Tobacco Corporation. Every time somebody sues because a loved one died of lung cancer, the tobacco people hire Barnes. They'll spend $200,000 on an investigation to squash a little summons and complaint, because once somebody wins, there's millions of people that can file. They did such deep background investigation that they would go back to see what the mother of the lung-cancer victim had ingested during her pregnancy. I'm sorry to say that when you go into court with such volumes of material, even it it's not specific evidence, the court's impressed. They never lost one.

There was one case I worked on for over a year, and that was the Howard Hughes will. We were hired by a law firm representing the matrilineal family, and my job was to disprove the Mormon will. For an entire year I did nothing but study Howard Hughes. Read everything I could find, talked to his old test pilots, his old engineers, everybody I could. The only thing that gave credence to the Mormon will was the fact that Melvin Dummar had insider information that no one would know unless he had really picked up Hughes in the desert and given him a ride, like he said.

Well, I found a great-uncle of Dummar's, and I talked to this old guy—missing teeth, about seventy-five years old—in Gardena. He said, "Yeah, it's really something what happened to old Melvin." He says, "You know, my wife used to work for Hughes back in the thirties."

I said, "Tell me about it. I hear he's really an interesting guy." He said, "Yeah, she had that book that nobody ever got to read." I said, "What book was this?" And he says, "You know when Hughes flew around the world, that copilot, Harry, he wrote a book about the whole thing. Howard wouldn't let him fly the plane because he wanted all the glory of doing the whole thing himself. So he kept taking stimulants, and Harry just sat there and listened to Howard talk the whole time. Harry wrote a book, it was a handwritten manuscript, and he tried like hell to get it published, but nobody would take it. We had that thing over here for years."

So that's where Dummar got it all from. It was beautiful. An unpublished manuscript that nobody even knew existed. So we were able to disprove the Mormon will.

Shortly after that, I had a bad dispute with Barnes, and ended my association with him. It was also around that time that my mother died—August 8, 1980, at the age of forty-nine. The specific cause of death was heart failure. It was my opinion that it was brought on by the effects of long-term alcoholism. I bore a tremendous amount of guilt over my mother's death. She died alone in a ramshackle little apartment. It didn't set well at all. We'd been corresponding regularly, exchanging letters once a week, but I felt like I should have been there. That incident with the cops in Santa Monica was the determining factor in her mental-health history—and I'd always felt responsible for that. But you eventually have to deal with the fact that the burden is gone, and no matter how much guilt you project on yourself, it's not going to change anything.

After I left Barnes, I opened up an office again in my own name. I started doing dope recoveries. Big dealers got hit, and they'd want their stuff back. They'd come to me and I'd PSE everybody and find out who was lying. The first one I did, I got almost a complete return. Boy, they heard about that. You talk about a grapevine. All of a sudden I had to get an answering machine. "Rhodes, I hear you do recovery work—on unusual items!"

I didn't want to be in that business, and was given an offer by a very rich firm in Orange County. They were interested in the PSE. Through many, many meetings, I learned that they ran massage parlors that were really whorehouses. They wanted the girls to be able to say, in a miked room, "Are you a cop?" And when the customer said, "No," they wanted that "No" analyzed, so they would know right away if she could go ahead and pitch the john, or the red light would go on and she would give a straight massage and get the guy out of there. I really got scared to death. Those guys were organized crime, and they were killers. One of their guys was working on a subsonic transmitter to scramble the brainwaves of critical witnesses. That's when I packed it in. I put it all down.

Through the years, the seediness of investigations, the slime, got to me. I felt as if I were as bad or worse as the people I was dealing with. Things that you did weren't normal. Your back against walls watching everybody in a restaurant. Running these machines. You see everybody as marks or johns, and I got tired of seeing the world that way.

When I finally got out of the business, I realized my childhood was cut short by events that occurred in my life. I chose to allow them to happen, but the fact remains that at eighteen years old, I wasn't driving around in a '57 Chevy. I had a sidewall haircut, a three-piece suit, and a big gun on, and I was living a very disciplined, almost monastic life. I discovered I really wanted to go back and get in touch, to try to live part of that life I missed, and just do what I wanted to do.

The first thing I did was to buy an interest in a treasure expedition. I took off for a year and went through Central America filming Mayan temples with a screenwriter friend of mine. We spent eight weeks in Panama sampling local ladies and bills of fare, having exciting times. Then we took off on this ship and lived on Greater Inagua Island, forty miles off the coast of Cuba, and spent six months diving every day, looking for treasure.

I got back and just started smiling again. Going to the beach, trying to enjoy things. In the past, I'd stepped on a lot of people because I was very busy, or maybe I was abrupt with them. So I tried to settle a few of those and tell them I was going to be a different person now.

I met Kimberley, my wife, in Marina Del Rey. She was going with a young fellow I knew, and they had just ended their relationship. She was looking to rent a room in the area, and I had a room to rent in a house I owned in Venice. She didn't like my looks and I didn't like her demeanor, so it didn't happen. Six months later I ran into her, and the room was open again, and this time she took it.

I couldn't believe the disgusting men that she went out with, all these swinging types from the marina. So I decided, I've got to do this girl a favor. She needs to go out with somebody who's decent. We started dating mildly at first, but we cared a lot about each other and began dating seriously. Before we left town and moved to the desert, I sold the house in Venice and started buying houses, fixing them, and rolling them over. Kimberley did that with me. Even though she was raised on a six-acre compound in Benedict Canyon, she was willing to roll up her sleeves and get dirty along with me. I like that.

Right now I'm a person who wears a multitude of hats. I write computer programs for billing and inventory control—application programs. I have a cleaning service here in Palm Desert that cleans condos. I'm an antique dealer. On the weekends, I cook at the Palm Desert Tennis Club, where Kimberley is the office manager. I really like to cook, and we're very slowly moving towards opening a restaurant. Also, I just began a job as an instructor at the Foundation for the Retarded of the Desert.

At this moment, career doesn't mean anything to me. I know at my age I should be thinking about it, but I'm really just happy and very content with my marriage, and with the changes in my life, and I'll see about that later. We've got a child coming, and now I can look at a small child and I can pause to reflect on the beauty of that little creature, whereas years ago I could not. I can see beauty now in my life that I could not see before. I'm still so ecstatic about that that I'm not really worried about money yet. I'm going to try to live my life on a good, positive note, and pause to take the time from now on to reflect on the beauty in the world around us, and that's something I never had time to do before.

After we had concluded our conversation, Rusty and I were joined by Kimberley and my wife, Flora. With our little boy running around, and with Kimberley being very pregnant, we talked at great length about prepared childbirth and the joys of parenting. But as the evening drew to a close, I couldn't help asking Rusty his informed opinion on a question that has never stopped bothering me: Who really did kill John F. Kennedy? Although Rusty's active involvement in the matter had ended several years earlier, it was obvious that his interest in the mystery had not diminished.

As for Lee Oswald, he was a man with an inflated ego, a troubled young man who was certainly the type that could be manipulated and guided. I could see that crazy little wimp firing shots that day. He couldn't have fired them all. He didn't have the training, and the rifle was a mess, but I would not be surprised if Lee Oswald did fire shots that day. However, there is no proof that he did. Either way, he was a patsy, in my opinion. His background raises a lot of questions, particularly his defection to the Soviet Union and his smooth return to the United States. We need to go to the offices of Naval Intelligence and get the files on his recruitment, and I'd like to go to the Soviet Union, sit down with somebody from the KGB, open up their file on Oswald, and talk about it.

However, the assassination of John F. Kennedy will never be solved until someone takes a long, hard, dismantling look at that symbiotic relationship that exists between the CIA and organized crime. That unholy marriage poses, in my opinion, the greatest threat to this democracy that we've ever witnessed. The Kennedy brothers had to be stopped. No attorney general in the history of this country has gone after organized crime like Robert Kennedy. The Kennedys were too rich to be bought and they were too brash to be intimidated. Even their old man couldn't stop them, and he was in bed with a lot of those people.

THE ACTIVIST:

Pearl Thomas Mitchell

I have heard it said that what became known as "the sixties" didn't really start until late 1966 or so, when the Vietnam War escalated dramatically and, with it, antiwar protests. In some areas of the country this was probably true, but for some people, particularly in the South, "the sixties" began much earlier.

"I don't know why they are protesting," said Edward Bailey, the white mayor of Demopolis, Alabama, on April 22, 1965. "We've integrated all the restaurants, cafés, public parks, theaters, and given them anything they wanted. When I asked them what they wanted, all they could answer was, 'Freedom.' "

The civil-rights movement, beginning with the Montgomery, Alabama, bus boycott in 1955–56, captured the attention of the media, not only in the United States but throughout the world. Camera crews and reporters rushed around the South to spread the news of the latest sit-in, march, or demonstration. Many towns experienced this sudden and short-lived glare of attention. But after the press packed up and moved on, the citizens of these towns, white and black, were left behind with their conflicts and hostilities unresolved.

Such a place was Bogalusa, Louisiana, a muggy paper-mill town near the Mississippi border. It is my habit when visiting a new city immediately to seek out the local health-food store and the local bookstore. This benign practice had sobering results in Bogalusa, where the paper business is dying, the population is declining, and many folks have to drive thirty miles or more to find work. There was a health-food store, but its shelves were bare except for some old dried fruit and a few bottles of vitamins. A new shipment of supplies was due "sometime next week."

Next door was the bookstore, but it sold only used paperbacks. If Boga-
lusans ever have a craving to buy a new book or a loaf of whole-wheat
bread, they have to drive at least a half hour to another town to meet
their needs.

In May 1965 most class-of-'65ers were buying dresses, suits, and
corsages for their graduation ceremonies and parties. At Central Memo-
rial High School in Bogalusa, however, many of them were busy demon-
strating for equal rights and integration, instead.

I found black Bogalusans quite willing to discuss the civil-rights
movement. I was told repeatedly that if I really wanted to hear about
what had taken place in Bogalusa in 1965, I should find Pearl Thomas.
This turned out to be easier said than done. It took two months of persis-
tent sleuthing to obtain the phone number of Pearl's home in Oakland,
California.

Initially, she resisted meeting with me. "White people have studied
black people to death," she said. Eventually she relented, and invited me
to her house. When I arrived, Pearl was wearing jeans and a Jesse Jack-
son T-shirt. Over the door to her bedroom was a sign, a souvenir from
Bogalusa, that read "Colored Women." Her television set looked as if it
had been hit by a tornado. She explained that her TV didn't work well
because she was always throwing things at it. "I buy old TVs at Good-
will," she said. "And I keep a rubber brick next to my chair, so I don't do
too much damage."

We settled down at her dining-room table and I asked her why she
admired Jesse Jackson.

She replied without hesitation. "Jesse Jackson's presidential candi-
dacy gave hope to black children. I had to eat my words about him, be-
cause I had always considered him a self-serving person. I was suspicious.
But he evolved and grew, and I became proud of him. I cried during his
whole speech at the Democratic Convention. My heart went out to him."

Pearl and I spent a few minutes exploring each other's political be-
liefs, and then I told her that while in Bogalusa I had heard that one of
the last lynchings in the United States had taken place just outside of
town. I asked Pearl if she recalled the incident.

I was in the sixth grade going into seventh grade. This black man, Mack
Charles Parker, was lynched, supposedly for raping this pregnant white
woman. It was in the spring, in April. That was a gloomy day. It was

dark, it seemed, at four o'clock. Everybody knew that it was going to happen. Everybody knew. Parents had their children in. You couldn't find anybody on the streets that night. Everybody knew that this was going to happen. And they were totally helpless—couldn't do anything about it. Sure enough, when the paper came the next morning—he had been taken out of the jail and he had disappeared. They didn't find the body for days. They dumped him in the Pearl River. That touched me. It really, really touched my life, kept me in knots, not sleeping at night, depressed for weeks.

The Klan in Bogalusa had organized the whole bit. One of the big leaders was a store owner; we had to run him out of business because he was supposedly a big mover and shaker. Supposedly his maid had washed his clothes and there was blood all over them. Whether that was true or not, it was spread like wildfire in the black community. And people stopped patronizing him. It wasn't a planned thing. It was word of mouth. He had progressed from a mom-and-pop-type operation to a big supermarket. And we shut him down without making any big fanfare about it.

By this time I had seen the meanness in the whole process. There were separate drinking fountains; we couldn't use the public library; we couldn't use the public park. We had colored and white benches at the hospital. The doctors had two separate waiting rooms. There was a white cemetery and a colored cemetery.

My blood father died in an accident when I was seven months old. I lived with my grandmother on a farm for a goodly portion of my early life and probably would have lived with her longer except that my family thought that the schools were better in Bogalusa, and I was always considered very bright. My grandmother and my uncles taught me how to read. I started living with my mother when I was six. She was a domestic and my stepfather was a milkman until he was declared legally blind because of cataracts. My mother had ten children all together and I was second. My mother and stepfather didn't hang out with the upper crust, if you will—if you could call anything in Bogalusa upper crust. You know, the teachers and the morticians and the preachers, and some of the Crown-Zellerbach workers. We always owned our own house, shabby as it may be, because that was important to my family.

We lived on what they now call the cul-de-sacs. We called them dead ends. The block I was on was all black, of course. But the next block was white. Out on the farm with my grandmother I didn't come in contact with white people. The area was all black. Nobody ever told me that if somebody hit you, you weren't supposed to hit them back. So when somebody hit me, I would hit back. The white kids would play with us and then the people in the neighborhood would tell you things like "You better not hit that white girl." That was a problem because I never stopped hitting when they hit me. They were really poor white trash. I mean they were renting their houses. So we thought we were better, because all the people on our block owned their homes or at least were buying them. They were more outcast than we were.

We would exchange comic books and that kind of stuff, and in the summer we'd have real good softball games. That was okay, but there were some boundaries. I remember my mother used to send me and my brother to the store, and this white boy—he was much older than we were—he lived in that next block from us and he was just mean. Oooh, he was mean. And he was a baby. He was the only boy out of a whole bunch of girls. My brother was probably around nine and I was probably around seven. We went to the store very peacefully, and when we came back, his father told him to go out and beat up my brother.

He hit my brother and he kicked him. And my brother was afraid to hit him back. We went home and I told my mama what happened, and she said, "Well, the next time, just walk on the other side of the street." That blew my mind. I said, "I'm not walking on the other side of the street." No. Not me. So I was constantly in trouble with the white kids. I think we had a little respect for each other because white folks knew I was going to fight. Simple as that.

A white girl worked at the corner store and she was friendly and would play. Talked with us and traded comic books, *True Confessions* and what have you, until white folks were around. One day I paid her and I touched her hand. And she said, "Oh, get that nigger off me." I forgot myself. I was twelve years old. I jumped over the counter and we were down between the wall and the counter. And we went to Fist City. The man who owned the store was Italian. Well, they couldn't very well make a big stink out of it because black people were supporting the store. Of course, I got into big trouble.

But I didn't care, because a long time ago I decided I wasn't going to be anybody's nigger. It was just a decision I personally made with myself. And when anyone called me a nigger at that time, he was prepared for a fight. If I had to go in white kids' yards to get them, if they called me nigger, we were going to fight. I'd come home, my dress was torn off at the waist, hair all over my head. And I'd get into trouble— but I was going to have these fights. I just had an attitude.

I would not take that treatment from the black-run school either, because black people can treat other blacks as niggers, too. I think I had more control over white people calling me a nigger than I did over black people treating me as if I were a nigger. I resented the caste system. Color, basically, was the essence of the caste system. The businesses for the most part in the black community were owned by fair-complexioned blacks. The Creoles. And Ray Charles can see that I don't look like any of that.

The summer after my junior year, Bogalusa celebrated its golden jubilee and they had a citywide essay contest for black students. I won the contest and got a trophy. In the meantime, things were happening around us. They had this biracial committee that the mayor had hand-picked. He had picked his boys and they were sitting around meeting and conferring.

One day we went to the café, the drugstore that had soda fountains and counters. We decided we would go in and order an ice-cream sundae. You would have thought that was the Second Coming. Within ten minutes the world knew it. I mean, the drugstore was closed immediately. They got us out of there and it was closed. Then the black leaders decided they would have to do something, because they could not keep us isolated from the rest of the world. Something was going to happen. But they were still meeting and conferring, meeting and conferring, and nothing was happening.

I was working for one of the black leaders at the time, one of the mayor's boys. He owned the Dairy Palace, a malt shop, and I was a waitress. He was always telling me that progress was being made and things were going to happen. We had a couple of meetings in January 1965, and students were getting restless. So we set up what was supposed to be a "test day"—that was something that the mayor's biracial committee had agreed to. We were going to "integrate" key restaurants in Bogalusa. We would go in all prearranged. The restaurant owners knew that we were coming and were asked to indulge these niggers for this one day. They weren't going to do it again: It was just going to be this one-day thing. They had this whole thing set up. They had the transportation here, there, and everywhere.

My partner and I went to this restaurant over at the wrong side of town, and we were supposed to be able to call back in. Well, we couldn't call back. And they were boiling grease in a deep fryer, and my heart was "thump, thump." But finally somebody showed up and we got our sandwiches and we left. Well, they ranted and raved about how smoothly things went. I mean, they had had it their way, and that was supposed to be the end of integration in Bogalusa.

By this time, representatives of CORE had come into town and started scoping the place, if you will. Giving advice and what have you. I was in school and hearing bits and pieces and slipping out, going to meetings when I could, because my mother had not become involved at that point. This was about the time that Selma was taking place. There were those who were dying to get there, and slipping off. My mother never knew that a group of us slipped off to go on the march with Martin Luther King.

The first big march in Bogalusa was April 8th. Our meeting place was at the Labor Union Hall. We started up Sullivan Drive, and they stopped us after about four blocks, and turned all these students around. They had this unlawful-assembly thing and crowd control. Some of the adult leaders went to New Orleans and got an injunction. It seemed like the fact that the police turned back the students got the adults really angry, and suddenly you had old people who could hardly walk, who were hobbling out there to get in the march. In many cases, they couldn't march all the way; they would march so far or would get in their car and come and join us. So April 8th became a real turning point in the whole thing.

The picketing began that afternoon. We got the court order saying we could. They got a concession that there couldn't be too many people. I think there were two people who could picket each store. We picketed both sides of the street from opening until the closing hour. There was always somebody there watching us. We would never be there alone. There was always somebody there with a gun. There was always a Deacon around.

I remember that night; it was my last night working at the Dairy Palace after I got fired. We couldn't make a telephone call. The telephone system was shut down in the black community because Bob Hicks was trying to call Bobby Kennedy, trying to get some federal assistance in there. It was like a state of siege. So the next day all the people who could pick up a gun got their guns and they formed the Deacons. Now the Deacons did not start in Bogalusa. They gained notoriety in Bogalusa; they started in Jonesboro. Their guys were frustrated in Jonesboro because that movement fizzled very quickly. They came down to Bogalusa and that's really where it was reborn.

So they got permits to carry guns. I mean, all these people got permits. And they would use them, and they would guard homes. On marches we had the FBI taking notes—that's all they ever did was take notes. We had the Bogalusa Police Department, and we had the Deacons. We had our own special police force. Our marches were never nonviolent. Nothing we ever did was nonviolent from that point on. I mean, we learned from CORE how to fall and how to protect ourselves. But, see, that just wasn't going to work.

I have the utmost respect for Martin Luther King. God rest his soul! But, see, there was something about somebody cracking me across the head, and me turning the other cheek, that just did not sit well with me. Those people were crazy. You know, they would have killed us. King never came to Bogalusa because he did not condone violence.

Some other students and I walked into the classrooms at the high school and called the students out to join us marching and picketing. We'd tell them, "If you're black, you're in it." And we'd call them by name and we would embarrass them. We'd tell them, "You're going to benefit from this, too." We were threatened by teachers and the principal: "If you don't leave, you're gonna get in trouble, get suspended. Worse, you're gonna get expelled." So we got across the street from the school, so that we were not on school property anymore. We called everybody out. Quite a few of them came, about 150. There were only about 500 in the school. And a lot of those who didn't come left school and went home because they were afraid. We did what we wanted to do. We disrupted the process, and we gave them something to think about.

So the pressure was on the principal from the superintendent to keep those kids in line. At the time, I didn't agree with him. I don't agree with him now, but I do understand a little more. Principles sometimes are tempered and compromised by reality. White people were forcing him to have control over something that he normally had control over. He had always had control over his students. That was his little empire. Suddenly he had lost that control with that group of '65. Not only were there marches and demonstrations going on but there were more girls in my class graduating pregnant than there had been in the history of Central Memorial High School.

Incidents during the picketing did not seem to start immediately. The more we were out there, the angrier they became. The name-calling, that was really no biggie. "Nigger" had been used so much that it suddenly had lost its meaning. We were not supposed to say anything to them—we left that to the Deacons—because we were displaying a certain amount of dignity on the picket line. Now, if they would hit you, you'd *forget* dignity, you'd put that picket sign down, and you'd go for broke and kick ass. There were some acts of violence. I knew this woman—this store owner came over to tear up her picket sign, and she was not going to give it to him. She literally picked him up and threw him through his own window. Oh, yeah! She was a big woman. We believed in direct action. But, you know, some of these white folks were walking around patrolling the streets like the Wild, Wild West with guns on, you know, with the holsters.

I lived very close to the downtown shopping district, so I would put my picket sign down and go home. I never really thought about it. But one evening I was followed, so the Deacons stopped me from doing that. Somebody would always take me home. It never occurred to me because, see, I had a weapon. I had a broom handle that I had nicked down and put razor blades all on the side. I would always swing my stick, just walking home with my stick. But there always was that concern that if any of us were caught in isolated places and were identified as being active in the movement, we would be subjected to physical and sexual abuse. There were horror stories about women who were put in jail.

My mother had this thing where if I left home, I had to have a dress on. She figured if I had a dress on, I wasn't going to do anything, because we wore jeans all the time. So anytime I left the house I had to pass inspection. I had learned to hide my jeans in a little bag at night on the corner. I would try to wear skirts so that I wouldn't have to do anything but go in the alley, put my pants on and put my skirt in the bag.

But this particular day, two weeks before graduation, I was late because I was supposed to relieve someone on the picket line. I was picketing, and this policeman took his nightstick and pulled my dress up. As luck would have it, *Time* magazine and all the other magazines got this on camera. Well, I was more worried about the trouble I was in at home than I was about this. So I sneaked to school. By the time I got there, the FBI was waiting for me, so they could get the rundown on this incident. The teachers were so upset at me: "You're gonna be in trouble." "Why don't you leave this mess alone?" And, "You've got an opportunity to go to school and be somebody."

I said, "Hell, I'm already somebody! I was *born* somebody!"

During this time, my mother lost her job. She worked for the people who owned the Western Auto chain, and I caught picket duty one day there. So I picketed. I guess that was pretty arrogant or stupid on my part. Her boss said, "Your daughter is really going to hurt you, because these white people are not going to pay people and have their kids picketing." They told my mother she was going to get fired. And she said, "No, you can't fire me." They said, "Well, why?" And she said, "I just quit." And she quit, and she became really militant at that point.

That same day, some of us went to the segregated park. Well, I don't know where those white people came from. There were no women. There were all these men. I think they were buried like moles in the sand. We were having a good time at the park and suddenly, out of nowhere, they came with their dogs and their sticks and their guns. It was unbelievable. I mean, women were fighting and struggling for their lives. This policeman hit me with this brass knuckle. And he was letting me have it, too. So I kicked him in the groin. Boy, my life wasn't worth a plug nickel, you hear. It was going to take him a while to get out of pain, but in the meantime, it was hard for me to run in sand.

I ran to Mr. Sam Barnes of the Deacons. Mr. Sam opened up the car door and said, "Run, Pearl, run!" I dove in that car, and blood was shooting all down my face. He wouldn't let them get to me. They took him and they beat him up. And really beat him. But he didn't let them get to me because they probably would have killed me. I mean, there was just that much furor. They put him in jail and beat him up, and they kept him in jail for a while. He protected me. He sacrificed what could have been his life, because he had an idea what kind of abuse I would have been subjected to had they put me in jail.

Three days later was our graduation. We couldn't even hold our baccalaureates in peace. They turned on the stereo at the Dairy Queen and played it all during the services. They threatened to shoot up the graduation. The Deacons were the thing that kept many people alive in Bogalusa. They told the chief of police, "You don't have to protect them, because we will. They are going to have a graduation. So if you don't want some dead white kids, you better keep their asses off that corner."

During this time the national TV and the newspapers and magazines were there every day. We were tyring to generate sympathy, so we were very definitely taught to be on our best behavior. But we were also told to protect ourselves. We were nine deep in the marches. The leaders tried to put the women in the middle and men on each side of them. The last four or five rows they tried to put men, so that women would be cushioned. The Deacons, of course, would be on either side. The counterdemonstrators were told not to get within so many feet of us. If one did, the Deacons would tell the police and the FBI that they better talk to him because if he crossed this line, it would be open season on him. We caught a couple of them across the line, and we had a field day on them down through the line.

You know how the media are. When they are sympathetic to your cause, they will never show anything that will make you look bad. So they would never have shown that, because they were generating sympathy. They'd show the policeman lifting my skirt or hitting me, but I don't think they'd show where I was kicking him back. Here I was, a defenseless little black girl, being brutalized by this policeman. It wouldn't have made good copy to show that I have been taught to defend myself. Later Bogalusa became old news to them and the riots in Watts and Detroit became focal points. But I think we had made our point.

It really, really got hot that summer. It was like all-out war declared on each other. A week after graduation they rounded us up while we were picketing. Forty-seven of us were arrested. They took us all to jail and we had a good time. We sang songs; we stopped the toilet up. The sergeant was stereotypical, fat and lazy, and he was begging parents to get us out. And parents had been told not to get anybody out of jail. We made him earn his money that day. Before the day was over, they dropped charges and let us out.

I had gotten a full scholarship for Southern University. Also my mom had worked for these white people, and they had met me and they were really impressed. One was a Southerner and one was from Minnesota. One was an attorney and one was a doctor. They liked my spunk and they had always been supportive of black education. They became sort of my patrons, if you will. They had always said that when I got ready to go to college, they were going to help me. Well, true to their word, they did.

I had to go to summer school. My mom didn't make me, but she sort of strongly suggested I go to summer school, because there seemed to be this thing that if I didn't go to summer school, I was going to get so caught up in the movement that I would never go to school. I would become a professional activist. So I went away to summer school at Southern in Baton Rouge. I would come home every chance I got and still participate in things.

It was at Southern that I first became aware of the Vietnam War, because guys who enrolled with me for summer school didn't come back in September. Then you'd ask about one of them and kids would get letters from home saying that he was killed. Remember there seemed to be a disproportionate number of black people going, and I resented that. You don't want us here, you don't give us our rights, but we can go over and fight your stupid war. I became acutely aware of it and hated the racist system in America for it, because I ran around with a group of students at Southern who were activists like me. You know, we find each other.

We were not the respected student leaders, not the ones the administration could count on. We had our underground movement. We were into a lot of heavy philosophical discussions. The war was beginning to be the topic of discussion, and lots of things were still going on in Bogalusa and around the country. Sometimes the students would have these little movements, where they'd be concerned about food in the cafeteria. I have always been selective about my battles. I never got involved with the "We need better food" movements. I guess having been a trooper and veteran of the Bogalusa war, it seemed trivial to me. And it was so hard to get a lot of people to talk about the war in Vietnam. They always thought you were crazy. It seemed so far away; yet black men were dying by the thousands. While I was at Southern, the war was only important to a small group of us; at that time we were called weirdos.

Meanwhile, things were still hot in Bogalusa. The Klan had been real strong, but we reached a point in '65 where we weren't afraid. They had tried to instill this fear in the black community about all these things that were going to happen. Nobody was afraid of them anymore because we had learned that they were cowards, and that the Deacons could deal with them. They weren't going to go in anyone's house because they knew that you were armed and everybody knew how to shoot. Their scare tactics lost their appeal.

So, in '66, while I was home for a semester break, we had a march where we wore white sheets and hoods. It was a riot. They had this stronghold for all these years and our march told them we don't give a damn about your sheets, could care less about your burning crosses, and even less about your guns. That really dealt them a dirty blow. That was the last nail in the coffin. Actually, while I was away at college, the Klan had one more march. They had a loudspeaker playing "Dixie," and when the black kids heard that they came running out and marched alongside and sang along. That must have been the really last nail in the coffin.

I majored in English in college. I wanted to be a lawyer. But one didn't get encouraged to be anything other than a nurse or a teacher if you were a girl. Regardless of what color you were, you were going to be a teacher or a nurse or a secretary. I didn't want to be a secretary, so I always felt that I'd major in English and I'd teach.

I was just getting ready to graduate from college, and I was doing student teaching, and had come in and taken a nap when the dorm just alarmed up. These girls started screaming. My roommates came in and said, "Pearl, King is dead!" And I said, "Such a sick, belated April Fools joke." But my roommate kept crying, and she said, "No, Pearl, I'm not . . ." One of my roommates had a TV, and we turned it on, and sure enough. I just wanted to drop out.

The next day, that Friday, the weather was beautiful, but it was one of the saddest days of my life. We had commemorative activities and chapel. Then we had a twenty-four-mile march to the Capitol. There were priests, rabbis, ministers, the whole bit. I just cried, because it was really hard. I didn't cry until Friday, and then I cried for a lot of reasons. I cried for . . . I cried for me, I cried for everybody. I cried for the hate, the country, the world. It really, really got to me. And as we were praying, the twenty-four miles got to me. I'm really sorry about this, but I was also praying at the time to see if anybody had a car to give me a ride, because my feet were hurting. Reality stepped in. I said, "Oh, God, please let somebody come through with a car because I've got to walk twenty-four miles back to Southern from the Capitol."

I tend to sleep when I get depressed. I went home because they let school out, and, basically, that whole week I just slept. Sort of like a zombie. King had never been my hero. I mean, I respected him and what he did, but Malcolm was my hero. Unfortunately, Malcolm didn't live long enough so that they could understand how they could both benefit each other for the good of black people—because I think there was a place for both of them. Later, when Bobby Kennedy was killed, I felt that was the final nail in the coffin for us. There went my dreams, my hopes.

I graduated college in three years. It was a combination of wanting to help the family and just wanting to get out and go on and do other things. My mother still had six kids at home, and my father was on a limited, fixed income. I felt if I got a job, it would take some of the pressure off. I wanted to go to law school; if that didn't work out, I was wanting to become a psychologist. And I did eventually get my masters in psych.

But first I taught for a year in Lafayette, Louisiana. Fifth-grade language arts. I really regret that. I missed being a near-adult. I suddenly had to become an adult, and when I was around kids my age, I didn't know how to act, because here I was having to be at work at eight in the morning and taking responsibility for thirty lives every day. I wished that I had spaced it out and had enjoyed it more socially for a while. I thought I was socially maladjusted.

So I taught a year and . . . see, Lafayette is one big caste system, like New Orleans. They believed they were as close to God as you could get because there was a disproportionate number of fair-complexioned ones there. They didn't get involved in the movement. And, of course, idealistic Pearl, right out of college, it was going to touch you, because if you're black, you're in it. So my thing was signs on my wall talking about "I'm black and I'm proud," and those people did not want to hear that. You know, we black people have collaborated in our own oppression. We have been very good collaborators, thanks to the white man's mind-control game. White people have encouraged our sense of self-hatred.

So one day I decided that I was going to start wearing a natural. My hair wouldn't act right, so I went and got me a wig. Big Angela Davis–type wig. And I cut me some African print and had me a dashiki made. It was a shirt, but dresses were real short at the time. And sandals were real popular at that time. The hippie sandals, as they called them. I put on big earrings and went to work. Well, hey, you would have thought World War Four had been declared. Those teachers would come into the room and they would be looking in. So the principal said there was a gas leak and closed the school down, because the superintendent happened to be on his way that day and the principal knew that before the superintendent got off campus, somebody was going to tell him that I was up there with all that hair. So he told me, "I'll give you a good recommendation, but at the end of the year, you've got to go." He told me that the South was not ready for me at that point. We weren't ready for each other. The marriage would never work. I told him I thought so too, and I applied to various graduate schools throughout the country and chose California. I chose San Diego State because they were more persistent in their letters to me. I thought San Diego was a nice place to make the transition.

I entered the graduate program in counseling psychology. I chose counseling psychology because I like studying people. And I thought it was good discipline, like reading and a lot of writing. I still had that dream of going to law school. I thought each little step would be in that direction.

That first summer I was there, I applied for a job at this clothing store in downtown San Diego. I filled out my application and the owner said, "Why are you doing this? You're obviously a very bright young woman. You're too qualified to be working here." He told me he had a lot of contacts at the school-district office and that I should apply for a teaching job and use his name. I did, and I got hired, but that didn't start until September and this was in June. He was sort of liberal and involved in sort of radical things. He knew some of the people that were involved. So I got involved in various community-type meetings.

I found it funny that they were so far behind in terms of what we had done. They were talking about segregated neighborhoods and red-lining. I mean, in Bogalusa we didn't live next door to white people, but we lived in the same neighborhood all of my life. So the mayor had appointed an interim city councilman, who was black, the first black city councilman, and he was up for election, his first campaign. I got the job being his office manager. I did that until school started.

But the big thing in San Diego—I guess that was true all over the country—was the antipoverty money. I had been led to believe that if you got an education, that was a key. But one of the real negatives of the money of Johnson's Great Society was that suddenly an education became a burden, especially for black people. The money was ear-marked for community people and people looked down upon you, suddenly attacked you, if you were educated. I remember one of my white professors at San Diego State attacked me, along with some of the black militants who were in the class, and said that I had been raised very "bourgie," you know, middle class. "How else can you justify being as young as you are and talking about getting a master's?"

So-called militants were running various community education groups and I tried to volunteer, but there was always somebody there trying to put me down. You know: "You are one of these little rich black kids." Then I sort of dropped out of it and concentrated on my education. I always did step to the beat of a different drummer, because I thought a lot of things they did were really trivial. I thought they were missing, in many cases, a bigger picture.

I met my husband while I was in San Diego. He was getting his doctorate from Cal. He had a very sharp mind. We were married in 1972. He did not like San Diego. After you've lived in the Bay Area, who would? So I completed my master's and we moved up north. After I married him, I realized he was a white boy in black skin. That's okay, but I didn't think I was marrying a white man. He got hung up on trendy things. There was no substance there. He's very bright—he has a scientific background. You know, we always tend to think of those who are good in math and science as being very smart. He could talk about a lot of things, and he was on top of the movement in Berkeley, and I was really impressed that somebody was actually doing something.

Much later I realized that this was just something to do, you know, like kids dabble in things like fingerpainting for a minute. I realized that he had no commitment to a real movement or to any social change. In short, philosophically, we were miles apart. We found that we couldn't talk politics and we couldn't talk sociology. So, animosity set in. We separated, and finally divorced in '79.

When we first moved to the Bay Area, I worked for a summer in a Bay Area school district. I'm glad I didn't get a regular job because mediocrity seemed to have been the standard, and I don't stand shoulder to shoulder with mediocrity. Either I would have burned out or I would have begun to accept their standards.

But I got a really good job in a neat district over in San Mateo County, where people were really into education. We had good, conscientious, hardworking teachers. I was a high-school counselor. We did some very good things in that school. It was an experimental school, as so many of them were in the late '60s and '70s. People *wanted* to be there, for the most part, and they gave it their all. We had good students—a little United Nations. We had everything there. So it was a neat place to be, for the most part.

But neighborhoods changed, and standards were not what they should have been for all kids. The change in color and the ethnic makeup had a lot to do with it. In many cases, when those parents moved to the suburbs they felt that they had given their kids all that they could give. I mean, they got them out of those inner-city schools in San Francisco, and they felt that that was enough. Their attitude seem to have been "God damn it, all you had to do was go and those teachers would teach you." That kind of thing. Parental involvement dropped off. And I had ideological problems with the new principal. So, after six years, it was time to leave.

I'm a risk-taker, so in '78 I quit the job; I took the plunge and went to graduate school. School of Education in Berkeley. I got fellowships, financial aid, and all that kind of other hustle. I worked as a research assistant. I always had two or three little hustles. It was never enough. So in '81 I went back to work full-time. I was a program director for a public-policy foundation for two years. Then I did campus public affairs for another foundation for six months. Now I'm with the Peralta Community College District in Oakland. I am working as a proposal writer, program development for the vocational school in the community-college district. Trying to get programs funded. That also means tightening up the programs and curriculum somewhat.

Now, in 1980, there was an incident that affected me deeply. To get a Ph.D. from the School of Education, you have to have an academic master's that's relevant to your work. Since I was getting my Ph.D. in policy analysis and administration, my counseling master's was not relevant. So I had to do a lot of working. I had to get an M.A. equivalent. Mine is in political science. Again that craving for politics.

Anyway, they had this conference for public administrators at the Hilton Hotel in San Francisco. A friend of mine from Bogalusa, who was teaching at a black college in Alabama, came out for this conference and she said, "You know, that will be good for you since you're dealing with policy." So I went to the hotel with her on Sunday and then came back Tuesday evening because the black caucus was having something. We had a symposium for like an hour, and then we went to have a bite to eat.

And I went on over to the hotel, not only to see what was going on, to see if there were any internships available, but to pick up Diane, my friend. I went up on the second floor on the escalator, and they said there was a party up on that level. I knew it was not a party because black folks would never be that quiet, not at a party. Whatever they were having was over. So I turned around and came back. And I see these two brothers. They had suits on.

I said, "Oh, hi. You here for the conference, too? Because I'm looking for Chicken." That's what we called Diane. I didn't know who the dudes were—didn't know they were security and didn't care. The guy looked at me and he said, "What are you doing up here?" I said,

"Well, I'm looking for Chicken." He said, "I don't give a damn what you're doing, you're going to have to get the hell off."

I thought he was just kidding. I said, "Don't get so uptight." Well, then, I get my attitude. I said, "Look, can't you tell that I'm going down this escalator?" He said, "Well, get on down." I turned around and I said, "Well, I *can* stop in the bar and have a drink, can't I?" He said, "If you can afford it." Phheww.

So I go down and I get me a glass of wine. The Hilton Hotel has some tables outside of the bar so you can watch what's going on in the lobby. I sat there, so I could see Diane if she came. Finished the wine, and Diane didn't show up. So I decided to go use the phone and call where I thought she might be, because she had a couple friends staying at the hotel. Nobody was in. When I got off the phone, the other security guard was leaning up against the elevator. I said, "What are you following me for? What's your problem?"

And he said, "You ugly nigger bitch, we're going to follow you everywhere you go."

And I said, "Yo' mammy," and, "We're going to send your no-talking ass back to Jamaica on that banana boat." He was Puerto Rican or something. We had this confrontation.

I left the hotel. I called the next morning to file my little complaint with the chief of security. Well, the next night, I was back at the hotel because Diane was supposed to pick me up there. She called and said the car wouldn't start—I had loaned her my car. I said, "You flooded it. Let it sit for a while and go back out and try." The friends whose room I was in had to go to someone else's room. I truck on down there and go down the steps, and the security guard who had stopped me the night before was standing there. He did not recognize me until I got down to the door. He whirled around and he went back to the desk. Diane never came. So I went back to use the phone, and that's where the shit hit the fan.

He said, "You can't come in here." I said, "Well, why not?" He said, "You're not a guest." I said, "I have some friends who are guests." I said, "You can't tell me I can't come in here." So we shadowboxed on over to this big desk. I said, "Well, can I use the phone?" He said, "Use the one across the street." I mean, if you know where the San Francisco Hilton is, you know that is not a place you can after dark go and use the phone. It's in the Tenderloin.

I went over, furious. I called and told my friends to come down and meet me. I got back to the hotel before they got down on the elevator. The security guard again stopped me and we went over to the desk of the night manager. I said, "Why are you treating me like this?" I said, "I don't have to take this kind of treatment." He said, "If you don't like it, take it up with the legal department."

I told him, "Sure as there is a God, Buddha, Jesus, Allah, or whoever you happen to believe in, you will live to eat those words!" I made him that promise that night. He then snatched my purse. I had my student ID, my driver's license, and a fifty-dollar bill. He took the fifty-dollar bill and said, "Sure you're a student at Berkeley, sure you are. What's a student doing with fifty dollars?"

So by this time, this friend came down. He's a doctor from Florida. The guard tells me that if I signed this little citation saying that I was either soliciting and/or trespassing, there would be no trouble. I said some foul things. I said, "I'm not signing this shit. I'm not going to do this." He said, "Well, if you don't sign it, we're going to call the police." I said, "Call the motherfuckers. Call 'em." I said, "Give me the phone; I'll call them for you!' And he said, "Just get her out of here."

So we went back upstairs and then I called a taxi. I was so furious. I went home and sat up all night long. At 8:01 A.M. I was dialing fiercely. I called the chief of security at the hotel. He calls later that afternoon and he says, "Well, I'm sorry that the incident occurred, but you have to realize where you were. That's the Tenderloin, and we have a lot of trouble with the prostitutes—black prostitutes. And that's the price that some women have to pay, for protecting our guests. And I'm sorry." He said the best he could do was to give me a meal on the Hilton. I said, "Hell, I didn't tell you I was hungry." I said, "Well, you've done what you had to do and now I must do what I must do."

Funny, I was taking a course from one of the law professors: "Sex Equity, Public Policy, and the Law." I called the professor and he found me an attorney, who subsequently got the assistance of another, and we filed this suit, which was later a class-action suit alleging that the Hilton had a pattern of treating black women that way. It happened in '80, and it was finally settled in '82. We got a consent decree. That means they didn't admit to any guilt, but they agreed to change the things we had accused them of doing in terms of their training of security guards. They would be more courteous. And it was settled for fifty thousand dollars' punitive damage.

Six weeks after that last day in court, I went to take my exams, and then everything happened so quickly. When the story hit the newspapers, the vultures came out, trying to sell me cars and all sorts of things.

I was disappointed in how people responded. I did buy this house, but I had given up the chance for more money, to get the structural change that was created by the class-action suit. I went through a real depression. I had been holding myself together for so long, and I guess you can't crawl out from under it all until you really hit rock bottom. I saw a therapist for it, for about a year and a half. He often asked the question, Why did it bother me so much? And it took me a while to answer that. That's the question he always started our sessions with: "Why would it bother you? Those things happen."

I told Tom, I said, "I made this decision a long time ago—I am not going to be a nigger. And as far as I'm concerned, they were trying to treat me like one." They didn't hit me. They didn't beat me up. But they did hurt my feelings. I'm black. I have no problems with being black. But there's a decisive difference between being black and being a nigger. I understand that difference, and I'm going to make sure that anybody that deals with me understands that. I'm going to demand that. And I don't allow black people to treat me like a nigger either. My autonomy is very important to me, and as a result I have problems, often.

What I've done is, for my own protection, I have narrowed my circle of acquaintances. I, once upon a time, would argue with a signpost. I still will argue, but I'm a lot more selective—I like a good one. Now I walk away. I'm learning to be tactful in my old age. I have superficial acquaintances where I don't touch certain things because I know some people think I'm weird. But I have people that I can talk with. I guess some people would say that's a snobbishness on our part, but, you know, we can talk for hours about various issues, and help each other sharpen our thoughts. We don't always agree. As a matter of fact, sometimes we have some bloody ones.

For example, I got into this discussion last week with this acquaintance of mine. We were talking about an institution that was having problems, and I said, "You know black people have so far to go. We collaborate in our own oppression." She immediately got defensive and said, "Well, you know, white people do it."

I said, "God damn it, I'm so tired of us rationalizing our failures based on what white people do. There are those things that we have control of and this is one that we do have control of." And I said, "A lesson that all of us should have learned is that there are two sets of rules in this society, one for them and one for us. And they have more opportunities to fail than we do. They're given more chances to fail than we as black people are." She said, "God, you are a radical." I said, "No, I'm a realist." I have friends who say that I'm a classic liberal and those who say I'm a populist. I hate labels. I draw from different sources to form my opinions, and issues determine the positions I take. Success for some is making money and having a fancy title by your name. But, for me, success is not the trappings of middle class. It is not "knowing my place." It is knowing my rights and making sure they are not violated. Success, for me, is being educated rather than being trained.

I advocate that black people read Carter G. Woodson's *The Mis-Education of the Negro*. It was written in the thirties, but it could have been written an hour ago. I personally feel *The Mis-Education of the Negro* should be a bible. That's the bible that we ought to adopt instead of that other stuff that the white folks wrote. I can't be overly critical of white people about certain things because I'm not white and I'm sure they do what is in their best interest, just as we must do. I know certain things they are responsible for, but not everything in our institutions can we lay blame. I think we have to start holding each other accountable for a lot more than we do.

Several times I've gone home to Bogalusa, I've taken books, particularly copies of *The Mis-Education of the Negro*. Most people don't know what I'm talking about. There's a sense of complacency there that bothers me. One of my professors asked me once, "What part of the world are you from?" I said, "South America." He said, "I thought so. Whereabouts?" And I said, "South of the Mason-Dixon." It is like Thomas Wolfe. You can never go home again. And that's pretty literal for me. I was always different anyway. I was a reader and always tended to be a little out of step with most people in my high-school class.

There's still a sort of insulation from the world—not understanding how close we are to a nuclear war, and not being concerned about the various threats to our safety. Not really being concerned about the environment, South Africa, and the insidious racism that is destroying our youth. Not even being concerned about the level of poverty. I think this country, it needs a nigger. Right now poor people represent America's nigger and most poor people are black. They still have blacks as their official niggers.

It's not just endemic to Bogalusa, or even small towns, because it happens here in the city, too. I could deal with it in Bogalusa for a couple of weeks. I can ha-ha-ha-ha-ha about things that we did, and what's going on here, and where the party is going to be, and that kind of thing. But after a while, the intellectual climate is just not right, because there are so few people who dare to challenge the bullshit—like too many black males in special-ed classes because they are aggressive and white teachers can't handle them.

I forget that not all of them were that involved in the movement, and it did not necessarily mean as much to them as it did to us. I mean, we took it personal. I still do. I was always amazed at how small that circle was when I got out of it and looked back in it. You know, Bogalusa is about the size of this living room, but there were people who were untouched by what happened. Those of us who were involved, we felt it was a great thing and that we were really on our way, and history was being made.

I do have regrets about the movement, though. The first one is the control that we gave up of our own destiny, that we, for whatever reason, traded off, by virtue of the outsiders coming in. It's the arrogance with which those white people came into our community. They felt they knew everything and it was like "We're gonna show you peons." They even labeled some blacks as "Uncle Toms." White folks just don't have the right to make those assessments for me. I was never trustful of white folks anyway. They didn't want to open their meetings with a prayer. And you just don't do that. You know, in black communities, we pray. The other thing, white folks were calling the shots because invariably we got more media exposure and more protection when they were there. So it was like we were in bed together not so much by choice but out of necessity, and it still makes me sick.

I regret the way our institutions were destroyed, our schools. Remember, when schools were desegregated, it was like the white system came down on the black community with a vengeance. They totally destroyed our institution—they even took away our trophies. We, Central, had been a very good school, and it had been academically one of the best black schools in the state. Out of a class of a hundred, at least fifty of us have a year of college or more, and twenty-five or twenty-six are college graduates. So education was perceived as a way out, and that doesn't seem to be the case anymore. Our churches and our schools were run by us. Now we have nothing left but our churches. We didn't destroy property. We didn't write on the walls. We didn't carve up the chairs. We were proud of our school. I think that was true until Central was no longer Central—until integration. You couldn't pay any of us to get off campus, where any adult couldn't see us. And now you see twelve- and thirteen-year-old kids walking the streets during school time, because they see that the black community no longer has control over its own. I'm not advocating mandatory resegregation. I'm saying that there should be a choice, that if a black community wants an all-black school, that should be its option, to have one. In Bogalusa, I never heard of special education at Central. Now you've got black kids who can't read. Whatever method those black teachers used, it worked. And now you've got half the black population being in special-education classes, especially black males.

I also think the movement led to a breakdown in respect for family and the extended-family concept that was so unique, because, suddenly, for the first time, you are put in a position to disobey your parents. When they say, "Don't get involved," you do. So it becomes easier and easier.

Now I'm thinking about getting pregnant. Suddenly the maternal instinct is there and I want to do it before I reach forty. I think I would have done it this year had I finished my dissertation. I do not have a father picked out, but I'm working on it. This seems cold and callous, but that's exactly what it's going to be. I would like a son, but I'm afraid to have a son because I've been told that I'm so strong that it would be bad for me to raise a son as a single parent. I don't think so, but I worry about that sometimes. I think if I had a healthy baby, I would be happy regardless of the sex. . . . Soon as I get this dissertation completed.

One more thing about the movement. I wish there could have been less violence, less confrontation, but I don't think it would or could have happened any other way. You almost had to be confrontational to get things done. People were so entrenched in their ideas. I think it's tragic that it had to be done that way, but I think if we had been non-violent, many of us would not be walking around talking about it today. It's much more civilized to sit down and talk about it, but then we aren't living in a civilized world.

ALL-STATE
QUARTERBACK:

Grant McElveen

*Across town from all-black Central Memorial High School was all-white
Bogalusa High School.*

   *At all high schools, at all times, there are certain students who are
almost public figures, they are so well known to the student body. At Bogalusa High, one of those standouts was the good-looking football star
Grant McElveen. Grant now lives on the outskirts of Jackson, Mississippi,
but I first caught up with him one unseasonably steamy night in Bogalusa.*

I was born and reared here in Bogalusa. My father's a workaholic, I
reckon. He's worked two jobs ever since I've known him. He owns a
small family business that his father and then his mother had operated.
It's a credit bureau. My mother works there, and my father works it,
too, when he's not working at the paper mill. When I was coming up,
he was in the insurance business on the side. At the paper mill I think
his job title is operator of the chemical plant. He's been there forty
years. Other than an engineer or somebody technical, he would be a
top man on his shift. The chemical plant makes the solvent DMSO.

   I used to be a little embarrassed about my name, since Grant was a
Union general. But, in reality, I was named after an army buddy of my
father's who had saved his life during World War II.

   When I was a kid I loved to play. Football, baseball, basketball—
everything. Played wholeheartedly and did well. Junior high, nothing. I
played a little basketball, then quit. Tried out for football and quit.
Just didn't seem to have what it took. Or the coaches didn't like what

76

they saw. I was a cheerleader in the ninth grade for the junior-high football team.

In high school I went out for football in the tenth grade and was resigned to be a second-team quarterback because I wasn't that good then. But I had a couple coaches that for some reason showed special interest in me. I wanted somebody to show a little extra interest in me, and I stuck with it. We had what we called a B team, a junior-varsity team. Halfway through the season they made me first-team quarterback on the B team.

Junior year we had what they call a jamboree in Hammond, Louisiana. That's where you have about four or five games that last about fifteen or twenty minutes each. Just kind of like a little preseason get-together. I was second-team quarterback and I don't think they expected much out of me. We drove down to like the 2-yard line and the other quarterback got hurt. We were about to score. Well, I went in and my first down I lost about three yards. Second down, I dropped back to pass and they tackled me and I lost about four more yards. Anyway, before it was over, it was fourth down and about fifteen to go and I just lost yardage every time I touched the ball. On the fourth down, I reckon I threw an incomplete pass or something. It was total devastation!

The season started and the starting quarterback had some problems the first game. They put me in there like the second game and I didn't mess up too bad. That was it. But the third game was a great game. Things went real well. I had five or six good games that year, and led the state in total offense in triple-A ball, which was the top class. I was chosen all-state quarterback and I got a lot of publicity right quick there. You'd think a little high-school football player wouldn't. But all during that year I would go to a junior-high football game and these little kids would be around and, you know, some little kid would come and bug the crud out of me. It was phenomenal. I mean, it was nice to get that kind of attention, but it got old, I would say. It got old very quickly.

When I was a sophomore we had a senior that was an all-state quarterback. I idolized the fellow. I thought, man, if you can be an all-state quarterback, you had life made! I felt that life would be a breeze from then on—a fantasy. And I was all-state quarterback in my *junior* year. I was on a mountaintop.

It wasn't long after that I found out that you had a senior year coming, and you had to live up to the billing and it was tough. My senior year I look on as a kind of disaster. Here I was learning about life a little bit, I think. I felt a lot of pressure. I worked very hard in the summer—running, throwing the football, getting in shape. I wanted to exceed my junior year. I really increased my physical strength and my speed. When the season began, I was ready. But I had overworked. I was beginning to feel emotionally pressured and I'd always been a nervous kid, I suppose. I just felt strained to produce.

I didn't throw as well in my senior year as I did in my junior. I think I was trying to be too perfect. I was trying too hard to throw just right, and you can't do that. The coaches tell you not to do that. Don't aim the ball. It's got to be a natural phenomenon, and it wasn't as natural because of the pressure, I think. And we had a good junior quarterback behind me. That put a lot of pressure on me, too.

I was hurt in the next-to-last game in my senior year, hurt pretty seriously. Right before the end of the first half. I just got a real hard hit in the hip and couldn't operate. They call it a hip pointer. If I pulled one side it would just catch and be a terrific pain. The junior quarterback came in and finished the game, really won the game for us. He was looking good. I was hurt all week, but I played the last game and did all right. But he went in and took over and won that game, too.

My senior year I didn't make all-state, but I was all-state honorable mention. Maybe I expected too much out of myself. The colleges were still very interested, though. I was recruited fairly heavily. I got letters from any number of schools all over the United States. Of course, at that time I didn't even consider any school that had an integrated football team. It boiled down to like three or four schools. Ole Miss, LSU, and Florida State. I chose Ole Miss. For one thing, I was a quarterback and Ole Miss was a quarterback school.

The last semester of high school was when integration hit Bogalusa. We had a big pasture out behind my house and a creek ran behind this pasture and the blacks lived on the other side of the creek. I used to play football with them and have BB-gun wars with them. Just a war. Nobody got hurt. We'd sit out there and smoke a cross vine and talk, and then get back to shooting at each other across the creek. Had a great time. They were some of the best times in my life.

So the marching and picketing came as a surprise. This integration thing, I would liken it to the Russians invading the country and putting their people in here amongst us. It was a cataclysmic thing. Your whole society structure was being busted up and you just don't see that every day. It was three hundred years of a certain way of life that they were saying was not anymore. "We are making this an edict from Washington, D.C.," and you thought the Civil War could start again if we had enough armament to fight with. I looked at it a little stronger than some others, but I know others looked at it stronger than me.

Me and some of my friends, we'd go out and holler at the blacks whenever they were marching. I went to most every march there was. Never saw a fight. Just ran along hollering at them, calling them names. Of course, I called them niggers at that time, but I wouldn't do that anymore. That was just what you called blacks in those days. That's what you called them for two hundred years, and I don't think it necessarily carried a derogatory meaning. At that time it may have started to, though. They called each other niggers, too. They called me a cracker. If I called a marcher a name, he'd call me one. Just laughing at who could call the worst name. I think we just wanted to get on television. I hollered the loudest when I was on TV. We were kids.

I may change my mind next week, but as I look back on integration, and we've had a lot of chance to look back, it had to be done, I reckon, it had to be just done. I don't know how you could have done it slowly, progressively. Nobody I know liked Lyndon Johnson, but he was a powerful man. He could get things done, and he got behind this thing and he did it. They put the FBI agents in here, and it never would have been done without them. The white police would have done their job, but it was asking too much of them to go in and fight their friends.

It was less than a week after graduation that we got a call at night, that my father had been arrested for murdering a black deputy. As it turned out, there was no evidence against him and the case never even went to court, but it was a traumatic experience. We got threatening phone calls. Black people, I suppose. It was a big shock to me and my family. We had to leave our house for a while. I saw him one time in jail. He didn't tell me anything. No talking at all. I had one of my father's friends come and tell me that he was sure my father didn't do it. That's the way it was. I just don't want to get into a lot of details on that. I don't think it's constructive.

Everybody thought it was beneficial for me to go to summer school at Ole Miss right away. They put me in a regular dorm. Had a roommate whose father was a well-to-do businessman in Alabama. Also there was this big guy, a junior, from Mobile, Alabama, that found out I was a football player and became like a big brother to me. His father was also a very influential businessman.

Anyway, freshman year I was the starting safety on the freshman team. I loved it. Less pressure. But I hurt my knee during practice before the last game. I just made a cut wrong and heard something pop in my knee. I didn't think much of it. I told the coach and he shook it around, said he reckoned it was all right. He was a tough coach. You had to be on a stretcher before he'd even listen to you. I went back into practice.

Well, next morning it was really swelling. I went up to a special orthopedic clinic in Memphis where they took care of all the football players. They put me in traction for about three, four days and put me in a cast for a month. While I was in the hospital, I was reading the paper, and it had there on the back: "OM Student Kills Self." Got to reading it and it was this big brother of mine. Well, when I got out of the hospital I was told from very reliable sources that he was drunk, apparently, and he had a .357 Magnum pistol and put one bullet in it and flipped it around—Russian roulette—and blew his head off. Happened to be that it landed on his number. I tell you, this guy had everything I had been taught that you want for success in life. You know, money was no object to this guy. And I know his parents must have loved him. The guy blew his head off. You don't do something like that unless you don't think much of life, do you? I tell you what, that threw me for a loop.

This other guy who was my roommate, a month later he was dead, too. I was told he "fell out" of a window in the psychiatric ward of a hospital. When it gets right down to it, you don't fall out the window, I don't think. You jump. I started thinking, "My goodness, man, what am I doing?" I'd just always been taught that success was having money and living in the upper echelons of society. And happiness—the American Dream—it's just that simple. These boys had it. And it just seemed that there was not anything to it. Another dream was shattered. I became disillusioned. I went on through my freshman year. I didn't study. I got with some boys. I wasted time and shot pool and went to the movies, for the most part.

My sophomore year, after these suicides, I started seeing that some things I had thought were important were not. The American Dream was not what it was made out to be. Nobody came and talked to me, but I remember I looked around and for some reason I really felt some kind of drawing to Christ, I reckon.

I was brought up in a Presbyterian church. When I was in high school, I would always try to be good during football season. I always prayed on Thursday night because the next day was a game. I'd pray on Wednesday, too, if it was a big game! And then when football season was over I forgot about Him and had a real good time. That's kind of how I saw God. If you wanted something you'd better pray to Him for it. If I didn't need Him, I forgot about God.

But after the suicides, just out of the blue, I went to a guy on the football team that was going to be a preacher, and said, "I want to be a Christian. I'd like to know how you do it." He took me to a Baptist church up there in Oxford, Mississippi, and I accepted Jesus Christ as my Lord and Savior.

Not long after I became a Christian I almost had a nervous breakdown. I guess it was everything catching up with me. I don't know how to explain it. I wanted peace in my life and I had the opposite. I had accepted Christ as my Savior, and now everything was going wrong and I didn't have any peace. Just feelings, I reckon, yukky feelings. Maybe I could have gone to a psychiatrist or a doctor and gotten a pill that would calm me down. I remember distinctly saying I was going to go to a doctor, but I felt a voice say, "No, don't do it." I was in bad shape, but I didn't do it.

I really gave myself to God completely. I wouldn't say that God made these things happen in my life, but, I suppose, in my thinking, He used them to draw me to Him. I wanted this peace in my life worse than anything in the world, and if there was a God and He was there, I was going to try to be obedient to Him, because I knew He was a loving God and He could give me the peace that I wanted and the Bible said He would give me. A very traumatic period of time—four or five months. It's been rough going at times since then, but never anything like that.

All during this period, I would go every night to the football stadium and pray. Had to climb a fence to get in there. I went there because it was empty and dark. Just quiet. Way up at the top end. I'd stay for thirty minutes to an hour. Pray, meditate, just spend time alone with God. I can remember on the weekends hearing the fraternity parties. Frat Row was about a quarter mile away, and I'd hear that noise and it didn't appeal to me. If that's all there was to life, there wasn't much to it. I'd look up in the sky and see these stars, and one time I finished praying and said, "If this God I'm praying to is real, if He is really God, and He really loves me like the Bible says, and He made all that up there and there's no end to it as far as we know, then maybe I don't have as much to worry about as I thought I did. If He made all that, then He'd take care of me. He'd give me peace at the drop of a finger if He wants to." And that's when I started having some peace of mind. If I thought that God was that great and He was as the Bible said, if He was that powerful and loving, then there wasn't anything to keep Him from giving it to me. And it became a reality to me. I felt God telling me, after things got wonderful in my life, I just felt God saying, "Go and tell other people." I felt the call to preach.

The next semester I transferred to Mississippi College, which is a Baptist school just outside of Jackson. They gave me a football scholarship, but I didn't play. I became disillusioned with football. It wasn't worth the sacrifice to me. That semester, a lot of my nervousness came back, not nearly as bad as it was before but a lot of doubts. I got sick, had allergies, felt terrible. It was spring of '69. The doctor gave me a patch test and said I was allergic to thirty things. Pollens, dust, synthetics, everything. I'd never had any problems before. The doctor put me on some pills and they made me real sleepy and I wound up missing so much class I flunked out. I didn't have to flunk. Most of the teachers said I could make it up. But I didn't want to. I just felt terrible. I went back home to Bogalusa and started working at the paper mill.

Then I got a greeting from Uncle Sam. A lot of guys I graduated with, we all were drafted at the same time. Went down to Fort Polk, Louisiana, and then they transferred us over to Fort Benning, Georgia. I felt patriotic and felt good. They took a count, a muster, and every morning they reported to Washington, D.C., just how many troops they had in every location in the world. They knew exactly, and I felt like I was serving my country. But I started getting sick. Had a pretty bad hemorrhoid problem, and my allergies were coming back and hurting me. I was sick the whole time.

But it was partly emotional, too. I wanted to be an officer, so they made me a platoon leader in basic training and I found I was going all the time. Just wasn't sleeping. I went to the doctor and they said there wasn't anything wrong with me. I did a lot of praying and finally I told them I don't care what that doctor said, I wasn't going back to training. I had been in the army not even a month. Then there was a lot in between me saying I wasn't going to training and me getting out, but after two or three months I got a medical discharge. As soon as I got out, I went to see my doctor here in town and he operated on me the next day! Really this whole experience had me depressed. I felt I must have been dreaming things. But I got out and this guy says I got a serious problem. And yet I respect the army. They were good to me in view of everything.

In the army I had a lot of time to think. I wanted to go back to school and get me an education. So I went back to Mississippi College and I made good grades after that. Here again, I felt a lot of pressure. Maybe I pushed myself too much. Maybe I thought I ought to be the best preacher in the world. When I was a kid I had a little problem saying certain words. I was a fearful child, and speaking in front of people just scared me to death. The Baptist Student Union at Mississippi College would send out youth teams of preachers trying to get a little experience. The first time I preached was at a rescue mission where these hobos and drunks stay overnight for two dollars. Give them something to eat and make them go to church. Still, when I go to preach—and I preach twice a week, at least—I always have that little uneasy, exciting feeling.

I was going to major in Bible; then I felt I shouldn't do it full-time, and switched my major to business. But I couldn't quit preaching. At the time I graduated from college in 1972, though, I didn't have anywhere to preach, so I started working for the Sanitation Department of the Mississippi Board of Health in Meridian, Mississippi, and I joined the church there. I taught Sunday school, but none of them knew I was a preacher, I don't reckon, until I said something about it. They didn't have a preacher and were looking for one. I went out and preached at the mission they sponsored on the outskirts of town, and the folks out there wanted me to be their preacher. So I did, part-time. I worked full-time for the state, then went nights and Sundays to preach at the little mission.

After two years in Meridian I got a kind of promotion and went to Jackson, the capital. I was one of three men that oversaw the licensing of child-care facilities in the state of Mississippi. Did that for about two years. I met my wife, Gail, while I was at church in Jackson. I proposed after about two months of dating and we got married in '75. She was sweet, attractive, a Christian. She was active in the church. That was a prerequisite. I just fell in love; there's no two ways about it. I don't know if I'd ever been in love before. Thought I had . . . sure told 'em I was. But it felt different this time.

Here, again, I was afraid of marriage—another fear. It was an act of faith, in my opinion, to get married. Let me say, I think the New Testament teaches a married woman should be submissive to her husband, that he is the head of the house. I don't believe men and women have the same role. I don't think this makes women *less* than men; I just think they have a separate role. The husband is to love his wife as Christ loved the Church—and He gave His life for the Church. Christ earned the right to be the head of the Church, and the husband should earn the right to be the head of the house. I don't believe if you've got some dog that's a husband that a woman has to put up with any abuse from him.

My wife and I have two children. A daughter, Leigh Alison, born in 1976, and a son, Jonathan Grant, born in 1979. I love my children. I can't wait to get back to them if I'm away overnight, but let me say this: I find it very hard, quite often, to play with them. I don't know how to explain that, but I guess it's work for me to play with them. It wears me out. But I love to be with them. We stay with them more than most parents. They're with us all the time. We very seldom do anything without them. We have a real good marriage. Had one tough period of time when I was working a lot. Gone all day at work and late at night at church meetings. Our relationship was strained. Just after our little boy was born.

After two years in child care, I spent a year and a half as administrator of a federally funded maternity and pediatric clinic in Jackson. Mainly low-income, primarily blacks. My attitude towards blacks started changing when I became a Christian. It's just been a complete reversal. I felt like they were subwhite. But when Christ comes into your life, you're a new person. Everything changes. They *are* a different culture; I don't have any doubt about that. They live differently than most white people: They talk different; they dance different; they eat different; morals are different.

After the clinic, I spent about two years as inspector or surveyor of hospitals and nursing homes for Medicare—still for the Board of Health. Then I transferred over into a job where I went back into sanitation, but did a lot of contract work for the United States Consumer Products Safety Commission. They'd contract with us to do investigations of people dying or being harmed by consumer products.

All this time I was preaching half the time and had a church most of the time on weekends. Around '81, my position with the Board of Health was eliminated. I could have bucked somebody out of a job, but after nine years with the Board of Health . . . if I had any own-your-own-business abilities, I wouldn't know it working for the state. I thought if I had these in me, I'd better get out and go into business for myself and see what I could do. I'm basically insecure, and there was a lot of security with the state, but I felt the Lord leading me to go out and get into a business. I felt like God was telling me to come on out and get away from all that security, and I'll take care of you.

I had a guy trying to get me in the insurance business for nine years. I called this guy and said I wanted to start working with him. He specialized in partially self-funded group medical insurance. New concept. To hear him talk, it was a booming business. You got to look out for salesmen. Boy, they can tell you everything. So you talk about a challenge. The insurance business is tough. I didn't have any income. It just got down to brass tacks. I was really worried for a while. But then I got this church.

I had let the Baptist Association know that I wanted a church. When a church comes along, they give them your name, along with five or ten other names. It happened that they gave this church my name and they wanted me to come and preach. I went there for about a month before they called me to be their pastor. Farm Haven Baptist Church is the name of it, between Canton and Carthage, Mississippi. It's just an old rural community. It's about fifty miles from my home to the church. You see, smaller churches can't pay enough to live on, but a fellow like me that's never been to seminary and not much training, they'll pay me something and I'll have another job. A "two-vocational pastor" is what they call it.

I'd say there's about a hundred in the congregation. We have anywhere from fifty to eighty people that come to Sunday school and study Bible. Then from eleven to twelve we have a preaching and worship service. Then in the afternoon we have a rap session, we call it. We talk about anything we want to talk about related to our Christianity. Then to six-forty-five in the evening we have another worship service. So I preach morning and evening and lead the rap session. I do visitation, counseling, marital problems, drug problems, alcohol problems, preach at funerals.

For the first two years it was a honeymoon. Then we had some very difficult times in the church, some real serious personal conflicts. It got to where I wanted to leave. I spent a lot of time outside with the Lord, as a result of it, looking at the stars. I'd gotten away from that and I shouldn't have. Can't go to the football stadium. Don't have one to go to. But this idea of being outside and spending time alone is good.

We've had differences of opinion—just how the church is led, priorities. Each church is autonomous. The congregation could vote me out on Sunday. It's a very insecure position. But I think the vast majority stand behind me. Since this trouble in the church, my insurance business has gone to just about nil. It's emotionally drained me. I just don't do a lot of work on my insurance business. I spend more time studying. I read the Bible a lot, and Karl Barth and other theologians. And I've been reading *The Decline and Fall of the Roman Empire* for at least a year.

All these emotional experiences I've had pushed me toward believing that a lot of people had them. God, Jesus Christ, met my need in that area, and if He is the Lord of the Universe, as I believe He is, then He's the one that can do something about that. He's got the power. He can heal.

If I knew I was going to have a rough Sunday, trouble in church, I fasted all day Saturday in anticipation of it. Fasting symbolizes an emptying of myself, of saying to God, "I know this is serious business." It's a sacrifice. I've not watched a football game as a sacrifice to God because I wanted it so bad. It was so important to me. Just let God know that we put Him ahead of these things.

I don't do a lot of counseling, but it seems like I do spend an awful lot of time at it. I feel extremely responsible about it. And nervous. I've never had any counseling courses, but I do read a good bit, especially on marriage counseling. I don't basically believe in divorce, yet you have some situations where you think that's the best thing. I have a lot of conflicts here about what is biblically right and what might appear to be right. That's an awesome responsibility. Alcohol is a big problem, real big. Tremendous counseling in that area. It takes power, and here's where Jesus comes in, gives power to overcome these things.

I believe in the Trinity: God the Father, God the Son, God the Holy Spirit. I believe that Jesus is the only way, that anybody who rejects Him rejects the Father, and to reject Him, you reject God Himself. I think He is our only way. Jesus Christ gave me life when I was a dead man. And I sure wouldn't say it's been easy since becoming a Christian. But everything seems to drive me to God and to find in Him everything I need.

A few months after our meeting in Bogalusa, I had the pleasure of spending a weekend with Grant and his family up in Farm Haven, Mississippi, where they stayed two days a week in a house next to the church. I attended all services and classes and accompanied Grant on his rounds, which included such diverse activities as visiting sick people, helping break in a new horse, and eating several delicious home-baked pies at a picnic.

Naturally, Grant used the Bible as the foundation for his sermons, but he also quoted freely from Billy Graham, Jerry Falwell, and others. One message I especially liked was part of his evening sermon on divorce. It dealt with the importance of not only loving *your wife but* liking *her as well. Grant's source for this lesson was Charley, a character played by Jimmy Stewart in the film* Shenandoah. *I thanked Grant for the reminder that spiritual lessons are not confined to places of worship, and can sometimes come when you least expect them.*

VIETNAM

Shortly after I began work on this book, a friend of my parents asked me what my current writing project was. When I told him that I was interviewing members of my generation, he said, "What a great idea— but you're not going to have too much Vietnam, are you?"

I was taken aback, but the conversation moved on before I could answer. I shrugged off the incident. But when I heard the same comment twice more within a few weeks, I became concerned. In each case, the comment had been made by an older male.

I began to sense the unpleasant implication that a portion of the generation of men who fought in World War II, and who continued the USA streak of winning wars by winning the big one, resented and felt contempt for our generation because we had lost "our" war. To them we were like the 1954 Yankees who finished in second place after the team had won five straight World Series. What was worse, from their point of view, was that so many of us had shirked our "duty" entirely, preferring to take drugs and protest.

When Vietnam veterans came home, there were no parades, no heroes' welcome. They were even shunned by many people. But a discharged soldier still had his family and his friends, even when his friends were against the war. I have heard some Vietnam vets say they could have won the war if it hadn't been for the protests at home. But I have heard many more say they were pleased that their peers had welcomed them back into the fold, although, with both friends and family, they preferred not to discuss what had actually gone on in Vietnam.

All this is to say that I'm afraid I must disappoint those who don't want "too much Vietnam." Every male of the generation, unless he had a legitimate physical problem, was confronted with the U.S. government's determination to send him overseas to help kill people and maybe be killed.

I remember seeing Lenny Bruce perform in Hollywood shortly before he died. He described the Japanese in World War II as the perfect enemy for most Americans. "They were small, they were a different color, and they attacked us first." It wasn't too difficult to hate the Nazis, either. And so World War II became the Good War.

The Vietnam War worked a little differently. It is true that the Vietnamese were small and a different color, but you had to be a fairly adept abstract thinker to figure out a way that they had attacked us first. Something just didn't wash—particularly if you were part of the generation that had been chosen to fight the war.

When U.S. military involvement began in Southeast Asia, the only Americans who opposed it were pacifists and left-wing intellectuals. Before long, though, antiwar sentiment spread throughout the draft-eligible generation. Then, in 1968, came the first major shift in public opinion. During the Tet Offensive, the casualty rate mushroomed. U.S. soldiers were dying at a rate of seventy a day. Military analysts have declared the repelling of the Tet Offensive a U.S. military success. But back home it made the war much more of a real event. Each day the bodies of American boys were shipped home in coffins. The coffins were dispersed to every corner of the nation. Bells were tolled; flags were lowered to half mast; obituaries were run in local newspapers; funerals were held; families wept. Almost everyone knew someone who had returned from Vietnam dead or seriously wounded. A whole new set of people were touched, and began to ask if this war was really worth it.

Then, two years later, came the shootings at Kent State, in which four unarmed students were killed by Ohio National Guardsmen. This shocking event awakened a new activism in a huge group of Americans who had previously steered free of the controversial debate between "hawks" and "doves." President Nixon had already seen the handwriting on the wall, and attempted to blunt the growing antiwar movement by reducing American casualties through "Vietnamization" and by replacing on-the-ground warfare with the air war and sophisticated "electronic battlefields." But antiwar sentiment continued to spread, and by late 1970 the national consensus had tipped in favor of withdrawing all U.S. troops from Vietnam within a year. Unfortunately, the Nixon Administration, and then that of Gerald Ford, failed to yield to this consensus, and another thousand American lives were lost before the fall of Saigon in 1975, not to mention the deaths of more than 400,000 Vietnamese, Cambodians, and Laotians.

The Vietnam War had been conceived and orchestrated by one generation and foisted upon another, younger generation who were expected to do the dirty work. I used to think that the Chinese Red Guards of the 1960s were the equivalent of student radicals in the United States, but I now realize that they were more like our Vietnam veterans. Both groups were made up of patriotic young people who were sent by their governments on a righteous mission to go to the countryside and destroy the lives and property of people they didn't know. But in both cases, the political climate changed while they were gone, and they ended up being criticized and reviled for doing nothing more than obeying authority and following orders. In China, most of the Red Guards were literally left out in the countryside to become a lost generation. The Vietnam veterans were allowed to return to society, but it is not surprising that so many of them quickly joined the ranks of disaffected, drug-taking youth.

One long-term result of the Vietnam War seems to have been the development of what I consider to be a healthy skepticism of government and an extreme wariness to send American troops to fight foreign wars. But it disturbs me that deeper lessons have not been learned. For one thing, this war wariness seems to be as much a result of fear of losing as it is a moral commitment. For another thing, American politicians, of both major political parties, still haven't learned that there are better ways to fight Communism than by giving military support to unpopular dictators and unpopular rebel armies. They have not learned the lesson that I once saw spray-painted on a wall in Berkeley, that "The Enemies of Our Enemies Are Not Necessarily Our Friends."

There is one more aspect of the Vietnam legacy that bothers me. In our current era, in which it is considered un-American to bring up bad memories or to be self-critical as a nation, there remains a taboo subject. For example, during all the ballyhoo and debates surrounding the tenth anniversary of the fall of Saigon, I never heard the subject mentioned, not even once. That subject is the My Lai Massacre, in which American soldiers, following orders from above, slaughtered 347 unarmed women, children, babies, and old men. Sadly, what happened at My Lai was not an isolated incident. Such massacres of innocent people were not frequent, but neither were they rare.

All of us, as individuals, make mistakes. We say things we wish we could take back, and do things we later regret. Sometimes we can just put them out of our minds. But sometimes, if they are bad enough, they keep coming back, and trying to ignore them only eats away at our conscience. When that happens, the only healthy thing to do is to face up to past mistakes, to apologize, and to promise to others and to ourselves that we have learned our lesson and will never repeat our mistakes.

I only hope that we, as a nation, can face up to what we have done, admit we were wrong, and pledge never to do it again. We have had no problem criticizing the Germans for the atrocities they committed, and we have had no problem criticizing Communists and terrorists for their atrocities. I hope that Americans can come to grips with the fact that we, too, are capable of killing children and babies, before another of our generations makes the same mistake.

THE QUESTIONER:

Richard Langdon

I arrived in Crawford County, in southern Indiana, two days before my scheduled meeting with Richard Langdon, so I was able to spend some time driving around and talking with people. Crawford County is the poorest county in Indiana, and has the highest unemployment rate. Like most places in the U.S., there are roads going in every direction. Yet the population is sparse enough that there is not a single stoplight in the entire county.

Driving the back roads through beautiful forests at the height of fall's bright colors, I crossed wooden bridges and saw handmade barges and rowboats resting against the shore. I also recalled the headline in the local newspaper one day about an enormous marijuana farm that had just been busted in the middle of the county. The area reminded me of Huckleberry Finn *with mind-altering drugs.*

If the United States is a nation famed for its ethnic and cultural diversity, you wouldn't know it in Crawford County. "Wallechinsky?" said one young carpenter. "Sounds like a Chicago name." As I drove through the town of English, near Richard's home, I saw a Filipino woman getting out of a car. I was so surprised that I almost ran a stop sign. She must have married a local boy while he was stationed overseas.

Richard came out to meet me in his driveway, guided me past a live wire crossing the path, and led me into his comfortably cluttered home. After I had dropped off my bags, Richard took me outside for a tour of the woods behind the house. As we walked, I asked him to clarify for me an unusual aspect of Crawford County: the fact that the inhabitants use two time zones at the same time.

Richard assured me that this was true and that when people made appointments, they would always specify whether it was "fast time" or "slow time." "The bank is on fast time and the post office is on fast time. The market downtown is on slow time and so is the hardware store. My friends the Burkhardts function on fast time because he works in Kentucky, but my other neighbor works in the other direction, so he's on slow time. I keep the clock in my kitchen on fast time, and the one in the bedroom on slow time."

After finishing our walk, Richard and I returned to the house and cooked dinner together, taking turns in the kitchen, since there was room for only one person at a time. We ate, cleaned up, and then settled down on his living room floor for some late-night talk.

Growing up outside of Muncie, Indiana, my parents, my younger sister, and I went to a Methodist church twice a week, on Sundays and on Wednesday evenings. I was always debating with someone over one fact or another, but I very much believed in the teachings. I prayed almost every night. In fact, I still do. As I got older I would just ask for anything I wanted, and at the moment I asked, I knew whether or not I was going to get it.

When I was ten or eleven my dad was saved and I was also. I can remember people praying with me at the altar, and I had seen enough of it happen to understand what's going on. I can remember it being something you're supposed to do, to show to God and to the people of the church. It was not an unpleasurable happening. It's like an opening of a *chakra* in your body—all of a sudden you've got this new energy level. It's real obvious and it's love.

When I was about thirteen, there was this young minister—everybody liked him. It was the first Sunday of the new year, and he gave this big sermon on how this new year we should take a new stance, a new attitude, and people in the church should read the Bible. I had never heard anybody say that in the church before. This guy always encouraged people to carry a Bible: "That's how you tell a Christian—they're carrying a Bible." He was trying to stress that people should take time every day and spend it in a spiritual attitude, consciously sitting down or walking or however they do it—but to do it, every day. If you're reading the Bible, that would make you do it every day.

At the end of the year, the minister asked the congregation, which numbered about a hundred for most church services, how many people had read the Bible from cover to cover. People had read certain books of the New Testament and one lady had read the complete New Testament, but there were only two people who could respond that they had read the entire Bible—my mom and I.

It was a really difficult thing to do, because a lot of what you read in the Bible goes on and on and on, and it doesn't really have a lot of sacred meaning. Some chapters go on and on with family histories, but I found most of it interesting. I don't disbelieve anything that's there. I can't say that I find it that incredible. I've seen some things that have happened in my life that didn't look like they should happen, but they happened anyway. There's a lot of energy in the universe that's making it all look like it is.

When I was in school, my father worked for Westinghouse in the department where they built power transformers as large as this house. He worked all these different jobs, then made supervisor, and remained that until he got laid off after twenty-one years. He made them lots of money, too. Now he works as a maintenance man for a friend of his who owns two motels.

My mother has always worked jobs at home, like hobbies that made her money. When I was very young, and my father was in the army, she made paper flowers out of crêpe paper and wire. She made beautiful bouquets out of paper and then plastic. She has also made other crafts, worked as a seamstress, and taken in laundry and ironing.

I always had a job. I was always selling something. When I was a little kid I would buy ice-cream bars in a box and take them home and sell them individually to the neighborhood kids. Or when they widened Highway 32 to four lanes, I put a cooler on my wagon and sold cold Coca-Cola to the workers for three times what I paid for it. From the age of about thirteen until eighteen, I worked as farm help, baling hay, driving tractors, hoeing beans.

My father and his brothers graduated from Selma High School, east of Muncie, and he thought it was one of the best in the area. So I attended Selma for twelve years. I started in the same building I graduated from. Our class had about ninety-eight or so. Some people were in a clique to such an extent that they had no relationships with anyone else. I knew everyone and everybody was nice to me. I wore nice clothes—ivy-league collars and white socks and pegged pants.

School was always real easy for me, so I would sit around in classes and think, Why do people think like they do? I knew what was in a guy's mind, but I was always wondering what was in a girl's mind. Until we got to be sixteen, the big thing was a Halloween party. You'd go out on a hayride and hug a little bit. I can remember playing spin-the-bottle and kissing a girl for the first time. Things changed real quick after that. When we got to be sixteen, then it was the automobile—buying gasoline and cruising the hamburger stands in your '55 Ford. You were on the make and running after the young girls.

The summer after graduation was when I first started at Colonial Bakery. I was on the bun crew. Our crew was always the best. We could outpack anybody. They couldn't keep enough buns on the floor for us.

When I was young I wanted to be a lifer in the military because I grew up as a little boy seeing my father train troops out the window when he was in the army. As I got older, I wanted something more glamorous—perhaps a spy or a diplomat—a dignified fellow, a James Bond type. At the time I graduated, I decided to work toward being a psychiatrist. I was interested in why people think the way they do. So I started college in pre-med, at Asbury College in Wilmore, Kentucky, near Lexington. My grandmother was going to fund me all the way.

Asbury was considered a Christian school. It was private, but run by a board of directors who were all Southern Methodists. The professors were excellent, for the most part, but Asbury was real confined at the time. One night I was in the Student Center, and it was raining and I had an umbrella, so I walked a girl back to the dormitory. I was stopped by a night guard and told that a gentleman would have given the girl his umbrella and would have walked back in the rain without it, because you weren't supposed to walk around with women after seven at night. Technically he could have given me a ticket or demerits. You could get knocked out of school for smoking, using liquor, or dancing. I thought that was really kind of archaic. They didn't even have intercollegiate sports because they thought we would get influenced by these other schools.

After a year I came back to Muncie and transferred to Ball State. I didn't let my mother know until just before school started. She considered Ball State heathen, Communist. I started working again with Colonial Bakeries and earned enough to buy me a new sports car, an MGB, and I was on the road anytime I could get away. During three years of college, I covered most of the area east of the Mississippi River between Quebec City and Key West. I stayed on pre-med that first year at Ball State, but I was working too much and falling asleep in class and my grades fell terribly.

I started to take more and more classes in history and ended up graduating with a double major in political science and world history. Most of the people I'd hang out with were members of the Young Republicans, but I have a tendency to meet a lot of people and listen to them, so I also knew the people who were into the alternative newspapers and politics that were brewing at Ball State in the sixties. And I used to go to the library every day and read the London *Times* because I could look good in the classroom and because it was the thing to do if you're going to be a diplomat.

Sometimes my buddies and I would end up sitting around discussing religion or philosophy late into the night. But sometimes we ended up with young ladies. I was very actively engaged in the process of chasing young college sweeties.

I was drafted twice and got out of it easily by going to summer school and keeping my credits up to the right level. There were a lot of interesting people at Ball State at the time, lots of international students, lots of blacks and ethnic groups, and there were a lot of people trying to stay out of the army. There were people who wouldn't have been in school if it hadn't been for grants and keeping out of the army. By this time I was very conscious of Vietnam. I had too many friends shot at and killed—I didn't want to go to Vietnam.

Then Uncle Sam decides to take away the credit requirements and instead you have to take a government test. This is right before the lottery. So I show up at Chip Whelan's house and he says, "Hey, man, I got something to drink here and the landlady's downtown, and we have a TV all to ourselves. There's a football game on, and let's don't go take that test!" So I said, "Okay." So we didn't—and both of us got our draft notices within the month. I've got six weeks to go until graduation, so I talked to a recruiter and signed up for delayed entry in Military Intelligence. I was promised that I would learn a Slavic language, but as it turned out, it was Vietnamese.

I went in on July 29, 1969, and I did basic training in Fort Knox, near Louisville. Basic was the most lonely I'd ever been in my life. Everything's green and drab and a kind of army paisley that they call "camouflage." You didn't know anybody around you, and if you did, they were liable to go in ten weeks, so it didn't really matter. And all the other people are hollering at you all the time. And they've shaved your head and they mess with your mind. At the same time I got a card from home, and I thought, Boy, I wish I weren't here. I wish I were there, or anywhere besides where I am.

I just went through this awareness of how you're really alone in the world and it doesn't even matter if you have a mother or not. So I had a good cry to myself, and after that it was okay. Kept on trucking. I was a holdover for another session, filling in behind desks for anybody that gets to take a two-week vacation. Then they shipped me up to Fort Holabird in Baltimore, which at that time was Military Intelligence Headquarters.

I was supposed to be an area specialist. They learn the language and do desk work for a while. It's a good starter for intelligence, real romantic, like James Bond. Right down my line as an historian. Well, I get there and find that the area school is very full and I've got to go to Vietnam first. I thought, Boy, they never told me that. So they give you an option: You can become an interrogator instead of an area specialist.

The course was very interesting. We learned the armament stucture of the United States military, the Chinese military, the Russian military. We learned everything from what guns they use and the makeups of the companies, battalions, brigades, and armies to how many men they have, where they're stationed, and how fast they move. If you're going to interrogate people, you have to know all this. We play-acted interrogations, trying to figure out from clues what information the other guy knows. That was fun. I did well and graduated on the commandant's list.

Of course, they teach you all the techniques, including things we're not supposed to support. Technically speaking, we don't torture, but obviously, shooting kneecaps off was very big in Vietnam. The way they'd present it was: "Some people might do this. Of course, we don't condone this, ha-ha-ha, but it is an effective way to get information." This was popular: You take two people in a helicopter. One person, you ask him a question. If he doesn't answer, you shove him out. The other person always talks.

We had instructors that were Green Beret; we had instructors that were CIA, FBI, Military Intelligence, Air Force Intelligence. I didn't always agree with them, but they were very knowledgeable about their subject. At the very end of the course, I learned that I wasn't going to study Slavic languages, and I was transferred to Vietnamese Language

School in El Paso, Texas. My classes were six hours a day, five days a week, for eight months.

I hadn't been in El Paso a month before I started meeting people who were applying for COs—conscientious objectors. These were all pretty reserved, laid-back, family-type people, a lot of them married. They were just your good American home-bred boys from the Midwest who said, "I don't really want to be a part of this killing. I feel that it's against my beliefs and my better judgment." I had already determined that I wouldn't go to Vietnam, but El Paso was where I learned that applying for CO was an option. I thought, well, this is an honorable thing to do. I would be much more proud of this than I would going to Vietnam and being discharged a hero. We also organized an antiwar coffeeshop while I was down there.

The main thing that upset me with the army was that there were so many people who seemed to like war. It's like a cop that likes demonstrations because he likes to go out and bang heads. There are military people like that. They like to go out and trash and pillage. The warriors used to rule only through their power, like the samurai, but now modern warfare isn't like that. There are simpletons in the military that are dangerous. It doesn't take much to pull the trigger on a gun. All these modern toys of war, it's so easy to make them go off.

After language school was over, I was called to be holdover for another four months. They put me on a missile-training brigade which was full of German officers. I basically answered mail and gave out Purple Hearts and other medals. I had a drawer full of medals. People would write in and say, "I was in Vietnam and I got shot," and I'd send them a medal. Or someone would say, "My son died in basic training, and I'd sure like to have a copy of this certificate that shows he was a good boy." So I'd send them a certificate that they could hang on their wall and have weird ideas of what patriotism is.

When I applied for a CO, I was required to be interviewed by a chaplain. I confronted him with his stance. I said, "Tell me how you can stand here and tell these young boys to go and die in Vietnam and that God's blessing is with them." I do believe that God's blessing *is* with them no matter what they do, but they're old enough to be responsible, and if you know much at all about this life, you know it's not normal to go out and kill each other for no reason. We had a good talk, and I respected that chaplain, but my CO application was turned down. They said I wasn't really a conscientious objector, but I knew that I was and I told myself that I had to be responsible for my own actions.

My next order, of course, was Vietnam. I went home to Muncie and my mom said, "Isn't it time you were supposed to report out there?" And I said that I decided not to go, to live up to my convictions instead and take a strong moral position. That's totally against everything my mom's lived with. I knew that if somebody called her about me, she'd tell them I was there, because as a Christian she couldn't lie. So I decided this is not a good place to be.

I'd always heard about Berkeley, that it was an intellectual center, and also a radical center, and I always wanted to go there. So I flew into San Francisco and was met by army friends who were studying Japanese in Monterey. They're getting ready to go to Japan, and I'm getting ready to go to Vietnam. I soon ran into a lawyer who turned me on to people in Berkeley, who let me stay with them.

According to the main press, Berkeley was *the* place in this country where political thought was changing. Politics interests me because it really affects our lives. But at the same time, it's also ridiculous and it doesn't function to help the people. It's obviously an organization for the sport of corporate enterprise, even in Communist countries. Politically, the thing that really interested me in Berkeley was the neighborhood politics: rent collectives, co-ops, neighborhood get-togethers to talk about problems and solutions. I was impressed by the way they were run, and by the involvement of the people.

When I had gotten to El Paso, I found myself not eating meat. Not that I should or shouldn't eat meat, just that my tastes were changing. When I got to Berkeley, I began reading about diet and health and taking care of yourself. Don't depend on a doctor who's going to take care of you when you get sick, like a mechanic takes care of a truck. Keep well in the first place.

In Berkeley I went to films and even the director or writer would be there to answer questions. I had never been around anything like that. And here were the bookstores. I had been going to bookstores and libraries, trying to find books on certain subjects, especially spiritual subjects or philosophy. And in Berkeley, there'd be a whole store of this. Cosmic consciousness, good translations of ancient Buddhist and Hindu texts. Anything I'd ever had an interest in, pretty much. So I got a lot out of Berkeley, and I've returned many times since.

I was AWOL for over seven months. As it turned out, when my

orders for Vietnam arrived in Oakland, somebody, probably a friend of a friend of a friend, took a Magic Marker and marked out my name on every copy. So they hadn't noticed I was missing. In all those months, the only thing they ever did was send a letter to my house saying I must have misplaced my orders.

I was still determined to get a conscientious-objector discharge. So I traveled across country and turned myself in at Fort Meade near Baltimore. The word was that, if you'd been AWOL a long time and you went back to Ford Meade, they usually gave you a general discharge. I went back on October 11th, and on the 13th they got a new post commander, and one of the first things he said was, "We're going to straighten this fort out, and no more people getting general discharges." And I thought, Oh, no.

But nobody treated me as a criminal. They put me in a limited-security facility. I could have easily walked back out at any time. We were able to get passes and do pretty much what we wanted. I got to be the gardener at the First Army Headquarters Chapel. It was a pretty good job until I decided to do a fast from speech and eating. If I had done it the week before, nobody would have bothered me, but, as it happened, right in the middle of the fast some sergeant wanted to talk to me—and I wouldn't talk to him. So he went and got the company commander, and he started giving me direct orders to speak. I just wrote him notes. How do you deal with a guy who won't talk to you? He already thinks I'm a little nuts because I'm the only person in my barracks that sleeps on the floor. After three months, they let me out of the army with an honorable discharge, which kind of surprised me.

I hitchhiked home to Muncie and eventually got involved with a friend doing a truck farm doing home-grown tomatoes. We would employ a couple people part-time to help hoe, and as many as six or seven during picking. Plus we had stands around town and hired people to run the stands, often in the front yards of their houses. We sold thousands of pounds of tomatoes. We also got into a natural-food store in southeast Muncie. If you were to look at Muncie, and know it as well as we did, you could ask where's the worst place to start a natural foods store—and that's where we put it. We did a good business, though, for a couple of years.

When I was in the army in El Paso, I was reading a lot about yoga, and I decided that I should be celibate. It's easy to say in the army, because you don't see any women, especially when you're living in El Paso. In El Paso I think they hide all the women from the soldiers. I kept celibate for a year and a half or so. But in Muncie the "evil women" came around and said, "Come home with me for dinner?" or for a cherry pie. . . . What can you do? One lady used to come in to the natural-foods store and rap philosophy. She was in the antiwar movement. She used to go crazy because I was celibate. "Oh, you're too young. Didn't you see *Last Tango in Paris*?" So I did have several girl-friends, but nobody like a steady.

In 1974 I went to India. You were supposed to go to India. I'd been reading these old Buddhist and Hindu writings, and I said, well, I need to take my tour to India. The only places I had ever been outside of the U.S. were in eastern Canada and in Mexico, and always by car, so that there was some interconnectedness to everything. And all of a sudden, I get on a plane not knowing what I'm getting into or how long I'm staying or, actually, where I'm going when I get there. I was very well dressed, I might say—a nice suit, sporting a tie, and the whole trip. I flew from D.C. to New York and straight to Delhi.

I soon find out that the quicker I take my nice clothes off, the better off I'll be. The cabdriver took me to a place to stay for five dollars a night, but I knew immediately that that was a lot. I mean, I had a toilet in my room. People in India don't have toilets in their rooms. I had applied to the University of Delhi because you could use your GI bill. I wanted to do religious studies, but they would only let me study history. So I decided, while I'm here in India, I'm going to go to Kashmir and visit Gopi Krishna, the writer on kundalini yoga.

I knew things would be real poor in India, but I didn't really imagine the population density, the great amount of people everywhere. Even on the sides of mountains. Everybody in the mountains seemed happier than the plains people. I took the train to Mussoorie and Jammu, and from there a bus ride to Srinagar that made me wonder if I'd get there alive. I was feeling quite sick when I arrived, but once I felt better, I found a book publisher, a bookbinder, and he knew Gopi Krishna, and took me to him. I was sick, I had diarrhea, and I didn't have enough energy to climb a mountain, but visiting with Gopi Krishna, sitting around talking religion and life and diet and everything else, that was a high point for me.

After six weeks in India, I flew straight back to New York. I was broke, and sick as a dog. I had a dime in my pocket. A taxicab driver, a black guy, gave me a ride from the airport to a good place to hitchhike from. And I hitchhiked from there back to Muncie. My last ride was from my dad, who saw me as he was driving to work. He and my mom left for Israel the next day and they left me a couple of basketloads of cantaloupe and a couple baskets of watermelons. The whole ten days they were gone, I pretty much played the recluse, ate nothing but melons, and sat around reading all these books I had brought back from India.

I decided to use my GI bill to go back to school at Ball State. I walked in and they were glad to have me. I studied world history and had my master's in a year, and then I went to Europe for the summer. Then I moved to Crawford County. Friends of mine first moved out here in '71. I came down because of the trees and the fall and the hills. I've always liked the woods, and every day, if you like, you can take a walk in the woods.

I worked with a friend, a young construction worker, traveling around restoring old log cabins. Then for the summer of '76 I took gainful employment as a youth counselor for eighty kids for the Summer Program for the Education and Development of Youth in Paoli. When they laid me off at the end of summer, I got to draw unemployment, so I went to California and spent the winter and spring on the beach, playing the guitar and thinking I should have something to sell.

When I came back to Indiana, I tried to get a job student-teaching. They told me I couldn't substitute-teach without a teaching license, which I later found out wasn't true. You can't substitute-teach when you come into their office in a denim jacket and long hair and a beard. But I went back to school to get my teaching license. I also applied for and got a grant in the history department to do doctoral work. I got my license in 1979 and spent the summer in California, a large part of it climbing in the Sierras.

When I came back, part of my grant was that I had to teach one class a quarter. The first quarter I taught a class in world history for freshmen honor students. We got along just dandy. That was the fall that they took our hostages in Iran. One day I picked up the school newspaper and read that the Iranian students were marching for something and the other students were really hassling them. So I thought this would give us a good moral issue to talk about in class—current events. But when I go in, I see that everybody's kind of looking at this one macho-type guy. And I look in the paper and he's one of the students raising heck with the Iranians. I realized the whole situation's going to have to be handled differently. So I tell them, "Okay, we're going to do this democratically." Basically the class wanted to go over and bomb Iran. Okay, we'll bomb them. I let them pick leaders and asked them what weapons they wanted. They're naming all their jets and stuff—they know which toys they want. So I said, "Okay, how are we going to get there?" And none of them knew!

None of the fascists in the class knew how to get to Iran. And these were honor students! One of them knew that it was an oil country in the Middle East. At this point, the other students, who had been quiet up to now, looked up with glee because they knew how to get to Iran. They were the ones that wanted diplomacy.

The next year I came back and they gave me "American History" and "Twentieth-Century Industrial Revolution." Meanwhile I had bought twenty acres in Crawford County for $7900. By 1981 my scholarship ran out and so did my GI bill. That was also the end of a four-year relationship with a girlfriend. Instead of going back to school, I bought this house next to my land. I like not being in a city. I like to be out in the country where the life-style is slow and I can garden. I feel more grounded; I feel healthier, more at ease, and more at peace with myself and with everything else around me.

Back in 1977, while I was writing a dissertation on folk artists in Indiana, I met an eighty-nine-year-old kitemaker named Ansel Toney. Every time I'd go over to see him, we'd make a kite and go out and fly it. Then I started selling his kites to friends, and then I bought some material and started making them at home and making them for friends. I got invited to show and sell my kites at the Broadripple Art Fair in Indianapolis. That was in the spring of '82 and I've been doing art fairs ever since. I've exhibited at over forty by now.

At first my mother and I made all the kites. I thought I would do it long enough to pay for my property and that then I would just stay here, grow my blueberries and raspberries, do wood-sculpting, play the piano, fly kites, and enjoy the beauty of the surrounding woods. But the kite business kept growing and now there are ten people involved. My dad makes the sticks. My mom keeps track of the seamstresses and handles the phone calls when I'm on the road at a fair. My uncle helps with the reels, one of my cousins sews, and even my ten-year-old niece has done secretarial duties, like rubber-stamping. This kiting is real serious stuff. My living room looks more like a storeroom, a factory, and a shipping area. I enjoy the fairs. You get to meet a lot of good people, and I get to travel. I've done fairs from Miami up to Madison, Wisconsin. The farthest west I've gone with the kites was Denver. I won an award of distinction there, a red ribbon and two hundred dollars, which just about paid for our gas. I would like to expand the business, but in such a way that I can spend less time on production and work more on prototypes and experiments.

Late in 1982, I was at a low ebb, romantically speaking. The three favorite women in my life had all gotten married. That means they're not free to go out to dinner anymore; you can't go to a play with them, or a movie, or even stop in and say hello. Their husbands don't like you to do that. Well, I helped a buddy move from Texas and met a friend of his—Jeannie. He warned me in advance: "She'll want to get married and you'll probably think about it. Don't! You don't want to marry her!"

I went down there and, sure enough, there is this brown-eyed, cute little lady. Her and I get to be pretty good friends. So I end up going back several times, and she comes up here, and we talk to each other on the telephone all the time, and the telephone bills increase. Finally we got to the point where we were talking about getting married. I was feeling lonely at the time and thought maybe it would be nice if I had a girlfriend or a wife. I looked at all the good parts of marriage. I thought it's got to be cheaper than having all these phone bills and trips to Texas. I rationalized that it would also be healthier since I wouldn't be out running after these other women.

Then, spur of the moment, she popped up with this idea that we should get married right away. The wedding took place in the minister's living room in Dallas, Texas, just the three of us there. We had a big party, then loaded up her stuff, and left the next day. Jeannie was very bummed out from the beginning, because things weren't working like her ideals: a marriage, a reception, a honeymoon. We didn't have a honeymoon, because it was the end of February and it was the busiest time of the year in the kite business.

Before we got married, we talked about every aspect of life we could think of. One of the things that came up was rings. I don't wear rings or jewelry. I don't even like to wear a belt. But she wanted wedding rings. She had a good job, but she didn't have any savings. I told her, "You've been in my house and you know we need plumbing real bad. If we buy rings, we don't have the money for the plumbing." She chose the rings. I told her exactly how much money we had, but she must have thought I really had more. We also bought expensive shoes and clothes for the wedding that I have never worn since.

Personally, I think when two people love one another and they make a commitment to live their lives together, that's what it's all about. It's not about marriage or what you wear or what kind of rings you have. It's a living experience, emotional and sacred. So we had a pretty rough marriage. The problem was, neither one of us wanted to change our life-styles. She left after we'd been together six weeks and we were divorced. Ironically, by then my busy time was over. My wife was gone and I sat here in English all alone. After she left, I sat here and cried for a while, not only because it grieved me that she was gone, but also I felt like I had hurt her, too. Up until this time, I had never really taken my emotions very seriously, or other people's emotions.

Since then I've gone back to my usual type of relationships. I meet women all the time and I have a lot of girlfriends, but they're in different places and I don't see them very often and then they've got another boyfriend or they're engaged.

I think that our generation grew up with good teachers who taught us the basics of education, so that when we got out we were able to make logical, rational decisions. I think that's what led to the antiwar demonstrations. I think the Vietnam War has done a lot to affect the consciousness of this generation, even though people may be in real straight jobs and pretty much conformed to traditional values. Our generation has looked into the bowl of soup and seen it's pretty thin. They are not people who have fought in World War II and believe America to be right in everything. They are people who have seen the military-industrial-complex foul-ups. Even though they are now a part of it, they know that it's not necessarily always right—it's just big and powerful.

LOST IN THE CROWD:

Bill Samuelson

I arrived in Leavenworth, Kansas, very late on a cold, cold night. When I entered my room at the Commanders' Inn, I headed straight for the heater. But I soon felt a strange presence in the room. Most motels decorate their walls with uninspired paintings of ducks or flowers, but the Commanders' Inn, in honor of nearby Fort Leavenworth, includes a plaque in each room honoring an officer associated with the history of the base.

I was in the Brigadier-General Leslie James McNair room. The caption beside General McNair's likeness described him as an unusually severe disciplinarian. "Short of stature, and with his beak-like nose and sharp, penetrating eyes, he was likened to a bird of prey and, by many, he was considered equally ruthless." According to Mrs. McNair, "While others partied, Whitey wrote textbooks on tactics."

I found it difficult to fall asleep with General McNair staring down at me, and actually stepped outside a couple of times to avoid his stern, disapproving gaze. When I woke up the next morning, he was still there.

I got ready quickly and headed over to Fort Leavenworth. I was directed to Bell Hall, the main classroom building for the U.S. Army Command and General Staff College, where U.S. and foreign officers learn the latest in military philosophy and tactics.

I waited in the hallway until Major Bill Samuelson emerged from a post-lecture discussion with an instructor. We walked to his car and then drove well outside of town to Bill's home, where his wife, Deborah, and their two children, Heidi and Jamie, were waiting with lunch. After the meal, Bill and I retired to the living room and began our more formal discussion of his life.

I was born in Puerto Rico at Ramey Air Force Base, which is where my father was stationed. He was enlisted and about that time probably an E6 staff sergeant. We moved fairly frequently, every three or four years. My father was in a sort of loop where he went from Puerto Rico to Indiana to Alaska to Florida to Indiana to Alaska to Florida. My high-school experience was actually outside Washington, D.C., in Clinton, Maryland. Surrattsville High School, named after Mary Surratt, who was hanged for her alleged role in the Lincoln assassination. My father had retired from the air force and was working in the security force for the National Gallery of Art in Washington.

We had a graduating class of over eight hundred. I doubt if my classmates would remember me well. I got lost in the obscurity of the situation. My teachers will tell you that. I lost interest in school at the end of my sophomore year. There were a couple of classes that kept my interest in my junior year. In my senior year, for all intents and purposes, I was just trading time for a diploma. I was pretty much a nonentity all the way through school. I had a close group of good friends, but I felt a very strong sense of loneliness.

I did meet my wife, though, the summer between sophomore and junior years. Beginning of July 1963. She was visiting a relative who lived about a block from me. I saw her for the first time as I was walking to the swimming pool in the apartment complex. She was walking on one side coming back from the pool and I was on the other side going to the pool. I thought I'd have to pursue this, so I thought up an excuse to go to her aunt's house, which is where she was staying. Unfortunately, I still remember the excuse.

One of my good friends was the paper boy who delivered the *Evening Star,* and Deb's aunt is a very gregarious person who loves to have company just drop in, the paper boy or whoever. So my friend and I took the door to the stall in the men's room at the pool and ran down there as though we had stolen the crown jewels and had to hide them someplace. That was our excuse for being there. I mean, nobody cared a damn about the door, and they knew where they could get it if they wanted it, anyway. It was immaterial that we had this treasure that must be preserved. You know, for a sixteen-year-old boy that was ingenious, and it worked. I'd not necessarily recommend it from the intelligence side of it, but the outcome was fantastic. We developed a relationship and it kept on going. Deb was living in Massachusetts.

She'd come down for a couple of long weekends during the year, and she came down for junior-senior prom.

With such a large graduation class, graduation was like a cattle call. As far back as I was, I could have dropped dead and they wouldn't have found me for a week. There was no emotion associated with it other than a sense of release. That night about five or six of us sat around and got very, very drunk. Just sat around and drank beer. The next day I spent recovering from a hangover. And the day after that I joined the army.

I went to basic training in Fort Gordon, Georgia, for eight weeks. I was with people who were basically as confused as I was. There was an immediate sense of "We need each other so we'd better be nice to each other." Then I went to advanced infantry training in Fort Polk, Louisiana, then to jump school at Fort Benning, Georgia. Then, in November of 1965, I went to Vietnam.

When I got to jump school, I had to fill out a dream sheet that said where I wanted to go. At that time there were several choices for airborne assignments worldwide and I picked Vietnam. The morality of the situation had never even occurred to me. It was strictly a continuation of the fantasies that I had grown up with, associated with World War II, to some extent Korea, combat on TV. I knew all about it. And if I stopped and thought, I thought we've got to stop Communism somewhere. That was the depth of my rationale. At that time Deb was going to the University of Massachusetts and she'd pretty much kind of gone her own way. We were still friends, but not making any plans for a collective future. At that point I really wasn't looking for any type of emotional commitment. I had sort of a romantic notion of riding off into the sunset, all that sort of stuff, and women just didn't figure into that.

So I flew off on a government charter plane full of the first real wave of replacements going to Vietnam. This was about the time of the Ia Drang Valley, and I was going to the First Cav, which had borne the brunt of the casualties. We were all very much into the gay, carefree, devil-may-care outlook, regardless of what we really felt.

Right after arrival, they put us on another airplane and away we went—on to An Khe, which was the base camp for the First Air Cav. The next day I was sent down to my unit, which was the second battalion of the Eighth Cav [Airborne] and I was told that because I was an infantryman and they needed replacements, I would go to the recon platoon. I told them, "That's not what I want to do. That sounds dangerous to me." And they said, "Oh, that's okay, you can make it." Then I joined my unit in the field and away we went. This was, like, within three days of leaving the States.

I started out as what was affectionately referred to as a "scout rifleman," which meant that I walked point and got shot at, basically. I worked my way up, and I say that with tongue in cheek, to radio operator, which meant that I got to carry twenty-five extra pounds of junk on my back and draw fire; to grenadier, which was carrying an M-79 grenade launcher; and a squad leader, which was the height of my ambitions at that time.

From my perspective, we would walk, and I didn't know where we were going or what we were trying to do. My job was to stay alert, and if I saw something that looked dangerous, it was my responsibility to bring it to the attention of someone with higher rank. If we got shot at, I shot back. I did whatever they told me to do.

The first time I was shot at, it was a North Vietnamese, I assume, and he just kind of stepped out from behind an anthill. There were very big anthills in the Ia Drang Valley. My reaction was, Why in the hell is he shooting? The fool is going to hurt somebody. Then I realized that I was down on the ground—it was just a reaction—and that people were shooting back at him. That was my introduction. It was very impersonal, but still very scary. A couple of guys got wounded. At that time, it was terrifying, but in retrospect there really wasn't anything spectacular, no life-threatening wounds. But it was my first encounter and I was impressed. It was serious.

The first time I saw somebody die, and I saw it actually happen, was in a place called Bong Song, on the coast. I saw several VC put up a little fight in the sand dunes to protect an area that we were trying to get to. And I saw several ARVNs, South Vietnamese soldiers, and a couple of Americans run up to them and actually shoot them. It was traumatic because I wasn't threatened at the time. It was a false sense of security, but I felt safe right then. I could see both sides the whole time. It was just like one very big picture. I was very detached, and yet the impact when I actually realized that they had in fact shot and killed these guys was devastating. Up to that point I had always been able to either turn my head, or was distracted at a critical point, or never saw the bodies until I walked up later. At night there was no body, no human being to associate with the violence of the action. There was never a direct link between action and reaction.

I went through AIT and jump school with a guy named Ferman

Saldana, who was from San Antonio, and he and I wound up in the same platoon. He got shot on the 20th of May 1966, just west of Que Nhon, during Operation CrazyHorse. It was one of these deals where the gunship landed and they threw him on the helicopter. He'd gone into shock and I just didn't recognize him. He died four days later. That, to me, was one of the single most traumatic experiences that I have ever had to deal with. He was the first friend who I knew had been killed in Vietnam. I was part of the action in which he was killed and there was a lot of recrimination on my part: I should have done this; if I'd only done that—that sort of thing. Who screwed up? Why did he get killed? Because he was a dynamite soldier, just first-class. That was very hard for me to deal with and I didn't. I literally did not deal with it for several years. I still haven't completely dealt with it. There are a lot of things that I have yet to bring out and work my way through.

For the most part, then, I ignored the fact that Americans were being killed. It was easier to live with—as long as it wasn't me. I learned from my parents to suppress my emotions and give back to people what I perceived they needed from me in order to make myself acceptable. In the environment in which I found myself in Vietnam, and in the army in general, that meant you don't show emotions. That's a sign of weakness. Because of that, I never really dealt with the fears, or the sadness, or the loss, or anything. Even the joys. I could only afford to experience them for a few moments and then I had to suppress them.

After twelve months in Vietnam, I returned to the States. I came back through San Francisco in November of 1966 and spent a couple of days there waiting for a friend to catch up. He was a couple of days behind me in leaving. All I had was a uniform, so that's what I wore in San Francisco. I had gone through San Francisco going over to Vietnam and wore a uniform downtown with no problem. People couldn't have been nicer. But it was a completely different climate when I got back. And I did not understand it. I could not understand why people were upset with me. Now I didn't exactly expect a brass band, but I also didn't expect the comments that they would utter under their breath.

Anyway, I decided that if I was going to stay in the army, particularly if I was going back to Vietnam, I didn't want to be in the infantry. So I went to Fort Sam Houston, Texas, to learn how to become a medic. Probably one of the worst changes I could have made was to become a medic, but at the time it seemed like a very, very smart thing to do. After all, medics don't walk point. They don't carry the radio, and they don't carry the M-79, and those things were just beating me to death. I hadn't rationalized to the point that if they aren't walking point, what is it that they're doing and where do they do it?

I decided that if I was going to be in the army, I did not want to be in the States, because it really wasn't a whole lot of fun. So I reenlisted to go back to Vietnam, which I did in September 1967. And I went to the First Brigade of the 101st Airborne as a medic. That lasted about five weeks. Then I decided this is not cool. I will do anything else. I'll walk point, carry the radio, M-79, all at the same time. Just get me out of here. Basically I found that what medics do when they're not walking point is they're going out and picking up people who *were* walking point. That was something that had completely escaped me the first time around. So I had a couple of exciting experiences that brought home to me the fact that the life expectancy for a medic was not all that great.

One of them was when I was sitting on a fire-support base waiting to go out to the field, and during the day they would bring in the casualties, the guys who had been killed from the line companies. We'd go down to the helipad and off-load the bodies there and stack them up. And that bothered me. It's one of the few things that I think of now . . . I can't deal with it. I can't even stop and focus on it. It bothers me a lot. And I realized then that if it bothered me there, where I could get up and walk away from it, it was going to bother me a lot more doing it in the field.

The other thing—and this kind of brought it home—probably more of a trigger that brought a whole lot of things to the surface. During one night the hill there was attacked, and the first grenade that was thrown landed on the poncho that I had strung over where I was sleeping. I heard it hit and I heard it roll off. Fortunately, I had put sandbags on either side, and I had the poncho over the sandbags rather than having the sandbags weighting it down, so it rolled off—about a foot and a half away from my head. And the poncho just disappeared. All of a sudden I could see stars and bright lights and all this other stuff. But I couldn't hear anything. The explosion just deafened me. I caught a small piece of shrapnel underneath my nose and it was bleeding. Of course it was dark and I didn't know how badly I'd been hit. But I could taste the blood and I knew something was wrong.

There was a lot of shooting and everything, and I thought, I don't like it here. I threw caution to the wind and went running to the bunker, only to run into somebody who wasn't supposed to be there. Somebody had gotten inside the wire, a VC or someone. Where I was, I was supposed to be safe, and I had convinced myself of that, so that was very upsetting.

In the calm of the next day, I was approached by a guy named Malone, who was a major at the time, who was recruiting for a special group, a special unit that he was putting together. I didn't care what they were doing or where it was; I wanted to be part of that organization because I knew it wasn't right there right then. So I went with him.

It turned out to be one of the first two long-range-patrol companies that were formed in Vietnam. Another was formed simultaneously in the southern part of the country. I was a team leader. I had a six-man team. We went out and did patrolling in areas where there weren't Americans working. Technically we were in areas where American influence by artillery fire or immediate-reaction forces just wasn't available in case you got in trouble. That was the disadvantage. The good part was that because it wasn't available, the other side tended to let their guard down, and they acted as though they owned the territory. So it was a much better environment in which to work. The people I worked with were just first-rate. Professionally, it was a good experience, developing small-unit leadership, small-unit tactics.

Around halfway through my second tour in Vietnam it dawned on me that not only were we not going to win; there was a real big chance we were going to lose. I knew we weren't going to win as in World War II. That was painfully clear. But it suddenly occurred to me that we might lose, with the same definitions of winning and losing as in World War II. It became obvious when I started going back to the same places on the ground where I had been on my first tour, or earlier in this tour, and doing the same thing. I started asking, "Why do I have to do it?" I couldn't come up with a good answer, so I started rethinking things at that point. But I stopped short of saying, Okay, we aren't going to win; let's ensure that we don't lose—let's get out now.

I started really coming to that sort of idea on leave after my second tour. I just didn't want to see anybody else get killed. Part of that was stimulated by the fact that a guy I'd gone to high school with, Marty Trailor, was killed the day after I left Vietnam. He was in the 101st, and while I was on leave I went to his funeral at Arlington.

I'd seen a lot of guys get shipped off and everything, but to see the family's experience, the trauma and the heartbreak, and to go over and

of it through their health-benefits programs, which means I pay a certain portion of it, which is financially difficult. But it beats the other option, which is paying for all of it. She's had fifteen major operations.

The way I dealt with Heidi's birth defects was to *not* deal with them. I literally checked out of the family. I didn't deal with her problems at all, and Deb had to deal with them. Consequently, I was going along, no problems; I denied everything. And everyone else was having to deal with it. I wrapped myself around the job. I had some very clear lines where I had my work, and the family had its things to do. They could go out and have a good time if they wanted to, which they didn't. They could do the family-type things and support me and enable me to go forth and be a super soldier. "I will support you financially and I will give you any time and energy that's left over after I've done my job." It was a very convenient way for me not to accept responsibility for what was going on.

I spent about five and a half years at Fort Myer. I was a platoon leader, a scout platoon leader, a company CO, battalion adjutant. I became an aide to a general officer for six months. I went back to the Old Guard and was a company commander. I was an operations officer. I wound up staying there through Nixon's second inaugural and the Bicentennial. I kept getting extended for obscure reasons.

At the second inaugural I was responsible for the alert platoon that was stashed in the Washington area in the event there was a riot or violent demonstration. We were the last shred of defense for the executive mansion and the first family. It went through the metropolitan police, special police, park police, White House police, Executive Protective Services, and then the Secret Service, and then us. So the chances of doing anything were very slim. But why take a chance? That was the rationale.

Later that year was when Deb's mother died of cancer. Not only was she a very stabilizing and important, as well as loved, factor in Deb's life, but she was in her own right a really great person. She was crazy about Heidi. She was the one person—regardless of what Heidi did, it was all right with her. She was a perfect grandparent. That was probably the lowest point in my life. Late in 1973 Deb had a significant miscarriage. It was long enough along that the emotional attachment was there. Our son, Jamie, was born eighteen months later, on the 15th of January 1975, in Washington, D.C.

At the time that the final offensive began in Vietnam, I was an aide to the deputy commanding general of the Military District of Washington, which in and of itself means that all I did was sit over at Fort McNair and not really do anything. But I had access to a lot of information that was being provided on a fairly real-time basis. They were briefing all general officers at that time with daily updates of the situation. At the discretion of the general officer, who could select anybody he so chose to be in on certain parts of the information, I was chosen to be let in on some of the things that were within my security classification. So I got a good chance to track what was happening from the time the NVA started making their move from the highlands around Ban Me Thuot and Pleiku, which is where I started the war ten years earlier.

So I suffered through the emotionality of the loss as they took the central highlands. I realized from my personal experiences that when they did that, it was just a matter of time. The rest of it was going to fall because that was what they had tried to do before. As Saigon fell there were a couple of really hardcore guys in the general's office who were hoping that we would recommit troops. Most of us took the attitude, We tried. We gave it our best shot. Let's ignore it as much as we can because it really is going to hurt us if we stop to think about it.

In 1976 I was with "A" company, and "A" company was stationed at Fort McNair, which is inside the District itself. "A" company had a Bicentennial unit specially developed, which was patterned after the Commander-in-Chief's Lifeguard—that's what they called George Washington's bodyguard during the Revolution. We had uniforms which were supposedly authentic reproductions, spontoons, like a spear, and big hatchets and the whole bit. We wore white wigs. We did this for just about every damn day for a year leading up to the Bicentennial. We were trying to gain credibility among the historical societies that had been at this for a lot longer than we had. Of course, we had a lot of money. We could afford the best of everything and we had a ready-made source of manpower. We marched in all kinds of parades and ceremonies. Every town in America east of the Mississippi had a Bicentennial celebration and we marched in most of them. As a matter of fact, I marched in the Patriots' Day parade in Lexington and Concord in Massachusetts, just as my wife had once, when she was a kid. It was very exciting and very rewarding because these people were absolutely, positively dedicated to what they were doing.

After Fort Myer, we went to Fort Benning, Georgia, for the infantry advanced course, which was six months of learning how to be a company commander. It seemed a good time for me because I had really become a type-A personality—you know, hard-driving, perfectionist, work before everything. I had really placed the job before my home life. But when I got down there and looked around at all these other guys—I was in a class with two hundred other captains, all charging along and thinking they were going to be general officers someday—I started asking, Is this really important to me? To get to where I want to go does not need to entail an ulcer, a divorce, a heart attack, or any of this other stuff. So I mellowed out a little.

I stayed on at Fort Benning and went to civilian school and finished up on a degree which I had been working on sporadically. I went to the illustrious Troy State University and got my degree in resources management.

Then to Army Recruiting Command as an area commander in the Upper Peninsula of Michigan. I had an area of 23,000 square miles. Because of the nature of the job, I spent a lot of time on the road. There were not a whole lot of good radio stations to listen to up there, so I was in the car by myself for hours on end, and I started doing some thinking. It was a little dangerous, I suppose, because I brought up some issues I didn't really want to deal with. But the foundation was laid.

After fifteen or sixteen months, I became the professional-development officer for the army's Midwest recruiting region, which is the thirteen Midwestern states.

During this period, Heidi had to go into the hospital for a major operation. And Deb, who by then was working and going to school, said, "I can't do it. I cannot spend the time with her this time, and emotionally I cannot handle it again."

So I said, "I'll do it. No problem." I had a boss who had made it very clear to me, when I had made it very clear to him that I had a family with medical considerations, that I should be with my family. He said, "Take the time you need."

And, for the first time, I took the time that I needed, and I experienced the emotional aspects of Heidi being in the hospital and spending time with her there, having to see her and her interactions with the nursing staff and the doctors. And I said, This is awful. This is what Deb's been going through for the last nine years on virtually a monthly basis. No wonder she feels the way she does about it. How in the hell has she managed to tolerate my absence for so long? Which is still an amazing fact for me. I'm surprised we're still married. I didn't jump right in, but I started easing into it. It was good because it was at a time when Deb needed to start having an identity of her own that wasn't just Heidi's mother, which is what she had been for so many years. So we started almost role-changing there. I owe Deb a great deal, which I'll probably never, ever really be able to balance out. I guess that's the way most marriages are.

From Chicago we went to Fort Ord, California, where I worked in the Combat Developments Experimentation Command. Basically, it's a test organization where tactics, doctrine, or items of equipment are tested using computers and lasers and combat simulation. Real-time casualty assessment is the big gig out there. I did that for three years.

By the time we got to California, I was the one who took Heidi to Stanford and San Francisco to the hospital, and I'm the one who got into verbal arguments with the doctors. Emotionally they wanted to shut her out and just deal with her physically. It's the damn system that teaches them to deal with the physical aspects of the problem as defined by the current powers that be. They just don't see people as anything other than an imperforate anus or whatever. They don't think of the *child* who's suffering the trauma. I guess they can't. There are those who can and we've been fortunate to have a couple of people who were like that.

In October 1982 I was promoted to major. Now I'm here at Fort Leavenworth attending the Command and General Staff College. Only about 40 percent of the officers in the army get selected to attend the resident course here. So it's pretty much a guarantee of a promotion to the next rank of lieutenant-colonel. The college is very much an attempt to provide a baseline for understanding foreign policy and the aspects of multinational operations. Now, that's a very innocent-sounding statement, but the reality is if you're going to have that baseline, you've got to accept a certain number of premises that aren't really that palatable. And they invariably take a very hard-line, right-wing approach to international relations. By going to school, I'm afforded an opportunity to stay in the army beyond twenty years and to go overseas. It looks like Japan for three years.

Eventually I'd like to retire and go back to California. I like every damn thing about California. I like the people, the climate. I like the way people tend to accept you regardless of where you're coming from. There is a built-in tolerance.

I feel that I could walk away from the army tonight and I wouldn't suffer a sense of regret or loss, providing I still had the means of supporting my family. That has to be there. But my emotional commitment to the army has pretty much run the complete spectrum of "Rah, rah, rah" up to "Okay, I'll do the job; I'll do the best I can; however, there's still a *me* out there that has to be satisfied." When the army is no longer a part of my life, I will still be a person and hopefully still be a husband and I will still be a father.

My son, Jamie, who is ten years old, wants to be a paleontologist. I fully support that. However, if he wanted to join the military, I would not be in favor of it. I want to be economically in a position where I can provide a means for him to do the things he thinks he would get in the military, such as going to school rather than the army paying for it. Education, travel, whatever. I am not opposed to people being in the military; however, I don't want my children to *have* to do that. If they were thinking about it, I would like to be able to dissuade them and offer them an alternative.

When Heidi was born with birth defects, we wanted to know why. We immediately ruled out things like drugs, because neither of us had ever done anything like that. There was no clean answer that the medical profession could give us. So we had genetic counseling through Johns Hopkins, detailed analysis, a workup. No answer there. There just wasn't a reason for it. We accepted the fact that it was "just one of those things" for several years. Then this Agent Orange issue began to get some play in the newspapers and maybe an article in *Newsweek* or something. It was Deb who started thinking there's a connection here that needs to be explored, if for no other reason just so we can rule it out if it is in fact not true.

In my first tour I was in an area where Agent Orange had been sprayed. I didn't know that at the time. I remember it because all the leaves had fallen off the trees, but not all the trees I could see. There was like a line beyond which they hadn't fallen off. I had no idea what that was all about. As a matter of fact, I rationalized why that had happened—that in the tropics autumn comes in waves, and sooner or later those leaves would fall off.

So about 1982 we started talking to people about Agent Orange. I became part of the lawsuit, which forced me to answer specific questions. I realized that, yes, there is definitely a link that satisfies the legal definition that this is the cause. So at this point, legally, I know what the cause is. In reality, the bottom line, I don't know what the cause is. But I have an answer that says this is it, and that makes it somewhat easier to deal with.

Physically, there's just not a whole lot left to do for Heidi. Barring any foreseeable improvements in the medical profession's ability to deal with such a thing, the way she is is pretty much the way she's going to be.

Back in Chicago, when I finally started realizing that there were things that I had to deal with centering around Heidi, I realized there were other things that I had to deal with, too. If I could acknowledge the existence of her problems, I had to acknowledge other problems, and it just started to snowball. Over a period of a couple of years I went through all the trips that other people who had dealt with their emotions went through in the late '60s and early '70s, the morality issue of Vietnam and so forth. I realize it's a very gross simplification of the problem, but it's like needing to discuss intelligently a football game a couple of weeks after it's over, which for some reason now has importance to you but which no one else really cares about anymore.

My big question now is, *Why?* Why me? Why Heidi? Who's paying for the problem? I've got a problem, but she's got a *real* problem. Is there somebody who's responsible? Was there a person in our government who said, "Use Agent Orange," and if so, what are we going to do to that person? Did he or she make that decision with the knowledge that birth defects could very well be an outcome? There's a need on my part to be able to work through that particular aspect of it.

In a different vein, Why Vietnam? *Why?* Why 58,000 Americans? I don't have a good answer for any of that stuff, and that hurts. I am a part of a generation that needs answers to everything. And now those answers either aren't forthcoming or aren't acceptable. I don't believe them.

THE NEW GIRL:

Deborah Samuelson

Two days after I talked with Bill Samuelson, I returned to his home to see his wife, Deborah. Bill and the kids were away at school, and the house, well removed from its nearest neighbor, was quiet and peaceful. Deborah brewed some tea, and I joined her in the living room as she assumed the same seat her husband had occupied when I had spoken with him.

My mother was an RN and my father, when I was a kid, was an elementary-school teacher. My parents separated when I was four. My mother was terrific. Although she never called herself this, I think she was very much a feminist, and I liked her priorities. I think she was very courageous and very much ahead of her time as far as the things she did as a woman. She went through nursing school and then she decided that she wanted to travel. So she got on a ship and went to France and worked at the American hospital in Paris for a year and a half. That sort of thing just wasn't done then. But she pretty much did what she wanted to do. She had high ideals and she lived up to them.

In the tenth grade I went to Lowell High School in Lowell, Massachusetts. Then I went to the eleventh and twelfth grades at King Philip Regional High in Wrentham. It was a strange situation for me because kids from three different small towns in the area went to that high school and most of them had known each other for quite some time. It was kind of a hard place to be the new kid. I didn't get to know a lot of people. I had a few friends that I knew well, and, other than that, I was very shy.

The summer of 1963 I spent with my aunt in Maryland and Bill just arrived one afternoon with this friend of his. I never knew until after we were married that we didn't just happen to meet. I never knew that he had planned this whole thing. It amuses me now because it was such an elaborate scheme.

I was fifteen at the time and I was immediately attracted to him. We talked about marriage a week later. I thought he was very attractive physically, but, of course, it was much more than that. It just seemed right. My mother, and this is one of the wonderful things about her, never belittled my feelings for Bill or his feelings for me, even though we were so young. She took us seriously. Nobody else did, but she did, and she understood how much I missed him. He wanted me to go to his prom with him, and she drove me down to Washington so I could go. That was five hundred miles each way. She was terrific and she understood. She didn't say, "This is silly. You're just in high school; what do you kids know?" I always try very hard to remember that, in regard to my own daughter, who's now thirteen. I think it's very important not to belittle children's feelings.

Bill and I had it all planned. He was going to go in the army and I wanted to go to college. We planned to get married about two years later—but that didn't work out.

I went to the University of Massachusetts, but I hated it from the first. It was large and impersonal, and at that time they still had a curfew for freshmen women—not for men. That was something new for me. My mother's system was "Use your own judgment," which really put the pressure on me to be responsible. And I always was. So suddenly being told that I had to be in at ten o'clock (not that I had anywhere to go, mind you), I hated it right from the start. I was homesick. I was lonely. I didn't want to be there. So I just got up one morning in March and went to see the appropriate person and said, "I want to go home today." She said, "You can't possibly do that." I said, "I guess I can." I called my mother and she said, "Okay, I'll be right there to get you." And she was.

I got a job working in a state hospital as an aide, but I quit the job and went down to Washington and stayed with my aunt. I wanted to be there when Bill came home. In the meantime, I met somebody else and I started going out with him. Bill had written something in a letter that annoyed me so I stopped writing to him. I never told him why. He had said he couldn't wait to get back to the land of "swinging doors, heated floors, and round-eyed whores." That annoyed me. Not that I took it personally; it just wasn't at all like him. In fact, I now know that it *really* wasn't like him at all. I guess it was just Vietnam and the guys and all that stuff. It seemed very crude to me. It still does.

When Bill came home, he didn't know what to do because he hadn't been hearing from me. His parents' house was just a couple of blocks from my aunt's house, but he never came over, because I had stopped writing. Typical kids—neither one of us knew what to do, and he didn't think he should do anything direct like call up and say, "What's wrong?"

We ran into each other at the store one day and we were just so casual. "Oh, hi. How are you?" and "How was Vietnam?" I said, "Would you like to come over for a cup of coffee?" "Oh, well, I guess I have the time to do that."

He came over to my aunt's house and we just continued along these lines, and he asked me to go out with him, and I said I wasn't sure—I was seeing somebody. He said, "Well, I can understand that," and I said, "In that case, I'm *engaged* to somebody else," which I wasn't, really. He said, "Maybe we can still be friends." So that was the end of that. He turned around and volunteered to go back to Vietnam.

I did become engaged to this other guy and I got married in March of 1967. We were married for six whole months. He looked like Bill—but he acted like a lunatic. He did some very strange things like burning holes in the palm of his hand with a lighted cigarette. He was unbelievably jealous. He was an electrician, but he would always leave work early and go to the office where I worked and stand out in the hall and watch me, which I didn't know at the time. He kept me awake nights questioning me about everything that I'd ever done with any boy, particularly Bill, of course. I felt like I was losing my mind. Whenever he'd leave me alone for five minutes, all I wanted to do was go to sleep because I was exhausted all the time. At the end of six months I weighed 90 pounds, and had started off about 110. I had bruises all over me, which turned out to be from a vitamin deficiency because I wasn't ever eating. I was a total wreck.

It wouldn't have lasted six months except that I felt sorry for him and responsible for him in some strange way. I knew I didn't love him, and I just told him one day to leave. I said, "Just go." And that was the end of that.

A mutual acquaintance told Bill that I was getting divorced. I think I wrote to him first and we started writing back and forth. I guess I just knew we'd get married even though we never said so. He came home from Vietnam in September of '68 and we got married in December.

What I remember most about the whole process of getting married is that it was my first experience with military bureaucracy and red tape. We were going to get married in the chapel at Andrews Air Force Base, which is across the street from where my aunt and his parents lived and where most of our mutual acquaintances were. It was the most convenient thing to do. As it turned out, we couldn't even reserve the chapel until we had had an interview with the chaplain and he had agreed to marry us. We had to take a written test, each of us, and of course we had to lie through our teeth because it was things like "How often do you attend church together?" Twice a week, you know, even though we live 750 miles apart. This was a compatibility test. After we had our interview, which entailed my flying down from Massachusetts and Bill's driving up from Fort Bragg, North Carolina, the chaplain agreed to marry us. Then and only then could we reserve the chapel. Then I had to fly down again so we could get the blood tests. It was just such a nuisance. I hate those sorts of things. We did get married in the chapel after all this. Then we moved to Fort Bragg.

When we first got married, Bill had a lot of friends who were also stationed at Fort Bragg, who'd been in Vietnam. Most of them were bachelors and they'd come over a lot and sit around and joke about it and all, and Bill never did that. So I knew it was different for him in some way. He never talked a lot about it. He would talk about experiences he had had there with his buddies, but never much about the actual combat. I never questioned him about it because it was hard for me, too.

I was very apolitical, very naive, very uninformed. However, I thought the Vietnam War had been a mistake from the start and just wanted it to be over with. I didn't care how. It really bothered me that people were so hung up on saving face, you know, looking for some graceful way to get out of it. I felt that the end was delayed for political purposes, and that was very upsetting. You see, my mother—if there was a war, she was sad about everybody, not just the Americans. There was never that differentiation. I always remember that from the time I was a child. It was that war was horrible—not just because of the American guys getting killed. So, because of her, I always had this awareness of the people on the other side. It seemed so strange to me that we never really heard much about that. After all, it was their country.

When Bill came home, that second time, his attitude was very different. He was sad about the whole thing and I felt sad for him, and still do. I don't really know how you cope with an experience like that. I'm not sure that I could. I know that he hasn't worked through it because it's almost as though it didn't happen. There are times ... You know that time just before you fall asleep at night and you think of something and it makes you sit straight up in bed. I feel that way even when I'm wide awake, about the fact that I know he's killed people. And yet I think it is a very big mistake not to differentiate between the U.S. government and the guys who went over there and did the fighting. I think it's wrong to blame the individuals who were involved in Vietnam.

When Bill and I first got married, I had had no exposure to the military at all—none. I guess I never thought about it. I was very surprised to find out about this whole niche cut out for me as his wife, and it was one in which I did not feel comfortable. At that time it wasn't optional. You were expected to do volunteer work, entertaining, that sort of thing. You see, Bill was enlisted when I married him and that was kind of odd because he was an E6 when he was twenty-one, which is very, very early. Where we lived on post at Fort Bragg, everyone else was at least ten years older than we were and had two or three kids, and here we were newlyweds, and obviously we didn't have a lot in common with anyone there. That was difficult. So when he decided to go to Officer Candidate School, I thought that would be a big improvement.

Well, the first thing we had to get used to was that, at that time, they were offering people cash bonuses not to go to Officer Candidate School. Vietnam was winding down and they didn't need all those second lieutenants the way they had a few years before. As a result, Bill had to hang around until enough people accumulated to make it worthwhile to have a class. I think they needed a hundred. So he was there for about two months before the class actually started. He went from being an E6, with a certain amount of responsibility and freedom and so forth, to being the lowest of the low, an officer candidate.

He was confined to post, but we were not authorized quarters on post. So I lived off post and I could only see him during certain visiting periods. We had already been married almost two years, so this was a very unpleasant change, as you can well imagine. This went on for a couple of months before they finally had enough people to start a class. So I already was not really thrilled with the whole program. And it went from bad to worse.

The guys never knew when we could see them. I think it was Wednesday afternoons that we had visiting hours, if we were going to have them. The wives would go out to the parking lot and sit in their cars and wait for some little guy to come and say, "Visiting hours are on" or "Visiting hours are off."

If they were on, we could go into the day room, and they had the chairs arranged all facing the same direction—like being on a bus. You were not allowed to touch each other. Guys who had children were not allowed to touch their children. You couldn't hold hands or put your arms around each other—nothing. You could just sit there in the day room for an hour and talk. If a guy did something wrong they would have him do push-ups in front of everyone, which, of course, was very embarrassing and uncomfortable for everyone concerned.

I don't know what their reason was for not allowing you to touch your family. It was just the whole idea of doing something because that's what you were told to do, and not to question it. This was very difficult for me because I don't come from an authoritarian background at all and it just seemed like so much nonsense to me. I was a colossal pain for Bill most of the time he was in OCS because I wanted him to quit. I thought it was absurd. He kept telling me he would if I really wanted him to, and I think he would have, but I'd say, "No. . . ."

Another thing they did was they wore fatigues and they had to be heavily starched to the point where you could put them on the floor and they would stand. They had to have all this stuff "on display" all the time and it had to be perfect. But the kick was, you couldn't get them through the army laundry fast enough, because it took a week. So what happened was all the wives ended up doing the fatigues, not only their own husband's, but the guys who weren't married would pay you to do theirs. The candidates would even do what they call "break starch"—put on clean fatigues for PT to go grovel around and do the low crawl in the mud. So, built into this are a lot of things that you are going to be a little annoyed about.

After they progressed to a certain point, the men could come home on Saturday afternoons, and that was a biggie. Then it went a little bit farther and they could come home Saturday nights and spend some time on Sundays.

When they were confined to post, there were only certain places you could go, like the library. The bowling alley was off limits. You couldn't go anywhere where there was any privacy at all. It was Georgia in the summertime so it was always about 110, so you'd sit in the car and sweat. A lot of people started going to church because that was one thing you were allowed to do together. Church attendance was way up.

They had two parties during OCS, an informal and a formal, and attendance was mandatory at both of them. Not only did the guy have to go; he had *better* have a woman with him. Now, the women fit into various categories: wives, fiancées, dates, and "other." We had name tags that were colored accordingly, and we went through the receiving line in that order. The only guys who were allowed to go without dates were what's called "geographical bachelors." That means they were married or engaged and the woman in question was not in the vicinity. Everybody else had to go out and beat the bushes, literally, for somebody to drag to this party. Of course there were always women around Columbus, Georgia, who were more than willing to go to these things.

Then—this got me more than anything, I think—at the informal, we were all told that the candidates and their wives, dates, whatever, were not allowed to sit the entire evening. Now, there were chairs, but they were only for the officers and their wives. There was one exception: if you were pregnant. But then only if you were showing.

Then we had the formal, and that was a lot of fun because the guys had been out in the field for about ten days or something and they got back the night before, like three o'clock in the morning. They were all exhausted. And at any kind of a military function nobody leaves until the ranking person leaves. So the wives were literally propping them up on the dance floor. It was ridiculous. I'm not sure all this prepares the candidates to defend our country, but they sure know how to act at a party.

The interesting thing for me about OCS was that they had a wives' club. I went and it was my first exposure to this sort of thing. It was hats and gloves, and we were supposed to help the lieutenants' wives off with their wraps, and serve them refreshments and not touch any of the food until they had all been served.

I said to Bill, "Does how you do in OCS have anything to do with me?" And he said, "No," and I said, "Whew. I will not be going back."

Well, I was told—threatened, really—all through OCS about how my husband just wouldn't even make it through the course because I was not making brownies and I was not going to these teas and one thing and another. Literally I was told that he would be taken out of the program because of me. And he kept saying, "No, no, that's not true. If I can't make it on my own, I don't want to go."

He ended up graduating first in his class. And they make a big deal out of the top guy. He got one bar pinned on by the general, and I got to go up on the stage and pin the other one on. And there were all these women in the audience with their hats and gloves—they just couldn't believe that he had done so well in spite of me! They have a luncheon at the end of the program for the wives and give them their PHTs—"pushing hubby through" diplomas. I was told that I had the dubious honor of being the very first wife not to receive a PHT. They didn't give me one!

Because Bill had graduated number one in the class, he had a choice for his next assignment, and he chose the Old Guard, which is a really prestigious assignment, very high visibility. At that time it was very stressful because if you made a mistake, you could literally be in Korea a week later—I am not exaggerating. So there was a lot of pressure on these guys. They worked terrible hours, and it was not a real fun time in that way. But it was a very close-knit group because it was small, only about fifty officers.

I went to a wives' club meeting there. I thought I'd give it another shot, and off I went. At that time, the colonel who was in charge of the Old Guard and his wife were a very formal couple. This woman used to wear a mink stole to walk her dog, and she had a long cigarette holder and you'd see her walking her poodle around. So I went to one of these wives' club meetings and there she was and I didn't go back for a year. When I finally did go back, it was a different colonel and his wife was a totally different type and I liked her. It was a different atmosphere at the wives' club meetings and it was fun. At that time it was expected that a wife would be mentioned in her husband's OER, which is officer-efficiency report, and if you weren't, then that was considered a lacking. But it never seemed to hurt Bill one way or another if I went to the meetings or didn't.

Heidi was born August 8th, 1971, at Walter Reed. I was awake when she was born, and she looked fine, so I had no idea that anything was wrong. I didn't see her again until the next day. Well, they had rooming in, where they bring the babies into the mothers first thing in the morning. They brought all the other babies, but they didn't bring mine. Nobody said anything to me, so I was very frightened. I had had a lot of hemorrhaging, so I was confined to bed. I asked some of the other mothers and they said, "Oh, it's probably just because of the shape you're in. Don't worry about it. It'll be fine."

An aide finally came in and she said to me, "Have they told you about your baby?"

And I said, "No. What?"

She said, "Oh, nothing. Forget I said it."

It was another couple of hours before they finally wheeled her in in one of those little bassinets, and she looked fine. She was sound asleep and I was terrified to touch her. I couldn't imagine what was wrong. Still, no one had said anything. Then the doctors came and they told me that she had an imperforate anus and she had something called a rectal-vaginal fistula, which means she had a tiny little opening that they thought would be sufficient until she was about a year old, at which time they would do corrective surgery. It wasn't until the next day that they told me she also had kidney problems—bilateral hydronephrosis. So that was that.

When they first told me about Heidi's birth defects I cried and said, "Can I go and call my husband?" and they said, "No, it's not the time when you can use the telephone."

I said, "Well, can he come?" and they said, "No, not until regular visiting hours."

They hadn't told Bill. So when he came, I told him. He didn't see Heidi until she was three days old. A new mother could only have one visitor, her husband. If he was out of the country or something, then she could have one other person. My mother said, "This is ridiculous. Nobody is going to keep me from seeing my very own grandchild." So she put on her nurse's uniform and just walked in! She went around saying hi to everybody and came over and sat by my bed and said, "How are you today?" She was a riot.

But there was nothing to be done. I mean, Bill tried to see Heidi— he was a second lieutenant at the time—but the nurse was a captain and pulled rank on him, which usually isn't done in these kinds of situations. We didn't know it at the time, but tests were being performed on Heidi and she was X-rayed forty times by the time she was six days old. Everything was just very impersonal. I went home at the usual time but they kept Heidi in the hospital a few more days. We could go only during visiting hours.

We were in a state of shock. It was just incomprehensible. We didn't really understand what was wrong and we had no idea why it had happened. I was the most careful mother-to-be that ever was, although I did smoke. I didn't smoke a lot, and at that time you weren't being told not to smoke if you were pregnant. Of course that has nothing to do with it anyway. But I worried about everything. I think I've relived the entire pregnancy in my mind a thousand times trying to think what could have happened. Not knowing was very difficult. I wanted to *know* what went wrong.

We did go see a doctor there at Walter Reed who talked to us about the statistical chances of having a child with these problems. Then later on the army sent us to Johns Hopkins to have chromosomal analysis and all that. At that time they really couldn't tell us too much. They did tell us that they couldn't find any genetic abnormalities with Bill or Heidi or me, and that supposedly there would be no problem having another child, although statistically when you have a child with birth defects, your chances do go up of having another child with birth defects. It was a real shock.

Heidi had this little fistula, as I said, this small opening, and when we took her home they gave us a series of graduated catheters. I was supposed to dilate the fistula every day to make sure it stayed open. I guess this was our first problem. They told me it wouldn't hurt her, but it bled when I did it, and she cried every time. I had to do it every morning and every night and it was unbearably difficult because I felt as though I was hurting her. But the doctors said no, no, no. Their attitude about a baby was that a baby doesn't really comprehend or feel anything. So, to make a very long story short, Bill went to the field when she was two weeks old—gone. And I was home alone with her.

Things went from bad to worse rapidly. She cried almost all the time and she wanted to eat all the time, and I knew next to nothing about babies anyway. She just seemed to cry more and more and more. My mother kept telling me that something was wrong. She would take me to Walter Reed to see the doctor and they told me Heidi had colic. Then they told me that it was the brand of disposable diapers I was using. Then they told me that they had found one of my hairs (I had very long hair at the time) in her diaper and she must have swallowed it and that irritated her, and that was the cause of everything. A hundred and one other ridiculous, absurd reasons to explain all of this.

In the meantime, she was hardly sleeping at all. I'd put her down and she would doze off and then she would awake with a start and start to scream. I was a wreck. My mother was working and coming to my apartment after she'd get through with work to take care of Heidi so I could try to get some sleep. The last straw, Heidi cried continually for sixteen hours. I really thought I was losing my mind. I would take her out to the hospital and they would just patronize me. Then I'd come home and my mother would say, "You've got to listen to me; there's something wrong with this child. You've got to get her taken care of." And I'd go back out there and they'd say, "There's nothing wrong with her. You're just a new mother. Calm down."

So I actually—I can't believe I did this—I looked up her doctor in the phone book and called him at home. I guess I was practically hysterical (according to him I was, anyway), and he said, "All right, Mrs. Samuelson, we'll put the baby in the hospital; we'll find out what's wrong. Don't you worry. We'll do all these tests." They actually brought Bill home from the field. They put Heidi in the hospital; they kept her for three days, then said, "Come and get her; there's nothing wrong."

So we took her home and she just cried constantly. She cried and cried and cried and Bill said, "I can't stand this." So we took her to a civilian hospital, Children's Hospital in Washington. A resident examined her and said, "She has to be admitted immediately."

Well, the next day we were told that she had this enormous intestinal impaction, that her rectum, the lowest part of the intestine, was ten times normal size, and that she was in agony, and that the reason she kept eating was because she couldn't differentiate between hunger pains and the pain from this impaction. That's why she wanted her bottle all the time. And they had told me at Walter Reed to just feed her all she wanted. I had said, "But isn't it unusual to gain eight ounces in a day?" and they said, "That's all right; she's a healthy baby."

Anyway, they tried to irrigate the impaction, but they couldn't do it. They had to perform a colostomy on her when she was four weeks old. When she was in Walter Reed for that three days, they had called Bill's commanding officer and said, "There's nothing wrong with the Samuelson child except a nervous mother." Then when she went to Children's Hospital, Walter Reed called Bill's commanding officer and said, "We'd be happy to have her come back here. We'll take another look." We said, "Thanks, but no thanks."

Then the big problem was trying to get medical coverage for her. Walter Reed claimed it was simply a difference of medical opinion, and they turned us down. Five times they turned us down. What finally happened is that there was a big shakeup at Walter Reed and something like twenty-three doctors were relieved, including the commanding general. We were told that eight of the doctors were relieved because of Heidi. Then we were finally issued an open-end nonavailability statement, which probably sounds like double-talk. You see, the kind of coverage you have in the military won't pay for you to go to a civilian hospital as an in-patient. You have to get a nonavailability statement, and that's what we kept applying for, and being turned down. The commanding general at Walter Reed had the request twice and refused to make a decision, just sent it back. So we went to *the* surgeon general in Washington, D.C., and he approved it. Usually you have to get one for every admission, but he gave us an open-end statement until Heidi's no longer Bill's dependent. So that was the good thing that came out of all this.

The colostomy was the first of Heidi's fifteen operations. The doctors knew they would have to do reconstructive surgery on her ureters, and her kidneys were already damaged when she was born. The idea was that they would keep an eye on the situation and let her put some weight on and let her go as long as possible without threatening her health. When she was five months old they decided it couldn't be put off any longer and they did surgery to reconstruct the ureters. The openings where they went into the bladder were much too small, so that the urine was forced back up into the kidneys, which is called "reflux," and damages the kidneys. She's had that operation three times. She has also had a long series of anoplasties, where they tried to construct the part of the intestine that was absent. That has not been too successful. She has no bowel control at all. She's totally incontinent. It remains to be seen whether she has enough musculature to ever learn any control.

My mother was the only person who ever just accepted Heidi. She'd say, "This is my granddaughter and she has these birth defects; that's part of her." You know, total acceptance. I don't think any of the rest of us have ever been able to do that. So they had a wonderful relationship and my mother was a very big help to me as far as Heidi was concerned.

My mother had been having some pains and she went to the doctor when we were living in Georgia, and they were going to put her in the hospital. But we were going to move the next week—I mean, we're always going to move the next week. So she said, "Well, I'll wait." And then she felt better, so she didn't go. Nurses and doctors, you know, are the worst patients in the world. She was a navy nurse during World War II, so she finally went to the VA hospital and told them she had a blockage of the common bile duct. The surgeons and internists argued back and forth and finally told her she had a blockage of the common bile duct. They did surgery to confirm that she did indeed have this blockage, and they told me after the surgery that that's what it was, but it was noncancerous. Needless to say, we were very relieved.

A couple of days later we got a call from the hospital: Would we please come over immediately. So we went over and the doctor told me he'd made a mistake. It was cancer. I didn't know they *made* mistakes like that. So I told my mother and that was very hard. She had chemotherapy for a long time and that was really difficult, and then she finally decided she didn't want to do it anymore. I respect her for that. She felt a lot better without it.

I had told her that I wouldn't take her to the hospital when she was dying if she didn't want to go. She was really only *very* ill for about five days. The next-to-the-last day I decided that I would take her to the hospital because her jaw was clenched shut and I couldn't give her her pain medication. I felt that she was in a lot of pain. I told her that I was sorry to go back on my promise, but I wanted her to be comfortable. So they put her on morphine and I stayed with her overnight and was very worried because Jamie, my son, was on the way. I was having problems and afraid I was going to lose him.

I finally went home the next afternoon, and of course I'd been home a couple of hours and the hospital called and she had passed away.

I had some regrets about not being there. My mother was the most maternal person ever and I'm not. I guess I feel as though she would have done much more for me had the positions been reversed. Before she died it got to the point where that body was no longer my mother, do you know what I mean? I had separated myself from her in some way, I suppose, in order to deal with her oncoming death. I didn't give her the physical care that I feel I should have. I just wasn't able to do it emotionally. I feel as though she would have done it for me, and I should have done that for her.

One of my big sadnesses about my mother is that she never was honest with my brother and me about her age. She always looked much younger than she was. She was always very energetic. When I was seventeen, I thought at the time she was probably forty. She looked so young. That was the first time she'd ever told us how old she really was. And it was such a shock because she was forty when I was born. I remember my brother and I both burst into tears and she said, "What's the matter? What difference does it make?" Both of us had envisioned having all this time with her, and suddenly realized we never would. And of course we didn't. I was twenty-six when she died, and she never saw Jamie.

I had four miscarriages, one before Heidi, and then I had three after. The farthest along was four and a half months. I wanted to have another child, but Bill didn't after that. When I had that miscarriage I lost a lot of blood and my heart stopped. Bill was there when it happened and it was very frightening for him. He was very afraid that I would die.

With my son, I did have some kind of hormones throughout most of the pregnancy because I kept threatening to miscarry. I am sure that's the only reason I was able to carry him. The army didn't want any part of us by this time and very happily gave us the chance to go to a civilian hospital, so he was born at Georgetown University. It was hard for us to believe that he was all right. We needed to be reassured all the time that there was nothing wrong. Every time he'd cry, we were worried. He's fine, but I'm still not convinced. Especially since we fear that Heidi's problems may be due to Agent Orange. That was one of my first thoughts when we made the connection. I thought, Oh, God, maybe something will turn up with Jamie.

When Heidi was little I was never able to do much of anything. I couldn't get a job or go to school or anything because she was always going into the hospital. Also, it wasn't as though I could get the teenager down the street to stay with her. So my life pretty much revolved around her.

When we went to Chicago I went back to school and I got a job working for a Mercedes-Benz dealer doing their inventory. Then, when we least expected it, Heidi went back into the hospital and was there for over a month. But I wasn't in a position to just drop everything and be with her the way I always had been. So Bill had to become involved with her in a big way.

Heidi had always been very cooperative in the hospital and put up with whatever came along. Then, once, when she was in the hospital in Georgia when she was about five years old, it was as though somebody had pushed a button. She had had surgery shortly before this and her IV came out of her arm. She just decided they weren't going to put it back in. She didn't want anybody to do anything to her ever again. It was very frightening. The doctor told me it was like a psychotic episode. He told me he didn't know if she'd come out of it. She became, to their way of thinking, totally irrational. To my way of thinking it made a lot of sense and I wondered why it hadn't happened earlier. She wouldn't even let the nurses come into her room to take her blood pressure. She'd had it. She's never been cooperative again. It's been very, very difficult because it's gotten to the point where she's had to be put to sleep with general anesthesia just to have an examination. When she was little, I couldn't take her into a bakery if somebody in a white jacket was behind the counter. She was terrified of anything that reminded her of the hospital in any way. I can't blame her, but it certainly made it very difficult to take care of her.

We used to take part in the procedures, like holding her down while they examined her. I'm sure to her it was just that they're hurting me and my parents are helping them do it. Or, even, my parents are hurting me. I would advise parents to remove themselves from these things. Of course, it's a great temptation to want to be there and make the child feel better. But the truth is, you can't make the child feel better anyway, so you are better off to disassociate yourself so that the child doesn't connect you with these things. We belatedly arrived at that conclusion.

Another time, Heidi was going to have blood drawn and Bill was in the waiting room. She was screaming, as usual, but there was something about it that just didn't sound quite right and he got suspicious. So he opened the door and walked in and here she was—she had just had a major operation—on the cement floor with a man kneeling on top of her pinning her legs down with one of his legs and with the other leg on her stomach and holding her arms down, while another man attempted to draw blood. Well, I don't know how Bill kept from being physical in this instance; I really don't. All the satisfaction we were able to get out of it was that the hospital has changed its procedure now. If a child is resistant, a doctor is called. I don't know what good *that* will do. They wouldn't fire these two individuals. The hospital said that by not going in there himself, Bill was tacitly giving his approval for whatever had to be done. I don't know how you explain something like that to an eight-year-old child. I'm at a loss to tell my daughter why something like this should have happened to her.

My mother was a nurse for over forty years and she never stopped being personally involved with the people she took care of. I don't think it's something inherent about being a doctor or nurse that makes people act that way. I understand that they have to have some distance just for their own survival, but I think that's not the same thing as ceasing to act like a human being. Heidi has just been a disease or a procedure to most of these people; she hasn't been a person. They've acted as though there were no head attached to this body. It's just amazing. She's been brutalized physically and emotionally. I have a lot of anger toward our medical system.

There was one more incident that occurred around that time that has had a lasting effect on me. We had just gotten to the army base, been there about two days, staying in a guest house with the kids. The guest house was part of a very large old building that also housed the officers' club.

We were sitting in our room one night and we heard some screams outside. We went out on the steps and we saw a small Asian woman on the steps of the officers' club being beaten by a man who was about twice her size, while two other men stood and watched. I had never seen anything like that before and I intervened. This man turned out to be a major. His wife was Vietnamese. They had both been drinking. When I went over to her she just held on to me and the two of us went into the officers' club and into the women's room. She told me, over the course of the evening, the story of her life with her husband, and to say I was shocked is a real understatement. I had no personal knowledge of domestic violence prior to that time.

My husband and I literally didn't know what to do. First of all, we were new at the base and didn't know anybody, didn't know who to call. We thought, Okay, we just call the appropriate people and get this taken care of. Nothing could have been further from the truth. Bill called the head chaplain, who was a full colonel, but he said he was busy working on a sermon and he couldn't come. We just couldn't get any help for this woman.

Her husband and his friends had gone back in the bar, but then they came to the door of the women's room and threatened us. Finally he agreed to go somewhere for the night and she went home and stayed with the kids. The three little kids were home alone in the meantime. She felt pretty confident that if he just slept it off, he'd be fine the next day. She said he really was violent only when he was drinking. It's very different in the military than it is in the civilian world. Women are in a much worse and more vulnerable situation as military wives. For one thing, in the military you don't want to rock the boat, and *everything* reflects on *his* career.

I was going to school at the time and was taking a class called "Philosophy of Women." There was a woman in that class who had been a battered wife and who was working on a crisis line in the area. I learned a lot from her and I started getting into it from an academic perspective.

When we moved to Fort Ord in California, I worked on a crisis line in Monterey. It was set up so you could take the calls at your house or your place of business and it was a very well-used line. We would take these calls, and if there was a woman who needed to be met, we would go out and meet her and arrange for someone else to cover the line. After a while we opened a shelter for battered women. Then we could meet the women and actually transport them to the shelter. We'd meet them at a police station or a hospital. But mostly it was talking to women on the telephone, mainly listening.

In California I attended Monterey Peninsula College and then transferred to the University of California at Santa Cruz. I felt like I was in a time machine every day going from Fort Ord to Santa Cruz. I can remember one day going to a rally for the Equal Rights Amendment and passing our neighbors in the driveway. They were on their way to a meeting of the National Rifle Association. That's pretty typical. I mean, I just couldn't interact with those people. There was no point in it, because they weren't going to like me and I wasn't going to like them. I am very guarded in military situations because if I were to say the things I really feel, and voice my views, they wouldn't fit in. I guess I've come to terms with it. It's not so uncomfortable for me as it was before.

Bill's so funny, you know. Everybody likes him and he'll say a lot of things, but he says it with a smile on his face and nobody ever really knows whether to take him seriously. Our last Christmas in California we had a party. We were making out lists of people we were going to invite and I had on my list a woman who I think the world of, who used to be a member of the Communist Party. And he had on his list a colonel and his wife whom he had known in the Old Guard. For whatever reason, when this guy showed up at the door, he said, "There aren't any Communists here tonight, are there, Bill?" Bill smiled and said, "Just one that I know of, sir!"

At Santa Cruz I earned a degree in women's studies and anthropology. Now I'm working on a master's in medical anthropology. It's an unusual field. I'm very interested in the concept of illness, partially because it seems to me that my daughter's physical problems are not the ones that cause her the most difficulty day to day. It's the other things, the social aspects. Nobody ever died from being incontinent, and yet that's what influences her day-to-day life. It's just gotten me thinking a lot about how afraid we are of differences in this culture.

Heidi was a March of Dimes poster child while we were in California. It had occurred to me somewhere along the line that every poster child I've ever seen has had some visible defect. I thought, Where does that leave kids like Heidi? With whom do *they* identify? I thought it's also dangerous because it allows the rest of us to believe that everyone we see who doesn't have braces on his legs or isn't missing an arm is well and normal. And that's simply not true. Most kids who have birth defects don't have any anomaly that can be seen.

I talked to Heidi about doing this and she wanted to. By that time she was selective about who she told, so by doing this she gave up her anonymity. I don't know if she'd do it again. She had a lot of mixed emotions.

It's been hard meeting people with whom to share our experiences. What Heidi has, there's not a name for it, not such and such a syndrome or anything like that. Then there's the fact that what she has is not something you can talk about. It's socially unacceptable to be incontinent. It's not something you bring up at a dinner party. It's kind of shameful, a stigma. We're so cleanliness-oriented in this society that it makes it very difficult to have any kind of a problem like Heidi has. We're so antiseptic about things in this society. I think we're quite absurd about our deodorants and such, as though we're trying not to be human or something like that.

I first made the connection with Agent Orange when I heard about a little girl named Carrie, who was one of the named plaintiffs in the Agent Orange suit, and became aware that among her multiple birth defects are the ones Heidi has. I knew from the genetic counseling we had had that having those defects in combination is exceedingly rare. That made me wonder as soon as I heard it. I had also read somewhere along the line about a connection between Agent Orange and children being born with an imperforate anus. Now I'm really quite convinced. It's not provable, but it seems, in the absence of anything else, a likely conclusion. If somebody gave me five million dollars tomorrow, it wouldn't make it up to me. I just want my daughter to be able to have the best medical care there is. I feel like somebody owes her that. I don't think I'm asking too much.

One time when Heidi was quite small I asked Bill, if he could have known, would he have wished that she'd been born or not, and he said he would wish she hadn't. And I said I wished that she still would have been born. Then we talked about it years later and it was just the opposite. He's just so crazy about her, he couldn't give her up. And I said I'm so crazy about her that I wouldn't have wanted her to go through this, had I known. I feel more and more that way as time goes by. It's harder and harder for me to see her hurt. I'm a big believer in the quality of life, and I hope that she has a very happy life ahead of her and a fairly normal life. But I've wished she'd never been born, and still wish it when I see her suffer.

Heidi's really pretty amazing. At some point we decided that even though she always knew about her birth defects, a time would come when it was going to hit her really hard. We thought that if she could do something that would make her feel better about herself physically, maybe that would help in the long run. If there was something she could do with her body, maybe she would say to herself, Okay, I've got this and that and the other thing, but I can do this or I can do that, so maybe it's not so bad.

We decided we would get her involved in sports. I guess she was about three when we made this decision. We thought we would teach her to swim. She turned out to be an incredibly good swimmer. She went through all those Red Cross lessons, and by the time she was seven she'd done everything there was to do, which was very frustrating. She wanted to do lifesaving, and you have to be sixteen. She was very strong, very well coordinated, and took to anything athletic. She plays softball and basketball and she skis very well. When she was eight, she started playing soccer, and now that's her favorite. It's really a beautiful thing to watch her play soccer. She loses herself in a way that she doesn't at any other time. She feels so good about herself when she's playing sports.

As for Jamie . . . It's funny, after Heidi was born, my best friend told me that Bill had wanted a girl. He had never told me that because he didn't want me to think he was disappointed if we had a son. I asked him why and he said because he didn't want a son to go off to war. I think we both always worry about Jamie in that regard. Neither one of us wants him to be in the military. I guess he's had a very different upbringing than other military kids. He's never had a toy gun. We both feel very strongly about that. We've taught him that war is not something you play at. Even though, for obvious reasons, that seems to be the game of choice for little boys on most military posts, he's never participated in that at all. He's a real good kid. He is very sensitive and intuitive. One of his teachers told me that Jamie's enough of a leader, and the other kids like him well enough, that he can get away with things other kids couldn't. I feel very protective of him. I want to be able to spare him the pain that I haven't been able to spare Heidi.

THE TOUGH GUY:

Mike Petty

While I was in Leavenworth, I also paid a visit to Lieutenant-Colonel Mike Petty, who lived on base and who was involved in another part of Fort Leavenworth: the United States Disciplinary Barracks, the maximum-security prison for all branches of the U.S. armed forces. Coincidentally, Mike Petty was Heidi Samuelson's soccer coach.

Mike and I ended up talking politics late into the night. Our opinions differed on almost everything, but we had a great time of it.

Earlier in the evening, over salad and pizza, he told me about an incident that occurred when he was a child.

My father was a salesman. He died when I was very young. He committed suicide. I was there when it happened. I was just turning nine. He and my mother were in the process of getting divorced and I still think to this day he did not intend to commit suicide. He had been drinking, in fact was intoxicated, and gave me a dime and told me to call my mother and tell her what he had done. And he then took a bunch of sleeping pills. When I did try to call my mother, there was no answer. I called his mother and she was just in utter panic.

We were living in an apartment house in Springfield, Illinois, at the time, and the woman running the apartment house heard me out in the lobby on the phone and came out and started speaking to my grandmother, saying, "Well, they were very mild sleeping pills," and she was sure nothing would happen. She had obtained the sleeping pills for my father, so maybe she felt scared. I can remember spending the rest of the night in the apartment of one of the men who lived in the house.

I went to school the next morning, and then they called me out of school and told me that they had taken my father to the hospital. I was told that he had awakened and did not feel well. When they told me that, I just knew that he was dead because he would not have gone to the hospital without having told me something was wrong. Then that evening all the people living in the boardinghouse, or apartment house, sat in the lobby and kind of entertained me all evening. One man was playing the organ and we were all singing. Then my mother, who had been living in Battle Creek, Michigan, came through the door and was crying, and that sealed it. I knew then that my father was dead.

Looking back as an adult, now, I don't think he was trying to kill himself. I think he was trying to somehow get my mother's attention, to scare her or shock her. He did not want to get a divorce—she did. For many years I carried a lot of guilt, thinking, Had I only insisted that they call the police. It's only been maybe in the last ten or fifteen years that I've really accepted the fact that I was only a kid and had done probably what any other kid would have done. So I think I have finally shed that guilt and accepted it as something that happened. Looking back, I think that most adults with common sense would have called the emergency squad, which did not happen. It was a real tragedy because it was a needless death. More so because it was my father.

I lived with my grandparents near Battle Creek and worked on their farm. I was very bitter when my mother remarried. Very jealous. I refused to accept my stepfather, which was quite unfair of me, but no one could replace my father. I refused to go live with them in Indiana. Finally my grandparents convinced me it was the thing to do, that I needed to be with kids my own age, and there were none near the farm where we lived.

My mother worked as a secretary, primarily. My stepfather was like a sales manager for Goodyear and later a tire salesman at Sears. I think he really tried hard to be a good father image for me. And I think I was just stubborn enough and pigheaded enough that I made it very difficult for him and for my mother. When I was maybe a freshman in high school, he started drinking very, very heavily and my mother started drinking very heavily and they started having fights. He never really beat her or hit her, but I was always afraid that would happen. When I was maybe fifteen or sixteen he and I had several fights because of the way he was treating my mother. He lost his job from drinking so much, so when my mother would come home after working all day, he'd immediately go to her purse to see if there was money in it.

Just before the start of senior year, they were finally divorced, and I was very glad of that happening. But then my mother continued to drink, and out of loneliness, if nothing else, she started hanging around at a couple of the bars in town. I think I knew then what was going on, but I would just not admit it. Now that it's all in the past, I believe she was probably sleeping around with just about anybody. Looking back at all that now, I think that was probably pretty obvious, not to my friends, my peers, but to their parents. It made for some difficulties since this was a very small town—Rushville, Indiana, population about seven thousand.

My senior year my mother moved in with a man who was the father of one of my friends and who was not married. That was well before the time that living together like that was acceptable. So the last half of my senior year, I lived by myself—I was an only child. I'd work nights at a gas station to keep some pocket change and worked on a farm in the country. But I couldn't pay the electric bill, so I was living in a house with no electricity. I couldn't flush the toilet, so I went out in the woods in back to go to the bathroom.

Looking back now, there were little things that were happening that I didn't realize. I had electricity in that house for months without making any utility payments because a friend's mother worked at the utility company and just kind of took care of that. Parents of some of my peers always managed to say, "Why don't you come by for dinner this evening?" Or, "Do you want to go with us?" I didn't realize back then that they were attuned so much to what was going on in my life. They really looked out for me and yet did not totally humiliate me by bringing the thing up and trying to make an issue of it. Probably if I would have really gotten in any serious financial difficulties or anything, one of them would have bailed me out.

As boring as I thought it was as a kid living in a little town with a little podunk movie theater, it really had some advantages. It was a very tight-knit community and people knew what was going on in other people's lives. There were a lot of people looking out for me, and I'm very appreciative of that. I think it's made me a better person in that when I see a young person today that needs a little boost or a little something, I try to do it. And I try to do it in the same way that people did for me—where I didn't know about it.

Of course, with all this going on at home, I still had a good time in high school. Freshman year, I was president of my class. I pictured myself as an athlete, though I'm not sure that the coaches did. But I played baseball and football and basketball. In a little high school, it's easy to be one of the jocks. I guess my junior year of high school was when I really discovered what sex was. I probably abused it because there were a couple of girls that there was no physical attraction or affection for whatsoever. We were going out to have sex. Now that I have daughters coming up to be that age, I cringe that they may find a younger version of me.

Every hero I'd ever had had been a coach or a professional athlete, or something like that. Then I got my first hero that was not a macho image. His name is Larry Kelly and he was a history teacher. He was short and he had a receding hairline and kind of reddish hair, and wore glasses, and did *not* present the image of being a jock. But he was so sensitive to people and their needs. He was the debate coach and drama coach. Up until that point in my life, I really looked down on people who were into that. I thought that my place in life was either being a jock or, you know, one of the guys. Larry Kelly taught me that you set your goals and be whatever you want to be. If you try, and work hard, you can be good at it and you can get a super feeling of satisfaction. He instilled within me a sense of pride and self-confidence that I had never known.

I can remember when I was in a play for him, *The Death and Life of Larry Benson,* by Reginald Rose. I can remember there were people in the audience that were crying because of the lines in the role that I had. What a feeling that gave me! He taught me the power of words. Through his example, I learned that it required more strength for a man to show his emotions than to hide them behind a false macho image. I still consider Larry Kelly to be one of the most influential people in my life. When I do things successfully, I do them thinking, I hope he knows.

I would have liked to have gone to college. I was taking a college-prep program and just assumed I'd go to college. Then when things started to deteriorate in the family, it started becoming real obvious to me that that was out. I just couldn't afford to go. I enlisted in the army before high school was out. I went in on the deferred program and took all the tests and everything before graduation. When I went in the army I had, like, eleven dollars in my pocket, and that was all I had to my name.

I went right into the army on the 14th of June 1965. Young punk, snot-nosed kid, you know, chip on his shoulder, going to be mean. Just really dumb. I enlisted for airborne infantry. I mean, I wanted to be the toughest guy on the block. I wanted to come home and be a paratrooper and strut my stuff and show off to the guys back on the block. When I went to enlist, the recruiter told me, "You test out for anything. If you want to go to college, the army will send you." He said, "When you get to the reception station, they're going to give you a lot more tests. You make sure you tell them you want to take the college-entrance exam." So I get to Fort Knox, Kentucky, and I go to the sergeant and say, "I want to make sure that I get scheduled for the college-entrance exam." When he started laughing, it was quite obvious I'd been had.

I remember, about the second night, getting on the telephone and calling my aunt in Michigan and crying and saying, "Oh, it's nothing like they said it would be." The shock of it was that in high school I was Mike Petty and people knew me as Mike Petty and they knew I was a good person and that I could be fun. I mean, I had made my little niche in life. And all of a sudden I'm a serial number with a burr haircut and there's hundreds of people just like me floating around, and not only do they not know us, it appeared as though they didn't give a damn. And that really hit me—what have I got myself into?

Then, as things went along, and we met each other within the platoon and the company, things started to smooth out again, and I told myself, "I can be good at this." And I was. Completing basic training, I received an accelerated promotion. They gave me orders to become a medic and go to Fort Sam Houston, Texas. You had to have good scores to get that. I remember getting up my courage to approach the first sergeant and the company commander because they were like God—you just stayed away from them—and I went in and said, "That's not what I wanted. I enlisted for the infantry," and both of them saying, "You're stupid, kid. This is good training. Anybody can be an infantryman." And in the back of my mind I'm thinking when I go back to Rushville, Indiana, I want them to see me strutting down the street with my paratrooper wings. I don't think young people have a reference point for time. You're immortal! God, I'm going to live forever and I'm never going to be old. How soon that changes!

So I had them change my orders. They sent me to Fort Polk, Louisiana, for Infantry AIT—advanced individual training—and I became an infantryman. Vietnam, at that point, was starting to pick up. We were seeing it in the headlines daily. You'd sit in the bleachers and the sergeant would say, "What you learn today may someday save your life in Vietnam," and we'd all prick our ears up.

Late one night I got a call from the Red Cross saying that my mother was seriously ill and would not live through the night. She had gone to her parents' house in Michigan, the grandparents I had stayed with. I guess she knew she was dying and she just wanted to go home to die. I rushed home and got there early the next morning. I could hardly recognize her. Her stomach was so distended from cirrhosis of the liver. She was comatose at the time, and hadn't eaten for several days. She wanted to die at home, she didn't want to be in a hospital. My grandparents had this old doctor, Dr. Funk, who was also a preacher and a mortician. I guess he covered all bases. I called him and insisted she be taken to the hospital. Within a couple days my mother came out of the coma and within a week or two had gone back home.

I went back to Fort Polk, but it wasn't long before I got another Red Cross message that my mother was dying. I went back to Michigan, but this time she did not come out of the coma. Her liver ceased to function with the cirrhosis and it was complicated because she had hepatitis. I mean, just what you think of as an alcoholic.

Meanwhile, it became quite obvious that if you are going to be in the army, there are better ways to go than charging up the proverbial hill every other day. Second lieutenants just seemed to have it made. They were always saying, "You guys do this . . . you guys carry that." I'm thinking, Hey, I can do that. That's a pretty good job. Besides, they make $244 a month. What could you possibly do with that much money? I was making $78.50 a month. So three of us applied to OCS—Officer Candidate School. I ended up going to engineer OCS at Fort Belvoir, Virginia. It was a challenge.

At that point I was thrust in with people much older than I was. I was a soldier—but I was a kid. I was in with guys that were twenty-five, thirty years old. I graduated from OCS right after I turned nineteen and was a second lieutenant at nineteen.

I went to Fort Lewis, Washington, and was a platoon leader and was the youngest man in the platoon. The unit was going to Vietnam. I didn't know that until I got there. I think I was smart enough to know that I didn't know much about what the devil we were doing. My first platoon sergeant, Cliff Simmons, was probably thirty-five or so and he told me early on, "You're the lieutenant and what you say goes." But he added, "I really run this platoon whether you think so or not, but if you'll give me the chance, I'll train you and I'll make you a good officer." And he said, "One of these days I'm going to tell you that you're ready, and that's when you don't need to come and ask me what should we do." I understood what he was saying. He and the other NCOs, noncommissioned officers, really did train me. I think they trained me well, better than what we may be doing in today's army.

I was still nineteen when we went to Vietnam. It was September of '66. A very popular song then was "See You in September," and that was kind of our unit's theme song because we'd gone in September and would be coming back in September.

We'd sent over an advanced party that went by plane. The rest of us went by ship and arrived three weeks after the advance party. We were in Quin Nhan harbor on the ship and we were going ashore the next day. You could see the flares in the distance and you could hear the artillery going off. I still remember that night. We were all in our own little world. No backslapping or anything. Everybody was very contemplative. What's out there? What's going to happen? You really did some serious soul-searching because you didn't know what was going to happen in the morning. I had thirty people that I was totally responsible for. What an awesome responsibility. I grew up very, very quickly. All of a sudden I realized that no one's immortal. We're all mere mortals and you don't know what's going to happen.

In the morning they put us in LSTs, Landing Ship Troops, and we had our steel helmets on and we had our M-14s locked and loaded. We were bumping against the waves and then hit the beach and everybody lurched forward as the LST crunched into the sand. They dropped the ramp and we came charging out. And there's Norman Adams, second lieutenant, one of our buddies who was in charge of the advance party, standing on the beach saying, "Hey, welcome to Vietnam!" He had all this beer stacked up there. We were all expecting, I guess, warriors or something, and there's Norm, with no steel pot, no weapon, and he's got these buses lined up for us to get on. Talk about anticlimactic!

About ten days later we started getting people killed. We were brand new and they married us up with another unit to go on a mission. We thought it was going to be kind of a gravy thing. We were going into an area called Tam Quan Beach to remove a bridge because they needed the bridging for another area and we were going to put in a different kind of bridge. We were there too long. The last night we were there, all the villagers left the little village and that told us, Hey, something's coming.

It started with probing by snipers. Then we started taking mortar and rocket attacks. My platoon had a perimeter and I had everybody in holes we had dug. But the other unit—these were "combat veterans"—they were sleeping on cots and in tents. We were under fire all night long.

I can remember the next morning, as it was getting light and the battalion surgeon had been working all night long on the wounded, I saw a man who had been hit in the head and the top of his skull was gone and his face had just collapsed inward. The skin was still there. People with gaping holes in their torsos. I never even imagined anything like that. I mean, death became a very real thing. It was just completely obvious to me that I could be one of those people. And, you know, it really made you think, What are we doing here? Why are we in Vietnam? What is the purpose of all this?

I don't know to this day if I really believed that we were there to provide the people of Vietnam with a free choice. I told myself I believed that, and I was willing to die for that. I believed that we were there fighting for a just cause.

I was not in an infantry unit that went on search-and-destroy missions. I was in an engineering unit. For the rest of my tour, we took a lot of fire, but it wasn't on a daily basis. It wasn't like being out in the bush, but we still got mortared and got rockets. What it did teach me, though, was, Hey, I don't like getting shot at. I don't like mortar attacks. There's nothing more frightening than being in a mortar or rocket attack. You don't know where they're coming from. You can't see them. All you can do is scrunch down behind a bunker or in a hole and hope that one doesn't come right in with you. You can't fight back. I had been wounded when we were at Tam Quan Beach. It was very superficial. I got hit on the hand. But it scared the living criminy out of me. It had a very sobering effect and I had not been drinking.

I've got a philosophy that there's really no such thing as courage. Courage is nothing more than controlling your fear. Probably 90 percent of the people that were in Vietnam did something that was very courageous but was never brought to light by anybody. But they knew themselves afterwards.

When I came home from Vietnam I extended my time in the army and went to jump school because I didn't want to go on leave until I could go home and say, "I'm a paratrooper." I went to the 82nd Airborne Division and less than five months later the brigade was alerted. I was right back in Vietnam again. This time I was in an airborne combat-engineer battalion. We had demolition teams out with all the infantry squads. We had the mission of clearing roads on a daily basis for mines, going into booby-trapped or mined areas, and base-camp security.

I was in Vietnam that second time for four or five months. I could have come back earlier, but the only two officers in the company that had been to Vietnam were the company commander and myself, and I just felt an obligation to those younger lieutenants, those platoon leaders, to stay there. As a company executive officer I was responsible to help train them. I turned twenty-one when I was there, so, you know, you're still very idealistic at that age.

I can remember when it was announced that everybody was going to Paris for the peace talks, and the elation that was felt. A couple of old NCOs said, "Hey, they talked for months and months and months in Korea before they came up with a truce or an armistice." And when they told me, I can remember thinking surely that won't happen in Vietnam—but surely it did. Another thing about this period was that President Johnson stopped the bombing in the North. I can remember writing Mr. Kelly, the high-school teacher, feeling so betrayed. Our forces in Vietnam were getting rocketed and shot and all this, and these supplies were being brought into the South down the Ho Chi Minh Trail, and yet we're going to stop the bombing. How can you expect us to be here to do something like this, and then you as much as tie our hands? I think that was my first touch with disillusionment.

I had met my future wife, Sherry, while I was at Fort Bragg. She was going to Methodist College in Fayetteville, North Carolina. We dated a couple of times, but she kept dating this other guy and I started dating a different girl. When I went back to Vietnam with the 82nd Airborne—this really sounds corny, but it's true—I had a dream, and in the dream I married Sherry. A couple of weeks later, I got a letter from her—just totally out of the blue—and we started writing.

We were married in August '68. We were both twenty-one. It just so happened that a bunch of my OCS classmates were at Fort Bragg at the time and they were the ushers. We had the crossed sabers and the military chapel and they were all in their dress blues.

By this time I had transferred to Special Forces—kind of a macho thing, I think. This good friend of mine told me he had applied to go to flight school and I said why and he said aviators make more money flying planes than the guys do jumping out of them. That made good sense to me. That was about the extent of the sophistication of my economics background. So I applied for flight school and was accepted.

Sherry and I headed for Fort Walter, Texas, and I was going to become a helicopter pilot. That's where our first daughter, Shannon, was born. From there we went to Fort Rucker, Alabama, to complete the flight training. I fully anticipated going back to Vietnam again as an aviator, because that was an automatic when you became a pilot. But after flight school they sent me to what was called the advanced course, which was a nine-month school mainly for captains and majors. That was in Fort Belvoir, Virginia, and my second daughter, Shaye, was born there.

Right after that I went back to Vietnam for the last time. That would have been Thanksgiving of 1970. The first two times when I was there I was a bachelor and I never really considered what would happen should I get killed. I didn't want to get killed, but I mean there was no long-range impact on other people. Well, now I've got a wife and two children and I'm thinking, If I get killed, what have they got? They've got some insurance money, maybe, but they don't have a daddy.

Out of all the tours, that was the tour when I really saw the most combat. I was a helicopter-gunship pilot. It was exciting, exhilarating, not necessarily in a fun way, but it really kept the adrenaline pumped up all the time. In the air at first light, on the ground long enough to rearm, refuel, then back in the air. It was not uncommon to fly twelve to fourteen hours a day. Sometimes the weather was so bad, you knew you shouldn't be flying, but there were American lives out there needing support and you tried to go out and give it. If someone on the ground was in contact and they were in an area that they couldn't get artillery to them, we'd go in and shoot for them. At that time, we were the only Cobra helicopters allowed in the DMZ, the demilitarized zone, anytime we wanted to go in.

My unit flew some classified missions in Laos—prisoner-of-war snatches and things like that. Basically we put people in and then went back either when they were discovered or at the end of a particular time to pick them up and bring them back out. You knew if you had to go get them before the time was up that it was going to be bad shit, that they were probably surrounded. You'd fly through anti-aircraft fire that was just like in the World War II movies. Black puffs of smoke all around and the concussions making your aircraft shudder. We were not anticipating the sophistication of the weapons they had—the ground-to-air missiles, anti-aircraft weapons. I can remember when we tried to make the extractions, watching the slicks, the supply and troop helicopters, go in to pick up Vietnamese soldiers and bring them out. So many would get on it that the slick couldn't even get off the ground. It was overloaded. They'd make some of them get off, and as they started to pull away there'd be Vietnamese soldiers dangling from the skids, they wanted out so badly.

When you were getting shot at and you were shooting back, your mind was so busy. It was afterwards you'd get the shakes. If you've had good training, then when the pressure comes, you resort to the things you've done through practice. So good training is one of the strengths, I think, of the American military. American ingenuity. One guy is always in charge, whether it be the captain or the lieutenant or the sergeant or whatever. If it's a captain that's in charge and he gets killed or incapacitated, somebody else stands up and takes over, and says, "Okay, let's keep going." And if they get hurt, somebody else does. And from everything I read and from my military training, that's the big advantage we have over the Russian forces. You know, if it's a bunch of young American soldiers, one of them's going to jump up and say, "Follow me." And the rest of them are going to do that. I see that as being one of the real strengths in our military system.

My oldest daugher, Shannon, was just beginning to talk and my wife would make tapes for Shannon to send to me. I was flying Cobra helicopters and she couldn't say that so she called them "Cobey copies." My wife would hold up a picture of me and I could hear Shannon's voice say, "My daddy, my daddy!" To get this tape and hear her voice, it would just rip your heart out.

During my last tour in Vietnam they started what they called a "mid-tour leave" and you could take a leave back to the United States. Sherry had gone back to school and her mother watched the kids while she finished college. I planned my mid-tour leave to come home for her graduation in May. As far as I was concerned, that was a momentous occasion. I was not a college grad, and I was so proud of her.

I came home for two weeks and I got to see the kids. Of course, they were very standoffish at first—who is this guy that's coming into our house? They knew I was their dad, but I was still a stranger for having been gone for six months. The kids did warm up to me, and it was such a neat thing. When I was going back to Vietnam, we went to the airport in Fayetteville, North Carolina, and we were walking down the ramp towards the little metal-detector thing and I was carrying Shannon. I was getting ready to get my hugs and my kisses, and Shannon wrapped her arms around my neck and wouldn't turn loose. And she was saying, "Daddy don't go . . . Daddy, don't go!" That's probably the hardest thing that I've ever done, was to have to hand her to my wife, knowing I was going back to Vietnam for the last six months.

It made that last tour very difficult because I had a wife and kids and I felt like I had something that I had not had before and I cherished very much. I certainly did not want to be killed in some kind of war in Vietnam especially when I no longer understood why we were there.

You know, we were supposedly taking people home and with-drawing troops, yet people were still in combat and still being killed. And the common saying then was, "God, I don't want to be the last person killed in Vietnam." It made you really start to question what we were doing, and as a soldier you're really not supposed to do that. But you couldn't help it. We tried to go through a Vietnamization process where we turned the war over to the South Vietnamese. I was really encouraged when that started, thinking we were going to get the Americans out, thinking the Vietnamese have had all these years of our support and training, and I just assumed they were going to be ready for that. And how quickly they were overrun. The speed with which that country was overrun by the Communists is just phenomenal to me. What had we been doing for all those years? Why were the Vietnamese Communists still so strong? I don't know what the answers were. But as we pulled out, it was just like a wave that overran the country. There was so much corruption.

After all of our years of involvement in Vietnam, to have been there that long and to have put that much into it and the amount of money, human lives, armament, everything else, and the Vietnamese still weren't holding their own. Should the Americans have stayed longer? In my opinion, no. I think the mistake was made early on when we went in and just nickel-and-dimed it. I'm not a politician, but I think Barry Goldwater told the truth and scared the hell out of the American public. Then Johnson came along and did what Barry Gold-water said he was going to do—only Johnson didn't do it all at once. He did it in phases. What if Goldwater would have gone in there with massive force right from the beginning and tried to treat it as a police action? Go in and kick the hell out of whoever needed to be kicked and move them back north and say, This is the line, don't cross it. Just like in Korea. I don't know. That's very simplistic. I don't even know if that would have worked.

All of us that were there as individual soldiers, we had no idea what was going on at the higher levels. I know my feelings were that we just kept doing the minimum amount because we were afraid the American public would not have been supportive of anything else, when in fact it escalated to that point and we *didn't* have the support of the American public.

I saw the peace movement or the protesters as part of America. I was a real Joan Baez fan. I still like her. And I had the highest respect for her husband, David Harris, because he went to jail for his convictions. A guy that ran to Canada I thought was a dirtbag. But those people that went to jail for their beliefs I respected. With my military friends, I think I was really in the minority. But that's what is the neat thing about our country. Everybody can believe what they want to believe. You can say whatever you want to about this country, as long as you don't hurt people. If you think the country's got things wrong with it and you want to protest them and try to change those things, you can do that.

So, anyway, it was just kind of a hard time. You hear about Vietnam Veterans of America and the guys are burned out and they didn't get welcome-home parades and waving flags. I don't buy any of that crap. I'm very bitter that we formed a Vietnam Veterans of America Association. If they want to join something like that, they've got the American Legion or Veterans of Foreign Wars. I don't care what studies show about post-Vietnam syndrome and that kind of stuff. I find those guys to be an embarrassment to me, personally. I went over there. I did what was asked of me. Whether I liked it or not, I did it. It was my job. It was my country I was doing it for, and I don't think I've been permanently brain-damaged having done that. It would have been nice to have had parades and all that kind of stuff, but it was not expected. I think what was expected was just to come back and be able to go on with our lives. I think I've done that, and I guess I don't understand why some of these other people haven't been able to turn loose of that Vietnam experience. You can't keep living in the past and blaming everything that's happening on the past. This sounds very hard and callous, but I don't think these people would have been successful in *anything* they were doing. Vietnam just happened to be the convenient excuse to hang their hat on.

Along those same lines, we had the settlement with the Agent Orange thing. I just don't understand that at all. These are men that went to war, were exposed to death and could have been killed. And they come back and they want to sue somebody because they've been exposed to a chemical agent, when in fact they could have been exposed to a bullet and killed. I understand that some men claim Agent Orange caused birth defects to their children, but I'm not sure that there's a lot of conclusive evidence either way. If, in fact, that's proven, I would have absolutely no heartburn with the Veterans Administration providing some type of a veterans' benefit to those children. But for a person to say, "I was in war and you exposed me to something hazardous, so I'm going to sue you," well, war itself is hazardous. So I feel somewhat embarrassed that people may associate me with some type of a bad syndrome because I went to Vietnam.

I finished my third tour in Vietnam and was stationed at Fort Lewis, Washington. I became a company commander of an engineer company. I was really having fun in the army. I mean, I was all of twenty-three and a company commander—I've got two hundred people I'm responsible for. It's a construction company. I've got massive equipment. Where else could I, with no college education, get a job like that? It was a ball, a complete ball. My third daughter, Maggie, was born there. But it was a scary time to go through, too. They were having what was called the RIF—reduction in force—meaning Vietnam was winding down, we had too many officers in the army, and they were removing some.

It became obvious if I was going to stay in the army and not get myself kicked out I had to get a college degree. I was going to school at nighttime and in 1975 finally graduated from college. St. Martin's College, Olympia, Washington. And I graduated *summa cum laude*. Sociology. Which did not sit well with the Corps of Engineers. About that same time, I'd made a decision that if I was going to stay in the army, educationally I was not going to remain competitive in the Corps of Engineers. As a Battalion S3, I was doing the plans for major vertical and horizontal construction and was getting in over my head. That's when I became a military policeman.

If I have any talent in life, it's working with and for people and bringing out their talents towards a common goal or a common mission. I just can't imagine doing any type of work where I'm not working with people. After becoming an MP, I was the station commander. If you equated that to a police department, I was like the captain of the patrol division, the cops on the street. Next I became the deputy of the stockade. Then we went to Germany, where I was company commander in charge of security of a nuclear-weapons site. That's probably the most demanding job I've ever had. We lived from inspection to inspection, and when you are dealing with nuclear items, there're no gray areas. When they come in to inspect, either you're right or you're wrong.

Then I became the deputy of the Mannheim jail, which was the largest-area confinement facility that the army had. I really was discovering that I enjoyed corrections. I think there's a real knack to dealing with people that a lot of people consider scumbags and trying to get something positive back out of them. You've got to realize that in the military we're not just talking about AWOLs; we're talking about felons.

I came out of Germany and went to San Antonio, Texas, to Fort Sam Houston. I worked for a couple of years with what is called the readiness group there, meaning I went out to National Guard and Reserve units and helped them with their training, helped them to meet the standards of the active army. It was a very rewarding job, but I was traveling 150 to 180 days a year, and most of that on the weekends and in the summer when my kids would have been home.

From that job I went to Health Services Command, which is the major headquarters for all of the army hospitals, medical centers, medical activities, throughout the United States. In that job I was responsible for security of the hospitals, writing the regulations about drug security, monitoring the crime within the hospitals, those kinds of things. Again, a really interesting job. We thought we might retire to San Antonio, so we started putting down roots. We bought a house and became members of the community. I was a reserve deputy sheriff for Bexar County. I was vice-president of the PTA, and was vice-president of the soccer association. A whole bunch of little things.

When I was promoted they said, "You've got to move because you've been there too long anyway." The army moves you every three or four years. I came to Fort Leavenworth here in Kansas and went to work at the United States Disciplinary Barracks. I was a director of classification when I first got here, meaning handling all the correctional treatment files, all the board actions, clemency, parole, finding the appropriate work details for inmates.

Then I became the director of training of the Disciplinary Barracks, which I am now. I have all the academic and vocational training for the inmates. Every inmate that comes into our jail is tested. If he tests below the ninth-grade reading or math level, it is mandatory that he be put in basic-skills education. Most of our people are in associated arts programs. We've got thirteen vocational training shops: shoe repair, upholstery, sheet metal, barbering, engraving, auto repair, auto body and auto paint, furniture, farming, screen printing, lithographic printing, and a greenhouse. We run a 2400-acre farm-ranch operation with livestock and crops. It's a tremendously challenging job, and I look forward to going to work every day.

This is the Department of Defense's maximum-security prison. We have 1300 inmates right now. About 60 percent of them are in for rape, murder, or assault. Many have life sentences and some have death sentences. I don't want to sound like a bleeding-heart liberal—I think I'm quite conservative—but I believe that every individual is capable of making a mistake in their life and I think they should be given the chance to atone for that mistake. They should be punished, but they shouldn't be warehoused. And when they are returned to society, they should be better equipped to become a productive member of society. If you can't get them turned around, then maybe you need to have selected prisons that are like warehouses. You don't want these people back in society.

But anybody can make a mistake, whether it be through immaturity or through passion, or through temporary insanity. They should be punished, but punishment is not what we do to them while they are there. The punishment is the fact that they *are* there. They're not going home with their families; they're not going to the movies or out shopping. Their punishment is being in jail. I don't like the word "rehabilitation." It gives me a connotation that we are doing something to change them. I believe we cannot change people. People change themselves. We are presenting them with a chance to change themselves. We can give them the opportunity to see different values and to see the consequences of what certain actions will bring. You teach them how to make decisions and how to prioritize. Then you've got to take the risk that they will make the right decision, and I really believe that in a lot of cases, people will do well.

I will be retiring from the military this year after twenty years. I've got one big thing going for me, I find, in talking with people about employment, and that's my age. They say, "Geez, you're only thirty-seven years old. You've got a whole career ahead of you." With one child in high school and the second one approaching high school and the third one right behind, I would like them to get into a high school and stay in that high school the rest of the way. My children really sacrificed for me to make my career in the military.

When I saw my first daughter the first time in the nursery right after she was born, I just stood there and cried. Here was a human being that I helped make, through the grace of God and a wonderful wife. I had no idea what was laid out for her or me for the next fifteen years. There've sure been some rough times along the way, but I would never trade any of it for the world. Every one of my daughters is a separate and distinct individual and every one of them has brought me the greatest joy. What better legacy to leave than a well-adjusted other human being who can enjoy life the same way that I have. I hope someday that they can have children that will bring them as much joy as they have to me.

Even though it sounds like I probably didn't have a good family life when I was growing up, and for a period of a couple years I didn't, I've got an aunt, who was my father's sister, and she and her husband have loved me, and worried about me, and cared for me. They have three daughters. I couldn't have had sisters that I could be closer to and I could not have had my own mother and father that I could be closer to than my aunt and uncle. So I do have a family. My children call them Grandma and Grandpa and Aunt Jody and Aunt Kathy and Aunt Jeanie.

My sister Jody is an unsung hero in America. She went to a very good high school that paid teachers a lot of money, and that high school tried to get her to teach after she'd been teaching at a little poor rural school. And she didn't go. She sees that they need her at the poorer school. I really respect her for having her set of principles and sticking to them. My sister is one of my heroes. I really hope that someday just one person will think of me the way I think of her.

THE YEARBOOK EDITOR:

Jody Owens

I liked Mike Petty's concept of unsung, everyday heroes, and decided I would like to pay a visit to his cousin Jody in Battle Creek, Michigan. I got lost while trying to find her house, and stopped to ask directions of a couple conversing in their driveway.

The man had never heard of the street where Jody lived, but his wife thought a moment and told me how to get there. When I arrived at Jody's house, I glanced to my right and realized that I was no more than thirty yards from the home of the couple I had asked for directions. This man had never heard of Jody's street, and yet a strong gust of wind could have blown him onto her front porch. A misthrown Frisbee could have landed on her roof.

When I told Jody what had happened, she explained that the man lived in a different subdivision and faced in the opposite direction, and I shouldn't get upset about it.

I set up my tape recorder while she went to get water and cookies. When she returned, I asked her to tell me some basic information about her family and her high school.

When I was born, my mother was a telephone operator and my father was an installer for the telephone company. I have two younger sisters, plus Michael, who's thirteen days younger. He calls me "the elderly sister." I was born right here in Battle Creek, and I went to Lakeview High School, which is a couple miles over that way.

Lakeview High School had a fully equipped fallout shelter for twelve hundred people. There was water, food, cots, blankets, everything, for twelve hundred people. There were certain rules in case of a nuclear explosion. Anyone who came to school could come in, but once the doors were closed, no one could go out. Even if your parents came for you, if the door was closed, you couldn't leave. As early as the first grade, we learned a little song about a turtle, and how to get under your desk and put your hands over your head. When you grow up and your whole life is getting ready for a nuclear war, well, I have to say I'm surprised that we made it this far. I never expected to go this long without there being a nuclear war.

When I was in high school, my mother used to tell me that I was born middle-aged. I took high school very seriously, and it was very important that I got good grades. It was really my senior year before anything significant happened to me socially. I was elected editor of the yearbook, which was a real, real thrill to me. But it did lead to my sad story. Since I was the yearbook editor, I was the chairman of the homecoming dance in my senior year. So I decorated all day—and then came back home. No one had invited me. I knew that night that my heart would break and I'd never live until morning. But, you do. I did have a boyfriend who was a year behind me, but you had to have a tux and flowers and dinner out, and he couldn't afford it.

I remember being really frightened at graduation. I'd already been accepted at college and had a scholarship, but the only thing you've really known for thirteen years is coming to an end. I knew the rules, I knew the ropes, I knew how to get from one class to another, and it was really frightening to think of starting all over.

I wanted to go to college somewhere small, where I felt like I wouldn't be lost in the shuffle. A friend of our family had gone to Hope College, in Holland, Michigan. I applied, was accepted, and decided that's where I was going before I ever visited there. I look back at some of the rules and realize how restrictive they would seem today. We could never wear pants to class. We had to attend chapel twice a week and that was grounds for expulsion. If we were going to be out of the dorm after 7:30 P.M., we had to sign out. As freshmen, we had to be in by ten o'clock on weeknights. Upperclassmen had to be in by ten-thirty. On weekends it was twelve and twelve-thirty. Of course, the rules were not at all restrictive to me. I didn't have anything to do after seven-thirty anyway.

I first became aware of the Vietnam War when Mark Lander died. He was in my high-school class. He'd come up through honors English with me and gone off to the University of Michigan. He felt compelled to quit school and join the marines—and he was killed when we were nineteen. I mean, people in my class were never going to die. War was in the history books. Then another boy I graduated with died in Vietnam. And my boyfriend's brother stepped on a land mine and was killed. And another boy from my class came home from Vietnam, but had a lot of problems mentally, and ended up setting himself on fire in his backyard and killing himself.

In Holland they had a "tradition" that as soon as a family was notified that their boy was dead in Vietnam, all the flags in Holland flew at half mast until the day of his funeral. Then, the day after the funeral, the flags would go back up. You are so isolated when you're in college, so involved with your own little world. But, when I was a junior, every day as I'd walk to class . . . it must have been about two months that the flag was never up, there were so many boys dying.

I had a cousin who was an active draft resister, and I took part in the end-the-war candlelight marches. It was more "Give peace a chance" than demonstrating against the soldiers who were in Vietnam. But it was Michael who really influenced my attitudes. The first time he went over as an engineer, he came home and was saying we were right to be there, and we were doing the right thing, and we were stopping the spread of Communism. He was sent back as a Green Beret paratrooper when I was a junior in college. I had his car while he was over there. That time when he came home, I remember how nervous he was. He couldn't sleep. He'd be up all night long, pacing the floor. If he did go to sleep, no matter how quiet you were, he'd wake up. He didn't talk about it as much anymore. Then he went back the third time as a Cobra pilot, and his attitude had swung around 180 degrees: There was no point in being there.

My goal in going to Hope was to graduate with highest honors. So for four years I was just tied to my books. I didn't see a newspaper. I could go a week at a time and not see television. I didn't make it, by the way; I only graduated with high honors. When I was a senior, I was nominated for a Woodrow Wilson. There were 24,000 nominated and then there were 1000 designates and 1000 honorable mentions. I was an honorable mention. I got an offer of a fellowship with pretty fair money to a school I'd never heard of in West Virginia. I decided I would go to Michigan State and work on my masters in English. All of a sudden I said, "That's not what I want to do." It was very flattering to be nominated. My poor adviser, I felt so badly telling him that I didn't want to go to graduate school. But he was very nice about it and got me into a student-teaching program that summer in Kalamazoo.

It was seventh- and eighth-graders who had failed English. It lasted for eight weeks and there were five student teachers in the room. So I had taught only eight mornings when I got my first job and they turned me loose with 120 seventeen- and eighteen-year-olds. The only school that called me for an interview was Athens High School, twenty miles south of Battle Creek. It was in a conservative farming community. Growing up in Battle Creek, I'd never heard of it. They offered me a contract and I accepted. There were twenty teachers on the staff and ten of us were new.

I taught English and I was yearbook adviser. My first day of teaching, Michael sent me a dozen roses, so that was really special and the kids thought that was neat. I was teaching twelfth grade, so I was only four years older than the kids. But it didn't make any difference because as soon as you cross the line from student to teacher, they never think of you as having any family or earlier life. I think they think you get rolled into your closet every night.

But I really didn't know what I was doing. I was just flying blind. The first year, all I knew to do was all the things that I had done coming up through advanced-placement English. So these kids read *Oedipus,* they read *Hamlet,* they read *The Grapes of Wrath,* and they read all the things that I read in advanced-placement English. They were very polite about it!

By this time, I had broken up with my boyfriend, Bob, after five years. He had gone to Michigan State while I was at Hope, and one of his friends told me that he was seeing another girl at Michigan State. So I called him and broke up, assuming he would know I'd found out. The same night I broke up with him, I agreed to go on a blind date. Why not? I'm a free agent. Within a month I was engaged to Bill. Bob never knew why I broke up. It turned out he hadn't been going out with anyone. His friend had lied to me. So a month later Bob saw my engagement in the paper and assumed I had broken up with him because I had been going out with this other fellow. Eventually we ran into each other and we began talking, and realized what had happened. But by then, we were both engaged. One of the world's sad love stories.

I was engaged through my first year of teaching. Bill was a super person, but it was just a rebound. We got engaged before I had a job. But then I taught for a year and I really liked it. All of a sudden I was on my own. I had an apartment, I had a car, and I had some money. He wouldn't stop pushing to get married, so I broke off the engagement. My aunts had had a shower for me, and then I didn't end up getting married, and felt terrible about that.

I met my husband, Gary, the end of my second year of teaching, and we were married in August of '72. He's a commercial truck driver. Class of '68. He didn't come on really strong and he wasn't real macho. Because he was shy, I felt I could be myself with him, because I'm really a shy person—when I'm not teaching. I taught for over seven years before I said anything at a teachers' meeting. I tell my kids that and they find it hard to believe, because, to them, I never shut up.

After I'd been teaching about two years, I was asked to interview for a teaching position at Lakeview, where I had gone to high school. I would have gotten more money. It's nice to have money, but that's not the most important thing. I liked it where I was at Athens. The school was $163,000 in debt and everybody was bailing out. I didn't want to be a quitter. I've been teaching at Athens ever since. I do teach adult education now one night a week at Lakeview.

In 1972 I wrote away to a place in California for a POW bracelet. Engraved on the bracelet was the name of Staff Sergeant David Demmon and the date 6/9/65, which was the day he disappeared. As it happened, it was also the date that I graduated from high school. I had planned to send him the bracelet when he returned, along with a letter I wrote him. But he never came back, and I still wear the bracelet every day. Just last night I had dinner with a former student who said, "I remember when the Iranian hostages were being held. You made a speech at an assembly and you talked about your prisoner of war, and how he never came home, and how you hoped that wouldn't happen with the Iranian hostages. You started to cry, and you couldn't go on." She said, "I felt sorry that it made you so sad, but I didn't understand what the big deal was about it."

I don't think the kids today are very political, but neither was I in high school. I feel there are a lot more ways that they're the same as we were than ways we're different. One difference I've seen is a dwindling respect for teachers. Not necessarily for me personally, but when I decided to be a teacher, I wasn't sure I could do it, because teachers were these beings that were set apart, and were so bright. Now the attitude is—what's the saying—those that can't, teach. I guess, when you come to look at it, why should they respect me just because I'm a teacher? I should earn their respect. But my teachers didn't have to earn my respect. Then it was, you get in trouble in school and you're in twice as much trouble when you get home. Now the parents often take the kid's side automatically before they even know what the problem is. And if a kid can't spell or can't read, it's my fault because I'm the English teacher.

There's also a growing lack of respect for property. There are no acts of violence at my high school, but there is a lot of senseless vandalism. They drive on the lawn; they shoot out the windows. The school's been broken into twice this year and the kitchen and the locker-room area were vandalized.

It was in the early '70s that the kids really scared me with drugs, and taking a lot of different kinds of pills. Now it's mostly just marijuana, and it's sort of swinging back to alcohol. Kids are so influenced by what's "in" and what's "out" in clothing and ideas and ways of defying the system. I don't think they ever think about their safety in terms of drinking and driving or mixing alcohol and pills, because it's never going to be them.

There have been some good changes, too. When it comes to dating, the girls are a little more bold about calling fellows and initiating the action. We had to be sneakier about it. You'd have to have your girlfriend tell his boyfriend and all that, instead of just picking up the phone and saying, "I'm not doing anything Saturday. Would you like to take me out?"

When I was in high school, there were no girls' sports teams. My girls can participate in basketball, in volleyball, in track. At the bigger schools, they can swim and become involved in softball and cross-country. I love it. I have a daughter, Alyson, who was born in 1975. My daughter the jock. She's a gymnast and she's going away to gymnastics camp this summer, by herself. She also plays floor hockey, which is like hockey in a gym. And this year she was the mascot for my varsity cheerleaders over at Athens.

Right now I teach "Practical English," where they learn survival skills: how to fill out a job application, how to write complaint letters or request letters. We have a listening unit where I try to talk about euphemisms and misleading statements in advertising and politics. We also read *Animal Farm,* because it's a fable with political implications, and they read *Johnny Got His Gun,* because I'm an old diehard antiwar demonstrator.

In my honors English class they still have to read Shakespeare, as well as *The Grapes of Wrath, To Kill a Mockingbird, Lord of the Flies,*

Death of a Salesman, Catcher in the Rye. When I first started teaching *Catcher in the Rye,* I used to have to send permission slips home for the parents to sign. I don't have to do that anymore. I also teach two ten-week classes each semester, what we call "quarter classes." That's a holdover from the '70s. In the '70s you could take virtually anything as an English class. You could take "The Bible as Literature." You could take "African Folktales," "Sports Literature," "Acting." Now it's the back-to-the-basics movement.

We've lost a lot of things from our curriculum. World history used to be a requirement, and it's not anymore. A lot of the quarter classes have been dropped, like Michigan history and Russian history. A lot of advanced classes like chemistry and physics are now taught every other year instead of every year. But at least now the school district is able to keep its head above water financially.

There is one incident that happened a few years ago that affected me deeply. I had stopped going to church when I was in college. I thought, If you're God, why do you let all these terrible things happen? Why are my classmates dying in Vietnam? I wanted nothing to do with church. Then, in 1980, two of my students died, two of my girls. It was an auto accident just before the start of their senior year. They weren't drinking; they weren't on drugs; they weren't driving too fast. They just lost control on a gravel road. I really couldn't come to terms with that. One was supposed to have been a cheerleader and the other was a state-champion runner in two different events. When the school year started, there were a lot of days when I just left school crying, because they should have been there.

A couple of months later, I agreed to go to this Presbyterian church with my mom, right across from Lakeview High School. I remember feeling so angry and so bitter and saying, "Okay, God, if you've got anything to say to me, I'm here." And it was like He was speaking just to me. The gist of the minister's sermon was, If something good happens, why is it our doing, but if something bad happens, it's God's fault? Cancer, pestilence, an automobile accident—we pin that on God. But a promotion or the birth of a child or anything positive— that's us, that's *our* accomplishment. That's what started the whole healing process for me. Now I attend church regularly, sing in the choir, and have become a deacon. Instead of believing God is up in the sky manipulating all of us, I believe it's each person's responsibility to know which of your friends needs a helping hand, and that God is working through you to bring comfort. It all comes down to this interrelated network of individuals helping one another and caring about one another.

A lot of people are really afraid of high-school kids; and the older they get, the more afraid they are. But I like the upperclassmen because they're poised right at the edge of the rest of their life, with all these decisions to make. The first year I taught, there was a teacher who seemed jealous of all the new teachers, who were all young and enthusiastic. Some of the kids would come to me with their problems. One day this teacher said to me, "They come to you now while you're young, but you just wait until you get older." Sometimes I sort of get scared that they *will* stop coming, but it's been sixteen years and they haven't yet.

While Jody and I were together, she told me that her cousin Michael had just retired from the army and taken a civilian job in Florida. I took down his new phone number, and when I returned home I placed a call to Mike in West Palm Beach. He was now a regional director for PRIDE (Prison Rehabilitative Industries and Diversified Enterprises, Inc.), the private corporation to which the state of Florida had turned over the running of its prison industries.

"Basically, I'm doing the same thing I was doing at Fort Leavenworth," he said. "Although I am enjoying myself, I must admit that I deeply miss the military. I guess I will always be a soldier."

MISSING IN ACTION:
Manuel Lauterio

At 2:10 P.M. on January 8, 1973, a UH-1H-type U.S. military helicopter took off in the area of Quang Tri in South Vietnam on what would later be described by the Department of the Army as a "routine flight" to "pick-up and discharge personnel at designated landing zones." On board were six U.S. soldiers, including three members of the class of '65: Elbert Bush, of Jackson, Mississippi; William Stinson, of Georgiana, Alabama; and Manuel Lauterio, of Los Angeles, California.

A few minutes later, the helicopter crew made its first pickup. They took off, headed for their second rendezvous—and were never heard from again.

At 3:45 P.M. a Vietnamese marine unit reported that a helicopter meeting the description of the missing aircraft had crossed the Thach Han River into North Vietnam and been struck by an enemy missile. However, a search of the area turned up no evidence of the helicopter or its crew.

Less than three weeks later, a cease-fire agreement was signed between the U.S. and North Vietnam. Several days after that, the North Vietnamese began releasing American prisoners of war. The last prisoners were returned on April 1, two days after the last U.S. combat troops left Vietnam. The six members of the missing helicopter crew were not among those POWs.

The official list of Vietnam War MIAs includes more than 2400 names. In actuality, about half of those are not really missing. They are referred to as "DBNR": Deceased, Body Not Recovered. These men were definitely seen to have died, but their remains were unrecoverable. Included in this category, for example, would be someone who was shot to death, fell into a stream, and was washed away, or soldiers whose bodies were spotted from the air but could not be reached because of intense enemy gunfire.

The remaining 1200 MIAs are truly missing. It is into this category that the six crew members of the UH-1H helicopter fall. To this day, their ultimate fate is unknown.

Manuel Lauterio left behind a wife, two sons, his mother, and seven brothers and sisters, most of whom live in the Hanford-Lemoore farming area of central California's San Joaquin Valley. The drive north from Los Angeles to Hanford is unremittingly dull, so I had plenty of time to be alone with my thoughts.

The previous day, the president of the United States, Ronald Reagan, had concluded a press conference by telling the nation that nuclear weapons were a deterrent that had "kept us at peace for the longest stretch we've ever known, forty years of peace." It was as if the Korean War and the Vietnam War had never happened. I wondered if the families of the 110,000 Americans who were killed during those two wars agreed with the president about the peacefulness of those years.

I also thought about the role of minorities in the U.S. military. Overrepresented on the front lines and on lists of casualties, they have received little recognition for their efforts. I had read *Bloods,* Wallace Terry's oral history of black soldiers in the Vietnam War, but Hispanic involvement has gone almost unrecorded.

It was hot and dry when I arrived in Hanford, but the home of Amparo Escalera, Manuel Lauterio's mother, was cool and comfortable. While we talked, Mrs. Escalera sifted through a box of family memorabilia, eventually turning up several letters from the army about her eldest son's disappearance. Afterwards, I drove on to nearby Lemoore and the apartment of Manuel's wife, Erminia, and their two teenage sons, Robert and Michael, who grew up with the nicknames Beanie and Titi. We spent some time talking, and then were joined by Mrs. Escalera and four of her other children.

Manuel Lauterio was born May 10, 1947, in Pomona, California. His father was a heavy drinker who used up whatever money came his way, making it very difficult for Amparo to raise her three children. Finally, she moved out, brought the children to Los Angeles, and, after much persistence, qualified to collect welfare. With a home of their own for the first time, the family was able to settle down. The children enrolled in a Catholic school, and Manuel and his younger brother spent a lot of time at the YMCA.

Amparo attempted to reconcile with her husband, but he continued to drink. "Every time we got together," she said, "it was worse and worse. It got to the point that the kids wanted to hit him. So I said, forget it, and completely left him alone." In 1962, she remarried.

Manuel enrolled at Benjamin Franklin High School, where he distinguished himself as a runner, finishing second in the Northern League Cross-Country Championships. However, he mostly kept to himself and showed little interest in his academic studies. His grades deteriorated with each semester, and in October 1964 he dropped out.

In the meantime, Manuel had fallen in love. At the age of fourteen, he met Erminia Escalera, the younger sister of his mother's second husband. He proposed to her the first night that they met. He told her he liked her legs. At twenty-nine, Erminia was twice Manuel's age, and only three years younger than his mother.

"I was shocked," she told me. "I told him he was crazy. I said, 'I'm grown and you're just a kid.' He said, 'When I get old enough, I'm going to marry you.'

"When he left school, he said he was going into the navy. I said, 'Fine. You do that. And when you get out, if you still feel the same way, we'll talk about it then.'

"He said, 'No, you're trying to put me off. You're trying to get rid of me.' He wouldn't take no for an answer."

Manuel's mother was dubious about such an unusual coupling, but felt that it would keep her son off the streets and out of trouble. So she gave her consent.

Manuel and Erminia were married June 16, 1965. Five days later, he joined the navy. Their first son, Robert, was born in February of 1967, and their second son, Michael, was born a year and a half later. During his four years in the navy, Manuel was never assigned overseas.

Manuel finished his service in June of 1968 and began driving a cab in Los Angeles. Erminia discouraged him from continuing at the job, because there had been a rash of fatal attacks on cabdrivers at the time. He took a position with AT&T, but was dissatisfied. His brother Alfred had already been to Vietnam and had told him that women could be rented there for a nickel. Manuel believed him. In February,

1969, he enlisted in the army. By April of 1970, he was in Vietnam, working as a helicopter mechanic. He found his tasks boring, and yearned to join those men who actually went up in the helicopters, flying missions to Cambodia and elsewhere.

When he first arrived in Vietnam, Manuel communicated regularly with his family. But then the letters and tapes ended. For months there was no word from him.

In November of 1971, four-year-old Robert Lauterio, who had an exceptionally high IQ, was playing outside when he saw someone walking down the street.

"I recognized it was my father. I went inside and told my mom, 'Daddy's coming!' " Erminia assumed her son was just imagining, just wishing his daddy was there.

"I opened the door," Robert recalled, "and there he was." The reunion, naturally, was a happy one. "I was in pre-school and the kids used to tease me. Because my father wasn't around, they used to say, 'You don't have a father.' I told them I did, but they still made fun of me. When he came back, I took him to school to prove it. I was so proud."

Manuel returned with a shocking story of being shot down behind enemy lines and spending almost six months slowly making his way back through the jungle until, exhausted and emaciated, he had reached a friendly camp. After a month at home, Manuel moved on to Texas and was back in Vietnam on April 12, 1972, assigned as a rear-door gunner on a helicopter. Nine months later, representatives of the Department of the Army appeared at the doors of the homes of Manuel's wife and mother with the news that he was missing. When his wife had asked Manuel why he wanted to go back, he had said, "I don't want some Russian, someday, to be telling us what we should do. I want my sons to know that I wanted to defend my country and that I wanted it to be free."

Before I left the Lauterios and the Escaleras, they gave me ten small reel-to-reel tapes that Manuel had sent to them during his first tour in Vietnam. The tapes were their last remaining link with Manuel. I promised to have them converted to cassettes, so that Robert and Michael could hear the sound of their father's voice. Seven of the ten tapes had deteriorated to such an extent that they were inaudible. But the other three tapes conveyed a poignant and painful verbal correspondence, in English and Spanish, between a soldier in a war zone and his wife and small children at home.

Manuel talks about everyday life at Bien Tong Air Base in the Mekong Delta, and he describes the native homes as being "sort of like the houses in Tijuana." He also speaks with some distress about the way that his fellow soldiers treat the South Vietnamese. "The GIs, in general, come here and say, 'To hell with the Vietnamese.' Just because they live like lower-class people, a lot of the Americans take advantage of them, make fun of them, and call them names."

"I'm counting the days just like you are," Manuel adds. "I think about you all the time. I sure do miss my babies."

Erminia and Robert respond with tears. "Papa," says the little boy, "when are you going to come back?"

The story of Manuel Lauterio has no ending, happy or sad. There are several theories to explain what happened to the twelve hundred missing Americans in Southeast Asia. Perhaps they died, their remains never found or else hoarded by the Vietnamese, to be used as gruesome bargaining chips in future negotiations with the U.S. government. Manuel's mother resists this explanation, convinced that her son is still alive.

There is also the theory, so popular in Hollywood, that some of the missing in action are actually being held prisoner in Vietnam. Personally, I find this possibility highly unlikely. I can't imagine why the Vietnamese would release most of the POWs but keep some of them. The Vietnamese government has a nation full of forced laborers. I can't see why they would need a few hundred more. If I am wrong, then the future for these men would appear to be bleak. Suddenly to release these prisoners after so many years of denying their existence would cause the Vietnamese tremendous embarrassment. However, is also possible that some U.S. soldiers may have voluntarily stayed behind in Southeast Asia. For example, Manuel, a loner, trained in the art of jungle survival, could have hidden in the woods, rejected his past, and ended up living with the Vietnamese, the Laotians, or the Thais.

I, for one, do not find it unreasonable to retain the hope that Manuel Lauterio, or any of the other MIAs, is still alive, somehow, somewhere.

MOST DEPENDABLE:

Michael Courtney[*]

THE PROPHETESS:

Melanie Courtney[*]

"Sex, drugs, and rock-and-roll" was a popular catchphrase to describe the recreational interests of the baby-boom generation. It is still an accurate summary for a large portion of the generation.

The mass media particularly liked the "sexual revolution." They played it up and gave it plenty of space: miniskirts and see-through blouses, free love and promiscuity. After a few years, the press reported the death of the sexual revolution. They declared it with glee, as if they hadn't built it up themselves in the first place. Some people even wondered if the sexual revolution had actually been a myth created by the media.

There was a real sexual revolution, but it wasn't the one that was covered by the media, the one with miniskirts and promiscuity. The real sexual revolution took place on the interpersonal level and was characterized by such things as a growth of tolerance for sexual diversity, a growing awareness that sexual partners can openly discuss their lovemaking, and an acknowledgment that lovemaking is meant to provide pleasure and satisfaction for both parties. This sexual revolution has had such a powerful

---

* These are pseudonyms made necessary, unfortunately, by the laws of the state of Virginia.

171

*and ongoing effect on American society that members of younger genera-
tions are often unaware that things were ever different.*

*I remember sitting in on a discussion between a woman from the
class of '65 and her sister, who had graduated high school exactly ten
years later, in the class of 1975. The younger sister had taken for granted
such things as calling a boy for a date, having sex before marriage, and
enjoying "at least as many orgasms as the guy gets." The older sister was
frustrated at being unable to make her younger sister understand that she
herself had had to become aware that such possibilities even existed, and
then had to struggle to have them recognized as legitimate personal rights.
The discussion reminded me of the complaints of our parents' generation
that they struggled to create a more prosperous world for their children,
and then their children just took it for granted. Now it is our generation's
turn to complain that we struggled for individual rights and sexual equal-
ity, and younger generations take that for granted.*

*When the class of '65 learned about sex, it was usually through
rumor and innuendo. We were taught the romantic myth that we should
engage in sex without being told anything in advance, and sexual partners
should know how to please each other properly the first time without any
verbal feedback.*

*Men would try to rack up conquests while women defended their vir-
tue and worried about their reputations, often saving intercourse as a re-
ward to be bestowed after marriage. Men tried to "screw" women or
"fuck" them. In any other context, to "screw" someone means to cheat or
take advantage of him or her. Likewise, the other uses of the word "fuck"
are equally hostile or negative: "fuck you," "fuck off," "fucked up."*

*Clearly we were raised, consciously or not, to view the sexual world
as a sort of battleground, with men penetrating women's defenses and
"scoring."*

*The changes that came with the real sexual revolution came slowly
and subtly, although, in retrospect, they actually happened rather quickly.
Maybe it wasn't necessary to marry the first person with whom you had
sexual intercourse. Maybe there was no need to feel guilty if you preferred
homosexuality to heterosexuality. Maybe you could "make love" to a
woman instead of "screwing" her. Maybe it was all right to say, "Dear,
could we try it this way?"*

*The real sexual revolution has included the acknowledgment that sex
need not be motivated only by lust or even by love but that it can also be
humorous, friendly—even therapeutic.*

MELANIE: When I was growing up, my father ran knitting machines at a hosiery mill in North Carolina. When I was twelve, he switched to real-estate appraisal. My parents were very affectionate to each other and to me. I was an only child and I knew a lot of love.

I remember one incident when I was two or three. I woke up during a thunderstorm, frightened. My father held me close to him and we looked out the window together. The rain was pouring down and turning the red clay dirt into mud. He told me that the rain and thunder were God's way of making the watermelons grow. I loved watermelons.

My parents made me comfortable with myself. One of the problems I have encountered with a lot of women in middle age is that they don't know how to accept love when it's there. A lot of women who are unhappy in marriages have a lot of distrust with men, or a lot of built-up angry feelings that come from their relationships with their fathers. I think the fact that I did have a very good, hugging relationship with my father, who treated me as a friend, has made me comfortable with myself and with my sexuality. Therefore, I can accept love, and I can give love, because I know how it feels to give and receive it.

MICHAEL: I'm also an only child. My parents tended to overprotect me. For example, I wasn't allowed to get my driver's license until I was eighteen. My parents were very religious—Southern Baptist. My mother in particular was very devout. One of the main things I acquired from the Southern Baptist religion was guilt. It was many, many years before I was able to overcome that guilt.

I went to grade school at a small, rural elementary school. My mother worked in a hosiery factory and my father was an upholsterer. About the seventh or eighth grade, he bought a small meat-packing company from an old fishing buddy. The primary product was liver pudding. After about ten years he went back to the upholstery business.

When we went on to high school, we country kids were generally accepted. I was a good student and also enjoyed sports. I was on the track team. My senior year I was vice-president of our class, and I was chosen "Most Dependable" in the class poll.

Some of our friends had decided that Melanie and I would be the perfect couple and were trying to push us together.

MELANIE: I was a very average, normal kid, with the in group, I guess. I was forbidden by my father to date until I was sixteen, and that was pretty much okay with me. A lot of my girlfriends played basketball, so I became the basketball manager. I was also a member of the French Club, the Beta Club, and the Methodist Youth Group, and I was vice-president of the Future Homemakers of America.

Senior year I was chosen to be the class prophetess, to predict what people in the class would be like in the future. There were about 115 students in the class and I didn't know everyone that well. So I asked the English teacher to have everyone write an essay on what they expected to be like in fifty years. Then I used those writings to make up my one-liners about them.

What I remember most is what my husband wrote. This was before I really knew him. I don't remember what he said about his career, but he added that he hoped to still be in love with his wife after fifty years. That, to me, sounded wonderful. It intrigued me enough to want to meet him.

We did meet at a basketball game in February of 1965. It was a tournament game at the end of the season. I was sitting at the end of a row of my friends and he was sitting at the end of a row of his friends, and that's the point where the two groups met.

MICHAEL: I needed a date for the senior prom. I thought that she would accept, so I asked her. First I needed to have a couple of dates before I asked her to go to the prom.

MELANIE: The first date we went to see *Mary Poppins;* the second date we went bowling; the third date was the prom.

MICHAEL: We did the prom and all the graduation activities together. We were dating pretty regularly at the end of the semester and through that summer.

MELANIE: After we graduated, I went to the International Institute of Interior Design in Washington, D.C. My goal was to become a show-room designer and go back to the furniture showrooms in High Point, North Carolina. I had a natural interest in design and rooms and interiors. I used to sit in church and redesign it—think about how it could be used for apartments or businesses. I frequently rearranged the furniture at home.

MICHAEL: I stayed at home and became a math major at High Point College, which was about a twenty- or twenty-five-minute drive from my house. We wrote regularly.

MELANIE: After seven months I decided that I couldn't handle the art-work. I couldn't get my ideas on paper well enough. So I left, and went back to North Carolina. I bought the line that everybody was feeding me: that I was going to get married and be taken care of, so I did not need my own career. That was a big mistake, and I've been regretting it ever since.

I went to the University of North Carolina at Greensboro, which used to be a women's college, and took a one-year secretarial course. Before I even graduated, my hometown doctor was looking for a receptionist, so I became a medical secretary and girl friday.

My father was traveling as a real-estate appraiser and my mother wanted to travel with him. They said we could have their house. So we got married on January 1, 1968.

Michael and I were both virgins when we were married—techni-cally. We did do a lot of heavy petting, which had helped me discover things about myself. I had had no idea that there was this well of en-ergy within me. I was delighted to find out about all that within myself. On our wedding night we had intercourse, and that was very disap-pointing. I enjoyed the heavy petting a lot more. After a couple years, we discussed that. Fortunately, I have a good husband who is con-cerned about my pleasure.

Michael's mother and father were very strict. No dancing, no smoking, no alcohol, no card-playing. Everything was a sin. I'm sure he married me because I was a way out. I was a fun-loving person. I didn't think any of those things were wrong or bad. I gave him the freedom to explore things that his family and his church considered sins. I opened windows and doors for him—and he just went way beyond me!

MICHAEL: Vietnam wasn't anything that was real to me until I was a se-nior in high school and I had to sign up for the draft. I generally sup-ported the government's position. I was deferred as long as I went to college. I thought we'd wipe them out before I graduated, and I wouldn't have to worry about it. But that didn't happen. I knew that as soon as I was out of college, I was going to be drafted. I didn't want to be with a ground crew and carry a rifle and get shot at. So I joined the air force—my form of the draft dodge.

I took a test and applied for officer-training school and was accepted in the computer field. I was very happy with that. I was commissioned in February 1970, and assigned to Keesler Air Force Base in Biloxi, Mississippi. I taught computer courses there for two years.

MELANIE: Our daughter was born April 12, right after we arrived in Biloxi. It was the thing to do to have a baby. Having been an only child, and not really having been around small children, I didn't know what to expect or how to handle a small child. So I spent the nine months of pregnancy worrying. I needed that nine months to prepare myself psychologically for having a child. I read all kinds of books.

When I went into labor, I was very surprised. It was easy. I have a collapsible cervix: When a baby gets a certain weight, I abort. She was about six weeks early. She just popped out—no problems. She was beautifully formed. After I had given birth, the overwhelming feeling was that I could take care of her. She was mine, and whatever she needed, I could give her. I'm glad I went through all the worry beforehand.

MICHAEL: Our daughter's birth had a much more intense impact on me than I had anticipated. I grew up believing that people got married and became parents, and that's what you did. But having a baby in the family suddenly changed our life-style. We'd always been free to get up and go on the spur of the moment. All of a sudden we couldn't do this. I felt very confined.

MELANIE: In 1971 my father had a sudden heart attack and died. I had a lot of problems in dealing with his death. My father adored me. He was my support. I felt I was being what he wanted me to be. It took me six years to deal with that grief, because I didn't deal with it. Whenever we had to go back to North Carolina, I would see my father in the backyard with his lawnmower. I could just envision him there. It was very difficult to face.

MICHAEL: In April of 1972, I was sent to Lowry Air Force Base in Denver. I worked there as an instructor, teaching computer courses. Then I transferred into the Air Defense Command, which also had a facility on the base. I was still in the computer field. We had thought that we needed a brother or a sister for our daughter, so Melanie became pregnant again.

MELANIE: I had a premonition that the baby was not going to be born. I would see the physician and he would do his regular checkup and say, "Everything's fine; you're going to deliver in September." Something in the back of my head said, "No, that's not the way it is." I didn't even get our daughter out of the baby bed and I didn't really prepare her for having another person come into her life.

I went into labor in July. I was very frightened that we were going to take the baby home and get attached to it, and then it would die. They gave it three full transfusions. I rationalized that it was much better to lose it before I really knew the child as an individual. She only lived twenty-eight hours. The doctors and nurses were much more concerned about it than I was, because they had been working hard and getting to know this person, whereas I had not really known the child. It wasn't as hard as dealing with the death of my father.

The doctors said that if I wanted to get pregnant, I should go ahead right away, and they would put me in a hospital for six months to keep me from spontaneously aborting. I didn't want to leave a healthy, active two-year-old for six months, so we decided that we were happy with the three-member family. Neither of us knew how to deal with sibling rivalry anyway.

I did find coping with motherhood was difficult. I felt isolated and unable to deal with all the negativism. There was a lot of "No, no, no," with an active two-year-old, constantly trying to create new ideas to keep her away from this, that, or the other in a positive way. I wasn't able to be the ideal mother I thought I could be. I felt like I was a failure. So I returned to work as a medical secretary for a psychiatrist. We used that money to buy a house and to travel to Europe and Mexico.

MICHAEL: I began going through a lot of changes in Denver—experiencing a dissatisfaction with the way my life was going, and considering a lot of my beliefs. One of the things that had a profound effect on my life was Watergate. I had held conservative beliefs up until that time. I had supported Goldwater in 1964, George Wallace in 1968, and Richard Nixon in 1972.

I used to have political discussions during lunch break with one of the guys that I worked with. He was certainly more liberal than I was. I was still defending Nixon at the beginning of all that. Every day something else would break. At some point, I just said, "Why am I defending this guy?" I really felt that my personal trust had been betrayed by Nixon, by all of his lying and cheating. Up until that time, I accepted things that I was told. If my parents said it, it must be right. If the preacher said it, it must be right. If the government said it, it must be right. I started questioning my entire belief system. I hope that is a process that is still growing.

After Denver, I applied for a grad-school assignment, and the air force sent me to the University of North Carolina to study computer science for a year, for which I incurred another three-year commitment. In Chapel Hill, communication began opening up between Melanie and me. I had become withdrawn and she pushed me to talk about the things I was feeling. I began talking about my curiosity about other women, and we began discussing the possibilities of an open marriage.

MELANIE: Having only made love with me, Michael was curious about what it would be like to make love with another woman. He did not want to do anything behind my back. He wanted my full participation and cooperation. He said, "We have to do it together, or not at all." This went on for at least a year. It was a very difficult, trying time of our marriage. It was very painful for both of us. I decided that if I said, "No, I don't want to do that," Michael would accept that decision— and we would be in a duty-bound marriage. I would never know for sure what he was brooding on. He would go along with me, but I would be the loser. I would miss out on his dreams and fantasies. So I said, "Okay, we'll try it." It was not until we came to the D.C. area that we actually did anything.

MICHAEL: I was assigned to a computer job in the Pentagon.

MELANIE: We moved to the northern Virginia area and immediately I started working again as a medical secretary for an ear, nose, and throat specialist. We both got involved with the NOW organization. Michael, I often say, is more of a women's libber than I am.

MICHAEL: Before we moved to northern Virginia, our social life had pretty much revolved around my friends in the military. When we moved to the D.C. area, that wasn't the case. It's a much larger, spread-out community. We tried merging into the larger suburban community and found it very difficult. People in the area tend to be pretty mobile and career-oriented. We found that we weren't finding very many friends that we could interact with socially on a regular basis.

I found an ad in the newspaper for a swing club and I talked Melanie into going. She resisted at first. I think the fact that it was potentially another avenue for social interaction is what finally made her decide to give it a try.

This club met in a hotel. They would rent a ballroom, a suite of rooms, and a couple of singles. They'd have a band and a bartender and people would bring their own alcoholic beverages. People would sit around the ballroom and talk or dance. It was quite a varied age group, from mid-twenties to fifties. We went maybe a half a dozen times. They also had a paper in which you could basically advertise yourself.

It turned out to be a good experience for both of us. I found it was ego-enhancing to have other women tell me I was a good lover.

MELANIE: I was frightened at first. I had to go through a process where I was willing to lose Michael. That was very frightening. But in the end, I felt that we were in a much better place having gone through it. I got a lot of positive feedback that I was an attractive woman and a good lover. It was a pleasing experience for me, and a very positive experience for our relationship. We could come back together, and discuss our feelings. We had the freedom not to be together, but we chose to be together. It somehow solidified our relationship. And we did make friends that we still see socially, even though we may not have sex with them.

One thing I tried briefly was homosexual experiences. I can't say that it is something that I seek, but I'm a great advocate of everyone trying bisexuality. It was such an eye-opener for me. Until then, I felt that if a man gave me cunnilingus, I should reciprocate and give fellatio. That was an unwritten rule. Then I discovered how much simpler it is to give cunnilingus than to have this large, throbbing organ in your mouth. Everybody should experience both. Then they would understand the other person's feelings. I think it would enhance their lovemaking.

MICHAEL: In February of '79, I decided that I was no longer philosophically in tune with the military, so I got out. I went to work with a consulting firm in support of a project at the U.S. Geological Survey, still computer-related.

By this time, Melanie and I had formed a relationship with another couple. We all liked each other a lot and found we were compatible, so we decided that we were going to merge our families and move in together. Including their two children, there were seven of us. It took us ten months to find a house, until November of '79.

MELANIE: We liked the idea of sharing expenses, sharing housing, child care, stimulation.

MICHAEL: Some people refer to it as a "group marriage" because we were sexually involved. We called it a "selected extended family."

MELANIE: But there were problems with this other couple.

MICHAEL: They fought and argued loudly. Melanie and I had never communicated with each other in that fashion. It was very difficult for us to be a part of that, so we moved out in 1981.

MELANIE: It was very painful, very much like a divorce.

MICHAEL: The job that I was working on ran out of funds, and I went on to a contract in support of the Defense Department. It was going to be temporary, but I had all the right experience, fortunately, or unfortunately—I'm not sure which. I'm still there, working as a computer analyst. Philosophically, I'm torn as to what I'm doing there and why I'm doing it, because over the years I have become more and more antiwar, antiviolence. I am a pacifist in the Pentagon.

I had a desire to be more independent, to have a place to get away from the city. We also had it in our minds for quite a while to have a cooperative community, a community of people who are at least philosophically accepting and supportive of each other. A community where people can pitch in and do things together.

MELANIE: We put a group of people together, which we called Expanding Alternatives, and we began looking for the land to build this community. We did find the land, but when we asked people for money commitments for the down payment, everybody started backing off. We were down to just us and the man of the couple we had lived with.

In the summer of '83, we bought 211 acres in northern Virginia, about two hours from D.C. It's a working farm: forty acres in peach and apple orchards, and sixty-five or so in pasture for sheep and cattle. The rest is woods. We have chickens and our daughter has a horse. We call the farm "Sojourners." The name derives from the idea that this land was here before us, and it will be here after we are gone. We are sojourners on the land. We see the farm as a stopping point along life's way, not something that someone possesses.

MICHAEL: Right now there are six adults and three teenagers living on the farm. I worked it out with my supervisor at the consulting firm that I could work twelve hours a day, three days a week. The computers are actually more available at other than regular duty hours. So we're able to spend four days a week on the farm, although our daughter lives there full-time.

MELANIE: A couple years ago, two therapists we knew, a husband-and-wife team, were looking for a sex surrogate, a practice partner, especially someone who could work with hearing-impaired men. Someone suggested me.

I have a long history of hearing loss on both sides of my family, and I wear a hearing aid. My hearing loss was gradual. I was spending a lot of body energy listening, and I'd get very tired. I was misinterpreting what people were saying. As I repeated what I thought they said, they would look at me in a real strange way. You start feeling like you're stupid.

When I was working for the ear, nose, and throat specialist, he encouraged me to get the work done and get the hearing aid. Being able to adjust to wearing a hearing aid at an early age is better than waiting until your hearing is really bad. One of the nice things about wearing a hearing aid is that I can turn it down and it will protect my ear. If I go into a noisy restaurant or a disco, I just turn it down and I can hear as well as anybody else. They can't hear at all, but I'm used to reading their lips and their looks and their body language. In the kitchen, I turn it off completely. My hearing loss is more annoying to my family than to me because they have to be in a room with me or I do not understand what they are saying.

So I began working with the therapist couple and they assigned me books to read about sex therapy and being a surrogate and supervised my training sessions. Now I work with several verbal therapists. I've had quite a number of clients since then, half of them hearing-impaired. Generally I have at least six sessions with a client, but the exact number varies with each person. We meet with the therapists, who give us an assignment. The client and I go together and do the assignment for one to three hours, and then come back immediately to discuss it in detail with the therapists for another hour.

The first session is a social meeting. We go somewhere and have a cup of coffee and just talk and get to know each other. A great deal of the surrogate work is teaching the client how to socialize with a woman. Most people who seek surrogate help don't have a partner, maybe because they're not that desirable. They're not the cream of the crop. For the hearing-impaired, their socialization skills just haven't been developed. Their fears of women are much stronger and much greater. I see many hearing-impaired people who have always been treated as if they were children. Some of them have had only homosexual experiences, which were initiated by other males. They want to be heterosexual, but they don't know how. They have a lot of fears about the physical aspects of a female and about their own sensuality.

The client is usually a person who is very frightened of women, has had little or no contacts with women, and doesn't know how to initiate or interact. I try to make them comfortable with just going out and meeting in a public place and talking.

Then we progress as a relationship naturally does—toward more intimacy—to hand-holding, to kissing hello and kissing good-bye in public. Then, when we're alone, we get comfortable with nudity. Either the client can undress, we can undress each other, or we can just be undressed, depending on their preference. It's a very gradual, step-by-step process.

Some of the exercises we do, like body-sculpturing, can be done clothed or unclothed. We stand face to face and feel the other person. We start at the top of the head with our hands and touch lightly. Generally I will start. I will sculpture the other person all over, then have them do it to me, and then we do it together with them following what I do.

Most of the sessions deal with sensate focus. We focus on sensations and feelings, and get back into our natural bodies, letting original and natural feelings come out, as if you were a child, instead of listening to all those tapes you have in your head about what you should or should not be doing or what you should or should not be feeling. I help the clients get into the natural flow of feelings and what it feels like to be touched, identifying for themselves where they like to be touched and where they don't want to be touched. Then we discuss those feelings with the therapists. Sometimes we progress to actual intercourse, but not always.

We live in a society where the males are supposed to know how to do it. And some women are very passive in the lovemaking role. They expect men to be aggressive, to know what to do and how to do it. It's very frightening for men to put themselves into that situation until they feel confident. Basically, that's what I do: give them the confidence that they can do it.

I see myself as a professional, carrying out the assignment each session. That doesn't mean I'm not caring and concerned as a friend, but it is not a romantic involvement. At the end of each session, I'm given a check by the client and make another appointment, which helps keep it very businesslike.

I'm frequently asked if I'm not just a high-priced prostitute. I do very little actual genital work. I am teaching the man how to go out into the world and interact with a woman of his choice, which is not necessarily what he's going to get from a prostitute. He'll only get whatever he asks for, a blow job or whatever. But not any how-tos or how to make love to a woman or how it feels to be a man. I would say that all of my clients come away with a better education, more knowledge, and more confidence in themselves than the average American who learns how to deal with girls in the backseat of a car.

I do find it very exhausting work because I am focusing on people and their problems. It's very draining. Most of the surrogates that I know are single people. I think it helps that I am married and I have someone who can give me support and help me relax after I've been with someone.

I didn't just go out and decide I was going to be a sex surrogate. But I feel that now that I'm doing this, I have found my niche in life. These are people who have a need, and I can fulfill it. They don't have knowledge or skills, and I find it very comfortable working with them, talking to them, and educating them. I find it enjoyable and it's great to be paid for work I enjoy doing.

I started going back to school in 1978, at George Mason University in Fairfax. I have one more semester to go and I will get my bachelor's degree in psychology. Then I want to do graduate work in clinical psychology. I want to be a sex therapist. One of the purposes for our farm is to have workshops and deal with sexuality, communication, parenting, family and marriage counseling. I would like to be able to do weekend and week-long seminars for couples who are having problems. I would like to do some premarital counseling, to counter what I call the Zap Theory. You're not supposed to know anything about sex until your wedding night, and *zap!* somehow you're supposed to know all about how to do it. That just isn't the way. Sex has to be learned.

I would also love to be able to do sex education, workshops, and counseling for the hearing-impaired, particularly for hearing-impaired children. This summer, I've been taking signing classes to help me communicate with my hearing-impaired clients and others.

MICHAEL: I've been trained as a surrogate as well, but I've only had one client. There seems to be less of a need for women to take on a male surrogate, or perhaps it is just not as socially permissible for women to admit that they want to enjoy sex, and that they are having trouble doing so.

I'm very optimistic about our future. I would hope that Melanie and I can have our workshop center and do our workshops frequently enough to pay our way and to be doing some good for some people in the world. I think if more people were making love, there'd be fewer people making war.

MELANIE: With all of our open discussions of sexuality at home, I wonder if we're taking away any of that luster of the unknown from our daughter. But I do think it's much healthier this way. Our daughter is just beginning to become interested in boys. Michael was saying last night that I should have another talk with her about birth control. And I was suggesting that he might do that.

Susan Pearcy, Normal Community
High School, Normal, Illinois.

Susan Pearcy, college sorority photo, 1967.

Susan (Pearcy) Mason
with Shad and Kendall,
1983.

ABOVE: John Higgins, Xenia High School, Xenia, Ohio.

BELOW, LEFT: John Higgins playing the air guitar, 1970.

BELOW, RIGHT: John Higgins, 1973.

LEFT: John Higgins, summer 1984.

LEFT: Rusty Rhodes, Santa Monica High School, Santa Monica, California.

RIGHT: Rusty Rhodes, 1985.

ABOVE: Pearl Thomas at home, 1968.

RIGHT: Pearl (Thomas) Mitchell, 1985 *(photo by Sug Mins)*.

Most Handsome
Senior Boy
Grant McElveen

ABOVE: Grant McElveen, Bogalusa High School, Bogalusa, Louisiana.

LEFT: Grant McElveen, Farm Haven Baptist Church, Farm Haven, Mississippi, 1985.

LEFT: Richard Langdon, Selma High School, Muncie, Indiana.

RIGHT: Richard Langdon, Fort Knox, 1970.

BELOW: Richard Langdon, at home in English, Indiana, 1984.

BELOW: Deborah Williams and Bill Samuelson at the Surrattsville High School junior prom, Surrattsville, Maryland, 1964.

BELOW, RIGHT: Bill and Deborah Samuelson, 1969.

ABOVE, LEFT: Mike Petty, Rushville High School, Rushville, Indiana.

ABOVE, RIGHT: Mike Petty in Vietnam.

LEFT: Lieutenant-Colonel Petty with wife, Sherry, 1984.

The Samuelson family, Leavenworth, Kansas, 1984.

LEFT: Jody Capron, Lakeview High School, Battle Creek, Michigan.

RIGHT: Jody (Capron) Owens, Athens High School, 1984.

LEFT: Manuel and Erminia Lauterio, 1965.

BELOW: Michael, Erminia, and Robert Lauterio, 1985.

Manuel Lauterio,
the last photo, 1972.

LEFT: Michael Courtney (right), Most Dependable, 1965.

RIGHT: Melanie Mason, the Prophetess, 1965.

ABOVE: Michael and Melanie Courtney, January 1, 1968.

RIGHT: The Courtneys on their farm, 1986.

LEFT: Jack Carter, Plains High School, Plains, Georgia.

BELOW: Jack Carter, 1985 *(photo by Charles M. Rafshoon)*.

MOUNTAIN PATHS

While visiting Calcutta in 1978, I was struck by the unusual manner in which the Bengali educated class viewed religion. Whenever I was introduced to someone, the first question I was asked was "What is your religion?" This was followed by "How do you perceive God?" They always showed great interest in my answers, and then explained to me their beliefs. There was never any attempt made to proselytize. The ensuing conversations were motivated instead by intellectual and spiritual curiosity and a desire to share ideas. It was much more stimulating than discussing current movies or TV shows (which we got around to eventually, anyway).

I was so impressed by these discussions that when I returned to the United States, I, too, began asking people about their religion and how they perceived God. But what works in India doesn't necessarily work in America. People viewed me with suspicion. Some seemed fearful that I was waiting for their answer so that I could pounce on it and try to convert them to some strange cult. Others reacted as if they were being quizzed, and worried that they would give the "wrong" answer. My questions seemed to make people feel uncomfortable, so I ended my little experiment prematurely.

Working on this book gave me the excuse to try again. I soon learned that many Americans don't think about spiritual matters at all. But those who do think about them exhibit those traits that are so pervasive among the class of '65: a questioning of established authority and a need to find answers that are personally satisfying. For all the publicity given the generation's involvement with strange, dogmatic cults, the intolerant religions were not nearly as popular as I had expected.

Claudine Schneider

I have a Catholic affiliation and attend mass occasionally, but not consistently. I like to read and learn about the religions of the world, so I have, perhaps, greater respect for other peoples' religions today than do many children who have gone through Catholic school and not had exposure to the other paths. At the time, we were taught that Catholics are the only right people on earth. The Crusades were something that were taught in history classes—that it was justified to kill for religion and wipe out heresy. I look back on that, and feel what a misguided lesson that was. God could never have condoned such madness.

During the '70s I learned how to meditate, and that interested me in communication with God. A lot of things came back—being a little child in Catholic school, being taught that God is within you. In school we had memorized prayers and were taught to pray. Usually when you're praying, you're either asking God for something or you're thanking Him for something. When you meditate, the communication is working the other way. You are opening yourself up to hear from God what it is He wants you to know.

I think that it is a Buddhist philosophy that says that all religions lead to the same God. All paths up the mountain lead to the top. My final conclusion is that God *is* there, the Superior Being, but our responsibility as His creations is to become more God-like and to try to improve ourselves, to be more loving and to see Him in others. By doing so, we are working to bring about Heaven on Earth.

Richard Langdon

Christians often use the text out of the Bible: "I am the Way, the Truth, and the Life. No man cometh unto the Father, but by me." I interpret it figuratively, that Christ is presenting himself as the spiritual path to the Godhead. It doesn't mean that you have to become a Christian. It just means that you have to become a spiritual person.

If someone asks me what my denomination is, I tell them I'm a Buddhist. Not only does it sometimes confuse them, but it makes for good conversation. I don't like the term "God" because it implies a dichotomy between male and female. I prefer what the American Indians call the Great Spirit, because you're speaking of an all-encompassing life-force. But what I refer to as the Great Spirit I don't think is really different than what the Methodists refer to as God. It's just that I've studied enough physics and science to know that this chair and my body and the dirt in the ground are all made out of the same stuff. We're all the same, and the life-force that holds it all together—that's the Great Spirit.

John Higgins

I hear that if you go to the Vatican in Rome and see the pope, you can get a certificate saying you've been there and seen the pope. I'd like to get one of those pope certificates. I think if you get one of those, you can present it in heaven and it's like a door pass. You don't have to wait to be checked out; you can go straight in.

Gary Liming

I'm one of those that in the back of your mind you're thinking, Maybe I ought to think there's a God just in case there is. You've got to cover all your bets. When I croak, I don't want to find out they slam the pearly gate in my face and say, "Hey, over there with the rest of the nonbelievers."

I don't know. My feeling has always been that if there is a God, he sure has neglected things. Who'd let little kids suffer, and all the other terrible things that happen on earth? I think that if there is a God, then he created it, and then just left it and went on to something else, because there are so many horrible things that happen that just shouldn't if there was somebody up there that was as kind and generous and forgiving as they claim he is.

I guess there's only one way to find out. But if I die and there's a God, I'm going to be shocked.

Mike Petty

Christmas Eve of 1966, I was in Vietnam, in a Montagnard village. I had got hold of some cognac and one of the guys had a guitar, and we were sitting around a fire singing Christmas carols. Out of nowhere came this Catholic priest. I don't know if he was Vietnamese or Montagnard, but he indicated for us to go with him. He took us to a crude building that was a church where they were having midnight mass. We could not understand their language, but I found it to be a moving experience. That two groups of people could reach out and touch, with Christ being the common denominator. Every year at Christmas, when we put up the decorations, it always brings back that memory.

Barbara Palmer

I do believe in the Lord. I just wonder if the Lord is there for me sometimes. I can't believe the Lord has to let someone suffer and struggle all their life. You've got to have a break in life sometime. Now I'm thirty-eight. When's He going to give it to me, when I'm sixty-two and can't move? I mean, if He's going to take the bad and send them to hell and keep the good, then why is He making the good on earth struggle and suffer and let the bad have it easy? God should help those that help themselves. If someone is trying, the Lord should be there to help you. People that are bums and all they want to do is collect welfare and they're too lazy to get out there and work, then I believe He should get strict with them.

Ramona Christopherson

When I was about fourteen years old, I was reading a novel and I came across the word "atheist." I asked my cousin, Karene, who was older, what it meant, and she said, "Someone who doesn't believe in God." I thought it was unimaginable that someone could not believe in God. I'd already gone through hundreds of reasons why you should believe in him—plus I had my five-year Sunday school pin—so I thought, I'm going to try to think of ten reasons why someone could not believe in God.

I laid awake in bed that night and thought of so many reasons that I talked myself out of believing in God. So, for a while, I became like a missionary against God. I thought, if I don't believe in God, I don't want my friends to be fooled either. It was a mistake. One girl became so upset it made her cry. I finally cut loose because people really don't want to hear it.

As they say, the thing about being an atheist is that you have to go around trying to prove something doesn't exist. It's a negative thing. So I became an agnostic. If you're an agnostic, either way, you'll probably be safe.

Katherine Mader

I have trouble believing in God. I consider myself very much attached to the Jewish heritage, but I don't feel comfortable going to temple. I just don't like organized religion. I don't like being told what to do.

I believe each of us, inside ourselves, has our own personal, moral conscience and that's our own God. So when I say I don't believe in God, I mean I don't believe in an *organized* God that we go to see every Friday night at the synagogue. I feel that many people use religion as a crutch to evade their own responsibility to themselves, and feel that they can just go to visit God once a week and somehow that makes them okay as people. I reject all that. I feel we walk around with our own God inside on a daily basis.

Tom Pierson

When I was growing up, we attended a Methodist church—what I refer to as moderate-to-left-wing Protestantism. I think the most valuable contribution of the story of Christ is the lesson of nonviolence.

Carol Iwata

I was brought up a Zenshuji Buddhist. Buddhism doesn't tell you what to do; it just gives you a path to follow. I believe in one God, but there are many different teachers for God. I don't think any one religion is better than another; each serves a purpose for the person who believes in it. Japanese society is one of little freedom of personal expression. However, Buddhism allows one this personal freedom of expression; it is not strict in terms of what you can or cannot do. Western society, on the other hand, allows you great personal freedom of expression; the religions that are dominant in its society seem to be very strict.

I don't think of God as having a physical form. It's someone, something, that's always there for you. I don't think he's going to make you do the right thing, but I do think he'll be there to help you make a decision.

David Hinkley

I was raised a Catholic and I remember what a real feeling of joy it gave me, as a child, to be grateful to God for everything that I saw that was beautiful in the world, and everything that I had been given. Even though I no longer practice religion, it's impossible for me not to think about it, not to wonder about it, not to feel a certain emptiness and longing in the face of my apostasy and the absence of a concrete spiritual dimension to my life. What I am, I suppose, is an agnostic. I don't believe there is no God; I just don't know how to get access to faith any longer. When my son went through an operation that might have been permanently damaging to him, but which had a good result, I was overcome with relief, but I had nobody to thank except the doctor.

Bill Samuelson

I have a belief in a Supreme Being which remains sexless and ill-defined because I don't know. It's not something that I need to define any further. It's more a confidant than someone who is at my beck and call, or my potential adversary, or someone who has to be placated. Kind of like in children's stories, you know, Harvey the Rabbit. It's a person with whom I can be myself. The expectations are low; therefore I am never disappointing to that being. It's a source of comfort. I don't have to be intelligent. I don't even have to be accurate. There are no questions asked. If I don't want to answer them, I don't have to. I can just relax.

Mike Petty

One of the hangups I had a couple of years ago . . . I remember going to my chaplain and very close friend and saying, "What if I die and Sherry remarries, and then later she and her husband die. Whose wife is she when we get to heaven?" So he put me into the Scriptures and we talked and now I don't think we're husbands and wives in heaven; I think we're all one in Christ, all one in God. And it's going to be such an exhilarating experience that we're all going to love one another.

Jack Carter

I am very much incensed by any reference to God as male. I think that is destructive to our whole society. I don't like the idea that God is the father, and I don't like the idea that the Church is the bride of Christ. All of these images really disturb me, where the male is the best one and the female drags along behind.

To me, the real Christian faith is saying that there is good news, and that good news is that God is in everybody, that you need to respect that part of God in everybody else, whether you respect the person or not.

THE SALUTATORIAN:

Jack Carter

Jack Carter and I wolfed down a big breakfast at a diner in downtown Evanston, Illinois, before returning to my hotel room to escape the zero-degree cold and warm up with some lively conversation. He told me that he did not have a high opinion of the press, and that he normally turned down interview requests. But he was intrigued by the idea of a book about our generation and was glad to share his perspective on the years gone by.

I am the seventh generation of Carters to live in Georgia. Two sets of my great-great-great-grandparents are buried within eight or nine miles of Plains. I was actually born in Portsmouth Naval Hospital, outside of Norfolk, Virginia. My father was a career military officer at the time, having graduated Annapolis the year before. My younger brothers were born in Hawaii and Connecticut. My sister was born much later in Georgia. My dad's father had some land and a small store downtown and a couple of warehouses for storing peanuts for the farmers.

When I was about six years old, my grandfather died and my dad made the big decision to give up his naval career and move down to Plains, and that's where we stayed. Right now Plains is a very warm spot for me. It's where I can take my kids. It's where I belong. That is where I can go and do anything I want to do.

When my dad took over the business, he started growing foundation seed on his land, and he started increasing the warehouse business and putting in some peanut cleaners, which take the dirt and stuff out of the shell, and a drier, which keeps them dry enough that you can store them. He had a little shelling plant where you take the hulls off, and the business just grew.

Peanuts is sort of what I did growing up. When I was young I started helping around the cleaner or the drier. I started driving tractors when I was thirteen and hauling peanut trailers around. Backing a four-wheel trailer is a real art and I got to do that fairly well. Then when I got a little bit older, I started running the drier or the cleaner by myself, or being in charge of it, anyway. During harvest season I worked several thirty-hour days.

You've got to remember how isolated Plains is. Plains is a town of six hundred people. It is ten miles out in the country, ten miles away from the county seat, which is Americus, Georgia, which had, at that time, maybe twelve thousand people in it. It was forty miles away from Albany, Georgia, which had maybe forty thousand people in it. That was a big town to us. It was about sixty miles away from Columbus, which had 100,000 or 120,000, and we were two hours and a half, 120 miles, from Atlanta. You're a *long* ways away from anywhere. In Plains, when I was growing up, your radio stations were all local radio stations, mainly country music, that shut down at sundown. The big thing in my high school years was *American Bandstand* on Saturday afternoons. The other big thing was WLS out of Chicago, which you could pick up late at night on your automobile radios on some sort of skip wave. That was where you would hear the latest kind of music.

In fact, I can remember the night that the Beatles came out. It must have been between Christmas and New Year's in 1963. I was driving back from a date in Leslie, which was about twenty miles from Plains. Nobody lived in Plains that you would want to go out with— not true, but our school was so little, in fact, that there were only eight girls in our graduating class of twenty-five. Anyway, I was driving back from this date on a Friday or Saturday night at midnight. I was listening to WLS and driving real fast in my grandmother's car, and here came "I Wanna Hold Your Hand." That's a very vivid memory for me.

Plains High School was a small, white brick building with the gym in back. All twelve grades were in the same school. The first-grade teacher, Miss Eleanor, the second-grade teacher, Miss Todd, and the fourth-grade teacher, Miss Elizabeth, also taught my mother and father. When I was younger we lived in an antebellum farmhouse out in the country and I took the school bus to school. There were always two school buses every morning—one bus that came by had a black grill, and one bus that came by had a white grill. I knew I was supposed to get on the one with the white grill. It never occurred to me that that was a sign of segregation. But at the same time my father was on the school board, talking about consolidating the systems. He was being perceived as a pretty big liberal in the area at that time because county-wide consolidation would bring integration.

I can remember in 1965 they had a congregational meeting after church service one day, and the question was, What response should the church take if some of these black agitators came up and wanted to come in and make a point of integrating our church? Dad got up and made a speech in which he said that we should accept anybody that wants to come in, in the spirit of brotherly love, Christian love. It was not a real excited sort of meeting. The church was just like the high school; everybody there had been there for years and years, and they all knew each other, and they all knew where they stood. When the church voted, there were six people who voted to let them in, basically my family and one other older woman. There were also a lot of people who did not vote, but there were obviously more than six that voted to keep them out. I don't really remember that that was tested until Dad got elected president.

I remember being in class when I heard that President Kennedy had died. I was wandering around the halls afterwards, because I was really cut by that. It must have been between classes. There was this big fat guy who was a year older than me that I always avoided. He came out into the hall and he was laughing about it: "Ha, ha, Kennedy's dead. Now we can go along with whatever we're going to be doing." The biggest regret I have in my life is that I didn't hit that guy. I was probably five foot ten and 120 pounds, a real small, skinny guy—not like the hulk that I am now—and I knew if I hit him that I was going to get really nailed. But if I had it to do over again, I would slug the guy just to make the point. That is probably the one thing that I would change in my life. If I had known that it was going to bother me this bad, even now, I would have done it as quickly as I could have.

The summer before my senior year, I was chosen to take part in the Governor's Honors Program in Macon—four hundred kids from all over the state getting together with the best teachers in the state. My main discipline was physics. I was sort of the top dog in my high school. I thought I was really something. Then I went to this place and I was just like everybody else, and couldn't compete with these guys. But I had a great time. It was just one fantastic mix of people.

I was salutatorian in my class—second-best grades—but I always beat the other guy on the achievement tests. I gave the salutatory speech at graduation. By that time I was ready to get away and go to Georgia Tech. Dad had been elected to the state senate in '62 and '64 and we all thought Atlanta was the best place to be. I majored in physics. I was sort of impressed that Dad was on a nuclear-powered boat, and math was what I was good at. But I really did not do very well at Georgia Tech. I played cards a lot and didn't go to class, and my grades went down a couple of tenths every quarter.

Toward the end of the spring quarter in '66, there was sort of a mixup in Georgia politics. One of the prime candidates for governor dropped out, and five or six people jumped in to fill the void. And Dad was one of them. So we started on a political campaign. During the summer of '66 we would all go in different directions in a car. I'd get in a car and drive through west-central Georgia, while my mother would go to north-central Georgia and my father would go down to the southwest section. We'd all take off during the week, and we'd stay with people that we knew out there—supporters.

You'd get up and you'd go into a town, into the town square. You'd have a trunkload of pamphlets, and you would go around the square and give everybody a pamphlet, and say, "Hey, I'm Jack Carter. My father, Jimmy Carter, is running for governor, and I'd like you to vote for him." And then you'd go to the next town. And if there was a radio station or a newspaper, you always dropped in and said, "I'm Jack Carter. I've been out in town handing out pamphlets, and my daddy's Jimmy Carter. . . ." We did that for six or eight weeks. That's where I met Judy, as a matter of fact. Every week in Atlanta, on Sunday, everybody in the campaign would gather and talk about what we needed to do and how it was going. It was always a real fun thing. Judy's father was one of our main supporters in northwest Georgia. He was on the game-and-fish commission. He brought his wife and Judy down to Atlanta for one of our weekly meetings.

I saw Judy one day stuffing envelopes when I came back to headquarters on a Saturday. I walked in and told her that she was doing it the wrong way—and that sparked a relationship that's lasted off and on since then.

The campaigning went on during the summer, and when we got down to the election, it was obviously going to be a runoff. The one candidate who had been in the race from the beginning was going to come in first, pretty surely. We figured if we could come in second, we'd get a runoff and could beat this guy. That was the strategy. When

I went to bed that night, we were in second place. But, during the night, Lester Maddox had a bunch of votes that came in from the sticks, and he beat us just barely. Maddox won the runoff and eventually became the governor. Dad lost, and that was really sort of a crushing experience, actually, because we obviously had the best candidate, and we had really busted our tails. Dad went back to the farm and I went back to Georgia Tech.

I think my sophomore winter quarter at Georgia Tech I cut eighty-two classes. I never really flunked out of Tech, but I decided at the end of that year that I didn't particularly want to be a physicist. So in '67 I got into Emory University for summer school. And the rest of '67 I went to Georgia Southwestern College, in Americus. I had to get a 2.5 average to get back into Emory the next quarter. By virtue of making 100 on a final exam, my average was exactly 2.5! So I went back to Emory in the winter quarter, and halfway through, Dad and I decided that college was maybe not made for me right now, so I dropped out.

I decided to join up rather than be drafted, so on April 12th, 1968, I reported into Atlanta for a physical to join the navy. My father had been in the navy, and I didn't think I'd have to go to Vietnam if I was in the navy. I came back to Plains and I had three or four days to get ready to go.

There's a little place outside of Plains called Joe's. The county was dry—but Joe's wasn't. I don't know how he did it. Apparently the state patrolmen who went by there looked the other way. Joe was a real conservative person. If you were black, you could buy beer from him, but you had to come around the back door. You did not come inside. Mr. Joe was also a skinflint. I drove over and got a beer one night, and we were sitting around the back watching the pool game going on and it came across the TV that Martin Luther King got shot. And Mr. Joe set up the house. Everybody remarked about how out of character that was. I thought awhile about taking the beer, and then decided what the hell, I'll take the beer. So the night that Martin Luther King got shot, I was out at Joe's Tavern for the first and only time . . . and I got a free beer.

I sort of agreed with what King was doing, but it was Bobby Kennedy who really hit me where everything lived. I mean, I believed in Bobby Kennedy. He was special. He believed in the things that I believed in, and he articulated them so well that whenever he said something, it was like, Yeah, yeah, that's it, that's where I am.

I went to boot camp at Great Lakes in Illinois. I did some ROTC in college, so they made me the assistant recruit chief petty officer in charge. I was a flunky for the drill instructors. The company commander of our barracks was a big black, about six foot six and about 240 pounds, and all muscular. He was an E6, the recruit petty officer in charge. He was a nothing, really, but he was raised up above the other nothings. One night he came in the middle of the night—I guess it was about three or four o'clock in the morning—and he woke everybody up and told us that Bobby Kennedy had been killed. I nearly hit him. "Don't fuck around with me that way. Don't say those kind of things. That is not funny." At Great Lakes you're pretty isolated. I couldn't find out about it because there was no radio or no TV. I had to wait six hours until I could go into the drill instructors' office. There was a radio over there and I turned it on and found out that he had in fact been shot and killed. I haven't had any heroes since then. That was the last hero for me. I know my dad too well for that.

I was really crazy when I enlisted. I signed up for six years to get into the nuclear-power program. So I stayed up there for about a year going to electronics school. I was an electronics technician in the navy, what they call an ET. Once I got my stripe I was an electronics technician radar—ETR.

When I joined the navy, my relationship with Judy didn't last long. I guess she felt I was deserting her. I went to see her at Christmas and she told me to sort of bug off.

In April or May of 1969, I left Great Lakes to report to a ship. I'd put in for the East Coast. Instead I got Hawaii, which didn't sound too bad. Again, I was really sort of trying not to go to Vietnam. So I went and met the USS *Grapple,* which was a salvage ship. ARS7—Auxiliary Rescue Salvage. It had an overstaffed crew at that time of about 110, which was pretty crowded. I was the electronics technician. I was supposed to fix all the electronic gear and everything else. We were stationed on the end of the runways on Hickam Field, right at the mouth of Pearl Harbor.

I was out there on the fantail one day, reading a book, and I heard this airplane coming. I looked up and it was a Japanese Zero. I thought, again? . . . And one quick clinch of the heart. It turned out they were filming *Tora! Tora! Tora!*

About a month or two after I got to Hawaii, we put out on what they call a "Westpack Cruise." So we went to Vietnam. Actually we spent most of our time in Taiwan and the Philippines, but we did go to the Tonkin Gulf and other parts of Vietnam. The only thing I ever really did from a war standpoint was when I was on the midwatch one night. We were about four or five miles south of the DMZ, and we were anchored about two hundred yards offshore, a little place called Qua Viet. We were trying to drag these barges off the beach. So I get a radio call saying that they think they've seen zappers in the water, swimmers, and I'm the petty officer of the watch. I sent my little messenger down to get the captain or at least the executive officer. So they both come up, and they're pulling on their clothes, and the captain says, "Cut the cables. Prepare to get under way." We cut the cables in the back, jerked up the anchors, and start taking off.

He told me to go throw a couple of hand grenades in the water for the shock effect. I rooted around until I found the grenades. I'd never seen these things. We didn't have any of this hand-to-hand stuff in the navy or ROTC. But it was obvious that you screwed this thing down and pulled the pin, and you threw it in the water. So my messenger and I went down there. I'm twenty-one or twenty-two; the messenger's probably eighteen or nineteen. I'm a second-class petty officer and he's a drip, so I'm trying to impress the guy. So I stroll along down to the foredeck, and I'm thinking about just pulling it out with my teeth, you know, John Wayne, right? If John Wayne ever pulled one of those pins out of a grenade with his teeth, I'd like to see that guy's teeth.

So I reached down to pull the pin out and gave it a nice little jerk. It wouldn't budge. Finally, I had to use all my leverage to pull the pin out. Then I throw it over the side fairly nonchalantly and it goes off in the water. And I'm thinking, Well, it's possible I've killed somebody. I don't really think anybody was close, but it's possible that I at least injured somebody. But it didn't bother me. Intellectually it bothered me, but really I didn't have these strong feelings of aversion like I guess you'd like to have.

There was an interesting article I read not too long ago about how men love war, and I really think that's true. It was an exciting, exhilarating sort of thing. I realized that I wouldn't have minded too much if I had to kill somebody. I don't really like that feeling in me, but I wouldn't have much trouble doing it.

When I got back from Vietnam, I took some leave. This must have been 1970. I still had four years to go, and I realized I had made some serious mistakes. By this time Judy had transferred from Agnes Scott College to the University of Georgia, and she had become a student radical. Right at that particular point, she was talking about bombing buildings. Not that *she* was going to do it, but she didn't mind that. She thought it was okay and useful. I wouldn't argue with her about that because I thought it probably was too. But one incident really grossed me out.

Back then I didn't care if people were against the war, and I didn't care if they were for it. I thought it was something that people could differ on. Besides, it didn't make any difference what I felt anyway, because I was there and was going to be there awhile. Well, I was sitting in the house that Judy rented with four other women. I had just come back from Vietnam and my hair's too short. There's no way that you fit in when you're in the military in 1970. I stuck out. Yet at this time I really empathized with the hippies. That's really where my soul was. The idea of love. The idea that the system, the government, was something that you should not take for granted. That the system's not worth our consideration except to restructure it.

But here were two guys a couple of years younger than me sitting in the middle of the floor with their long hair and their wire-rimmed spectacles, and they were talking about the war. They're ignoring me because they know what I am. They're talking about eating soap to develop ulcers so that they can beat the draft, which was just totally unacceptable to me. I thought that if you were going to be against the war, you had one honorable choice: You stood up. You said, "I'm against the war. I'm burning my draft card right here. Lock me up." I never had any problem with anybody like that because I felt that they were standing up for what they believed in. But, boy, these two guys!

I went out to drive around a little bit after that, and that's what really sparked the big conversation with Judy. I was never really pro-Vietnam, but I was against the way these guys were getting out of it. She thought it was not going that counted more than anything else, and this was their way of making a statement, and that was okay. So we really got into it then. Needless to say, I did not spend the night.

I got shipped to Vallejo, north of San Francisco, where you took nuclear-power basics in classroom form. I used to go to San Francisco and play Ping-Pong at the USO. You couldn't do anything else. No girls would look at you because your hair was too short and you were a military guy. You were a total outcast. I became very much a loner, which is what I've always sort of been anyway. I used to go into San Francisco and just walk by myself for miles and avoid people. It was at this time that my religious experience happened.

I felt there had been some coincidences in my life that were a little hard to believe—like when I needed somebody, somebody showed up.

I decided that if my Christian background had been correct—you know, knock and it shall be opened—that I ought to be able to devise an experiment. If God is really there, and if God wants to be known, then it/he/she ought to come to where I am. If it's too damn hard to find this character what difference does it make?

So I decided that to be scientific about it, I had to let God's hand show somehow, and what that meant was I had to pretty much do away with my will—what *I* wanted to do, what *I* thought should happen. That was the tough part. What I decided on is this: I would do whatever somebody else asked me to do, aside from giving them money and this kind of stuff. But if they wanted to do something with me, I would do it. There really are sort of a lot of drips in the armed forces, people who are not particularly personable. And for some reason I always seem to be the target. If I don't really watch myself, I end up having to listen to them for a long time. Well, those are the people who came out of the woodwork—people I'd been halfway avoiding or putting off. Those are the ones I'm dealing with now. The cool people don't ask you to go out and do things very often.

So I start on this project, and, just as I thought, these guys come up and ask me to do things. "Play cards with me, Jack." "Okay, sure." "Hey, I'm going to San Francisco. You want to go to a movie?" "Sure."

I didn't want to go with these dopey people, do these dopey things, and not have a good time, but I was willing to make that sacrifice in the effort to find out whether there's a God or not. But it was not working the way I expected. Somehow these people would ask me to do these dumb-sounding things, but when I would go, it would be almost an exhilarating experience. I was wrestling with a philosophical problem— like, What is sin? And I'd go to this movie with some character and somebody would say something which was the answer to what I was working on. It struck me as so totally mystic that from that time on, I've never thought there was no God. I was absolutely convinced.

In three days I felt I had gotten so much more out of the entire process than what I was putting into it. I stopped the experiment after three days because I felt like if I continued it for longer than that, God was going to trap me into doing some of this damn religious work, and I knew that I did not want to be a minister. . . . But that was an outstanding experience.

My next duty station was Idaho Falls, Idaho. I got there around October of 1970 and studied sort of cookbook engineering—how heat conductors work, how a nuclear reactor works. Idaho Falls is where all the prototypes of nuclear plants are. You go there to get your on-the-job training, and it was a real bitch. Interesting, nice people, but the prototype is about seventy miles away and you had to be there at seven-thirty in the morning. You had to catch a bus at like four-fifteen in the morning, work from eight to five, ride the bus back, and get back about seven-thirty at night. There was only one real bar in town, and we'd go out there and close that place down, get three hours of sleep, then sleep on the rest breaks. There was nothing going on in that area, just desolation.

They had a drug bust and they started bringing them in like flies. They came in and took depositions: "Have you ever smoked dope? If you answer this question untruthfully, then you will be falsifying government records, and that's subject to ten years in Leavenworth."

And you say, "God, let me think about it a minute." They got probably sixty people, including a lot of people close to me. When they finally got around to me, I decided to be truthful about it. I told them that I had. I mean, I'm a child of the times. So I admitted to it. That was about it.

They gave me some orders to go down to Treasure Island in San Francisco Bay to spend a month there before getting out. I was supposed to report to Barracks X. When I saw it, it had a ten-foot-high wire fence around it, chain links with barbed wire on the top. So I picked up my sea bag and walked around the back and sneaked up on it. I turned around the corner and there on the side was a big "X." I thought, I'm in for it now. I walked up to the front, slowly, and here's this E1, which is as low as you get, slouched down in the guardhouse by an open gate, and he doesn't have on a gun. He's a sloppy-looking guy.

I said, "Hey, I'm supposed to report at three o'clock." And he said, "What'd they get you for? Drugs?" And I said, "Yes." And he said, "Well, you want any dope?" "Nope." "LSD?" "No." "THC?" "No." He gave a list of about fifteen drugs. I said no to all of them. Finally when he got down to the bottom, he looked at me and said, "Well, you're not going to have a very good time around here." It was a very lenient place.

I got out about Christmas Day of '70. By that time Dad had been elected governor. My parents don't get mad; they get disappointed. It wasn't that I had let them down or brought dishonor on the family; I think they were more concerned about what it was going to do to me in my life, that you can't do some things later on that you want to. It was never any big deal.

I started going back to Georgia Tech, and I picked up my old major of physics because that was the quickest way to get out. I started making decent grades, let my hair grow out, and returned to normal. I really had a pretty good time as the governor's son. There were a lot of women that wanted to get to know me. I was living in the Governor's Mansion and had people waiting on me there—never had that happen before. The GI bill took care of all my financial needs. It was good to be out and be alive. I was being integrated back into what I considered the real world. Just a good time had by all.

Judy, at this point, was gone on a world cruise with something called World Campus Afloat. One Saturday afternoon I came back from a big raft race down the Chattahoochee River, and Judy was there at the Governor's Mansion when I got back. We never really left each other after that. We got married in November, about six months later. I knew that I wanted her the first time I saw her. I think I proposed to her when she was still sixteen. I think she finally decided I was going to love her, no matter what, that other guys may win over the short term, but I had the long-term pull.

She was a teacher, and was also getting her master's in early-childhood education. We were living in the Governor's Mansion, and in '72 all of the Democratic presidential candidates came through Georgia to see the governor. I guess it was sort of a courtesy, since Atlanta was a decent population center. McGovern, Humphrey, John Lindsay, "Scoop" Jackson, Muskie. All those guys came down to see Dad, and we made it a point to go meet them. We were not very impressed with any of those guys, except Humphrey. Most of them, we felt, were sitting on the edge of their seat trying to figure out what answer you wanted before they gave it. After you've been around these people for a while, you think, Hey, I can do that. They are never as big as you thought, which is really a sign of the parochial view that we started out with.

Another visitor to the Mansion was Bob Dylan. When we heard Dylan was going to do a concert in Atlanta, my brothers and I suggested to Dad that he invite Dylan to come out to the Governor's Mansion the night of the concert. My parents listened to Dylan's albums. So he did come by. He was very, very quiet.

I finished up at Tech in August of '72 and applied to law school. I was really afraid I wasn't going to get in because my grades were so bad. But I did real well on the LSAT. That, plus the fact that Dad was governor, was enough to get me into law school. That summer was the last time I ever worked at the warehouse during the peanut-harvest season. Then I started law school.

Judy and I were living in Athens, where Judy was teaching. I remember when we were at the Governor's Mansion over one weekend, Mom and Dad were sitting in one of the rooms upstairs, watching TV. Judy and I walked in, and Dad turned around and said he was going to run for president. Our first reaction was, "That's great! You'll do better than anybody else we've seen." It did not strike us as being awesome. From that moment, we felt that we had an excellent chance to win. We thought that our main competition was going to be Teddy Kennedy, and, in fact, Teddy Kennedy was scheduled to give the Law Day speech at the University of Georgia Law School on May the 1st. None of my feeling for Bobby rubbed off on Teddy Kennedy. Dad was going to give a speech to a luncheon following the Law Day exercise. All the big lawyers and judges would be there, as well as the money people at the law school. We thought this is going to give us the chance to see one versus the other.

As Law Day comes closer, we hear the important news that not only is Teddy Kennedy coming, but covering him is going to be the Lone Wolf, Hunter Thompson. I mean, Teddy Kennedy didn't mean much, but Hunter Thompson was something else. So Judy and I made a point to be in Atlanta that Friday night. Teddy Kennedy comes in, and he was tired and not impressive. We wind up talking with a couple of his entourage, who were pretty neat people.

Next morning we all go down and we have breakfast. The Kennedy party, our party, and some other people—maybe fifteen or twenty people sitting at one of these long tables in one of the big dining rooms in the Governor's Mansion. The guard from the gate calls up and says he's got some weirdo down there who claims he's been invited to breakfast with Senator Kennedy and Governor Carter. He says his name is Hunter S. Thompson. I said, "He's okay; send him up."

So I go out to meet Hunter. He's wearing a T-shirt and blue jeans, tennis shoes, and no socks. And a windbreaker. He's got a leather thong around his neck, and a Brazilian fist hanging down from it, dark glasses, and his hair real short. And he's raving about the Watergate papers. The tapes had just been released, and they'd been printed up. He goes around to the back of the cab that he came in, gets his airplane-travel bag, opens it up, and there's three or four volumes of the Watergate-tape transcripts that are obviously just right off the government press. And he's raving about the stuff that's in there. Also in his bag is a bottle of Wild Turkey and a six-pack of Budweiser.

So I take him into the Governor's Mansion and he continues to rave about this. He sits down and they talked about it for a while, but Dad and Hunter get into this discussion through Bob Dylan. I knew Dad was well versed on Bob Dylan because I turned him on to that in 1962 or '3. But I didn't know he knew so much about these other guys. Everybody at the table, even though they may be carrying on little conversations with the people next to them, are trying to hear what Dad and Hunter Thompson are saying at the other end. Ted Kennedy is still there, but he's essentially vanished. It was really an amazing situation.

At the Law Day exercises, Kennedy gave a pretty innocuous speech. He said nothing for a long time. I thought, The guy's supposed to be an orator. If this is the best he can do, we're going to blow him away. We left there and went over to the lunch where Dad was supposed to speak. Stage two of the preview of the 1976 presidential election. Dad has written out a speech, which he has now torn up, and he writes another in the bathroom—just scribbled notes.

He starts giving this speech to this assembled group of high lawyers in Georgia, and it is devastating. It's just a scathing indictment of the legal system as it was then. It still makes me tingle when I talk about it. When he got through, there was a long silence, and then there was a spontaneous standing ovation. I've never heard another speech that moved me that way. It was a combination of sincere style and sincere subject, and it was unbelievable. Well, Judy and I are just ripped up. It was such a powerful thing, and we both feel so fortunate to have been there. Dad has never come close to doing that again. I don't think anybody will in my lifetime. Judy wrote Dad a poem about it, and it still hangs on his wall. Hunter Thompson wound up with the only tape of the speech and the text of it is in his book *The Great Shark Hunt*.

In December of '74, Dad announced his candidacy at the mini-convention in Kansas City, to which I was an elected delegate from my own district. I began doing work for the campaign on weekends, going to South Carolina, meeting people, and trying to set up an organization. I graduated law school in June, and we moved to Calhoun, where Judy's father was an attorney. He hired me and paid me $10,800 a year, which was sort of disappointing. I would go down to Atlanta and do "cold-calling." You get a list of people that you never heard of before, and you call them up and you ask them to give money to somebody they've never heard of before. It's not real successful.

Then Jason came along in August. Judy had had a couple of miscarriages, and one of them was pretty serious. She was bleeding, and they couldn't get the bleeding stopped. We thought she was going to die. With Jason, we got into the Lamaze classes and we were going to Emory University Hospital, which was the only one in Atlanta which would allow the husband to participate in the birth process. Judy started having pains one night, and we left in the fog and got to the hospital at three in the morning. This big Harley-Davidson drives up and a doctor gets off of it. Dr. Bottomy. He's about sixty, driving a big Harley in from the lake. I don't know if that made me feel better or not. But, boy, he was great. This doctor has been delivering babies at a major hospital for forty years. God knows how many babies he's delivered, and it's still exciting to him, and I'm in the delivery room and he's imparting that to me. That was really a neat experience.

After Jason, I pretty much went on the campaign trail. That was a lot of fun, but it was real hard work. You'd hit a factory shift at six in the morning, and you'd run until dinner at eight at night or eight-thirty. Then you'd go home with somebody to spend the night, because it was cheap and also effective in building an organization. But when you got there, they likely would have over some of their relatives and close friends, and you'd wind up getting to bed at ten o'clock and then have to get up at five the next morning.

My main state was Florida, but I'd take a break every once in a while and go somewhere else. I went to Columbus, Ohio, in December of '75, and I'm met by a politically unsavory character. He's not a bad guy, but he's not somebody that you'd pick to run your campaign. He tells me that we have nothing scheduled that night, which is lousy. I'm not so sure I like this. But the next morning we've got this press conference. Well, I know what that means. I've had press conferences before. There's one guy there from a local radio station, and there's a young kid there from a local newspaper who usually does obits and he's now going to do a little paragraph on a presidential candidate's child comes to Columbus. So until the next morning I'm thinking this guy's a real jerk.

I walk into this hotel and the place is packed. There are three TV stations, all of the newspapers. Looking back on it, this guy must have let them believe it was going to be Dad that was going to be there instead of me. At the time I thought this was just a sign of how good our campaign was going. I had about ten microphones in front of me and I was sensing the power. I start telling them I just came from Dade County in Florida, where our steering committee runs the range from old McGovernites to people who could be in the John Birch Society or the Ku Klux Klan. So this one guy in the front, a newspaper writer, jumps on the KKK and says, "Are you seeking the Ku Klux Klan vote in Florida?" And I said, "No." And he said, "Well, would you take it if you got it?" And I said, "We're not turning anybody away, but we're not going after the KKK vote." He said, "Well, would your father ever appoint a KKK to the Supreme Court?" I said, "Of course not; that's ridiculous." So he shuts off, and we go on with the rest of the press conference.

I get back to Georgia three or four days later. I walk into the headquarters and nobody's looking at me. When I walk in, they all turn away. Finally I grab somebody and say, "What is going on here?" And he said, "You haven't seen the article?" So they pull out the biggest newspaper in Columbus, Ohio, capital of the state. The headline is CARTER'S SON DENIES FATHER TO APPOINT KKK TO HIGH COURT. I couldn't believe it. At that point, I'm trying to be an honest person and say exactly what things are. That told me that you can't do that, because not only is it a bad article, all about the KKK, it's also, in today's modern political world, Xeroxed and distributed by your opponents. It reinforced the idea that because we're from the South, we are all racists. If it had happened six months later, that could have really made a lot of difference. As it was, nobody cared about Jimmy Carter yet.

Now if I were to be asked the same question, I would say, "Florida's steering committee runs from very liberal to very conservative. All work together in a harmonious fashion." When they ask you about the KKK you say, "That is a ridiculous question and I'm not going to answer it." I would make sure not to use the phrase "KKK" so that some newspaper person couldn't pull it out of context and use it as a quote.

Our strategy was to win the Iowa caucuses to get the notice, and win in New Hampshire because it's first and in the North, and win in Florida because that was Wallace country at the time. When we won in Iowa, people were unprepared for it. But when we won in New Hampshire, we decided to shift into a Massachusetts strategy. It surprised us a little bit to win so big so early. There was only a week between New Hampshire and Massachusetts, but we thought maybe if we could win in Massachusetts, then we could put it out of reach all at once.

The Florida primary is one week after Massachusetts. My argument in Florida was that if you were liberal, you had to vote for Carter because he's the only one that had a chance to beat Wallace. And if you were conservative, you had to vote for Carter because he's the only one from the South that had a chance to win nationwide.

I took a week off after the New Hampshire primary. I hit Orlando, which was our state headquarters, the afternoon of the Massachusetts primary. I find out that Dad's in town. So I go over to the hotel where he is, and me and Dad and Jody Powell watch the Massachusetts results come in. There's a snowstorm, so all of our soft poll support doesn't show. We've got no organizational equipment there, no people, no setup, no buses. The results were coming in so bad that it was funny. We were sitting there making all these morbid jokes. Dad had to get up and go tell the television folks what happened.

Well, I'd sort of been in charge of Florida, and I'm a little bit worried now, because what I'd been saying in Florida didn't hold in Massachusetts. Wallace, who we are saying in Florida has no chance to win in the North, is in the lead there, over the busing issue. Scoop Jackson, who we are saying has no chance to beat Wallace, is close enough that he may win, which he eventually did. We came in fourth.

The Florida election is on Tuesday. Monday noon, I can't stand it anymore, and I leave. I drive straight through from Fort Lauderdale to Calhoun, which is six or eight hundred miles. I was flying. That was right about the time when CB radios were really coming in, and I had one. I got to Calhoun about two in the morning, tapped on the window until Judy woke up, and I slept until late the next day. I was real nervous about the whole thing.

The polls closed at six o'clock. At something like six-o-two, they called us the winner, and we broke out the champagne. We wound up just beating the tar out of Wallace and Jackson.

At that point we felt we had beaten Wallace in his own backyard, and we really felt good about the rest of the campaign. We always felt like we had the best candidate; it was just a matter of getting people to know him.

I can remember the Pennsylvania primary was where the last of the old guard really set up its stand—a big Northern industrial state. The press was playing it up as the first big test. Can Jimmy Carter, a Southerner from a right-to-work state, win in a big union state? We did it. We blew them out again. That was really a fun time. By that time the family had six or eight accomplished campaigners crisscrossing the country. We had dealt with all our press problems early. We had turned from people who spoke the truth to the mealy-mouthed kind of politicians that I always didn't want to be. But we found out that you had to be that way or you'd have a problem being misquoted or mistreated in the press. We discovered that early, and then didn't have to worry about it.

I didn't particularly like the general election against Ford. It was not as much fun. In the first place, the primaries were sort of like a game where you were scoring all the time. The general election didn't have that. It was how the press took it, and the polls. We started at such a high level in the polls, and we were dropping all the time, so it got a little bit sensitive. And everybody was afraid Jimmy Carter was a closet racist. People from the South were really suspect.

The campaign got real exhausting. You get on a plane one place, go to the next place, get off the plane. You meet a guy who tells you everything about the area. You drive from the airport to wherever you're supposed to go. They tell you what kind of group you're speaking to and how big or little, and it really doesn't make any difference to you. You've got the same sort of things to say, and they're all interchangeable. Everybody's about the same in one sense. But when you've done that enough, and you're on display time after time after time, and you're talking all day, at some point your thoughts become disconnected from your speech, and your sentences literally come out garbled. You just interchange words, and there's nothing that fits anymore. At that point, you've had enough. You can't do anything else. It's not that you get tired in the physical sense; it's that you get tired of being on display. You get tired of watching whatever you're saying, whatever you do, whomever you're with. You've just got to go and wait for a couple of days. I'm sure that for a candidate, it's a lot worse. They can't stop as easily as I could.

Election night, John Belushi and Dan Aykroyd happened to be in Atlanta, and they came up to the hotel where we were staying and joined us. I had met Belushi at a *Rolling Stone* party at the Democratic Convention in New York. That was really exciting, though. It was a pretty close race, but we won.

That first day when Dad got inaugurated, and we walked down Pennsylvania Avenue, that was a great experience. Everybody there was looking at us. I felt like it was deserved. They ought to have been paying attention to us, because we went out and we did something nobody thought we could do that year before, and we felt like we did it pretty much on our own, or, at least, each one of us had a lot to do with it. We started walking down that street, and there's all these Roman columns and Greek architecture, and I had the feeling it was like Julius Caesar coming back to Rome to take over the town. That was really neat.

I'd never been in the White House before. We all walked across the yard to the White House. That was a real thrill. It's a nice place, a lot of rooms, very comfortable, very easy to get used to. Antiques didn't bother us. We had the same sort of thing in the Governor's Mansion. And they're well made. Sturdy furniture. There was a lot of real good service. They had a little movie theater downstairs; you could order any movie that you wanted. I remember watching *Alice's Restaurant.*

We also got Secret Service protection. It wasn't quite so bad as people think. Most of those guys were my age. I liked my guys. It was fun a lot, and it wasn't that bad the rest of the time.

But I decided not to live in the White House. I was too old to go back into my mother and father's house. I was almost thirty years old and I had my own life. I went back to Calhoun and got into the grain-elevator business. I thought I knew something about it, and I had some good friends that were in it. I didn't particularly like the law. Law is too much dealing with other people's problems. So I determined to make some of my own, and I was exceedingly successful. The business went broke three or four years later, and I had to settle a lot of debts. But it was interesting while it was going on, and it got me interested in the commodities market, so I guess something good came out of it.

On December 19, 1978, Judy gave birth again, but the second one was a little bit different. Same doctor, Dr. Bottomy. Sara was his last baby. He had some sort of deteriorating spinal-column condition and he died within a year. Judy was in labor for a long time, and it was draining. But here's Dr. Bottomy, as confident and experienced as ever. He sticks his hand up inside and says, "Ah, this baby's coming face-down." Ordinarily you'd have a shock of fear, but with him it was like, "Oh, I haven't had one of these in a while. Here's what we do here." It was always obvious that he was totally in control.

I thought Dad was doing a pretty good job. We argue all the time about one thing or another, in a fun way, but my basic attitude was that I was not enough of an expert on anything to disagree. I wasn't really that interested in politics, as a matter of fact. I didn't want to deal with it. I always had complete confidence in Dad's judgment, in what he was doing, and why.

I'm often asked what it was like when Dad got criticized so harshly while he was president. If you're going to be a public official in this day and time, you're going to get ridiculed. You have to understand that when you're going in, and I think he did. I voted for Dad, a lot of people did, and I always appreciate it when they say that they did.

Aside from the drawbacks of being the president's son, there are obviously a lot of pluses, too. We got to do a lot of things and meet a lot of people. But I think the only difference between my experiences and those of others is that I've met enough people to know that nobody's particularly different from anybody else, and it doesn't take anything to be on television, except standing in front of a television camera. It doesn't mean you're smarter or more intelligent than other people.

It's the campaigns that I enjoy, particularly being in on the strategy part of it. A campaign is one of the only occasions where I ever really get a chance to get back at the media, to fight on equal terms. However, I didn't do much in the 1980 campaign. I had my own life going at that time and I was having to struggle with the grain elevator. I did make a couple of trips to farming areas to defend the grain embargo. I think Dad would have been a better president than Reagan. I think the American people made a mistake, but then I don't *know* that. I'm certain that Dad's more qualified for the job, more intelligent, more knowledgeable. I'm not sure that that's what makes a good president.

So Dad got beat, and the grain elevator folded. We were fairly well undercapitalized to start with, and the first year was the worst drought in twenty or thirty years, and we started going downhill from there. Aside from the weather, it was probably poor management that did us in. I was the manager. We sold the place for a good bit less than we paid for it.

Ultimately somebody gave me a job at Archer Daniels Midland–Taber Commodities. They suggested I come to Chicago and work on the floor at the Board of Trade. I got here in June '81 and later moved to the Continental Bank. I run their Board of Trade operations. I am what they call the "floor manager." Every big clearinghouse has somebody on the floor that answers the phone, takes the orders, puts them into the pit, makes sure they get executed properly, reports when the orders are filled, and who also keeps an eye on the market—what's going on, who's doing what, what the price action is like, what it feels like. I'm also a technical analyst, dealing with chart patterns. I look at price movement to make some projection of what the market's going to be doing. I tell people how to speculate in bonds.

I had a rough time at age thirty-five. I had not accomplished the kind of things that I thought I was going to accomplish back when I thought there were great people in the world. I thought maybe I would be one of them. It turns out that not only am I not one of them, but there aren't any! Lately—and this may be temporary—what I do for a living is not as important to me as it once was. I seem to enjoy just being around a lot more. The kids are getting into new things. Judy's got a new job that she really enjoys, and it's fun for me to watch her do that.

Judy used to write a column for *Redbook* magazine; then she went to this PR operation downtown. Now she works as a consultant for a privately funded operation here called Family Focus and an allied program called the Ounce of Prevention Fund. Family Focus is focusing now on teenage pregnancy, teenage parents. They've got a couple of centers where they have courses for would-be parents on what to expect. They'll keep your small baby while you finish up high school. They're really doing a good job. I told somebody that I lost the prestige of having a wife that worked down in the Loop, and that she's become a social worker. She didn't like that description, so we finally settled on calling her a "social thinker," which is what she does.

Our marriage has grown by passing responsibilities from Judy to me, in terms of housework. When we got married, we both had standard ideas that I was supposed to go out and work and Judy was supposed to stay home. After she put me through law school, she was supposed to stay home, take care of the kids, and clean house for me. After a while, it was obvious it wasn't going to work for long. So now we both do the housework, we both work, she gets the kids off to school in the morning, and I get them back at night and fix supper. It all balances out.

The kids get out of school around 3:15 P.M. and stay in a day-care center associated with the school for an hour or so until I get home about four-thirty. At one point Judy said she felt like she wasn't really being a good mother because she wasn't there when they came home from school. My response was, "What you're giving up, I'm getting." I've got a chance now to be with my kids, by myself, from four-thirty in the afternoon until five-thirty or six. If the mother is always there, the father goes and watches the TV. But if you have to be there and get their supper and look at their homework and listen to them complaining about what went on at school, or what they enjoyed, the whole relationship changes. I think that we're much closer than we were before Judy started working.

The kids have a chance to see both parents in different situations. To give an example of how this is working, Sara made a comment a few months ago about how she was glad she was going to grow up to be a woman because women didn't have to wash dishes!

Men tend to approach things from a very aggressive standpoint. I see that in myself. I compete; I want to get the better of somebody else. Even though I do it in a genteel fashion, it's there—it drives me. I want to be able to buy the things I want, even though I know that most people can't. I want to be the best at what I do. But masculinity is not the form that's going to keep this world together. Femininity may not be it either, but it certainly lies somewhere between the two. We masculine people have got to move towards feminism to eliminate the aggression and to understand the concept of nurturing—what we now call "mothering." This is the way we're going to have to go if we're going to get out of the confrontational, aggressive world situation where we always go from war to war and which has now become too dangerous to put up with.

The way that we treat each other within a loving family has to be expanded to encompass the workplace, all workplaces, and the nations of the world. Not that you have to give up competition, because competition is fun. But confrontation at an international level is dangerous, and feeling that you're the most important because you are the United States is not necessarily a good thing.

Our generation witnessed the questioning of the system. We came along and we were righteous and with reason. We caught the tail end of the civil-rights movement, took that civil-rights virtue and put it to work really quick in the student movement before any of it wore off. We grew very intolerant about anybody that didn't agree with us. We watched the system crack and we watched it grow back. I don't think it's been put back any better than before, at least not yet. But it's much more important now than it used to be to look at the other side of the argument with a serious eye, to try to understand why people hold the views they do. Maybe there is a time when you really have got to say, "This is where I draw the line." But you've also got to recognize that it's *your* line, for you, and it's not for everybody else.

After Jack Carter and I had concluded several hours of conversation, Jack led me through the snow to the Blind Faith Café, which, he chided me, would be my kind of place since it was a sanctuary for hippies and counter-cultural types. The vegetarian fare was delicious and I ordered an extra meal to go.

Then we trudged back to the Baptist church that Jack and his family attend, and arrived just in time for Jack to don his costume for a church talent show. Most of the talent was raw and the jokes corny, but I found it delightful that the participants ranged in age from four to eighty-seven.

Afterward, I accompanied Jack and Judy to a couples' reading group that they took part in each week. I felt quite honored that the seven couples involved allowed me into their lives.

It had been a long time since I had been part of such a group discussion, and I found it quite stimulating. The Carters dropped me off at my hotel, and as I watched them drive off, I felt encouraged by the reminder that members of my generation were still at it, still exploring, still searching. I hope it is a process that never stops.

TEACHER'S PET:

Katherine Mader

If I had to choose one movement or cause associated with the upheavals of the '60s that has had the greatest, most enduring effect, I would choose the women's movement. There is still much to be done, particularly in the political realm, but the growing awareness of women's issues has already strengthened the whole society enormously.

One aspect of the women's movement that found the class of '65 on the front lines was the sexual integration of the workplace. During the mid-to-late '70s, I heard tales from my wife's family about being the first woman on a road-repair crew or on a railroad crew, or in a previously all-male department of a factory. It wasn't easy being among the first, but it was worth the problems.

I decided to visit an old friend of mine, Kathy Mader, who also had direct knowledge of being a pathfinder in her field. The setting for our talk was very familiar to me. It was the same house that Kathy lived in when I used to visit her more than twenty years earlier in junior high school and high school.

My parents were European. My dad went to the University of Vienna, got a Ph.D. in chemistry. He got out of Vienna in '39, right at the end. He had people in his family that were killed by Nazis, but he was able to get into Switzerland and come here, by way of New York. He was chief chemist of the Air Pollution Control District in Los Angeles. He did all the initial work on smog, when they didn't really know yet what smog was. My mom came earlier from Germany, ended up going to high school in L.A., and UCLA. She was a school nurse.

I was an only child. I did what my parents wanted, and they wanted me to be a lawyer. But within the legal profession, I chose an unusual way of practicing, as close to being an outlaw as a lawyer could be. I've always been interested in crime. I always loved Nancy Drew and the Hardy Boys. In junior-high-school journalism class, we had an assignment to interview someone. So I interviewed Mickey Cohen, the gangster. My parents made me do everything so safely, but it was okay to talk to Mickey Cohen because it was part of my assignment.

I think that a lot of my parents' strictness came from their European background. They were very loving, too, and I was very wanted, but they were extremely strict. They used to forbid me, for instance, from riding my bicycle in the street. So when I rode my bicycle to Brentwood Elementary School I'd have to ride on the sidewalk, even though riding a bike on the sidewalk is illegal. I'm surprised that I didn't rebel more than I did during the '60s.

As a child I rebelled in my own way, as much as I could within very defined boundaries. My parents made me practice the piano. I always hated the piano; I hated it since I was five years old. In fact, going back, I found my mother saved all my Mother's Day cards from when I was six and seven years old. I'd say, "You're a wonderful mother and everything you do is great. However, I hate the piano and I always will."

When I think of my first years, I think of being dominated by the piano. I took lessons from five years old till I was about sixteen or seventeen. My parents made me play half an hour right when I woke up and right after dinner, six days a week. So from the moment I got up, my whole day revolved around when I was going to practice the piano. This wasn't just practicing the piano and doing what you feel like. This was my father coming in and setting the timer twice a day on thirty minutes. Or he'd sit down in a red chair right in back of the piano and he would watch his watch and I couldn't end a minute before thirty minutes.

I used to devise all sorts of ways to get around playing the piano, even while playing it. My parents would be getting dressed in the bedroom and I learned how to play the scales while I was reading books. So I could read and just have my fingers move up and down the piano and they really didn't know the difference. My great-great-great-great-great-great uncle was Felix Mendelssohn, so they always thought I had this great musical genius that skipped generations—that it was my turn.

They could always make me play, but they couldn't make me play with any kind of emotion or any type of feeling. Looking back at some of the things my piano teacher used to write, she'd say, "Kathy is so technically proficient she can play anything. But she plays like a martinet. She has no feeling whatsoever." Well, I knew that I played with no feeling, and I knew that I had the feeling inside me, but I felt that if I showed feeling it would be the ultimate capitulation to my parents. So I played as rigidly as possible, so that they wouldn't get the satisfaction of knowing that they had beaten me.

In high school, I created an aura about myself of being rather unapproachable, as a defense mechanism, because I didn't want to be rejected. I was aloof with a lot of people that I probably would have enjoyed being friendly with. I really felt kind of out. Looking back, I think there were a couple of things that I did to make myself *feel* like I belonged in some way, so that I wouldn't feel badly about myself.

One thing was to become teacher's pet to Mr. Keech, the geometry teacher. He was wild and crazy and accepted by all the students. I thought that if I was his teacher's pet or whatever, that that would give me some sort of status of being accepted also.

Mr. Keech was really into skiing, so I became president of the ski club. He ran this ski service called Sierra Skiers Service, where he took busloads of people up to Mammoth and other different ski areas. I became a tour guide on his buses, so every few weekends I would get to go up to Mammoth and I would collect the money. Here I was, about fourteen or fifteen years old, and I'd have a couple of thousand dollars, sometimes in cash. Everyone thought I was real cute. I was the mascot of all the buses. For me it was really neat, my first job, and also really neat because he was twenty years older than I was.

Everything that he said was gospel. I thought he was one of the most intelligent, charismatic, charming people that I had ever met. And if only when I got older he would still be available, because he was a bachelor then. He was always totally proper in his behavior towards me and treated me more like a daughter than a potential girlfriend. He taught me how to write his signature and I used to sign all of his report cards. I still make my *K* exactly the same way as the way I learned from Mr. Keech. Of course, I got A's in geometry two semesters in a row, even though I never learned a thing.

Well, I continued to stay friends with him, and when I got married, he gave us a trip to Mammoth for a week as a wedding present. After that, though, I didn't have any contact with him for fifteen years.

Then a babysitter was over and she was talking about somebody in high school that she had a crush on, which keyed me on Mr. Keech, and I told her my story. She said, "Well, you should call him up, check him out." I said I didn't think so. I didn't really have anything to say to him.

She said, "Oh, come on. Do it." And I was sitting there, the phone right next to me, so, okay, I dialed a few numbers and found him. He, of course, remembered who I was, and we had this nice talk and he said, "Why don't you come by and we'll have lunch or talk?" He had an office in Inglewood. Sierra Skiers Service was still in existence. So on my way back from court one day I stopped by and it was such a disappointment. Here I am thirty-five and he's fifty-five, and I had all these great expectations as to what this hero of my youth was going to be like.

Well, first of all, he was doing the identical thing he was doing twenty years ago. He had never married. The way he was running his ski service was totally disorganized, disheveled. He was having arguments with the bus driver—the exact same thing that I used to hear him doing years before. No progress. I was there probably about an hour and I talked with him about his views on different subjects. Here was a man who I thought intellectually was so far my superior in high school, and I was so disappointed at his perception of things. Not only did he not seem particularly enlightened or thoughtful, but he was extemely racist in some of the things he was saying about the neighborhood where his office was.

I said to him, "I don't remember you being this way. I don't understand this." I probably gave him a hard time about it because I told him about how my perception was that he had really changed quite a bit. And he said maybe he's just gotten more bitter over the years because he hasn't done what he's wanted to do. I left feeling kind of discouraged. What I thought was going to be a very up experience was just a bummer. I was very disappointed, so I put it behind me.

It wasn't more than a week later when I was in court and one of our other high-school teachers was there with his government class down to watch my trial. I brought up the subject of Mr. Keech and he said, "Oh, didn't you hear? Two or three days ago he was driving in Colorado and he had a massive heart attack. He pulled over to the side of the road and he died." Just like that. He didn't ever take very good care of himself. I just hope that my confronting him with how, in a sense, I didn't like how he turned out didn't cause him emotionally to be upset and contribute to what happened. But I just can't believe that that could have been the case.

So . . . back to high school. The other person I became involved with to help my self-esteem was my boyfriend, Fred. He was an unusual person and he always seemed to fit in. Me being attached to Fred in a way made me fit in with people that I wouldn't by myself. I think we became friends way back in eighth or ninth grade, and we just started spending more and more time together. He was always a very interesting person, but I think also that my relationship with Fred was, in a lot of ways, a rebellion against my parents. Here I am, an only Jewish child, and here he is, coming from a family of fourteen brothers and sisters, not Jewish.

Our relationship was basically platonic. He would kiss me goodnight and that was like a big deal. There was never anything beyond that. We used to hold hands—that was it. Thinking back, it's hard to believe that people actually get married when, in a sense, they didn't have anything more in terms of experience together than Fred and I had. But at the time, even though we had just kissed each other goodnight, it seemed very normal that we were just going to go through the process of getting pinned and engaged and we were going to get married.

One of the things that didn't endear Fred to my parents was that he couldn't drive. I used to have horrible arguments with my parents about this. I thought he couldn't drive because he didn't want to pay for the insurance. My mother said the reason why Fred can't drive is because his eyes are so bad. "When you two get older, you'll be married to a blind man and have to lead him everywhere." Fred used to be really into running. He was on the track team and the cross-country team. What he used to do is run from his house to my house. It was a long run, about ten miles. He'd arrive all sweaty—our Saturday-night date. He'd come and we'd sit down and watch a movie on television together. That was it. Then he'd hitchhike home. My parents used to say, "What kind of a relationship is this? He never takes you anywhere; all he does is sit at your house." We'd have dinner Saturday night, me and my parents, and we'd save an extra dinner for Fred when he came running in. Now that I think about it, he would never take a shower or anything.

After graduation, Fred went off to college at Berkeley and my parents forbade me from going to Berkeley because Fred was there. So I went to UCLA. My first or second week there I met Norman at a fraternity party. My parents thought Norman was wonderful, thought he was everything they had hoped for for their daughter. So they were really pushing Norman on me. Of course, I was not the slightest bit interested, because I had Fred. The more my parents pushed Norman, the more I gravitated towards Fred. Fred and I used to write all the time. Then what happened was that for the summer after our first year of college, Fred got a very good job as a lifeguard at a swimming pool in Berkeley.

I got angry and said, "Look, we spend the whole year apart and if you're going to be up there in Berkeley, what's the point of the whole relationship? I thought you were going to come down to Santa Monica for the summer." So Fred changed his plans and decided to come down to Los Angeles. Maybe about a month or two before the summer, I started thinking to myself, "You know, Norman is really a pretty great guy. I think in some ways, despite the fact that my parents like him, I kind of like him, too." You see, Norman was dating somebody else at the time, and I felt very competitive in a way with this other girl. I was interested in having Norman more to myself.

Norman was a year ahead of me at UCLA, so he was already integrated into the whole campus scene. He was president of a service organization, he was very active in campus politics. He ran a speaker's program and he was in charge of taking people around, so by being his girlfriend I could meet all these people, too. This was before the women's movement, and the idea of gaining recognition or gaining respect by being the girlfriend of somebody who had a lot of status was very acceptable and commonplace, something that I aspired to at the time. So Norman was a good "catch" in that vein, and he was good-looking besides.

Well, Norman had made plans to go with a friend of his to University of Hawaii summer school, so this friend of mine and I decided we were going to University of Hawaii summer school, too. At the last minute my friend couldn't go and Norman's friend couldn't go, so Norman and I both ended up at University of Hawaii summer school, and poor Fred ended up working as an orderly at Santa Monica Hospital for the summer. He could have been a lifeguard in Berkeley. I've felt really bad about that ever since. Fred and I have joked about it since, but it really was a terrible thing to do.

So Norman and I went off to Hawaii and I studied physics with Dr. Edward Teller, and economics because I could get rid of the courses in six weeks and avoid taking them for twenty weeks at UCLA.

Norman had a Honda 50 and I was forbidden from riding his Honda 50. My parents came over to Hawaii for a visit and they were going to check things out. Norman was working at a department store there selling shoes, and I told my parents, after I greeted them at the airport and went with them to the hotel, that I was going to see Norman and would take the bus home. They said, "Okay, but don't ride that motorcycle."

I said, "Of course not. I wouldn't ride that motorcycle." Well, of course, I rode home on the back of Norman's motorcycle and I still remember going across an intersection and here comes this car at the left and Norman says, "Oh, shit, we're dead!" We plowed right into the back door of the car. Motorcycle, just creamed. It has to be, of course, the night that my parents arrive in Hawaii. We're taken to the hospital in an ambulance and had a full set of X-rays. Luckily neither of us broke anything. But we were totally banged up. The black and blue doesn't come out for a day or two. We couldn't move. I guess the shock to the system. Anyway, my parents were going to be there for two or three days and we had to act like nothing had happened.

I have pictures of me wearing these dresses all the way down to the floor and long sleeves. I refused to go on an outrigger canoe. I said it was for tourists and I wasn't a tourist. But the real reason was that I just couldn't move my arms. The only thing we could do was go out to eat with them. It was terrible. I had a big bump on my head, which fortunately was covered with my hair. So we did great for about three days and they left. About a week later I get a phone call from my parents. They were hysterical. At the hospital I had given both addresses, the Hawaii and Mainland addresses. And my parents got the bill for skull X-rays for the night that they arrived in Hawaii! They were just livid. They ordered me home immediately. It was really the first time in my life that I defied my parents. I didn't go home until the agreed-upon time.

Back at UCLA I continued to date Norman, but he always felt like he couldn't be tied down, and there was always this tug between us because I *wanted* to be tied down. I was getting a lot of pressure from my parents. You know: "What a nice boy; you should get married." The next summer, 1967, Norman went to Washington, D.C., on this Washington internship program and worked for the National Students' Association. I spent the summer in Los Angeles, and got a letter on my birthday from Norman telling me that he didn't want to go out anymore.

I was real upset, and during the fall Norman said that we could only go out if I understood that it was never going to be any permanent relationship between the two of us. Or there might be, but it would be years down the line and we should be free to go out with others. So that was fine and I went out with other people. Norman and I used to see each other every week or every two weeks. Then one night he was sitting by himself in his apartment, feeling very lonely and thinking to himself, "I really don't have a friend to talk to except Kathy, and why am I pushing her away?"

So he called me up and he came over and wanted to live together. Because I was the obedient daughter that I was, I said, "Oh, no. My parents would never allow it. If you want to live with me, you have to get married to me." So he says, "Fine, then we'll get married."

And we got married ten days later in the den, right over there, with a portable *huppah.* His mother and father and my mother and father held the corners of the *huppah,* with the rabbi and us underneath. I think his parents were relieved because they thought that this would bring some stability into his life—they thought that he was a crazed, maniac radical, which he really wasn't. At that time, parents tended to totally overreact to anything. It took my parents a few days to get used to the idea. Then they thought, I think, that it could be a lot worse. So they became fairly supportive except that they really treated us like children for a long time.

After we graduated college, and after spending almost two years with both sets of parents meddling into everything and having very fixed opinions about everything, we decided for our own sanity that we had to get out of Los Angeles. When you're both only children, and you're both the center of your parents' lives . . . Our parents were both older people, too. My dad was forty when I was born, my mom was about ten or twelve years younger. Norman's dad was forty also and his mom was ten years younger. We're both left-handed. We're both only children. We're both nearsighted and we were born in the same hospital.

Norman didn't want to go to law school. Norman wanted to drop out and live in Berkeley. I, again, as a good, dutiful daughter, wanted to do what my parents wanted for me, and I didn't see that I could ever be comfortable really living on the streets in Berkeley or the Haight. It just wasn't me. I think Norman always regrets that he didn't just do it. So we both went to law school at the University of California at Davis.

What happened when we went to Davis was that he did his dropping out the first year of law school. He had a motorcycle, never bought any books, never went to class, always riding the motorcycle up in the hills. And I was the stable one. I was the one always trying to keep him functioning responsibly. At the end of the first year, he would have flunked out except for the fact that it was the period of the invasion of Cambodia, there was great turmoil, and the evaluations were postponed. You didn't have to take your tests the first quarter of the second year. That summer he went away on a motorcycle trip without me for six weeks up in the Pacific Northwest. We were up in Lake Tahoe with some friends for the weekend. I rode back with our friends in the van and he took off on his motorcycle, and when I came home he had left me a note explaining that he had to go find himself.

I think Norman will always be in the process of finding himself. I don't mean it necessarily in a negative sense. I mean he's the kind of person who always questions who he is and whether or not he's happy doing what he's doing. He's actually taught me a lot about myself in the process; through Norman I've learned not to be ashamed or embarrassed about "feeling" things and expressing my feelings to others. I've also learned to be much more honest in the way I relate to people. One difference, though, is that I wake up in the morning and I'm happy to be alive, functioning, whereas Norman wakes up not really sure about himself, not really sure whether or not he's feeling fulfilled doing what he's doing. I think that would be a very difficult way to live. I'm not used to it. I had been thinking for a number of years with Norman that it was just around the corner, that he would turn the corner and he would be happy, content, fulfilled. I think I've just recently come to the realization that his personality is such that he will always be seeking, he'll always be looking around the corner. Actually Norman, in many ways, provides a good balance for me; he's thoughtful when I tend to be impetuous, thinks of the good in people when I sometimes am petty. He's been an awfully warm and supportive friend.

But he did come back from his motorcycle trip deciding that he really wanted to be a lawyer, and ended up, after getting D's and F's the first year, getting only A's and B's for the rest of law school.

I basically didn't really excel in law school. I never cared that much about going to law school. What I cared more about was learning how to be a lawyer, and Davis has really good clinical programs. You could take twenty units of clinical programs to get yourself out of the law school, which was quite a bit at the time. I took every unit that I could. I worked in a Vacaville Prison project, and I worked for a while as a district attorney's assistant in Yolo County. I worked for a lawyer in Davis. I did whatever I could to get the practical skills.

I think that law school was a gradual process of me becoming more and more clear about who I was, apart from Norman. Law school was a really enriching experience in a lot of ways, and one of the ways was sensing my own strength as a person. I was feeling pretty good about myself. However, I still was feeling, I think, that I had to have a man. I had to have Norman in order for me to feel complete.

When I got out of law school, I became a public defender in Sacramento. The assistant public defender told me they had had a bad experience with the woman before me, and they weren't interested in hiring other women. Looking back at it, I'm real surprised how blatantly they were discriminating against women at the time, which was '72 and '73. We formed the first women's caucus at the law school. There were about 10 women in my class of 140 or so. Now it's half and half, at least.

I got my job in the public defender's office by the same way I've gotten a number of other jobs, which has been through persistence. I am probably the most persistent person on the face of the earth if there's something that I really want to do. I have always been very lucky, or not necessarily lucky. In some ways I feel that we all kind of create our own opportunities. My feeling is always that if you *really* want something, and if you really excel at something, there is always room for people who are good at a particular endeavor.

I never really worried about either getting jobs or doing what I wanted to do. I think I owe a lot to my parents, who kind of imbued me with the idea that I could do anything I want, and I never felt from either of them that there were things I could only do because I was a girl. I think my father wouldn't have treated me any different if I were his son. As a result, I didn't grow up with a lot of these preconceived notions about what a woman's job was or what a man's job was that a lot of people did.

My first jury trial was a petty theft, and I won. I was going to make sure that in the public defender's office—how should I say?—that they weren't going to have another bad experience with a woman and they weren't going to say, "Oh, she's okay, but she won't do this kind of case or that kind of case," or "What do you expect of a woman?" So I always did my share and more of the lousy cases.

When I got into the felony section, I think that they intentionally used to give me a lot of the child molestations and 288s, which is forced oral copulation, and that kind of stuff, because my supervisor wanted to load down the women and validate his opinion that women couldn't hack it. Myself and another woman were the first women who had gotten into that felony-trial section. The other woman couldn't handle it, basically. She left and joined the Foreign Service. We did everything. Rapes, arsons, fetus murder. That was real interesting.

A man was charged with stomping on his wife's stomach, causing her to abort. I was the public defender at the time. There was some question as to whether or not the person was really guilty, whether it was him or somebody else, who was a lover of the victim, who actually had done the deed. He ended up pleading no contest to assault with a deadly weapon—his foot—as a misdemeanor. He had spent ninety days in jail and got out that day.

It was particularly interesting because he insisted that he was not guilty, and I always have felt badly about that. See, when you're a public defender or a defense attorney, a lot of times you have to make a judgment whether or not it's worthwhile taking the risk to go to trial. Here's a person that was going to go to trial for second-degree murder or manslaughter. And I had to make a judgment. He could get out that day or he could take a chance and go to trial and possibly end up in prison. He was vehement that it wasn't him. It was one of the only times I've really, really twisted somebody's arm to plead no contest or guilty because I didn't want to take the chance of losing that case and having him go to prison for a substantial time.

I was a public defender for three years. Then I was hired by Dr. Jerry Lackner, Cesar Chavez's physician, the new director of the California Department of Health. Governor Brown had put him in charge of 23,000 employees in the Department of Health and he had this idea that he was going to establish a patients' rights office in the director's office of the Department of Health in Sacramento. I was put in charge of enforcing the rights of patients in any licensed facility, which included state hospitals, nursing homes, board-and-care homes. There was a whole group of us that he included from the outside who really didn't have any long-term vested interest in state service.

Since I was only going to be there for a short period of time, I and the fellow I hired decided we wanted to focus the public's attention on conditions in the state hospitals for the mentally ill—as opposed to the developmentally disabled, or "retarded," as they are commonly known. Generally the conditions for acute care, people that come in just for short stays, mentally ill people, are very, very bad. We tried to think of a way that we could focus public attention on what was wrong.

Every day we would get what are called "special-incident reports." If any facility within the state has anything unusual happen, you have to write out these special-incident reports. They would generate maybe thirty or forty a day. We started reading them and would come across, occasionally, deaths that occurred in the state hospitals that seemed kind of suspicious. What we would do is we would show up at a hospital at two o'clock in the morning. Generally we would walk into the pharmacy—that would be the first place—and grab stuff off the shelves. It was supposed to be controlled substances in the pharmacy, but they were not properly monitoring anything. We wanted to demonstrate how lax the procedures were.

So we took a whole bunch of stuff and walked into the director's office and put all this stuff on the desk. Then we'd walk into the file room and start taking people's files out, and put the files upon the desk. By this time they were starting to say, "Who are these people?" We'd show our identification from Sacramento, and would walk on into the wards, usually where they had the mentally ill. They had restraint and seclusion rooms where people would be taken off the wards and put into these small rooms and tied with restraints. Acutely psychotic people are supposed to be checked every fifteen minutes—all sorts of things can go wrong. They get themselves twisted so they end up suffocating. They need to eat; they need to go to the bathroom—all these different things.

Some of the people who work in these hospitals, especially during the nighttime, don't want to check these people at fifteen-minute intervals, so what they do is write up the charts as though they had been checked all night long. So if you catch the chart at one or two in the morning, it's been marked up until six o'clock in the morning, when the next shift comes on. So we would go and look who's in what room and grab the charts that had been already marked up, and go to the director's office. By that time the director had already been told we were there and we would say, "Look, this is what's going on in your hospital," and basically just stir things up. It was a wonderful, heady kind of experience.

What we decided to do was request inquests on the deaths of our own patients, where we felt that the death was suspicious, which was a fairly unusual thing to do because generally the state Department of Health always wants to make themselves look as good as possible.

There were three inquests in a row on the deaths of patients that occurred at Metropolitan State Hospital, and the juries all came back "Death at the hands of another." By the time of the third inquest, there was all sorts of media coverage. Then we initiated this invesigation into deaths of patients in the state hospitals. We had all the deaths that occurred over a five-year period investigated. We had teams of investigators going to all the different hospitals. They found numerous, numerous suspicious deaths and problems. For a period of time, there was really something happening, at least in the state-hospital system. Unfortunately it didn't last because there was a change of administration. Jerry Lackner was gone and the new person wasn't as interested in patients' rights.

I feel that I had some impact there for a while. Then I left and went into private practice in Sacramento. Most of the time that I was in private practice, I represented this one client by the name of Alfred Sosa—one of the defendants in the Delia murder case. The preliminary hearing alone lasted about a year. Michael Delia was the director of the Get Going Project, which is a halfway house for ex-cons in Los Angeles. His wife, Ellen Delia, was going up to Sacramento, supposedly to inform state legislators about the fact that money that was given to these halfway houses was being diverted and used by prison gangs to finance prison gang activities. She was picked up at the airport in Sacramento and executed. My client, supposedly the hit man for the Mexican mafia, was charged with killing her. It was a very complicated case because her killing was supposed to be just one killing in a kind of cleaning-house month for the Mexican mafia in which there were probably seven or eight killings up and down the state.

During the preliminary hearing we were able to establish that the police officers who originally arrested my client had falsified a police report related to the vehicle stop. The police that made the stop wrote that my client made an illegal left turn in front of their patrol car and that's why they stopped the car. We were able to show, and convince the judge, that in fact they were deliberately following this car. The stop was made as my client's car was turning into Michael Delia's driveway. The two officers that made the stop claim that they didn't know that that was Michael Delia's house, that it was all totally coincidental. We were able to show that, in fact, they were out that night specifically looking for Michael Delia, that one of the officers was actually Michael Delia's cousin, that they had received a teletype from Sacramento asking for help in locating Michael Delia, and that that's exactly what they were doing.

Everything that occurred as a result of the vehicle stop was suppressed—thrown out. There was a gun in the car, and the gun ended up being suppressed. There was a person in the car with my client, and the person ended up turning state's evidence. His statement was suppressed because he would not have been arrested had it not been for the illegal vehicle stop.

One of the things that has disturbed me most about my whole career is what happened to two officers who were at the Monterey Park police station the night that this occurred. They came up to Sacramento and testified that the other two officers *were* really looking for Michael Delia that night, and now those two good officers are no longer on the police force. They were ostracized. They were basically hounded from the force by the chief of police. The bad officers who had falsified the report, nothing ever happened to them in terms of disciplinary actions. The two officers who told the truth, their careers were ruined—and they were good officers. It's really a sad thing. Justice did not prevail in this instance. The two officers with integrity will never recover. The case was still going when I left Sacramento.

We had an organization in Sacramento that I started called Women Advocates, which is a group of women lawyers that used to do things to call people's attention to discrimination against women. The Sacramento Police Department initiated a practice of arresting prostitutes for unlawful assembly. If there was a group of two or three women standing on a street corner, they were all arrested. So our group decided to call people's attention to the fact that we felt it was unlawful to make these arrests.

So a whole group of us stood on street corners one evening, dressed as we perceived prostitutes would dress, and we had men from the public defender's office pick us up in cars and drop us back down. Of course, none of us got arrested for anything, but it created this big hubbub. The man from the Sacramento Police Department in charge of arresting the original, real prostitutes made all sorts of outrageous statements about how our conduct had distracted his police officers from their normal work, and a robbery victim had ended up dying of a heart attack and it was all our fault because his officers were busy checking out the fake prostitutes. Unfortunately, this man is now the police chief of Sacramento. He referred our case to the district attorney's office for prosecution—for impersonating prostitutes. In fact, there was nothing we could be prosecuted for. And all the real prostitutes had all of their cases dropped, so we ended up accomplishing what we had set out to do.

Another action that we took was that we totally disrupted a sexist play that was being given by the Sacramento County Bar Association annual dinner. They did it every year, and every year it was obnoxious and demeaning to women. We had gotten hold of the script prior to the play and we made cue cards that said "GROAN," "HISS." There were maybe five hundred people in the audience, and we got up and down the aisles with our cue cards, and whenever it got to a particularly sexist comment, we held a sign saying "HISS," and the audience thought we were part of the play. The people in the play were all confused because there were all these sounds coming from the audience. After a while, people started shouting and just created a big problem. At the end of the play, the sign said "VOMIT" and everybody went "Blaaahhh!"

It was while I was in private practice in Sacramento, in 1978, that Julia was born. It was right when I got the Delia murder case. About three weeks before she was due some friends of ours arranged to have a brunch, like a shower for us, and a number of our friends came up from San Francisco. The night before the brunch, everybody gathered and we all went out together and I had a huge dinner—prime rib, chocolate cheesecake, baked potato. And I made jokes with one good friend named David that I wanted him to cut Julia's umbilical cord. We knew he was real, real squeamish. And he said, "Oh, no, I couldn't possibly do that. And it's going to be too difficult for me to get to the hospital from San Francisco." So that night when I said goodnight to everybody, I turned to David and said, "You know what? I think I'll just have Julia tonight, since you're here anyway."

I woke up at six in the morning, after having a good night's sleep, with labor pains. I thought it was just gas because I'd eaten so much the night before! And it wasn't consistent with what we had learned in these classes about the first part of labor. You are supposed to have about twelve hours at home first. So I didn't tell Norman right away. But these were really kind of incapacitating pains. Finally we called the doctor and she said, "You probably should come down to the hospital."

Well, Norman drove to the hospital and—I don't think I'm as bad as I used to be, but I don't like to spend money unnecessarily on things—so I didn't want to pay for parking at the parking lot. I, of course, didn't want to go to the emergency entrance because that would be too weak and it was too early in my labor. So I made Norman park the car a good distance away and started walking. I got about to the middle of the parking lot and I said to Norman, "I just can't walk anymore." And he said, "You insisted! You walk! I can't carry you at this point!"

So I continued walking, and we came up the back elevator and ended up in the maternity ward, and I said, "Excuse me," but I think I'm pretty close to having this baby." And I had the baby about half an hour or an hour after I got there. Norman called David and he made it down to cut the umbilical cord. The brunch was set for eleven and Julia was born at ten-thirty, so everybody came down to the hospital. I felt great because I'd had a good night's sleep and hadn't had any drugs. So we moved all the food down to the hospital and had a big party. I went back to work when Julia was nine days old. Now, seven years later, I'm pregnant again.

My dad died of Parkinson's disease on January 1, 1980. He had it for several years. It was really terrible because my mom cared for him all the years before he died. My mom was totally drained by the whole experience. Norman and I started thinking that maybe we should move back to Los Angeles. Norman didn't want to be a criminal-defense lawyer anymore. He'd always been interested in business and finance, so he went back to school and got an advanced law degree in tax. When he got done, we had to make a decision. If he started a practice in Sacramento, it was like we would be there forever. So we decided it's now or never. Our reason for leaving Los Angeles didn't seem compelling anymore: to establish ourselves as independent people. We had a child, and parents who were old, and my dad had just died and my mom was really lonely. Norman's dad was in his late seventies. If we came down here, it would be nice for them to spend time with their grandchild. So we packed up and moved.

When we came down here, I wanted to get involved in some kind of criminal law. Gerry Chaliff had just been appointed a couple of months before to the Hillside Strangler case, in which Angelo Buono was charged with killing ten women, and someone I knew said, "You should contact Chaliff because he needs to have another attorney on the case." So I did, and insisted, of course, that I would be the best person. I ended up being appointed also, and did it full-time for three and a half years. The trial was two years—the longest criminal trial in history, supposedly. I'm still recovering.

My potential client, Angelo Buono, wanted to have time to check me out. Well, people in prisons have a network, so Angelo Buono sent a message to somebody who was an associate of Alfie Sosa's, asking what Katherine Mader was like. The message came back "She's okay," and I was on the case.

I think there has never been a multiple-murder case where there has been an acquittal. In our case we had a lot going for us in terms of the evidence not being as strong as a lot of other mass-murder cases. There really were some legitimate questions in my mind and the minds of others as to Mr. Buono's guilt. I think there is also a tendency when you're going to work as long as I did on a case to be overly optimistic or to see things a little brighter than they really are. Possibly, I talked myself into being optimistic in order to do the case, and also to not confront the fact that my client could have possibly committed these kinds of crimes—because this case was really different in my book than representing persons charged with rape or a murder in the heat of passion. These were really sadistic, calculated, horrible acts. We're talking about women that are picked up on the street using the ruse that they're being taken to a police department, when in fact they were supposedly taken to my client's home and blindfolded, gagged, raped, sodomized in some cases, tortured with electrical cords, gas inhalation, injections of cleaning fluid, and then strangled and their bodies just thrown by the wayside.

I think there is a tendency in that type of a situation for me, sitting next to Mr. Buono, to not believe that he could possibly be capable of this kind of act. I also made a particular effort throughout the trial to do what is normally done by criminal-defense attorneys, which is to humanize the client—to talk with him and put my hand on his arm and whisper and laugh and try to look as though I enjoyed his company and I wasn't afraid of him. If I'm going to sit next to him and appear to be frightened of him, what is the jury going to think? However, the fact that I was a woman and "touched" Mr. Buono was something that made the prosecution furious because they thought I was faking friendliness, which they couldn't counter. At the trial, there was one beefy, alcoholic, and unethical cop who invented vulgar stories about my supposed attraction to mass murderers. The press also continuously focused on my "relationship" with Mr. Buono—for example, asking, "How does it feel to touch him?" when they wouldn't have mentioned it if I was a man trying to humanize my client. Much criticism of me also was made about the fact that I wore "feminine," flouncy dresses and smiled a lot. It's a difficult criticism to counter. I am who I am. I know inside me that Mr. Buono had a great defense and I feel good about it. I think, despite the fact that we lost, we really did a good job representing him. There were times in the case where I could have laid back, when it was very uncomfortable for me to persist in a particular line of questioning. There was a very uncomfortable period of months where I could have let a situation go where I felt the sheriff's department had hidden some important evidence, that an eyewitness was located in a mental hospital. It really wouldn't have made that much difference to the end result of the case, but I felt that if I saw something that was wrong, then it was my responsibility to persist until it was righted.

I don't find it to be a problem defending people that I know are guilty. What I believe in very strongly is the process by which a person cannot be found guilty until it can be shown beyond a reasonable doubt that the evidence is there. If we lessen that standard because the defense attorneys feel that some clients are more deserving than other clients, then it really destroys the whole system of justice that we have in this country. I haven't seen that many situations wherein I've gotten off a person who really should not be out on the streets. It has happened on occasion, but I've represented hundreds of people, and that is the price to pay for living with the kind of justice system we have.

The first year or so after my dad died, my mom was really, really depressed and was just beginning to come out of it and, for the first time in her life, to have women friends. She always thought that associating with women was boring. She never found any women that she could enjoy, and then she developed a whole group of women friends. She went on a trip, camping across Africa, across the Sahara Desert, and it was shortly after that that she noticed her hands didn't have much color in them. Kind of yellow—not pink. They did a bunch of tests and told her she had myelofibrosis, a bone-marrow disease, a hardening of the bone marrow, when the blood stops producing red cells. There's no cure for it. There's basically nothing that can be done for it. In six months she died.

It's really strange not having any parents. Being an only child, I don't have any close relatives either. Just an aunt in Vienna, a cousin in Switzerland, some second cousins I don't see very often. I thought that having a mother, or having parents, kept me kind of stable, that I was a good person, an honest person, because if I wasn't, my mother would be angry at me. It was a very strange feeling after my mother died, realizing I had no controls on me, and realizing I was the exact same person I was before my mother died, and I must have been that same person for quite a while. But I didn't realize that, that I had grown up.

After my dad died, my mom wanted someone to live in the house to keep her company, so she found Chao Di. My mother thought like this: Who would be the most honest person to have live in my house? Someone from mainland China, because they don't know crime in mainland China. Someone at UCLA recommended Chao Di, an architecture student who had just arrived in this country a week before. He spoke no English whatsoever. Yet he took all of his classes at UCLA in English and at the end of the year ended up with the highest grades and got a scholarship. Mind-boggling. He sings opera and was the captain of the University of Shanghai basketball team—just an exceptional person.

Chao Di became a part of our family when he took care of my mother after she became ill, and I told my mother that I would always make sure that Chao Di was taken care of. After my mother died, and we moved into the family house, we absorbed him as part of the family. I really feel that he is part of our family.

I have the luxury right now of having inherited from my parents a house that's paid for and having some income coming in. I don't have the pressures that a lot of people have in which they say, "I can't really do this or that because it will antagonize my boss." I'm fully aware of the fact that I can afford to be outspoken, and I can afford to be persistent about a lot of what I believe in because there's very little that can threaten me in terms of financial security—although I wasn't really any different when I didn't have the house or didn't have some money.

I think I've mellowed out a lot the last few years, which is probably characteristic of our generation. When I first became a lawyer, first became a public defender, I was really adamant about how the system oppressed criminal defendants, and I used to be very shrill in the area of women's rights. I'm not like that anymore. I'm much more accepting of other positions that are different than my own. There was a period of time when I could only have been a criminal-defense attorney, and now to me it really doesn't matter at all. I'd be just as comfortable as a prosecutor. I used to view with disdain any woman who chose not to have a career, and now I'm totally accepting of the fact that everybody is different and everybody has to do what's comfortable for them. I wouldn't ever presume to put my values on another person—where I would have years ago.

I do feel that one of the most important things that any of us can do is to take a stand when you see something wrong and to try to correct it in any way you can, and to never give up. I feel that as individuals we each *can* really make a difference, in a lot of different areas, if we devote the energy and enthusiasm and persistence to correcting things that we believe to be wrong, and not be afraid of the consequences.

Kathy Mader and I continued to see each other regularly after the interview was finished, and I was amazed by what an active life she led. In the year that followed, Kathy sold her house, gave birth to a son named David Paul, co-authored a book about noteworthy crimes in Los Angeles history, and began working as a prosecutor for the Los Angeles County District Attorney's Office.

THE SINGER:

Marty Kaniger

One of my clearest memories of high school actually occurred after hours. It was Wednesday night, November 27, 1963, and the annual Palisades High School "Hootenanny Holiday" was being held in the school gym. After numerous acts, including a flamenco guitarist, the Burgundians performing "La Bomba" and "Freedom Calling," and headliner Randy Boone (the following year's headliner was a local singer named John Denver), it came Marty Kaniger's turn to perform. His entrance onstage, with his guitar, provoked laughter and jeering from the large group of seniors behind whom I was sitting. Their comments about Marty's thinness and his pompadour hairdo were crude and insensitive. Although Marty was only a casual friend, I began rooting for him wildly, but silently.

Marty's first song was "Passing Through," about Jesus, George Washington, and other men who devoted their brief stays on Earth to making a better world. The moving lyrics reminded us that, less than a week earlier, the nation had lost another leader. At the end, Marty added a verse of his own about John Kennedy. When Marty finished, the audience burst into applause. He performed one more song and left the stage. Brought back by shouts of "More" and "Encore," he confessed that he had no encore. Never in my life had I witnessed a student's public image change so quickly. From jeers to standing ovation, Marty had gone from wimp to hero in five minutes.

More than twenty years later, I sat across a table from Marty Kaniger. Ironically, although his appearance had gone through many changes over the years, his current mode of employment had led him once again to wear his hair in a pompadour. I asked Marty if he remembered the 1963 hootenanny as vividly as I did.

Oh, yes. That hootenanny was a major turning point in my life. Actually, up until that time I had never, ever sung in front of people. I used to lock myself in my room alone. Sometimes I'd let my sister, who was five years old, listen to me. But if I thought someone was walking by the door I used to stop playing.

When I heard about the auditions, I just decided that was it. It was very unlike me to jump into something like that. I don't remember one second of being onstage at the hootenanny, I was so scared. My mouth and my hands were going, but my brain was numb.

I was shocked by the response I got. It was tremendous. I used to look at the jocks and the guys who were better scholastically, but there was nothing that made Marty Kaniger memorable. Now, all of a sudden, people were coming up to me who had never had anything to do with me before. I had found something *I* could do. It put me on the map.

Before that, my main enjoyment in school was pulling off practical jokes with my friends. Like the Cow Eye Caper. We stole a cow eye from physiology class. In the cafeteria at lunch they served a sort of pudding, like a blob of whipped cream and a cherry in the middle. So we got one of those cow eyes, put it in a round plastic dessert dish, and slipped it in among the puddings. I seem to remember a girl grabbing it, putting it on her tray, and then screaming, dumping the whole tray on the floor.

I also remember what we did to Dr. Opitz, the German teacher, poor lady. She was . . . odd. Every period, every day, she would count the desks in her room before the class came in and then again after the class left. I guess she was paranoid that someone would steal a desk. So one day we got a bunch of people to walk in front of her, and Mike Kaliger and I picked up the last desk in the last row and took it outside and around the corner. About three minutes later, we saw her come huffing and puffing out of the classroom, down the stairs and down to the office. As soon as she was gone we put the desk back in the class. She came back with the boys' vice-principal and a couple others and, lo and behold, the missing desk was still there.

Actually, the best practical joke was one at my expense. Dr. Aigner, the principal, was so bad at reading the PA announcements. He never looked at the sheets before he started reading. We thought if we worded something serious enough, he'd read it before he realized what it was. So we got hold of a stack of PA-announcement sheets and decided to compose an announcement for a Senior Class Garbage Fight. Two of my friends, Mike and Art, said, "We'll take it home and write it. It'll be great; you'll see."

The next day, second period, I was sitting in Contemporary American Problems class listening to Dr. Aigner read the daily announcements and all of a sudden it came on. I still remember the text: "I would like to congratulate Marty Kaniger, this year's recipient of the George F. Weenie Memorial Scholarship. This scholarship is given to one student each year for high scholastic average and outstanding athletic ability." Mind you, at the time I was about five foot eight and weighed just over a hundred pounds. I was also on the verge of failing Contemporary American Problems. The class happened to be full of football players and they all turned around and looked at me with the most incredible looks on their faces. I turned bright red. I was throbbing. The teacher was absolutely flabbergasted. But he did come over and shake my hand and congratulate me. Once I recovered from the embarrassment, I just smiled and thanked everybody.

Anyway, the hootenanny convinced me to get seriously involved with music. I began thinking about a musical career. So four of us formed a band called the Spectres and played Beatles songs. Really terrible. None of us could play lead guitar, so whenever we performed we told everyone that our lead guitarist was sick and didn't show up. It was terrible, but it was fun. The standards weren't that high back then. Then one of the guys, Bob Linden, said, "Listen, let's form a real band." So we started jamming with some better musicians. At first we called ourselves the Executioners. After about two weeks, we realized that wasn't going to sell, so we changed to the Voyagers and then the Loved Ones.

Eventually we got hired to play the senior prom. Actually we got to play while the main band took fifteen-minute breaks. It took us five minutes to set up and five minutes to break down, which gave us maybe five minutes to play. We were there because a lot of people wanted a rock band and the other band just played standards. We lost money. I think we got paid twenty-five to thirty dollars total and we had to go rent tuxes which cost us that much each. I couldn't find anything to fit me. I looked like the hanger in somebody's tuxedo.

When I was fourteen I developed ileitis, an inflammatory condition of the ileum, part of the small intestine. I still have it, although I haven't been hospitalized since 1974. Back in high school, between lunch and going home, I was in pain all the time. Always after lunch. Come to think of it, maybe it was the food in the cafeteria. I don't know. Anyway, it did get me out of the draft. At my draft physical, when I gave the doctor my medical records he said, "Please, no. When the Chinese land we'll give you a call."

After graduation I went to Santa Monica City College. Anthropology major. What was real exciting to me was to go and buy the books and start the class. The first time a term project or something came up, I used to stop going. One day I couldn't find a parking space and I dropped out.

By this time the band was sort of breaking up, getting down to just Dan Peyton and myself. The girl that I was going out with was working in a record store in Beverly Hills. The bookkeeper there was married to a record producer. So we went to his house to play for him and he liked us and he introduced us to some people at Screen Gems. One of them was Lester Sill, who was the president of Screen Gems Columbia Music. At that time you could walk in with your guitar and play for somebody instead of having to go to a studio and cut a sixteen-track demo or master. We found out that Lester liked us but hated the guy who had introduced us, and that that was stopping him from following through on a contract.

Dan and I went down to try to catch Lester in his office. It was one of these real typical show-business things: We couldn't get into his office. So we got into the elevator and rode it up and down with the light off so that when the doors closed it would suddenly be dark. When Lester finally got in and the door closed, he realized that there were two people in there with him. Later he told us that he thought he was going to get mugged or killed. When we turned the light on and said, "It's us," he was so relieved he brought us back up to the office and we got our first recording contract. Promise not to kill 'em and they'll sign anything.

So Dan and I were writing songs and recording—with friends and studio musicians. We recorded four or five singles. Soft rock. We always did well in the Midwest. Kansas City played the hell out of our records. We never had any real hits, but it did lead to our first album— a soundtrack album.

It seemed like at that point everything was getting screwed up. Nothing was going right. We were over at RCA studio mixing down something when we got a call from one of the people at the Screen Gems publishing department. I remember he said, "How would you like to do a soundtrack for a movie? . . . The name of the film is *Getting Straight.*" So the title was a turnoff right away. But as soon as he told us Elliott Gould was in it, we went over there immediately. I think it was right after *M*A*S*H.* It was Elliott Gould's year.

We went over there and it turns out the reason we got it was because nobody else wanted it. They already had a melody for a title song and all the big writers hated it and wanted to write the song from scratch. It was a terrible melody. Some kind of schmaltzy Czechoslovakian love song or something. Just awful. But we said, "What the hell. We don't care. We're not proud." So we wrote the title song. Turned it into a sort of Simon and Garfunkel–type tune. Drastically rewrote even the melody. We went into the studio and spent about a week recording.

So we got the soundtrack album—most of it was our music. It didn't sell very much and we didn't make much money, but I'll never forget sitting in the theater when *Getting Straight* first played. Seeing the huge Columbia lady with the light coming from her torch, and the first thing I heard was my guitar, my twelve-string guitar. Dan and I were sitting there grinning from ear to ear. I could even see my name on the screen if I looked fast enough. That was wonderful.

Right after, Dan and I were signed as staff writers for Screen Gems. We wrote a song for *The Partridge Family* that was used on their show. Then we wrote six songs for Bobby Sherman's TV show. Even though the show was dropped quickly, we seemed to be on a roll. We wrote for Screen Gems for a year or two, but nothing happened with our songs. Nothing. So we got out of the contract.

At that point I wanted to start performing again. I missed it. But Dan wasn't interested. I decided to start performing as a single, which I hadn't done since high school. It was strange, but I got to like it real quick.

The first job I got was at Regular Jon's pizza parlor. Immediately it started to work. People were coming in later. The place was getting a late-night crowd. So the owner built a stage and I put in a PA system and I was there three and a half years. Most of that time I worked five nights a week. I was doing things that were popular on the radio and sneaking in some of my own stuff. Some nights were great. It was fun, lots of energy there. But then some nights you'd get a strange combination of people. It was right near the Veterans Administration home, so you got a lot of old blowouts from the VA sitting in there. They'd be on medication, tranquilizers. Then they'd come out and start drinking beer. They'd take a bottle of scotch out of their pocket and pour that into the beer. And a lot of the jocks from UCLA would come in and drink beer until it was coming out of their ears. Sometimes it was impossible. And I didn't have that ace in the hole where I could get through to these people. In fact, I needed something.

Well, a friend of mine, a girl that I'd met at Regular Jon's, used to love to come over and sit in and play together. She was a hostess at a local restaurant.

She came in one night and asked if she could sit in. I said, "Hey, if you want to kill yourself. Nobody is listening tonight." It was one of those VA-drunks-and-jocks nights. But she got up anyway and sang a song I had never heard before called "Why Don't We Get Drunk and Screw?" The drunks sobered up and started listening to her and the jocks shut up—she had them. Then she went on and did her regular, straight stuff, mostly country. But she had them.

I said, "Where did you get that song?" I found out it was a Jimmy Buffett song. So I ran out and bought the album, learned the song, and when people weren't paying attention, I found that if you threw a dirty song at them, they listened. I started writing some songs of my own and that began Marty's brief blue period. That was in 1975, living in Malibu at the time. By the way, an historical footnote: The girlfriend who sang the song and inspired me to write dirty songs was Patti Reagan. Daddy at that time was *only* the governor of California. A lesser job.

Anyway, I wrote these songs. Like "Peaches and Cream in My Jeans, I Had a Wet One Over You." That was good. Or the sadomasochistic love song "I'd Like to Do You In for What You've Done to Me." But the big one, the one that's gotten around the most, was the very first dirty song that I wrote: "It's So Hard to Say I Love You When You're Sitting on My Face." That's been a big song for me.

> It's so hard to say I love you when
> you're sitting on my face.
> I could tell you what I'm thinking
> of you if you'd just sit some other place.
> For just a moment, just a breath
> of air, just a little change of pace.
> 'Cause it's so hard to say I love you when
> you're sitting on my face.

That's just the first verse. It's never been recorded, although I've heard that there's been some unauthorized recordings. I gave the song to a lot of bands and it's gotten around. Somebody heard it being sung in a bar in Australia. When I wrote the song, I started performing it and it worked. It was a winner. I took it down to a friend of mine who was working for a publishing company that was part of the CBS group. Marv is real emotional and if you tell him you've written a tearjerker, he'll start crying before you even play it. So I called him up and said, "Marv, I've done it. I've written a love song. I think this is it." I really built it up. I went down there and he loved it. Everybody from all the offices came in and started listening. I assigned the song to that publishing company and I would say that it's the most almost-recorded song in my history. All I've made from it is three or five hundred bucks, something like that. But it's been a good song.

So I was singing these songs at Regular Jon's and they were very popular. Also a few drug songs. I like to sing songs that make people cry and then songs to make people laugh, and songs that shock people. It's fun. It breaks up the evening. But after a while it was actually kind of bad because I think that's what people were coming in to hear instead of my regular songs.

Eventually I started playing other places as well, including about a year and a half at Monty's, a fancy restaurant in Westwood. But then I became burned out playing bars. I don't drink and it was just getting real depressing. These were nice places, but people want to buy you drinks. If you don't drink, it's very intimidating to drinkers. They get real upset. I'd tell them, "Since I started shooting heroin, I don't drink at all." But some of them were just too drunk to know that I was joking.

Then I went up to Sun Valley, Idaho, for a while. A very nice little break, playing during the summer. But it's very, very dry up there and if you're not a drinker . . . I got a real bad cough that lasted for months, almost like a dry pneumonia. You know, when you're on the road and you get sick, there's nothing you can do; you just have to sing anyway. When I got back my voice was blown out, just a wreck. I did someplace down in Newport Beach for three months which totaled it. At that point I asked myself, "How much do I really want to do this?"

I started doing other jobs. Like a friend of mine owned a flower shop, a job where I didn't have to think, just do it. And when I got finished I could walk away and not even think about it. So I was driving the delivery truck, which was fine, for a few months. Then I started working with my father in the textile business as a salesman. That lasted about three years, I guess. Nothing wrong with that kind of work, except it's not me. It was torture.

Meanwhile I got into merchandising. You see, I had a dog named Elliot. He had a knack for getting multiple tennis balls in his mouth. Started out with two, one on top of the other, and that was his thing. A friend of mine took a couple of pictures of him and it looked like there was a lot of extra cheek. Got two more balls and he had four in his mouth. I thought about those photos for a couple of years, thinking, "There's money to be made here." I finally contacted a photographer up in Malibu. I took the dog out there and we did a photo session for about an hour and a half and got some great shots. Tennis balls, racket balls, tennis hat, sunglasses on, all kinds of things.

Then I contacted some people in the music business and they turned me on to a merchandising company that handled rock groups. This was their first animal—besides some of the rock stars. We got buttons, posters, transfers for T-shirts. All with pictures of Elliot and the captions YOU'VE GOTTA HAVE BALLS and TENNIS ANYONE? I was living with my parents at the time. Still do. And Elliot the dog became the star of the family. We had a contract to do a calendar with him—a different sport for each month. But then he died.

It may seem silly to some, but when Elliot died it was probably the lowest point in my life. From 1969 to 1979 the dog was always by my side. No matter what else was going wrong, that was a stabilizing influence. I mean, we had to go through a whole list of people and call them and tell them that he had died. He had more friends than I did. It was nice having all those pictures of him. People wearing him on their shirts and hanging them in their houses. It was an opportunity to share the dog with people around the world. They're still enjoying him.

I got back into the music business kind of by accident. I decided to go see Lester Sill, who was still the president of the Screen Gems publishing group. Just to visit and give him some Elliot buttons. We talked about how close we came to really getting off the ground. It was nice to think that someone in that position still believed in me—then there's no reason why I couldn't believe in myself.

I started to write songs again and playing with other musicians. We recorded "It's So Hard to Say I Love You . . ." but we didn't release it. An old friend from Palisades High School, Bob Wayne, had a recording studio. Rhino Records was doing a lot of work in Bob's studio and one of the owners of the record company had always wanted to do an album of contemporary hits done '50s doo-wop style. Back when I was at Regular Jon's, Bob and I used to get together with a bunch of friends, dress up, and do oldies. We called ourselves Big Daddy. So in 1983 we revived Big Daddy and put together an album for Rhino Records.

We took contemporary hits and rearranged them. For example, "You Don't Bring Me Flowers," the Barbra Streisand/Neil Diamond hit, we did in the general style of the Coasters, up tempo. "Super Freak," the ultimate in funk, we did an Everly Brothers treatment on that. "Hotel California" we did the way Del Shannon might have done it. For the album we had to think of a good reason why we do everything in the style of the '50s. The reason was that in 1959 we were an up-and-coming group whose manager booked them on a USO tour of Southeast Asia, hoping for publicity, and not realizing that there wouldn't be any publicity because our military presence was limited to "advisers." So we went and played for the advisers. Became lost in the jungle, captured by Laotian revolutionaries, and held for twenty-four years. Then we were rescued by the CIA and brought back here. So that the culture shock wouldn't be too severe, they didn't play us any contemporary music, but they did give us lots of sheet music. Naturally we didn't know how the arrangements went, but in our minds and souls we were still back in 1959, where time stopped for us. So everything we did came out the way we thought it should be done circa 1959.

I had had a beard for twelve years, but I shaved it for the album cover. I mean, in the '50s who had a beard? Rabbis, yes, but . . . When I first shaved, it scared the hell out of me. The first couple of days I could *feel* people walk by. My parents thought it was hysterical. But, you know, parents don't care if you're bad or good; they love you anyway. My mother keeps pinching my cheek.

When the album came out, it got rave reviews. John Tobler of *Music* magazine in England said it might be the best album of 1983. The Mainichi *Daily News* of Japan gave it a tremendous review. *People* magazine went through the premise and described some of the songs, which is important in any review of the album. They called it "both musical and funny, a perfect album for a surprising change of pace at a party."

We did the album as a lark, a one-shot, but there was some magic with all the people involved. Just the right combination. So since the album we've been playing clubs here in Los Angeles and it's been great. We keep the story about our captivity going through the show. We played Harrah's in Reno, which was a real high point. It didn't really hit home until we got into Reno and saw the marquee. BIG

DADDY on a marquee two or three stories high. Across the street, on the other marquee, was the SMOTHERS BROTHERS, who were a big influence on me. It was wonderful. I hope they didn't feel bad about that.

Club owners on the whole don't treat musicians very well. They take them for granted. We have a lot of dressing and makeup and hair stuff to do. Some fancy clothes. There are some places where we've been getting dressed in greasy kitchens and bathrooms. At Harrah's we had three dressing-room suites, color TV, soft drinks, and coffee and tea and beer and room service. A lot of places actually make you pay for your own parking. Not like Harrah's.

In February of 1985, our British record company flew us to England to promote a single, "I Write the Songs," in the style of "At the Hop" by Danny and the Juniors. They asked us to bring over something new to add as a bonus cut on the album, and we chose Bruce Springsteen's "Dancing in the Dark." Our version is reminiscent of Pat Boone's "Moody River." It's actually a very pretty song that stands on its own. At that time, Springsteen's video had just come out, and the song was back in the top ten. So we performed our version on British television and it was a hit. We went up to number 21 on the charts.

If you do one or two television shows in England, everyone recognizes you. It's like instant stardom. We played some clubs and they were packed. People reaching for the stage and grabbing. It was scary. It was also wonderful. Of course, anyone from America has got to be a star anyway.

Performing has its fringe benefits. I don't like to call them groupies. They're friends, actually. Sexual friends. Friends are people to share things with. However, I have been going out exclusively with one person for the last couple years. Vicki and I had already been friends for almost ten years when we got together, which makes it easy and comfortable.

To perform well there's a fine line. You've got to be up, the adrenaline has to be going, but you've got to be within your senses and relaxed to a certain extent, too. Once I tried to perform on cocaine. It didn't work. First of all, I didn't sing well. It affected my nose and throat right away. And my hand on my guitar. I was pressing so hard and my muscles were so tensed up that it stuck in that position, cramped up. I had to peel my fingers off the neck of the guitar. Natural adrenaline is enough for me. I get real up. You've got to be physically up and mentally up. You have to have your senses about you and think about what's going on, and part of your mind has to be on a dozen different things: the equipment, the audience, who's standing behind you when you take a step back, should we cut a song short, what song comes next—a million things. I used to want to be a star, but now I'm happy just to be making a living and having fun.

A couple of weeks after our meeting, I drove to the San Fernando Valley to see Marty and Big Daddy perform at a trendy nightclub called Sasch's, which was not one of their regular clubs. Marty appeared on stage wearing an outrageous oversized white suit, with glitter in his hair. Other members of the eight-man band were dressed as characters of the '50s: a beatnik, an Ivy Leaguer, a tourist in Bermuda shorts.

The audience at Sasch's is not known for its intellectual sophistication, and many of the young men and women seemed confused by Big Daddy's premise. The humor went right over their heads. After one of the band members mockingly described the tastes of Valley kids as "Cool . . . but simple," many of them walked out. However, those who remained seemed to have a great time, responding with particular enthusiasm to a Duane Eddy version of "Star Wars," "Ebony and Ivory" in the style of Little Richard, and Cyndi Lauper's "Girls Just Wanna Have Fun" transformed into a variation of "Duke of Earl." More than two decades after Marty Kaniger's debut at the Palisades High School Hootenanny Holiday, he was still getting calls for encores. This time he was ready.

After the show, I went over to congratulate Marty, but just as I got to him, he was approached by a very attractive young woman who appeared to be barely half his age. I withdrew a couple of steps and watched as she spoke to him softly, smiling seductively all the while. Finally, she held his hand, kissed, rubbed, and squeezed him, and said good-bye. After watching her walk away, Marty raised his eyebrows and let out a deep sigh. Then he turned to me, shook his head, and said, "I love show business."

THE VALEDICTORIAN:

Tom Pierson

Another member of my own high-school class who pursued a career in music was Tom Pierson, the class valedictorian. The valedictorian was the student with the highest grade-point average. In a class of more than five hundred, that meant that there was no room to slip or let up. Tom Pierson just got A's. But Tom wasn't just a scholar. His real forte was the piano. He was the champion at that, too. For all his distinctions, though, Tom was basically an unassuming fellow, gracious, friendly, and without pretension.

When I visited him twenty years later in Santa Monica, Tom was preparing to pack up and move to New York City. He had little interest in talking about high school.

I was hardworking, ambitious to achieve the goal of being a concert pianist. That was what was laid out to me by my parents as a path, a path that I came to desire to take very strongly myself. I played with the Houston Symphony when I was like thirteen or fourteen. "Excitingly prodigious" was my review.

In high school I practiced the piano only three hours or so a day. But I also had the highest grade-point average in the class, so I became valedictorian. I didn't want to give a speech and the school would have let it pass, but my mother went into the principal's office and insisted. So I had one period to write it. It was about individuality.

I applied to Juilliard and Northwestern, where my father had attended graduate school, and auditioned in both places. Never been away from home before. Got on a plane, went to Northwestern, played the piano, went to New York, stayed at the Sloan House YMCA, went up to Juilliard, played my audition, came back, and that was it. I was accepted by Juilliard. I don't recall if I was accepted by Northwestern.

At Juilliard I practiced six to eight hours a day. I loved practicing the repertoire. I had a great deal of difficulty performing and I never had a technique that was competitive with my colleagues'. I gradually became aware that I didn't have the ability to accomplish that goal. I began to write.

When I first arrived in New York, I was terrified of the city. I didn't go out of the space between the room I was staying and the school, about three blocks away, for several months. I was totally square. No eyes, no ears, just going about my business. I later became a victim of crime near Juilliard, which was up on 122nd and Broadway. Mugging. Later—I'm quite proud of this incident—I saw where these ... kids, really, hung out. So I got some friends and we marched uptown and got a cop. The cop wouldn't do anything without me making a citizen's arrest first, but he would come up later.

So I went up to this kid, and he'd been one of three guys, one of whom had held a knife to my throat. He was on a stoop, and I went up and he turned to go in—he didn't remember me, I'm sure—and he turned and I said, "Aren't you the guy that held me up like two or three months ago? Yeah, yeah, it was you." And the cop came up and I said, "Yeah, that's the guy."

We went to court and I testified against the guy, and he went to jail—for the summer. Then he came back, and I walked out of school and there was this guy, Rafael, and some of his friends. I said, "Hi," and just walked. I was scared shitless for about six months, but nothing ever happened.

I got married the summer of 1969, prior to my last year at Juilliard. I met Christine in high school. The first girl I ever dated, I married. So I'm in school and Christine is supporting me working at Bloomingdale's. I also got involved in politics at Juilliard. A friend and I sat in the student lounge for two weeks, passed out teacher-evaluation questionnaires to the students, typed up the results, and sold them for a quarter.

Around Kent State time there was an organizational boycott in school, and I was thrust into prominence. I was chairing this meeting of all the faculty and students of the school to decide some undefined agenda of things which had to be done, which in the opinion of some was to close the school, as Columbia did. We finally passed some resolutions that included some rather subversive notions of how the school itself should be organized.

Then I applied and tested to become a conducting major, having realized that I would not be a pianist. I gave what I felt was a brilliant examination, was applauded by the orchestra. Later found out that the head of the conducting faculty had accepted me, but that the president of the school had intervened, I would imagine because of this prominence in a disruptive proceeding. So I lost my scholarship, but, even more importantly, I wasn't accepted into the conducting program, which was a great blow to me. I felt some satisfaction four or five years later when I was chosen over a Juilliard doctoral graduate to conduct Leonard Bernstein's *Mass* at the Metropolitan Opera.

Like so many others, when I graduated college, I faced the draft. On the advice of an attorney I took my physical in Pittsburgh. I avoided the draft by feigning insanity—specifically, I refused to undress. When I got alone with the chief medical officer, the guy said, "Well, haven't you ever been to a doctor?"

I just said, "I don't take my clothes off in front of a bunch of guys." He said, "If I give you the examination here, will you strip?" And I agreed to it. So then when I stripped, I was wearing frilly pink, women's panties. He was angered, greatly angered. This sergeant came and took me around to the other stops, and they moved me out of there quick. I received a 1-Y classification, and they never called me again. I'm *not* proud of that. The real reason that I didn't want to serve was that I felt that it would hold me back in my career. I'm more impressed by those who went to jail or Canada, rather than those who dodged it. But I'm not saying I would do something different.

So then I'm not at school. Then I'm working as a pianist accompanying ballet, accompanying Broadway shows; I'm working as a musician in Broadway shows; I'm working as an orchestrator in Broadway shows; I'm working as a conductor. During this period I also conducted the *Mass* and conducted the Houston Symphony, but I didn't pick up my conducting career. That was a funny lapse. Also, all this time, I'm becoming a writer. I first began to write jazz pieces and this music evolved into other, more classical endeavors.

I've worked with classical forms incorporating improvisation. Usually in classical, a composer will use improvisation as an effect—in other words, to get a texture. But improvisation as the main event, as the core of the work, that's jazz. But jazz has progressed stylistically to being as complete a music as classical. In other words, freely chromatic, no limitations. There are sections of modern classical composers that really sound like free jazz, but free jazz has the rhythmic accuracy and spontaneity.

The first film I did was *Hair*. I was the unnamed producer of the soundtrack. That's the movie business right there. I had worked with the composer on other shows of his. We were very close, and he wanted me to do the film. Then another good friend of mine wanted someone with a classical background to write some music for *A Perfect Couple*. I did that one for Robert Altman, and then he had me do *Quintet*, in which I got to conduct the London Symphony Orchestra playing my own music. It was thrilling. It was so thrilling, in fact, that I became convinced that I would never have as good an experience. I had total creative freedom. I was alone with the reels for thirteen weeks, plenty of time to write. And at the same time as I was writing that score, I was constructing an orchestral suite in my mind. André Previn was quoted in the paper recently as saying, "Some critics will forgive you for being an ax murderer, but not for scoring a film." On *Quintet,* though, I wrote my real music, and the London Symphony Orchestra had 105 musicians playing what I believed in my heart was good music.

After that, I adapted Gershwin for Woody Allen's *Manhattan*. But working with Woody Allen was much different than working with Robert Altman. Allen had his way of doing things. It was not as satisfying an experience. After *Manhattan*, I turned down the movie *Fame*. Or, let's put it this way, they wanted me to do the coordinating and orchestrating for the work of other songwriters, and I wanted to do all the writing. They rejected me on that basis. I turned down another picture—and that was the end of my film career. That's all it took. I've since done additional scoring for one film, *Popeye*, for Altman, but I no longer see myself as really having a future in film. Not that I wouldn't do one, but music in a film will always be just wall paint. Also, my beliefs have become very clear that homicide is not entertainment. This is very important to me.

This period coincided with the breakup of my marriage. I would describe it as she and I gradually growing apart in values, though that puts too much blame on her. Then, finally, I met someone that I fell in love with, a singer, like my wife. We saw each other on and off for a couple of years and then lived together in L.A. for a year. But she couldn't take me.

The system divides a man's life into his family and his work. For most men, I would suggest that the work has no thrill beyond accomplishing the task and being rewarded for it. And the greater enthusiasm would lie outside of the work. An artist's work encroaches on this boundary. For example, when I was married and I wanted to realize my own music in addition to these musical jobs I was working, my wife would feel that I was taking something from her. "He doesn't love me because he would rather be organizing a band, or he would rather be in a room composing." Renée felt the same way. I would get ill-tempered when I would work, and this ill temper took its toll.

When I got my *Manhattan* check, I took a six-month sabbatical to write my symphony. I got one movement of the symphony done and now think of it as a kind of symphonic prelude. It's never been played. I thought I would continue to get job offers, but I also didn't have a telephone service for about six months, so psychologically I was definitely turning my back on it. I didn't have any doubt when I chose to write my symphony. I was too familiar with talented individuals who put off their real ambition until it was too late.

I have come to a kind of peace within myself concerning the life of my work. I had to give up ambition on certain levels a few years ago, when I wasn't getting any jobs, and it was a relief. I've become very accustomed to a reduced cash flow. Also I felt more focused towards my *real* job, which was not to promote my music but to write it.

About three years ago, I was living alone in Los Angeles and I had a feeling I was going to be unemployed for a while, a feeling which was accurate. A friend of mine, unbeknownst to me, was a practitioner of martial arts and I happened to see him in the studio one day while I was walking down the street. It looked exciting so I went to a karate studio near here. I studied for two years. Though I'm a long way from being really dangerous, it changed my entire outlook—philosophical, mental, emotional, physical—on life. I had never pursued an athletic discipline. I think the study of karate is medicinal. I could go into class sick and come out well. What is taught at Master Han's studio is complete. It is a worldview—"world" is almost too limiting. *Ki* is some substance of existence of which the human is made up, and not only the human but all life. And not even limited to life, but to everything that reaches man through his senses. The unity which contains diversity.

When I first awoke to the spiritual dimension, largely a result of study of karate, I was horrified at what I saw: the emphasis on control, on dirty tricks, on group identification, on military imagery. This is on a spiritual level! The function of a group is to maintain its power, to exclude the outsiders, and to regulate the insiders. This is true of *all* groups. Conflict is inevitable and insidious.

My eyes and ears were opening and I think it happened too suddenly. I was gone. I called my father long-distance in the middle of the night. I mean, if I can't call my father in the middle of the night, what kind of relationship is it? I thought he was trying to communicate telepathically, and I kept trying to figure out what it was. This conversation supposedly lasted forty-five minutes, largely silence on my part. I'm not denying that I was gone, but it was something else. I thought I was having a spiritual . . . I *was* having a spiritual experience. Meanwhile, my parents called the police because they thought I was smoking too much pot.

I was smoking a couple of joints a night. I'm not now advocating smoking pot. I would agree that consuming a substance on a daily basis slants your whole life to a certain degree. But that isn't what was happening. What was happening was that I was hearing sounds and seeing sights that were not due to drugs. I get the same information even better now without any drugs.

So this policeman shows up at the door and he hands me a card that has one digit of my parents' phone number wrong on it. Then this friend of my brother's shows up and says, "We're taking you over to this hospital. Now just be cool. We'll tell them you had an overdose of drugs, something like that. We'll just get you in and out." I'd expressed an interest to my father in the Masons—as you know, Mozart was a Mason—so I thought this was the initiation, the hazing, if you will, to get in the Masons. So we go over to the hospital and I say, "Okay, I'll check in. I'll go through with the plan."

So then I got tortured. It was just a drug program. With smiling faces they subjected me to a kind of torture which is called "negative conditioning." They don't tell you that, though. They just smile at you and give you drugs that fuck you up. They give you these shit drugs; then they take you off them and put you on a schedule and you feel so good once you're off these drugs that the idea is you don't go back to smoking pot or whatever. I loved being in the hospital. I met a girl up there. I took my piano and gave a gala concert for the inmates. I was there a couple of weeks. I went right through with the program and everything. I stayed there until I realized how much money it was costing.

Professionally, I have had some great achievements: the scoring of films for Robert Altman, the adaptation for Woody Allen. I conducted *The Wiz* on Broadway. I've orchestrated music for Leonard Bernstein, co-orchestrated with Michel Legrand. I have composed music that has been released on recordings. I have had commissioned works played by various orchestras.

But the single action I am most proud of was during the summer of '83. I had gone to Westwood to see *Zelig.* It was sold out, so I'm walking around and I go up to this viewing box, this preview box in front of a movie theater on the street. It's showing coming attractions of *Rumble Fish, Scarface.* I'm watching this violent shit, man, thinking this is unbelievable. I believe that the mind is the source of the physical reality. As in the belief of Zen, right thought is a coordinate to right action. So I watched this bullshit, and I'm walking back to my car and thinking about *Hair.* Not the movie *Hair* but the stage play *Hair,* where, at the end of the first act, everybody takes off their clothes.

So I go back, and I look at this thing, and I watch it through, and I turn around, and I take off all my clothes and I stand next to it. This is a Sunday afternoon in Westwood, children on the street. Pretty soon cops drive up—"What do you think you're doing?" Bam! Down onto the concrete. Bam! Hands behind my back and the cuffing technique reserved for sex offenders. "What do you think you're doing?"

Another cop comes up and finally I spoke, which was to say, "I came up here, I saw this violence being proclaimed on the street, and I had to do something about it." So this cop took my shirt and he put it across my cock so that I looked like an Indian fakir. The rest is them taking me, booking me, keeping me overnight in jail, releasing me the next day with the description of my offense as "exposure of self," which I felt was a very articulate rejection of the notion of "indecent exposure." I wasn't brought to trial. They dropped charges.

I have continued to occasionally stage my protests against violence as entertainment, homicide as entertainment, but I have not engaged in any further public nudity. Most of my energy is devoted to my music. The piece I spent last year on I'm very excited about. It's a piano concerto with the solo part totally improvised. It's not jazz, though. The orchestral parts are all written out, but why have the pianist come out and play some part that you've written and he practiced a million hours in order to play when good pianists can extemporize with greater force than can be created by making the pianist a machine? I also have my jazz band, and perform around town. But mostly I'm trying to be a good composer and trying to write the best music I can write. I would also like to teach some seminars, based on my jazz compositions.

Another thing I would like is to find a woman. I miss women. I'd pay for sex if I could afford it. But it's not the act of sex I yearn for; it is the physical closeness. And yet, at the same time, I feel wary of that closeness.

I know that people think of me as crazy, and I don't like being despised. I don't like hearing people rattle on about me in the background. But I feel very strongly about what I see and what I hear around me. It is terrible that appearing naked in public should be considered a crime, whereas displaying violence in public is not. When *any* nonviolent behavior is judged as a greater crime than violence, then violence has moved one step closer towards legitimacy. I think that the act of homicide should be so extraordinary, so rare, that it would be front-page news.

Authority is a habit-forming drug, and authority legitimizes violence. The authoritarian structure requires becoming part of a machine, giving up your judgment. We need for every individual to be the leader of himself. I fear what I call the New Fascism: extreme emphasis on group identification, less tolerance of difference, more demands of the law, greater emphasis on punishment and humiliation, less gentleness. Right now, the gentle are humiliated.

A few months after our conversation, I visited with Tom in New York and attended a performance of his sixteen-man band at a jazz club above a bar in the West Village. At the end of the first set, he stepped up to the microphone and spoke out against violence in newspapers' advertisements for movies. "Why must all men in such ads carry guns or rifles?" he asked. No answer was forthcoming.

THE "A" STUDENT:

Barbara Sellars

New York is a city that seems to attract outstanding people. If Tom Pierson had a perfect academic record in high school, Barbara Sellars was not far behind.

In an ideal society, everyone would earn a living at a job that was satisfying, fulfilling, and helpful to others. Such is not now the case. I found it a pleasure to meet and talk with a member of the fortunate minority.

I was born in Tulsa, where my father was working for an oilfield-equipment company. My mother had worked during World War II on the graveyard shifts in airplane factories in Tulsa, going to college during the day. They got married after the war was over and had four kids in five years. I am the oldest.

I think the most traumatic time in my childhood was moving, between grammar school and junior high school, from Tulsa, where I had gone to a little bitty grammar school on the edge of town, to Baton Rouge, Louisiana, where I was thought of as a Yankee because I was from Oklahoma. My father took a new job and we moved kit and kaboodle to the Old South. It was a real different culture, and it was very hard for me to adjust. I felt like a little ugly duckling. Making new friends was real hard—riding the bus and having nobody want to sit with me.

By eighth grade I knew some people and it wasn't so bad, but the oil business changed again, and before ninth grade we moved back to

Oklahoma—to Oklahoma City. By the time I made the second move, I didn't fear it anymore. I looked upon it as a new beginning. I went to Putnam City High School, where there was a great deal of pride in scholastic excellence. I didn't kill myself studying, but I got only one B in high school—in chemistry. The rest of my grades were A's. Oklahoma has a scholastic meet every year with tests in different subjects. I remember winning Oklahoma history—best in the state. I won a couple of others, too.

The summer before I was a senior, I began to date a fellow who had graduated two years before and was at Yale. He and his friends told me about college boards. I didn't know that such a thing existed before that. They said, "You can go to college in the East." I said, "Who, me?" They said, "You've got good grades, a lot of school activities, and you've got geographic distribution on your side. Take these college boards and you can probably go."

I had one girlfriend who was interested in going to school out of state. She was dating a guy who was at Harvard. So we had our little strategy. We would not apply at the same schools because being from Oklahoma was going to be our unique feature. She applied to Radcliffe, Wellesley, and Mount Holyoke. I applied to Vassar, Smith, and U. Conn. for my safety school.

My mom got *McCall's* and *Ladies' Home Journal* and *Good Housekeeping* every month. I read the fashion and the fiction in those magazines, and most of the stories are about New York City, or *maybe* Greenwich, Connecticut. So that, and Mary McCarthy's *The Group*, was my knowledge of what the East Coast was like. It was kind of romantic and New York became my Oz, my fairyland.

In February of '65 my friend and I came up on the bus to interview at colleges. We rode the bus for thirty-six hours from Oklahoma to New York. I was filled with advice from people who had told me how to be careful in New York City because people were going to take advantage of me. Well, ever since I was a kid, I'd had problems with my nose bleeding, and by the time I'd ridden the bus in the winter with dry heat for thirty-six hours, someplace in New Jersey, I got a nosebleed which was unstaunchable. I went through everybody's Kleenex on the bus. I stepped off the bus at the Port Authority with this incredible nosebleed, and eighty people tell me, "Do this, dear," "Do that, dear," "Let me help you, dear." All my fears and my stereotypes were shattered immediately. Nobody tried to mug me because I had a nosebleed, and nobody tried to take advantage of me. Everybody was really very, very helpful and very kind. So I interviewed at Smith and nearly froze to death, and interviewed at Vassar.

A couple of months later we got our acceptance letters. I was accepted at both Smith and Vassar. Well, we were delighted. I was totally oblivious to what it meant to my parents for me to be going away to school. And it never crossed my mind to even ask about the money involved. We were delirious at the thought of escaping and about this wonderful new life that we were going to start in the East.

The day after we got our acceptance letters, we were interrupted in class and told that the senior counselor wanted to speak with us in his office. We thought he was going to congratulate us. We marched down the hall to his office and he sat us down and says, "I want you to think very hard about what you're doing. There's no reason you have to leave this wonderful state of Oklahoma. Everything you need in an education is here. Why aren't you going to Oklahoma State or O.U.? There's plenty of time to make an application, and I'll help you." We were a bit taken aback, but it wasn't enough to stop us.

I worked full-time that summer as a dental assistant and then I took the bus up again to Vassar. I stayed in a dormitory there; people were not unfriendly. By that time I was dating the person I married. He had also graduated from Putnam City High School two years ahead of me and was at Yale. He sent me a congratulatory telegram when I got into Vassar, and that was the neatest thing that had ever happened. So at Vassar I was on a five-day-school, two-day-weekend schedule. Art history ended at two-thirty Friday afternoon. We'd get out and run for the bus, and it would be an hour-and-a-half ride over to Yale—come back Sunday afternoon and try to get your homework done for class on Monday. Bill and I got engaged the summer after my freshman year.

The program that I had gone to Vassar to pursue was early-childhood education. But at the beginning of my sophomore year, they took away the major in early-childhood education and it became a subspecialty of psychology. I was really left without a major. I felt that the rug had been pulled out from under me. Bill was an English major. I wasn't getting anything out of it, so getting married seemed like as good an idea as changing my major again, quite frankly. Our wedding was December 31, 1966. I took my finals and got out and moved to New Haven.

I got a job as a file clerk in the Yale Student Health Center, and we lived on my take-home pay of two hundred dollars a month. It was real tight. Bill always wanted to be a college English teacher. From the moment I met him, that was his goal in life. He was in love with literature. But the Vietnam War was clanking its chains. In Oklahoma in 1967 Addie May Lewis ran the draft board, and Addie May believed that Oklahomans were good old boys and they are going to fight for their country. So two or three months before graduation, all the young men from Oklahoma who were seniors at Yale went home for spring break—all of them except two, my husband and another young man who was married.

The day after spring break started, the reclassifications arrived in the mailbox in Connecticut and they said, "You have ten days to appeal." The other guys were not going to be back for fourteen more days. Bill and Jimmy called as many of their friends as they could, but some of them were unreachable. Bill was able to appeal and maintain his student status, but with Addie May on our tail, and without any money to go to graduate school, it looked like he was going to be drafted, so he decided to join the navy. He entered Officer Candidate School in August of 1967.

We made a conscious decision that since we wanted to have kids sometime, we might as well do it while we were young and poor, particularly since we had health coverage for the next several years. So I got pregnant immediately and spent three months going to work and eating constantly so I wouldn't barf all over the desk. When I was growing up I never could think of what to say when people said, "What do you want to do when you grow up?" other than to say, "I want to have kids." I guess it was because I'd never seen a woman doing anything I wanted to do, other than being a mother.

When Bill graduated from Officer Candidate School, I joined him in Newport, while he went to navy communications school. We left there in May '68 and moved to Norfolk, Virginia. Very hot. A lousy place to be very pregnant. This was when I first experienced obstetrics. I remember going to the navy clinic, standing, waiting, for hours it seemed, with thousands of other young pregnant women, and finally seeing somebody for thirty seconds who tells you, "You're still pregnant; come back next week."

There were no classes in childbirth preparation. The navy did have a wonderful movie in three parts: "First Trimester," "Second Trimester," and "Third Trimester and Birth." The first part showed a navy wife puking in glorious, living color, with this shot from the point of view of the toilet bowl! If you stayed past the first two reels, you saw a very edited version of birth. But it did mention in passing that it was probably a good idea to keep on breathing while you were having your "labor pains." I remember reading a college biology textbook and Dr. Spock, and that's all I could find to tell me what it was going to be like to have a baby. I asked my mother and she said, "Oh, I don't remember. I'd get to the hospital, they'd give me a little white pill, and I'd wake up later and they'd tell me that I had another kid." She said, "People live through it. Everybody has babies. Don't worry about it." So I didn't.

I was about eleven days late and enormously pregnant when I woke up with contractions about three in the morning. I went through the day at home. I did my toenails. I rolled my hair in those great big rollers and put the dryer on so I'd have curly hair. Finally I decided we'd better go to the hospital. So we drove to Portsmouth Navy Hospital, which was built in 1846—a real modern facility. At that time there was a waiting room and then these big double doors that said something to the effect of "Only the Future Mothers of the World Go Through These Doors." Nobody else. No husbands, no mothers, no sisters, no support people whatsoever.

They were really busy that night—thirteen babies, I think. There was a big thunderstorm, and people's membranes rupture when the barometric pressure goes down. They had me walk around for a while and then, after what seemed like an eternity, somebody came for me. I was trying to do some breathing while someone was doing an examination. They said, "What are you doing?" I said, "Breathing, like in the movie."

They said, "Don't do that! You'll hyperventilate and you'll hurt your baby!" So the only thing I knew to do was taken away from me.

I got into this labor bed and was given a shot of what must have been at least a hundred milligrams of Demerol. I was on a roller coaster—oblivion alternating with really excruciating pain. I woke up with one contraction with this different feeling. Could not move, could not turn over and get the call button, beached whale that I was. So I must have made some horrible bellow. Some poor nurse comes in and says, "What do you want?" I said, "I don't know. Something's different."

So she lifts up the covers and she says, ever echoing in my memory, "John! Get the gurney!"

I had no idea what was going on. I was moved onto a stretcher, rolled down two corridors, and asked to sit up. I learned later that I was being given a spinal block. Nobody asked me; nobody told me.

I'm sitting on the edge of the table and this little nurse is saying, "Just lean over and arch your back out." I have my arms around her neck and I'm leaning down on her shoulder, and I got a hell of a contraction and screamed—and I bit her! I don't know if I bit her shoulder or lower, but she wasn't very friendly with me after that.

Then I lay back, and they said, "Push." There were drapes all over, and a big light, and some man I'd never seen before behind a mask at the end of the table. I did something, but because of the spinal block I was not able to feel anything. Like a rabbit from a hat, they held up this baby that I didn't feel being born at all—that just sort of appeared from the sheets. I couldn't touch her because my hands were strapped down and I couldn't get closer to her because my legs were strapped up. They said, "It's a girl!" And that was it. She was gone.

I went to sleep again from the Demerol, and I woke up listening to the sound of the rain coming down on the recovery-room windows with this nurse saying, "What's your name? What day is it? Did you have a boy or a girl?" Beats me. I didn't know the answers to any of those questions. Finally, when I could answer two out of three, I guess, they put me on another stretcher and took me down the hallway. My husband was allowed to walk alongside the stretcher, while I was talking ninety miles a minute on a Demerol high. I was as white as a sheet and he thought I was dying.

I was put into this very old-fashioned high bed that you had to use a four-step ladder to get out of. I remember a nurse coming in and saying, "Have you urinated yet?" I said, "No."

She said, "If you don't urinate we're going to catheterize you." I wasn't really quite sure what that meant, but it didn't sound good. I had no feeling in half of my body, and I couldn't sit up because my head was supposed to lie flat for twelve hours because of the spinal block. But over a period of about an hour, I got enough urine out to keep them from catheterizing me.

At five-thirty in the morning: "Up and at 'em! It's the morning—this is a navy hospital! You're going to get up and take a shower and clean yourself up!"

I had had a spinal block seven hours earlier, I had an 8½-pound kid, and I must have lost quite a bit of blood. I sat up. I went down the four steps. I staggered into the bathroom, bled all over the place, almost passed out, came very close to drowning in the toilet. Luckily, I hit an emergency bell on the way down. Someone came in and bawled me out for being so sloppy, and having bled all over the floor. Threw me into the shower and marched me off to breakfast.

That night I had mandatory rooming in. They brought the baby in and said, "Here, take care of it; feed it." I was lucky enough to run across a breast-feeding book during the pregnancy, so I had decided to do that. The baby's about twenty-four hours old and she cried a lot. I would breast-feed her and she'd go to sleep. I'd put her down in her bed and she'd wake up and cry again. This went on all night. By three in the morning, I was totally exhausted. So I decided to breast-feed her in bed with me.

I threw her into the bed, climbed up the ladder, settled into bed, and snuggled her up against me—and it was terrific. It was the nicest thing that had ever happened to me. She was quiet. I was quiet. I was drifting off to sleep when suddenly "Nurse Ratchet" came back and said, "What are you doing in that bed? You're going to smother your baby! If you're going to have that child with you, you'll have to sit up in a chair." So I sat up in a chair for the rest of the night with the baby in my arms.

Luckily, they were so busy that they discharged me the next day. Emotionally, having the baby was certainly not a satisfying experience. On the other hand, it gave me an enormous amount of respect for myself. It made me think that there had to be a better way. I had not the slightest idea what that better way might be; it just seemed that that couldn't be the way God meant it to be.

Shortly after Amy was born, my husband's parents came to visit for two weeks. While they were staying with us, my husband left and went on a cruise with this navy refrigerator ship that took lettuce and steaks over to the Mediterranean. So I was there with my in-laws and a six-week-old baby when the Democratic Convention occurred in '68. We sat there every night and watched what happened in Chicago. I was sitting in front of the television just not believing what I was seeing—and having to listen to my in-laws goad the police on the TV. "Come on, get 'em!" It was really awful. I was in tears. They thought I was very naive—bleeding-heart. I had to leave the room every evening.

Bill came back after three months, just before Christmas. In the navy, when you're an officer, people wait on you. So he came home after being waited on for three months—and his clothes are on the floor, and his socks would go in the closet. I didn't like that. That was the first time things were kind of rocky for a while.

I got pregnant again in March '69. Then, in October, Bill was assigned to shore duty, which was great because we were going to be settled. He'd be able to help me. There wouldn't be any other changes before he got out. We'd have the kids. The navy was going to pay for it. When he got out he'd be able to go to graduate school because he'd have the GI bill.

So we moved to a little bitty town called Port Deposit, Maryland, and Bill became the person in charge of a naval training school for radiomen. It was really quite a plum for a junior officer. It was going to be a temporary thing while the guy who was in charge recuperated from a heart attack. Bill was very enthusiastic and trying to make some reforms. This was a time when a little more social action was allowed in the navy. We couldn't march, but we'd send telegrams and write letters. When Nixon invaded Cambodia, we sent a telegram of protest to the White House, and got a message back saying "Thank you for your support"!

I met a whole new group of people, and one of the women I met was a navy officer's wife who said, "You've got to take these childbirth classes." I said, "Classes? I had a baby. I know what it's all about." She said, "Well, read this book," and she shoved *Thank You, Dr. Lamaze* into my hands.

I read that book and was enthusiastic enough about it to drive to Baltimore, which was sixty miles away, once a week for six weeks, to take Lamaze classes. When Jennifer was born, three weeks late, we'd had a lot of time to practice. The whole experience was so different emotionally. I did have to go to the delivery room and have my legs up in the straps, and have a million drapes, and my husband was not allowed to come in the room, although he was allowed to be with me during labor. But I didn't have a spinal block, and I did understand what was going on, and I felt more in control.

I remember being fully dilated, and feeling the head go into the birth canal, and saying, "I've got to push!" The doctor came in and said, "No, no, you're not quite fully dilated." But I knew he was lying. He had to go put his gown on and scrub. I was panting away, not pushing. Finally everybody gets ready. I remember the doctor getting down to the foot of the table and saying, "Okay, you can push now."

I took a deep breath, just like they teach you in the classes, grabbed on to those hand-holders, and looked up. And just before I pushed, I thought, *I'm* having this baby! And I gave a big push and out popped nine-pounds-seven-ounce Jennifer!

I couldn't hold her, but at least they didn't whisk her off, and I was not feeling so terrible afterwards. After an hour in the recovery room I told them I was hungry. They said, "Eat? You're hungry?" I said, "I'm starving, I've been working all day." So they gave me some of their midnight rations and I had scrambled eggs, bacon, toast, milk, everything on the tray.

A couple of hours later, they brought the baby in and said, "Now, don't breast-feed her. Just give her water." By this time I had enough sense to say, "Okay, thank you very much." They shut the door and I started breast-feeding her.

The difference between the two birth experiences was like night and day for me. I turned into this zealot. I'd see a pregnant woman in the street that I'd never seen before in my life, and I'd go up and tell her that she had to take these classes. I was obnoxious!

Then the man that Bill was replacing got well after three months and came back, and the navy had nothing for Bill to do. Even though it was going to be more than a year until he was out, they didn't want to transfer him, because he was a short-timer. It was very difficult for him because he got kicked out of this little niche where he had made all these improvements. It was great for me because now I had two little kids and I needed help. He could help me go do the grocery shopping and take the kids to the pediatrician. I liked it. We didn't have much money, but we could drive around the countryside. At that time I don't think I understood how personally involved one could get with one's work, and how devastating it can be when one doesn't have a sense of self-worth about what one's doing.

But because Bill was in this no-job job, I could indulge myself in going through training to be a childbirth instructor. I drove to Baltimore, sort of apprenticed with somebody, did all the reading, and passed the written test. Then one of the doctors from the base came and listened to me give my classes, and it was okay, so I started teaching. I was doing two or three classes a week, and I had a booming business going.

Bill's hitch in the navy was over in August of '71 and he was accepted to graduate school with a teaching fellowship at the University of Texas in Austin. I got dragged kicking and screaming halfway across the continent. I did not want to go back to what we used to call the Middle West. But I didn't have much choice. That was it. Austin was much more pleasant than I had ever hoped. There were a lot of parks and lakes nearby, the climate was nice, we didn't need to lock the doors. As a place to have little kids, it was marvelous. But here we were in a new town and my husband was going to do what he had wanted to do all his life—embark on a career towards being a college English teacher. He felt a lot of pressure to do well and it's very tough to be a teaching assistant and take your own courses in graduate school, but it was also something he very much wanted to do. He would get up in the morning, take the shuttle bus into school, and be gone all day. He disappeared from my life at that point.

I had two little kids, under two, very little money—it was a good six months before I was able to start teaching classes again. I would spend the day taking care of the kids. When he came home there was nothing for us to talk about. He was delving deeply into Renaissance literature and I was mopping up spilt milk. I'd want him to spend more time with us, but he was too busy. I'd go through these big teary things and say, "When will you have time?" and the answer always was "You have to understand that it's never going to be different, because I have to work on my Ph.D., and once I get my Ph.D., then I have to publish or perish. I'll always have to be grading papers and I'll always have to be doing my own research papers. It's never going to be any different." There seemed to be very little to look forward to.

After a year and a half of that, I spent a whole month crying. I just couldn't see continuing this way for an indefinite eternity. After a month of crying every goddamn day, I said, Enough of this, already. You can't live your life this way. You've got to do something. We had no money to go to a psychiatrist, but the student health center would take students' wives for limited counseling. So I went to see this sweet little man who took a while to understand what was the matter. The way he saw it, the problem was that I was causing a problem for my husband. He said, "Well, what would you like to do?" I didn't know. Out of the clear-blue sky I said, "What I really want to do is to be a midwife." I had met a woman who was a midwife. Before that, I didn't know there were modern midwives.

But I said, "I can't be a midwife. I'd have to go back to school and become a nurse first. I have two kids and no time. I can't afford to put them in day care." We had another couple of sessions, and the kindly old man suggested that Bill and I go swimming together with the kids on Sundays as a togetherness sort of thing, and that I go back to school. We never addressed the lack of communication and the whole basic relationship. The way to take care of the problem, which was me, was to keep me busy so that I wouldn't bother him.

I took two courses that summer and I got A's, and I met a few people that talked to me. So I registered the kids for a nursery school and we worked out this elaborate schedule. Bill was very supportive. As long as I could still do the shopping and the laundry and clean up the house and get the kids to bed, I could go to school. He would pick them up from nursery school and sometimes watch them for me. So I went back to school to get the prerequisites out of the way.

I started riding my bike around. I lost weight. I managed to do the studying. I'd wash the dishes with a book propped up, run the bathwater with a book propped up. I was real tired, but it was the most wonderful thing that had happened in a long time, and I didn't feel depressed all the time. I felt angry sometimes because I was definitely doing more than 50 percent, but it was so much better than what I'd been before that I would just continue.

I never wanted to be a "nursey" nurse, but I had to go to nursing school to be a midwife. I had become so frustrated teaching childbirth-education classes and telling people what was possible and how to negotiate with their doctors, knowing that it wasn't going to work. I was not listened to by any of the doctors and nurses in the hospital because I didn't have any letters after my name.

I graduated from nursing school in December 1976 and took a job as a labor-delivery nurse in the County Hospital, working nights so I could still be with the kids as much as possible when they were awake. Boy, then I was *really* tired! It was acknowledged that nurses would sometimes have to catch babies, especially on the night shift. So I asked one of the residents, Bob Matthews, to talk me through one that's controlled so I'd know what I was doing when the first one came flying off the street.

So somebody came in and it was an old-fashioned delivery-table delivery. The poor lady's legs are up in the stirrups and she's flat on her back. I pulled on the gloves, and I stood there with Bob right behind me. When that baby's head started emerging, the whole world spun. I could hardly see straight to know which way to catch it. Bob put his hands on mine and that baby slipped out. We pulled down for the shoulders, and I held that child in my hands, and it was just the most euphoric moment.

I applied to midwifery school at Yale, Georgetown, and Downstate in New York City. I was turned down at Georgetown and Downstate because I didn't have two years' nursing experience. Yale had a three-year program for non-nurses, so they didn't have that requirement. But they were only taking twelve that year and I was fourteenth on the list. I was depressed. About ten days before a planned vacation to Mexico, the pot boiled over with Bill. We started talking for the first time. I was angry a lot of the time, feeling that we had nothing in common. We cried and screamed and talked about whether we were going to get a divorce or separate or what. We decided we didn't want to subject the kids to a "broken home," so we would try to stay together.

We made it through the summer, attempting to be cordial to each other and doing all right. In September, five days before classes started, I was notified that one of the people had dropped out of the Yale program, the first person on the waiting list could not come, and I could go to midwifery school. They said they would find me scholarship money and housing. So when Bill came home that afternoon, I basically said, "I'm going. If you want to come, come. If you don't, okay." It was not an easy decision, but he had finished everything but his dissertation, so he decided that he would come and bring the kids. I packed up quickly and went to New Haven and Bill and the kids followed three weeks later. That started the best part of my life since high school.

School itself was not the most pleasant experience, but I loved the clinical part. The next summer I was able to get a part-time job in a doctors' office in Middletown, Connecticut. I would do prenatal visits for their noncomplicated clients, and I would be allowed, for credit but no pay, to be on call for those women who wanted a midwife at the delivery. Bless their hearts, letting themselves be delivered by a student nurse-midwife. I really have to thank them.

The first time I did an official delivery at school, at Yale–New Haven Hospital, it was quite a scene. It was supposed to be an easy one, but there was a little complication. The baby's head was still quite high when the mother was fully dilated, and there's a possibility of the umbilical cord prolapsing and coming down before the baby's head if the water should break precipitously. We had to be ready to do a cesarean if this should happen. So here I was, student nurse-midwife, with my instructor, the resident, the attending physician, a pediatrician, an intern pediatrician, an anesthesiologist, an intern anesthesiologist, a nurse, the father of the baby, and the mother down on the table. There are eleven people in the room. We should have sold tickets.

I was certainly intimidated by the scene, but I had caught fifteen babies in Texas. When the water broke and the cord didn't come down, it looked okay. I had enough presence of mind to say, "Okay, now push. You're doing very well; that's great; hold your breath." I could hear it going around the room: "She spoke to the patient!" It worked out fine. That was kind of fun.

Meanwhile, Bill got a job at this prep school in New York. By this time, with a Ph.D. in English and seventy cents, you could get on the subway. If he hadn't spent those four years in the navy, if he'd gone to graduate school right out of college, he would have been in the job market. He's a wonderful teacher. He would have beaten the competition. By the time he got a Ph.D., enrollment in college English was way, way down. Everybody's taking computers by then. He had won a prize for the best dissertation in the Humanities Department at the University of Texas, but he was not able to get a position at the college level. So we moved to New York City and I commuted to New Haven.

In my second year at midwifery school, I negotiated to have a clinical site, where I could get my hands-on experience, in New York City. I was very, very lucky in that one of the women faculty members at Yale had taken a job at North Central Bronx Hospital. I got there a year after the Obstetrics Department opened. We worked twelve-hour shifts. By the time you do reports in the morning and in the evening, it's well over twelve hours. Sometimes you ran your tail off the whole damn time. You never sat down. But experience—fantastic! Twins, breeches, preeclamptics, complications, normal deliveries, you name it. By the time I finished that semester I had more deliveries than anybody else in my class.

My last semester at Yale, I was not only a student; I was also a lecturer on the faculty. I was a clinical supervisor covering first-year students in the clinic and at deliveries. I graduated in May of '79 and got a job at North Central Bronx Hospital as a staff nurse-midwife. We lived in the Bronx and the kids were able to go to the private school because of their father's position on the faculty. I worked at North Central Bronx for two and a half years, and delivered about three hundred babies by myself and did about three hundred more with students of various sorts. But it became very frustrating to work for the city because of the enormous bureaucracy of the Health Care Administration.

There were pregnant patients who'd come in for a checkup, and you'd ask them the last time they'd eaten, and it was two days ago. They didn't have any money to buy food. Now, when you're pregnant, it's very important to eat at least something every day. We would steal trays off the meal cart to feed them. After two and a half years, I was very much ready to go into private practice. I happened to connect with a woman physician who had been a nurse-midwife, and had just been appointed to the faculty of Columbia Presbyterian Hospital and was looking for a nurse-midwife to help her in her practice. I began working for her in 1981, and had a wonderful time for three and a half years.

Along the way, the marriage went kaput. I was getting more and more depressed. I'd walk down the street toward the house and not want to go in. The kids were older. I didn't feel quite so sure that they would be terribly devastated if we were to separate. I came home from work one day and I said, "We have to start talking about this." And we couldn't talk. We spent four hours trying to explain what we really meant. This went on for about six weeks, and I finally said, "We're going to have to go to a marriage counselor or a therapist to learn how to talk to each other." So we made an appointment. Bill came home two days later and said, "I don't want to do that. I just want to separate." I thought it over for about thirty seconds and I said okay.

The first year after that was hard. For the first six months, it was euphoria for eight hours and then the depths of depression for eight hours. It was like a roller coaster. Then, over time, it evened out a little more. I learned how to shovel snow better, and to fix things better, and my upper-back muscles got a lot stronger. And the kids did okay. They had obviously known that things were not great for a while. They made jokes in the beginning. They said, "You're supposed to take us out to dinner and tell us, like in the Judy Blume book." Or, "Don't I get a bicycle out of this?" I couldn't see that Amy was terribly upset by it. By that time she was fourteen and she had her own social life. Jennifer had a couple of nightmares about hurting and being hurt. We talked it through. She was very angry with me for a while, but I don't feel that she's angry with me anymore.

Both of them are wonderful kids. I couldn't have more wonderful, neat, intelligent, funny kids. They went to Washington to join a protest demonstration and got back at one o'clock at night, and Jennifer went out and sat on the Columbia University steps all night to protest the policy of South Africa. The only tough time I had with them was just before puberty when they got absolutely estrogen-poison crazy for a few months. They couldn't decide about anything; they would scream and rage and act irrationally. They drove me nuts. Once that was over with, they've been wonderful ever since. Amy just graduated high school and is about to enter Yale.

I've just started a new job, working full-time in a nurse-midwifery practice with two other nurse-midwives in Greenwich Village. This is the first autonomous nurse-midwifery practice in the state of New York. The other two set it up and I'm the new girl in their practice. We are self-employed. The patients pay us, and we pay our bills and we pay ourselves.

I feel so lucky to be in a job where I get paid for catching babies and being with people at some of the most wonderful moments of their lives, meeting people I never would have met, and getting to play with babies a lot. Another reason I feel so blessed is that I can give women what I never had. That's one small injustice in the world that I am constantly working on—to have your birthing experience not taken away from you.

AN AVERAGE GUY:
Arthur Miller

Most high schools in the United States have very little soul. Architecturally, they reflect the same degree of imagination that is required in prison-building. Standing in the central quad of a typical American high school, one soaks up about as much history and emotion as standing in the parking lot of a shopping mall. Those campuses that really do exude a sense of history are usually prep schools, reserved for the wealthy and elite.

Yet, scattered across the country there are a few public schools that have maintained an atmosphere of history and continuity, and which students enter with as much excitement and pride as they would a major university. One such school is—or was—Erasmus Hall High School on Flatbush Avenue in Brooklyn.

Among the quarter of a million people who have attended Erasmus High are Susan Hayward, Jeff Chandler, Eli Wallach, John Forsythe, Barbra Streisand, Neil Diamond, Gabriel Kaplan, and Beverly Sills, not to mention chess Grand Master Bobby Fischer, author Bernard Malamud, columnist Dorothy Kilgallen, Olympic champion swimmer and actress Eleanor Holm, Hall of Fame baseball pitcher Waite Hoyt, Hall of Fame football quarterback Sid Luckman, basketball star Billy Cunningham, Nobel Prize–winning botanist Barbara McClintock, and Janelle Commissiong, Miss Universe of 1977.

Construction of the school, named after the Dutch Humanist scholar Desiderius Erasmus, began in 1786 on land donated by the Dutch Reformed Church. Early benefactors included Alexander Hamilton, Aaron Burr, John Jay, and John Vanderbilt. Their family crests can still be seen on the stained-glass windows of the library. The school opened the follow-

*ing year under the supervision of the church. Girls were first admitted in
1801. In 1896, Erasmus was turned over to New York City and converted
to an open school without tuition. By 1905, with immigrants flooding the
area, the school was already operating on triple session. Although new
wings and buildings have been added over the years, the original Academy
Building, built in 1786 and restored from 1938 to 1952, still stands and
has been designated a national landmark.*

*The Erasmus Class of 1965 included 1801 graduates, far more than
any other class that I studied. So huge was the class that when I read off
to various class members the names of the students who had been voted
Most Popular and Most Likely to Succeed, the typical response was,
"Who? Never heard of him."*

*In the twenty-plus years since the class of '65 left, Erasmus High has
undergone drastic changes. The grandeur and glory have all but disappeared, washed away by the punishing tide of urban poverty. Three members of the class of '65 returned to the school as teachers, but only one,
Arthur Miller, has stuck it out and observed the entire transformation.*

*I visited Arthur at his home in the Flatlands section of Brooklyn on a
Sunday afternoon, while his wife, Leya, and his four-year-old daughter,
Sheryl, were off enjoying a day in the country. Arthur ushered me into the
living room, offered me a seat, and then settled into his "Archie Bunker
chair" by the TV set. I began by asking him about his old neighborhood
of Flatbush around Erasmus High.*

I was born in Flatbush. My father owned a cleaning store, and my parents, my younger brother, and I lived in an apartment building on
Dorchester Road, two blocks from Flatbush Avenue. My mother's
mother lived with us until I was eighteen. I'm glad I grew up with my
grandmother. I think it's important for generations to know about each
other.

We lived in a mixed neighborhood, but most of the kids we hung
out with were Jewish. We didn't know anybody who owned their own
house then. Everybody was in big apartment buildings. Within a radius
of a square city block you're talking eight to ten apartment houses, and
it seemed everybody had kids. You're talking about a pool of maybe
fifty or sixty kids and you didn't even have to walk off your block. I
could just go down to the street corner and meet ten or twelve different
buddies. I enjoyed growing up with a lot of kids in the street. You

didn't need your parents for anything—just to call you when dinner was ready. My daughter won't have that. Where we live now there's ten or fifteen houses on the block. Some have kids and some don't. My daughter, you have to drive her around everyplace. You don't walk as much.

Back then we used to play ball in the street between parked cars. Punch ball, slap ball, football. There were some private homes in Flatbush that had basketball hoops. Every afternoon we'd go play there until the owners would come home and chase us off. When I bought this house, the first thing I did was put up a basket and play ball, telling myself, "No one's gonna chase me here."

As kids, of course, we were all Dodgers fans. The sports pages of the *New York Post* was how I got involved in reading. I remember when the Dodgers left Brooklyn and moved to Los Angeles. I was really just a kid, so I always thought they were coming back to New York. Now it's thirty years later; I guess they're not coming back.

Going to Erasmus was a big deal. Every time we'd walk up Flatbush Avenue and pass Erasmus, my mother would say, "This is where you're going to go someday." That whole summer before, it was a real big deal. Finally we went and got our programs. There were three different shifts. Sophomores went from 10 to 5. It was a big school, 7000 kids. The school was open from 8 in the morning until 5 at night. Tenth-graders got the late shift.

Right away we got involved with rooting for the basketball team. Billy Cunningham had just graduated and we knew that we still had a very good team. We went to a few games, but we were really intimidated by the crowds. If you had a front seat, the tough kids would push you to the back. We knew that our main team to beat was Boys High. The first two years we couldn't beat them. We must have lost to them five times. Then, the last year, 1965, we beat them and we went on to win the city championship. That was fun. Kids parading in the streets up and down Flatbush Avenue until maybe eleven o'clock.

My friends and I would go to the movies a lot on the Avenue. We also played a lot of cards and went bowling. But doing well in school was very important. Senior year my friend and I got this note to come to an Arista meeting—that was the school honors society. We wondered what we were doing there. We were afraid to talk to these kids, they were so smart. We figured it was a mistake, but really my grades had been high junior year.

The other exciting thing that happened senior year was that I got an early acceptance to college. A friend of mine told me to apply to Stony Brook, this new state university that had opened up on Long Island. Everybody else was sweating out getting accepted to college and here I got my acceptance in January. I had no idea why. They told us later they had accepted some kids with lower averages, like myself, as an experiment. I would have gone to Brooklyn College or Queens College like everybody else. My parents agonized whether I was mature enough to go out of town because I'd never been away. I wasn't too good at cleaning up my own room, you know.

We decided, okay, we'll give it a try. I got all sorts of lectures about being good. And it worked. That was a very good period.

At the time that I went to college in Long Island, it was really very countrified, very quiet. Not like it is now. That was the first time I found out that people didn't exactly like you if you were from New York. I never realized it before—that we weren't God's gift to the world, that there were different ways of doing things. The townies didn't like the university students coming to their bars and clubs. As always, they got to know us and we got to know them. It all worked out.

The first day as a freshman, the administrators told us, "Look to your left and look to your right. One of you is not going to be here for graduation." They were right. I had two roommates freshman year, and one of them didn't make it. I had to work very hard at college because I was with smarter kids. The first year or two I was so scared about flunking out. I was lucky. There were some upper-classmen in the dorm who took an interest in me and, besides fooling around, they taught me how to study. The classrooms were open at night, so a group of us would go out every night on our bicycles and study. After the first two years I caught on and then I didn't have to study so much. Still, I didn't get too involved in the antiwar protests. I was really in above my head—it was a very demanding school—and I was too busy just trying to keep up.

I majored in history because that was my best subject in high school. I was going to major in Latin American history in college until the war came. The boys older than me told me, "You'd better take education courses or you're going to get drafted." So I did. I concentrated more on education. To be honest, if there had been no draft, I think I would have gone to law school instead.

At that time, if you got your state certification you could get a substitute's license. It was January 1969. I hadn't student-taught yet. I knew nothing about teaching. We got our provisional licenses right there, guaranteeing us licenses in June if we sent a transcript. And that was the last time they gave a regular sub license. They haven't given any since 1969 so that they don't have to pay full benefits.

I did do my student-teaching at Middleville Junior High School in East Northport, Long Island. Very conservative. I once wore a sweater and I was called into the administrator's office about two weeks later. "We heard you wore a sweater. It's very nice, but you ought not do that." I said, "Okay, I won't do that anymore." They really wanted a sport jacket.

As soon as I graduated in June I visited a few schools looking for a job. One principal promised to give me a job if I came back in September. I came in September and she said, "I'm sorry, there's nothing I can do for you." That same week I had gotten my 1A notice in the mail. So I went to a couple more junior high schools and I went to Erasmus. The principal there said, "Son, next time you come, you should wear a tie." I had just been walking on the Avenue. It was the beginning of September, and hot. That day I also went to the history chairman and he said, "Maybe something will come up." Sure enough, after the first week of the term, he calls me up and says, "You come in Tuesday morning. I got a job for you."

I did get a teacher deferment and I thanked my lucky stars. I felt bad about it at first, wondering if it was bad to have someone else fight for you. But I decided, with help from my parents, that I didn't want to fight someplace that I knew nothing about.

At Erasmus they gave me five classes and said, "We'll see what happens at the end of the semester." I was twenty-one years old and I was very proud to be teaching at Erasmus. I took home $500 to $600 a month, I lived at home. That was a lot of money. I was really pleased. I thought I was a hotshot.

I had a much better beginning as a teacher than most people do. The kids were responding pretty well. They were mostly middle-class Jewish kids. In some cases I had gone to school with their brothers and sisters. One girl came in once and said, "My sister said I don't have to say anything to you because she knew you in the sixth grade when you were a little schmucky kid!" Those kind of kids were pretty good. The chairman would say, "Good rapport." That was the word. "Mr. Miller, a first-term teacher, shows good rapport with his students." But it was because they responded. If a kid was bad, I would say, "You can't take the test tomorrow." That was a punishment to those kids. It wasn't until I'd been teaching two years that I had my first bad class. But back then they were few and far between.

During Thanksgiving of 1971 I went to a dance put on by the UFT, the United Federation of Teachers. I think it was $2.00 for girls and a dollar for guys. That was my type of dance. That was where I met my future wife. She was a math teacher, already appointed at a high school in Queens, whereas I was just a sub. I was impressed by the fact that she had a purpose in life, that she was serious and goal-oriented. She wasn't flighty. I also found her easy to confide in. And, let's face it, I thought she could probably take care of me the way my mother had. We got married about a year later, in December '72. That same year, I got appointed. That meant more money, a pension, more benefits.

The following year I became the assistant union rep for Erasmus. I just wanted to learn the ropes, never thinking I'd someday become the actual shop steward. In 1975 we decided the time had come to buy a house. At the same time, there were huge layoffs. I came within fifty to a hundred names on a citywide list of being laid off. So I started going down to the union hall to pay more attention to what was going on. I started to get more involved. In 1980 the union head at the school went on sabbatical and I took over while she was gone. I subsequently ran against her and won. All these years later I'm still the union man at the school. I'm the union rep for over 270 members: teachers, guidance counselors, lab assistants, secretaries, and paraprofessionals who work on special programs like remedial math or special ed. I handle salary disputes, counseling on sabbatical rights and pension rights—a wide range of problems. It's very difficult, but also very rewarding.

All this time, the school was changing. Part of it was ethnic changes. When I was a student, Erasmus was about 90 percent white and 10 percent black. By the time I started teaching, the composition must have been 75/25. Now it's 100 percent minorities. There are no white students in the school. But the real changes had other causes. In the early '70s the New York State commissioner of education, in order to integrate other schools, made the decision to allow minority students the right to bypass Erasmus and go to white schools in the borough. That took away our best students. All the best students go to other schools. The second problem was that we became an open school. While other schools have neighborhood admissions policies limiting

274 // MIDTERM REPORT

the number of students from outside, we have to take anybody who moves into the area.

Erasmus is now almost a non-English-speaking high school. Out of 4000 students, a thousand are from Haiti and another 1500 or so are from other islands: Jamaica, Trinidad, etcetera. We used to have Southeast Asians, but they had a lot of problems with the other minorities. They were used to trusting their neighbors. They weren't used to locking their doors. It didn't work out, so they all moved to Pennsylvania.

When we were in school, we knew we were there to learn. Now there's so much else going on that it's hard for the kids to concentrate. They bring a lot of problems to school. A large majority of our students have only one parent. They have to take care of younger brothers and sisters. They have other things on their mind which makes school second, and it doesn't work. And there are petty crimes all the time. We call them "untoward incidents." Lockers are broken into constantly. Last month seven kids came in and robbed the classroom next to mine. I didn't hear boo. The other teacher told me about it in passing during a break.

These kids today are pretty sharp streetwise. I give them credit for that. In certain ways they know a lot more about the world than we did. But the average student at Erasmus is just not prepared to go to high school, even though he's old enough to go. They don't have the reading skills to read the text even though it's easy. And if they do, they don't remember what they read. And they don't have the confidence and the verbal skills to answer a question. You can run into a lot of flack by calling on a student: "I didn't raise my hand." They don't like to be called on. They put earphones on and listen to the radio in class. It would be amusing if I wasn't trying to teach them. But when you're serious about it, it's not too amusing. If I don't put notes on the board, if I just talk to them, they think of it as bullshitting. They don't take it seriously. So I put up notes on the board until their hands get tired, and then they get mad about that. And that's not really teaching. Teaching is where you're asking them questions and they're responding. They don't respond. They have no interest in history or where they came from or what they are going to do. These students have no goals. Going to college doesn't mean anything to them. They are very present-oriented. Whatever makes them happy today is all that matters. It's their future, but they haven't bought into it. Teaching at Erasmus can be a very humbling experience, believe me.

In some ways they're no different from students at other schools. They're used to TV and the media. They don't want to interact. They just want to sit there and listen and be entertained, as if the teacher was a television set.

Every now and then we do get a good student. We call them "throwback kids," you know, throwbacks to the '60s. I try to give them encouragement. They make me happy and I try to remember to say thanks to them at the end of the day or the end of the week. But I'd say that in a typical class, about 40 percent receive a failing grade, usually because they cut too many classes. They're just not there.

I do my best to try to reach them by having good work habits myself. I'm there and I'm there on time. I try not to be absent unless I'm really, really sick. I had some very good high school history teachers and I use them as role models. I try not to go so slow that it bores them, but I also teach only one lesson a day, one topic. I try to relate it, when I can, to what's going on today. But it's not easy. I don't always succeed.

Certain lessons just don't go. They don't work. The students have no interest in European history, for example. They're interested in wars, World War I and World War II, but not in the Holocaust. They're not quite sensitive enough to understand what really happened. The New Frontier goes and so does the Great Society. Current events, the Bill of Rights, consumer economics.

People say, "Why do you do it? Why do you keep teaching?" Because every once in a while you teach a good lesson. At the end of class everybody's buzzing and discussing what you talked about. Nobody leaves right at the bell. The chairman of the social studies department, Stan Neuwirth, is a man I greatly admire. He told me once that if you can have one good laugh on your job every day, it would be worthwhile. Maybe that's the trouble. There's not that much amusing anymore. There's not a laugh a day. I do enjoy my colleagues, though. There's about fifteen of us in the department who have taught for fifteen years or more. We have a lot of good times.

But it's tough on teachers these days. Society is measuring worth a lot more now by what they pay you. Starting salary now is $20,000, which is fair, but twenty or twenty-five years later, you're still making $40,000. Teachers want to be part of the American dream like everybody else. You can't buy an automobile or a house on respect or prestige. And we're really on the defensive. The kids aren't doing well and we get blamed. And we don't actually have that much to say as to how the school is run. The school is run like a factory, from the top down. Even the principal has very little to say about the building that he's running. It's all controlled by the board of education; a few people who may have no idea of what's going on. Maybe it's a computer that runs the system. If I could have my way, the teachers would have more input in the way the school is run. The teachers deserve more trust. If you show teachers you're interested, they'll give you all the time and work that's necessary.

This term, for the first time, I'm going to be a dean. I'll be in the halls most of the time telling the kids to get to class. And yet, one thing about my career is that I want to be thought of as a good *teacher*. Everybody's saying how good the deans are or how good the basketball coach is or the grade advisors or the union rep. The one thing that I want to be known as is a good teacher. Not because I was a super-teacher who gave the greatest lessons, but because I was there every day and I tried. Even when there is no response from the kids at all, I hope that maybe a few years later, they'll think back and remember that we teachers were good role models.

There was a noise at the door and in marched Sheryl, home from her outing. Arthur lit up with joy. In an instant, it was clear that the little girl was the highlight of his life. While Arthur went outside to help his wife bring in packages, Sheryl entertained me with somersaults and almost-cartwheels. When Arthur returned, I asked him about his thoughts on parenting.

You always want your kids to have it a little easier. I don't know if that's good or bad because what I see now is sometimes kids have it too easy, have no drive. They just wander aimlessly. I thank my parents for giving me that drive, for not giving me everything so that I had something to shoot for on my own. Without it, it's a tough world out there. If you're not sharp, if you're wishy-washy, you're going to get eaten up, especially in New York. Of course, having said that, I do spoil my daughter rotten.

I've done a lot of the things I wanted to do. Now it's us instead of me. You do it for your kids. I realize that whatever I do now will be for her. I've had my shot. It's her life now.

Kathy Mader, Palisades High
School, Los Angeles,
California.

Katherine Mader with former boyfriend Fred Reinsch and husband, Norman Kulla,
at her twenty-year high-school reunion, 1985. *(© 1985 Los Angeles Times.)*

ABOVE: Marty Kaniger, Palisades
High School, Los Angeles,
California.

RIGHT: Marty Kaniger, keeping the
faith, 1985.

LEFT: Tom Pierson, New York City,
1985.

BELOW: Tom Pierson, valedictorian,
Palisades High School, Los Angeles,
California.

ABOVE: Arthur Miller, Erasmus Hall High School, 1986.

LEFT: Arthur Miller, Erasmus Hall High School, Brooklyn, New York.

LEFT: Barbara Sellars with Daniella Gallo Bailey, New York City, 1983.

BELOW: Barbara Sellars, Putnam City High School, Putnam City, Oklahoma.

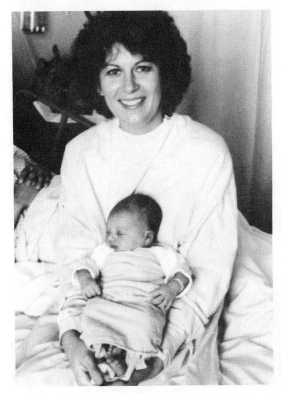

LEFT: Gary Liming, Fairborn High School, Fairborn, Ohio.

RIGHT: Gary Liming, dressed up for his daughter's eighth-grade graduation, St. Mary's, Ohio, 1985.

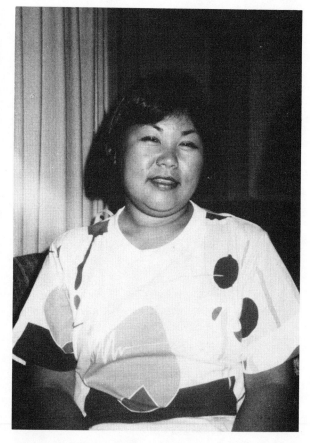

ABOVE: Carol Iwata, Waimea High School, Kauai, Hawaii.

RIGHT: Carol Iwata, 1985.

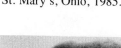

ABOVE: Charles Thomas, Ferndale High School, Ferndale, Michigan.

RIGHT: Charles Thomas, 1985.

ABOVE: Linda Christopherson, East Dougherty High School, Charleston, South Carolina.

LEFT: (Linda) Ramona Christopherson, at home on the Farm, Summertown, Tennessee, 1986.

LEFT: Barbara Palmer, at home in Pleasant Ridge, Michigan, 1985.

BELOW: Barbara Palmer, Kingston High School, Kingston, New York.

ABOVE: Paul Glover, Ithaca High School, Ithaca, New York.

RIGHT: Paul Glover, Venice, California, 1983 *(photo by Erin Fitzgerald)*.

ABOVE: Claudine Cmarada, 1970.

RIGHT: Claudine Cmarada at the Winchester Thurston School senior prom, Pittsburgh, Pennsylvania.

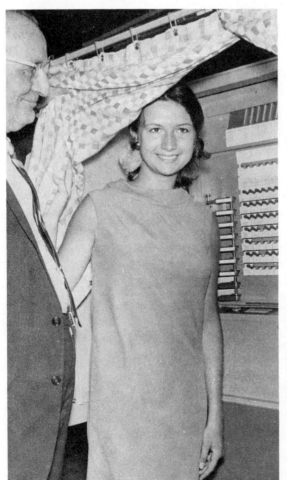

LEFT: Claudine Cmarada, 1968, voting for the first time.

BELOW: Claudine Schneider, 1985.

RIGHT: David Hinkley,
Yosemite Falls, 1965 *(photo
by Michael Keplinger)*.

BELOW: David Hinkley, at his
desk, 1985.

THE HUNTER:

Gary Liming

It wasn't easy interviewing Gary Liming. It was not that he was hard to find or hard to talk with; it's just that the living room of the Liming home in the small town of St. Mary's, Ohio, can be a very busy place on a Sunday afternoon when it's cold outside. His children showed a mild interest when Gary brought out his old high-school yearbook. When I pulled out my tape recorder, it became necessary to halt activity at the stereo and the computer. A compromise was reached with the television in the den, which was allowed to remain on a football game as long as the sound was turned down.

My father was a civilian employee at the air-force base when I was born. His family's all from southern Ohio, which is redneck country, ham and beans and cornbread type of people. My mother's family are all German immigrants, bakers by trade. My great-grandfather had a bakery in Fairfield before it became Fairborn. Dad's family is from the hills, and I think that's where part of my love for hunting comes from. He took me out with him for the first time when I was thirteen. Then he had a heart attack when I was a junior in high school and he was forty-two. Of course he was confined to the house, and I'd gotten a job as a Fuller Brush salesman, my first job. He let me have his work car, and it more or less became my car. So he figured by that time I was smart enough that I wouldn't blow my foot off, so I started to go hunting alone. My father died in 1974.

Fairborn High School students were about half military and half civilian, and there were very few people that crossed the lines. I mean, if you were civilian, you had to be the class president to run with the military kids. The military kids all thought they were better than the civilian kids, and of course that created resentment amongst some of the civilian kids. I crossed the line a little bit as far as I dated a couple of girls that were military. But I couldn't deal with all the "Yes sir" and "No sir."

For instance, this one girl I took to the senior prom, her dad was a major. She had told me beforehand, she said, "You know, be nice to Dad, and 'Yes sir' and 'No sir.'" Well, I didn't say "Yes sir" or "No sir" to anybody, really. My dad didn't expect it. But I did it to please her.

I was an average or below-average student, B's and C's, only two or three D's in my life, because I was scared to get my butt kicked. See, my father went to the eighth grade in school and he had a thing about his kids getting an education and all that. He didn't mind B's and C's, but if you came home with a D, look out. He was from the old school—into the woodshed with a belt. Fortunately, it was only for report cards. If it had been for tests, I'd have been dead years ago. Best thing that ever happened to me was when I got into high school, they started to use those mimeographs—you know, carbon. A carbon sheet's inserted and you get like the third copy, like W2 forms. So you lay a piece of carbon over it and you can change the D into a B. If I got a D, I just changed the darn thing and saved myself a lot of trouble.

Girls, of course, took up a lot of time. I wasn't sophisticated enough to talk them out of their virginity. So I didn't get too far. I was a late bloomer by most standards. Not that I feel like I've missed anything, because there are a lot of people who have had a lot of problems because they got into that sort of thing early. How's that for a good rationalization?

I played football in school. In the lower grades, eighth, ninth, I was on the starting team, but when I got to high school I was second string. I was guard or tackle, depending on how much I weighed. Now I'm about 255. Back then I was anywhere from 213 to 260, depending whether I worked out with weights. Now it's just all fat. I had a back injury in my junior year and I didn't play football my senior year. I thought it was unfair because I felt like I could play, and yet the doctor said no and my parents said no. So I said to hell with the whole thing and didn't want to have any more to do with it. I didn't even go to the games in my senior year. That's when I started to do a lot of hunting.

I didn't have a profession in mind. When anybody would ask, I'd tell 'em I was going to be an architectural engineer. I mean, I didn't know what the hell an architectural engineer was, but it sounded good, you know. I wasn't any great shakes as a Fuller Brush salesman. I spent the money faster than I could make it. It was a way to make money for me; that's all I cared about. I would go out and work until I thought I had enough money to buy gas and go out on a date, and the heck with it.

The summer that I graduated, I drove a truck for the Fairborn Lumber Company. Then I quit and moved up here to St. Mary's. We had a cottage up here from about the time I was six years old, so I lived in the cottage and got a job at Hoge Lumber. A factory-type thing, assembly line. I hated that job. Repetitious, the same thing every day. They had me on a job making carpet strips, and to this day I don't know what carpet strips are. I just made them for eight or ten hours a day.

While I was working at Hoge Lumber Company, Alan, the guy that I ran around with, got his draft notice and he went to see if he could get into anything where he could get schooling rather than going directly into the army, and they offered him a deal that he could go to avionics school to become a helicopter mechanic. So he came to me and he said, "Gary, you're going to get your draft notice anyway. Why don't you and I join on the buddy plan and we can go through basic and go to the school together?" That seemed reasonable to me at the time. In '65 and '66 it seemed like the thing to do. Vietnam had escalated from a police action into a full-fledged war where guys were going to fight *for* something, and you're floating around in between high school and no-man's-land wondering what to do. And you think, Well, hell, I ought to just get into this thing and you feel like it might do something for you—that's how smart you are when you're eighteen or nineteen. It gets you killed is what it'll do for you!

This was the marines, so we went to Cleveland to take the physical and Alan passed and they swore him in while I proceeded to flunk the physical because of my back. So I went and applied for his job that he vacated and got it. That's how I happened to leave Hoge Lumber and went to work at Midwest Electric, which is a rural cooperative. I got a job as a warehouse accountant and stayed there for a couple of years. The only qualification was you had to be able to count up to a hundred. Counting nuts and bolts. But the title was "warehouse accountant."

I'm happy as hell I didn't get into that Vietnam mess. Then along came '67, '68, '69, and you're picking up the paper and here guys you knew around town are dead. You think of a war as going over there and being the guy that charges up the hill and all this crap, and then somebody you know comes home in a wheelchair and he's going to be in that wheelchair for life, and all of a sudden there's no glory or anything. That's the realization that I got out of it. One guy I knew growing up got killed, and it wasn't just his getting killed so much as the stories that went with it. He had stepped on a land mine and was so mangled that when they had to have an identification, an uncle had to look at the body. The army wouldn't let the parents do it.

Around this time, I started dating Joanne, my wife. I've known her ever since we started coming up here when I was six. Her dad owned a grocery store out at the lake. Known her for years and years and years. Never paid a damn bit of attention to her, and all of a sudden one day I thought, Hmmm, maybe I ought to ask her to go out. Her parents are Catholic to the core, and at that time she wasn't even allowed to date Protestants. They finally relented and let me date her, and when we decided to get married, the qualification was that I convert. We were married in September 1969. Joanne's the oldest in her family, and now she's had three other sisters that married non-Catholics and there was no talk about conversion, because I think they saw that it didn't really help.

Joanne was going to college at Ohio State and I thought, You know, don't be a dummy; go back to school. So I quit out at Midwest Electric and got a job as a construction worker building grain silos for the summer to make enough money to go back to school. Then I went to Columbus Business University, which wasn't all that it was cracked up to be. They spent most of their money printing brochures. When you got to the facility, it was rundown. They used part-time teachers, subpar professionals. I didn't feel like you were getting your money's worth. It was a business for these people more than it was a school.

While I was going to school I worked for a retail-credit company as an insurance investigator on the near south side of Columbus, which was an eye-opener for a small-town boy. Carried a gun. It's all black and Fairborn is predominantly white and St. Mary's is all white, and I'd never dealt with black people. You got a one-sided impression because they weren't the cream of the black crop. They were people that weren't paying their bills.

I did a lot of credit-card collections, which I did by choice because they paid you twenty-five dollars for every credit card you could get. I worked out a scam for that. I'd go to the door, and these people hate to be taken. They might not pay their bills, but they don't like to be screwed either. So you go to the door and you tell this guy, "I'm from such-and-such credit company, and somebody's been using your credit card, and we want to find out who."

He'd get all bent out of shape. And you'd say, "Can I see your card? I want to check it against the numbers on the card." And if he was dumb enough to hand you his card, you'd walk to the car and drive off as fast as you could. I got twenty-five dollars for each one I could turn in.

After school I got an offer from American Budget Company, one of these small savings-and-loan outfits in New Bremen. They offered me a job as assistant manager. After about six months, they promoted me to manager, traveling manager. I went around all of their seven branches and filled in while the other managers took their vacations.

We dealt with a lot of blacks down there, too, and I found out they were a whole different type of people. Just like us. They were people that came in and borrowed money and paid money back. And they had families and jobs, and the only difference between them and me was that they were black. I had assumed up until that time that they were different. You know, to these old Germans around here, they were niggers. That's all it is. They wouldn't give one of them a break in a hundred years.

So I didn't know anything about black people. Then it turned out I actually had more respect for a lot of them than for the whites. If a black man told you down there "I'll be in Monday with the money," nine times out of ten, he's there with the money. Now if some of these white guys told you "I'll be in there Monday with the money," they were usually back in Kentucky with the car by Monday and you had to go down there and repossess it. I got altogether a different picture. A lot of people's attitudes are formed just by the fact that they don't have any contact with them. I learned that in a hurry. You had to meet the right ones, whether black, white, red, green, whatever.

Then I got offered a job at a bank in Coldwater as assistant manager in their personal-loan department. They found me. They were looking for a collector. They had a real problem with their delinquencies and I was always real good at collections, so they made me an offer I couldn't refuse, I guess. I did that job for about two years, never did like it. It was too restricted. That was a small town where you had to be

nice to everybody because they either were customers or potential customers. And if I have a problem with somebody I would just as leave
be able to tell them about it as have to bite my tongue and forget
about it.

Also, I just didn't like the suit-and-tie-type atmosphere. Major
complaints I had from the board were that my shoes weren't shiny
enough. It's the little things that count with them. They expect you to
do your job and do it well, but they also expect you to attend the
Soroptimists Women's Hamburger Fry and all that kind of crap. It all
fell on you because the manager had already done it for years, and if he
could pawn it off on you, he was going to make you do it. I just got
tired of going to these little social functions and all that stuff. It was a
real downer for me every day, and I guess when I'd come home, I'd
more or less take it out on my wife. I was not my usual jovial self. So I
just quit cold turkey. That was 1973. My wife told me it was the best
thing that ever happened when I quit that job.

I picked up the paper one night and saw an ad in there that they
were looking for a truck driver. And I thought, What I need to do is
make a complete reversal of what I've been doing. So I went and interviewed and he asked me if I'd ever had any experience with trucks. I
said, "Oh, yes, straight trucks." And he said, "What about semis?"
Well, when I was a wee little kid we lived by the cement plant there in
Fairborn and I used to go over to Schwerman's on weekends and
they'd pay kids to wash the trucks. That was my experience! "Oh, yeah,
I've had some semi experience." He said, "All right, can you start tomorrow morning?" and I said, "Sure."

Boy, I was scared to death. I mean, just getting in one of those
things out of the blue scared the shhhh right out of me. You had to take
a driver's test—ninety miles, and the guy that owns the company, he
went with me, and he drove when we went to Columbus to a meat-
packing plant. He drove up, and on the way back he pulled over on the
side and he said, "You might as well take it. It's about ninety miles till
we get home. You'll have your test done, all right?"

Oh, God! So I got in the driver's seat and he proceeded to fall
asleep, sound asleep—saved my butt, because I didn't know how to
change gears or anything. But he just laid back there and snored. Slept
like a baby the whole time I was driving. I drove all the way home
without wrecking the damn thing, so I passed the test. Been driving
ever since. Of course, once you get out by yourself with nobody looking

over your shoulder, it's not so hard. You can make a little mistake with the gear or something and you don't panic.

I drove there about six months and was gone all the time. The wife didn't like that. I had a brother-in-law that drove for Sturgeon Oil Company, and they were gone like three days a week, and he wanted to be on the road all the time, so we just traded jobs.

One thing I remember, though, before I changed jobs—we used to go into Baltimore, to the docks, and pick up meat and stuff. I took a load of turkeys in one time, and when you had an overload, the driver got to keep it. So I had like thirty big tom turkeys. There was this little black kid, and he was a humper, one of the guys that help unload the trucks, just a little shit. I had all these turkeys left over, and I thought, What am I going to do with them? And he said, "Well, can I buy them off you?" and I said, "Well, I suppose."

So we made a deal and I said, "What are you going to do with them?" He said, "Come on with me." He had a bicycle, and I had to follow him in the truck. We went down into some part of Baltimore, a black section, and this little boy took those turkeys and went around and gave them to his neighbors. Just gave them away, like Christmas. It was right around Thanksgiving time. I was so moved that I didn't charge him. He was a peach.

Anyway, I drove semis for the oil company for about nine years and straight trucks for two years after they cut out the semi part of it. That's why I quit. I didn't like the straight trucks because it's drive fifteen miles and unload ten cases of oil, then drive another fifteen. With the semi, basically you're going to make one or two stops, and it's all driving. We ran West Virginia and Chicago, Fort Wayne, and we went into Indianapolis, Cincinnati, Michigan. Now, in the wintertime I've been driving trucks for St. Mary's Trucking. They've only got rights for Ohio, so that's basically Cleveland area. The rest of the year I work for Conay, which is a stone quarry north of town. I run a front-loader down in the hole. It's a machine that loads dirt or stone, digs about sixty ton, which I enjoy. Anytime I get around machinery, I'm happy.

To me, truck driving is hours and hours of boredom, interspersed with seconds of terror. Any day that you didn't get killed was a positive experience. I've had a couple of bad wrecks that weren't my fault. The worst wreck I was involved in, I was going down to Oxford. There's a back road that goes from Middleton, and I was going across there one night. It was raining, and four girls in a little Toyota ran a stop sign, and I hit them broadside. My truck went down through a field and out into some guy's yard there. I jumped out and ran back and their car was wrapped around this telephone pole. I ran up and got to the back of the car and saw this stuff running down the back window and this lady's laying back there, and I thought, God, it's her brains! I can't look in there. Why me, Lord? You know, there's no traffic around, just a back road. And I stood there and stood there and thought, Well, I got to see if I can do anything. So I walked on up and looked at her, and she looked all right, and I looked again and found out they were on their way to a wedding shower, and it was a crock pot full of baked beans they had sitting on the back window! Baked beans!

I saw a guy burned to death one time. It was the worst experience I ever had. That was on the other side of Columbus. Guy was driving a pickup truck with the gas tank on the inside, you know, behind the seat. He changed lanes, and he clipped another truck and rolled over on its side, and it slid and caught on fire. I was coming from the other direction, just left Buckeye Truck Stop, and I got there just in time to see the door open and he jumped out and, just like you see on TV, arms waving and stuff. He fell on the ground, and I ran over with a fire extinguisher, as did a bunch of people, but just too late. To this day I can't watch anything on TV when they show these people on fire. I can't handle that.

I have always considered myself to be fortunate in that I'm satisfied with the way things are. I feel sorry for people that haven't found what makes them happy. I feel sorry for them because I'm well satisfied. Of course, my expectation of what makes people happy might be a lot lower than some people's. I don't know. Maybe I'm just a born-again nerd.

I spend a lot of time in the woods, even when it's not hunting season. I do what's commonly known by deer hunters as scouting. All it is is a way to get out of the house and get into the woods, and that's prior to the season and postseason. You go out without a weapon, just see where the deer are at and what they're doing and sit around and watch the squirrels, and people think you're nuts or wasting your time like that. It's relaxing to be outdoors. I'm really not that big on killing things, but I just get a kick out of hunting. If the purpose was to kill things, they would call it killing, not hunting.

I don't drink as much as I used to, now that I have a wife and four kids. My wife is the guidance counselor up at the high school, and along with the job goes the drug- and alcohol-abuse program. And it's not real good for her husband to be fooling around in the bars around town. If I wanted to do any serious drinking, I'd have to leave town. So I just occasionally have a beer now and then.

I love being a father. Of course it helps having a more or less professional child-handler in the house. My wife deals with them all the time and she can sit down and talk to them. It makes a lot of difference. I think the kids were more of an aggravation when they were little than they are now. Once they get to the age where they can dress themselves, it seems like everything gets easier—to me, anyway.

One boy set himself on fire one time out here in the garage, playing with gasoline. I was in the shower upstairs and he came up, and when I opened the shower door, he looked like one of those cartoon characters that you see after an explosion on TV. The black holes and the smoke and the hair. I thought, What now! And the youngest was up there, she was about four and he was about six. I started giving him hell right off the bat, you know, as any good parent should—"You ought to know better!"

And she's going, "Dad, Dad," and I'm giving him hell. "Dad, Dad!" I said, *"What?"* I was mad. She just stood there. So I started in on him again.

Finally I turned to her and said, "Kelly, what's the matter?" And she said, "The garage is on fire." Oh, shit! There's a bale of straw in there that I use with the dogs and that had caught on fire. Well, the neighbor's out there and he had the fire out, but Kelly wasn't going to tell me. She's still like that. If you give her any shit, she won't talk to you. She has an animal which I would like to take to the woods and use for target practice. It takes dog food and changes it into shit. That's his whole purpose in life.

My wife and I share the family and our relationship, but as far as recreation, we have different interests. I think you can spend too much time together. It's just my opinion. She likes to shoot a little bit, but as far as her interests, I don't cross over on that side too much. She's a 10K runner and she enters triathlons. To me, running is right up there with truck driving, just hours and hours of boredom.

I'm just laid back enough and easygoing enough that as long as I get up in the morning and I'm still breathing, I'm happy. The future's here as far as I'm concerned. This is as good as it gets.

MOST TALKATIVE:

Carol Iwata

The United States is such a huge country that it is easy for many Americans to become very provincial, to forget that their view of the nation is only one of many.

More than five thousand miles from New York City, on the west coast of the island of Kauai, is Waimea High School, the westernmost high school in the United States. Although the graduates of Waimea High may seem like "foreigners" to some people on the mainland, they are all U.S. citizens, who vote in national elections, pay taxes to the Internal Revenue Service, and are eligible to be elected president of the United States.

I met with Waimea High graduate Carol Iwata in Honolulu, during what was for her a journey of rediscovery and a time for reflection.

My family came from Hiroshima to Hawaii as contract laborers in the 1880s. I grew up in a plantation camp called Wahiawa, which means "red dirt." It's all dirt roads; you wouldn't be able to find it unless someone told you how to get there. The sugar company built these little camps for its workers in the middle of the sugarcane fields and would charge nominal rent which was taken out of their paychecks every month. The residents of this camp were mostly Japanese with some Filipinos. My three brothers and I went to regular school during the day and then would come home and go to a Japanese-language school which was connected to our Buddhist church. As my grandmother lived with us and could speak little English, our house was pretty bilingual.

My father was a surveyor for the sugar company. He died of a brain hemorrhage when I was seven. After he died, my mom had to support the family, so she started working in the sugarcane fields as a laborer. She also had to take care of my grandmother, her mother-in-law, who was not an easy person to get along with. Looking back on it now, I realize how her world really fell apart. My mother came from Honolulu; she was a big-city girl who, when she got engaged to my father, thought her future was going to be in Honolulu. Then she had to come to this small immigrant town where there was no indoor plumbing, indoor baths, or hot running water, because my father had to return to Kauai. By the time I was born, the family had moved to a row of houses called "New Houses" because they had indoor plumbing, although we had an outdoor bath, which was connected to one of our neighbor's, and no running hot water.

It was such a shock when President Kennedy died. The one thing I remember most about his death was seeing the funeral on TV. I saw Mrs. Kennedy and I thought, That poor woman; her husband's dead and she has two small kids to support. Then I thought, Carol, you're really stupid; President Kennedy is dead and of course it's sad, but Mrs. Kennedy doesn't have to worry about how she's going to feed her kids. It made me realize what my mom went through; her husband died, she had four kids and an in-law to support, and had no money. It made me appreciate her a lot. I feel bad that it took me that long, but I'm glad it happened then instead of later in life. I think it's a tribute to her that she protected us and that we were basically happy. Also, coming from a camp life where your neighbors were like your extended family made a difference.

I was voted the "Most Talkative" of my high-school class. I was up for a couple of other things, like "Most Friendly" and such, but they decided that everyone could be in only one category, and everyone knew I should win for "Most Talkative." I was jolly and funny. I was really fat, and I think when you're fat, you sometimes compensate by being jolly. It might hide a lot of insecurities that you don't realize are there, but as you get older you realize how it was. When I came back for my twenty-year reunion, the first reunion I've attended, some people didn't recognize me because I had lost weight and wore contacts, but once I opened my mouth, they knew it was me. I call it "diarrhea of the mouth"; I can't help it.

Since I grew up in a basically Japanese environment, I decided, while in high school, that I wanted to know what it was like to live in a Caucasian-dominated society. At our high school and in our camp, we were the majority. So I decided to go to college on the mainland. I thought if I went to the West Coast, I would hang around with other Japanese and wouldn't really experience what it would be like to be a minority, which is the norm for the Japanese-Americans on the mainland. One of my classmate's sisters had gone to Northern Michigan and said it was really nice, so I applied there and was accepted. When my mom and I talked about it, she said, "If you go there, you can't come home for four years because I can't afford to bring you back." I know it was very difficult for her to say that to me, her only daughter.

I had never been to the mainland before. First I went to California to visit a relative and then went to Detroit, where I had a pen pal and visited with her and her family. I was really homesick by the time I got to Detroit; everything was so different. Then I flew up to Northern Michigan. I was so bewildered that I was going crazy. I had this image of Michigan being in the middle of the country, so I thought it would be easy to travel around once I got there. But not the Upper Peninsula of Michigan! When I got there I thought, My God, what did I come to? I couldn't believe it.

By the time I reached my dorm, I still hadn't met anyone. I didn't know what to do. Then a girl came up to me and said hi and invited me to go to orientation with her and her mom. I was so nervous and relieved that this girl was friendly. While we were walking along she said, "What's your name?" I said, "Carol Iwata. What's yours?" She said, "Robin Hood." The first person I met in college was named Robin Hood. It was the funniest thing in the world, but I was afraid that if I laughed, she would get mad. I thought, "My God, these *haoles,* these Caucasians, are really kind of weird!"

I remember walking around the campus during orientation with tears rolling down my cheeks because I was so homesick and I knew I couldn't go home for four years. Looking back on it now, I realize that it was probably one of the hardest experiences I've ever had but also one of the best.

The college was almost all Caucasian. Coincidentally, this other girl in my high-school graduating class, whom I had gone to school with since kindergarten, also chose to go to Northern Michigan. She and I and a few foreign students were the only Orientals. I remember one Thanksgiving I went to a girlfriend's home. She said, "Carol, we're going to my uncle's house for dinner. Don't ever tell him you're Japanese because he fought in the war and hates Japanese people. He'll go berserk. Just say you're Hawaiian." Of course, I went nuts. I had never experienced anything like that. I was so scared through the whole evening, but I did it.

During my first year, members of the Job Corps were housed on our campus. A lot were American Indians, and I sometimes got mistaken for an American Indian. I didn't mind that, but when I went to town I was sometimes treated differently because the American Indians and the Job Corps people were looked down upon and made fun of.

The first semester I did really bad. I had two roommates who were very close friends and I was always the odd man out. My first couple of months were just miserable. I couldn't get adjusted to my roommates; they would go to bed at nine o'clock at night, and I'm a night person. So I was practically living out of my room. I changed dormitories the second semester and things got a lot better.

During the summers I would work on the mainland. The first summer I worked at a resort in Rhode Island. Then, beginning the summer of '67, I started to work as a secretary at a law firm in Chicago and returned every summer.

During my sophomore year, I began to feel that I really wanted to go home and see my mom. So that summer, I worked I don't know how many days straight to make the money for the flight home at Christmas. Looking back, I can't believe how much I worked, but I did save enough money for the plane fare in addition to money for school. When I returned in the fall, my teachers all agreed to let me take my exams before Christmas so I could have a month at home; they were all really nice about that.

I flew back and surprised my mom; she was shocked. I think it surprised everyone else too, because they always thought I wasn't a very serious person and wouldn't have been able to do something like this, as the fare was really expensive.

I worked in Chicago during the summer of '68 at the time of the Democratic Convention. I had written to the governor of Hawaii, John Burns, on a lark asking if I could get in, and he helped me get an alternate's pass. I did get to go down on the floor and see Paul Newman and some other celebrities. On the way back from the Amphitheater, riding in a bus with the Hawaii delegation, I could hear the rioting. When we got off at their hotel, which was right across the street from the Conrad Hilton, people were fighting and I was very frightened. There were lots of cops on horses lined up in front of the Conrad Hilton. The demonstrators would throw things and the cops would hit them. It's one thing to see it on TV, but it's another thing to be right there.

I thought these people had a right to demonstrate; they really did. No one wanted the war; we wanted to get out. I felt bad because here were people fighting for others to come back and they themselves might get killed. I felt very sympathetic toward these demonstrators, and yet, because in Japanese society you don't do that, there was a conflict within myself about it. No one wanted this kind of demonstration to happen, but it was somehow right it happened in Chicago. Mayor Daley was a tyrant of a leader and it really showed him for what he was.

The war had really come home to me when one of my girlfriends went to Hawaii to meet her boyfriend, who had a one-week R-and-R from Vietnam. She told me that although it was wonderful seeing him, it was difficult because sometimes she'd wake up and he would be having nightmares, beating her up and not even realizing it. He had been seriously injured and had nightmares about survival and would hit her black and blue in his sleep.

Later, it was very important for me to honor the journalists who were missing in Vietnam. I believe it was because of their reporting from Vietnam that we got out of the war. I thought about this for a long time, wondering what I could do. Then one day I picked up a *TV Guide* which had an article about journalists missing in Vietnam. It mentioned Dana Stone and Sean Flynn, who had disappeared on April 7, 1970. That day, as I was walking on Madison Street in Chicago, I passed a jewelry store. I went in, bought a bracelet, and told the clerk, "I want you to engrave these two names on it and, in between, the date of 4/7/70." I put that bracelet on and for twelve years took it off only once, when I had surgery. Every year on April 7, I would go to a church and pray for them and the MIAs, something which I still do. Then in 1983 Walter Cronkite, who was the president of Journalists Missing in Action, came to town on a promotional tour, and I gave him the bracelet and asked him to give it to one of the families.

After college, I came to Chicago and worked at a different law firm than the one I had worked at during the summers. After a year I changed firms and about a year and a half later I was asked to become a paralegal. At that time, no one knew what a paralegal was. I took care of our clients' personal property and capital-stock taxes—whether they should file returns, pay the taxes, seeing the state's attorney to settle the case if they were sued for nonpayment of the taxes. A couple of years later, one of the attorneys in my department needed someone to organize and monitor the cases of a new client. I transferred to that position; I'm still working for him and another attorney. I now do all their client billing and other odds and ends that need to be done. I've been with the same firm since 1971.

I like Chicago except for the winters. It's a hardworking city, the people are real down to earth, and the politics here are never boring. When we were in grammar school, one of the big events for me was when the Honolulu Symphony came to Kauai. Cultural events like that were really a luxury. In Chicago I can take advantage of all sorts of cultural activities, which is such a joy. I get to go to a lot of plays and movies; I belong to a couple of film societies and attend a weekly film class. Last year I went to 269 movies! I don't think I'll ever break that record!

I used to volunteer at the Historical Society. I would dress up as a pioneer woman and make candles. Can you imagine me in old-time pioneer garb, having an Oriental face, trying to explain to visitors that I was an example of a pioneer woman?

I live in Lincoln Park, where a lot of the yuppies live. It seems a lot of them are not very happy; they seem to be on a treadmill going nowhere and it must be difficult for them. They've got it all, but then, what do they have? Our parents' luxuries are our necessities. I think most of the yuppies are younger than I am and did not grow up with the '60s generation. If there's one thing I'm happy about it is that I am a '60s child. It was an exciting time—a time of real caring and commitment. I think we were the last generation able to freely do something about that caring and commitment as a whole. I don't see it now in the younger generation.

Most of my friends are single. Although I don't date a lot, I seem to be busy all the time. I don't go to bars; it's just not me. Back in college, I'd have close friends; then they'd get married and I wouldn't hear from them again. I'd think, "Well, what was I?" Now I'm happy that women are realizing that you don't have to give up your friends when you get married. It would be nice to be married; however, it's not a major concern in my life as it's something you can't predict or plan on. I'm glad I live in a time where being single and having close male friends are acceptable.

A few years ago, the sugar company began encouraging people to move out of the camps in Wahiawa and to build their own homes on some land they set aside about a mile away. When the time came when my mother said she wanted to move, my older brothers and I got together to help her. I took all the savings I had and dumped it in for the house. We're paying the mortgage, splitting it evenly with my mom.

I told my mom that when she dies, I don't want her to leave a penny. I want her to do anything and everything she wants. For all the hard work she did, she deserves it. In my parents' and grandparents' time, their big purpose for sacrifice was *kodomo no tame ni,* "for the sake of the children." You endure any hardship for the future of your children. Now, for me, it's "for the sake of my mom," who is now seventy-three years old. I'm so happy she can now take a hot shower whenever she wants, instead of coming home from work, like she used to when we were living in Wahiawa, and having to go outside to warm up the heater and wait for half an hour. It may be a small thing but it means a lot.

I come home to Kauai at least once a year. I love coming home to see my mom and my neighbors, all of whom are in their seventies and eighties. They have all had hard lives; I cherish all these people and am very proud of them. It's a part of American history that people don't know about—the Japanese immigrants coming here almost like slave labor, working for nine dollars a month or less. I feel bad for people who reject their childhood and their past, because the only way you can measure yourself is to go back where you grew up. When you reject your past, you're really rejecting a part of yourself.

There's not a lot of outlet for me to indulge the Japanese side of my heritage when I'm in Chicago. The only time I eat Japanese food is when I go to a Japanese restaurant. But when I come home, it's different. We speak Japanese, eat Japanese food, and I get to catch up on my Japanese TV shows. I'm pretty comfortable being a Japanese-American. I think a lot has to do with the fact that our parents were not interned like those on the mainland and we grew up in a place where the Japanese were the majority. When I'm on the mainland, I'm on the American side of my hyphenated nationality; when I'm here, I'm on the Japanese side. I'm lucky most of the time to find a middle.

I came home this time to attend two reunions: my class reunion and the Wahiawa reunion. Then, this past week, my mom's aunt died, so all her relatives had an unplanned reunion.

I think the best part of the class reunion was when we honored the five people from our class who have died. Coincidentally, they are all buried in the same cemetery. Persons who had been close to those who died spoke about what their friendship with that person had meant to them. Then we went to each grave to put flowers on it and speak with the parents who had been invited. For some it was painful; however, they told me it was wonderful to have their child remembered in this way.

In Buddhism, death is a natural progression in the cycle of life. It's not a mystery; it's a passage. Every summer, each Buddhist church has a *bon odori,* a festival where men, women, and children folk-dance in a ring to honor the memory of the dead, memories of the happy times they have provided and shared with you. This ties in with the Wahiawa reunion.

The sugar company is going to tear Wahiawa down by the end of the year; sugar is dying and they want to do some experimentation with macadamia nuts and tea. The house I lived in will be destroyed. It saddens me, because physically my whole past will be gone. But I'm glad we had this reunion, because it was like a happy funeral, if there is such a thing. A funeral is very necessary in life because it's an outlet for people to deal with their grief of someone who has died. If I had to come back and Wahiawa had all of a sudden not been there, it would have been hard to deal with. But this reunion, like a funeral, gave us a chance to say, We're letting you go, but the memory will never disappear. It was in remembrance of those who came before us, thanking them for all they have given us.

I never forget that I'm a very, very lucky person. I'm lucky with my friends. I'm lucky with my family. I'm really lucky with my mom. I'm really glad that I have deep roots in my family and my Japanese-American background. In this age of uncertainty, that background has anchored me. My mother once gave me a wall hanging that said, "There are two things you can give your children: One is roots and the other is wings." After a while, you have to go, but if you have strong enough roots, they will never be broken.

THE LADIES' MAN:

Charles Thomas

I first met Charles Thomas at the unemployment office in Royal Oak, Michigan. He told me it was a place with which he was all too familiar, yet he continued to express more optimism than bitterness. Later that night he joined me in my motel room for a few hours of relaxed and easy conversation.

I was born at Helena, Arkansas, the second out of four. My father worked at a paper mill, but we came back up to the Detroit area right after I was born. I had a healthy childhood; I really did. We didn't have a lot, but our clothes were always clean, and I had fun.

My mother always has been the dominating factor in our house. There was never any of this "I'm going to tell your father on you" or "You wait until your father gets home." If you did something wrong, Mom'd take care of it herself, right then and there. In the type of neighborhood we lived in, if I was supposed to be in school and I wasn't, my mom's phone's going to ring: "Hey, I see that young man of yours floating around." Then, it ain't about waiting until I come home—she's going to come out and look for me. And wherever I was at, she'd do her thing there. I think it helped me growing up because I never became a troublemaker.

The only hard time I had in school was beginning high school in the ninth grade. I grew up in an all-black neighborhood. We were a community of black people surrounded by white people. I went to an all-black elementary school. I think there was one white teacher at the school I went to, and she was the music teacher. Everything but the walls was black. Then I went to Ferndale High, which had about three thousand students, and there might be five hundred of us black, just from that one little area. All the teachers were white. I don't remember any black teachers being there. Out of all my buddies, I had the worst time getting adjusted. Freshman year, ninth grade, I messed up so bad that summer school wouldn't help, and I lost a year. I just didn't take classes seriously. I'd go to sleep.

But I was in school every day. I had fun talking to people, growing up, checking it out. I didn't want to miss nothing. During that time, if your young lady wore your jacket, then you're "going steady" with her. Going steady? I'd never heard of that. There was a whole different terminology. Another thing: In the neighborhood I didn't see black couples walking around holding hands. When I got to high school, white couples, they go hand in hand. I thought it was really cute; I really did. See, the blacks, they hugged up, and they can't walk properly. They're always stumbling. Holding hands, you can swing. So that's what I started doing. I started holding hands with my girlfriend. I liked that. I still like it. I'll hold hands in a minute. In high school I mostly went along, messing with the chicks, but after my freshman year my grades was fine.

My sister's right below me, and we graduated in '65 together. I had made up my mind to quit when my class graduated in 1964. Then, after summer vacation was over, I was going into the service. The morning of the beginning of the next semester, my sister got up to go to school, and I was still in bed. I said, "I don't have to get up so early today because I'm going to the recruiting office." But Mom came back and said, "No, you're going to school." I said, "They're going to be mocking me." She said, "You're going to school," and that's what I did. My mother put so much emphasis on school because she didn't get a chance. Mom only went up to the fifth grade because she had to work in the fields. So she'd say, "Learn something. Don't be a dummy." She didn't even allow us to work, except in summer.

If I hadn't been in school that extra year, I wouldn't have met Maxine, my wife. She was a real sharp chick. Everybody thought she was white. I didn't pay close attention to her at first because I thought she was a white girl, too, and I didn't date white girls. My mom spoke on that, too: "You stay in your own race, boy. Don't be crossing."

After graduation I got a job with a small company that chrome-plated bumpers. My job was to attach them to this rack so they could be dipped in cleaner and then in acid. I worked there about a month and it scared me because of the hot metal and the acid.

I wanted to stay away from the Big Three—Ford, Chrysler, and GM—but all my buddies, they got them '64 Chevy convertibles and I had me a '55 Buick! So I said, "Wow, I got to get me one of these." So I finally went out to Ford Motor Company and applied. I took some tests and they hired me on to do inspection. They gave me a pencil and a clipboard with a pad of paper on it and took me over and told me to fill in here, make sure the screws is here, make sure the bolts is there, and if it's not, make a mark here and they'll get it. I don't believe this. This is sweet. Here we had all these myths about the factories: You get dirty; you get sweaty; you get tired. And this is sweet. I was working six days a week. Took away my night life, but I was enjoying it.

I was on a ninety-day probationary period. After eighty-seven days, they come around and say, "We have a reduction in force. We'll have to put you over here." No sweat. They put me on the line, assembling the brakes, putting bolts on the brake shoes. Dude showed me a few times, and fine, I can keep up. But as soon as he left me alone, and the line was running, I couldn't go fast enough. I was just missing so many. I kept calling for the foreman or someone to help me, but no one ever came. So I picked up my hat and my coat and walked out of that joint.

I stayed off a whole month and then I went back out there to the union. I told a little white lie. I said I was having a problem on the job and they told me to check out and go home. The union man brought me out to the engine plant, and it was sweet again. I was over there torquing engines, after they put the pistons in and the caps. It was every third motor, and as you go, you get quicker.

About April of '66, I got my draft papers. I took it up there and showed my foreman, and he sent me to Labor Personnel. They said, "As long as you come back to work within ninety days, the job is yours." Well, I partied, partied, partied for the next month, until it was time to go.

Maxine was pregnant. I didn't deny it, because I knew what I had done. Me and her got married May 21, 1966, and I left to go in the army May 28th. I took basic in El Paso, Texas, and then went to Fort Ord in California for Morse Code training. The Vietnam War was really brewing up, so they were shipping people around. They shipped me right to Fort Gordon, Georgia—teletype school. I didn't get to come back home on leave.

When I was going out to California, my mother told me, "Have a good time. I wish I could go to California." But when I called home and told her, "They're shipping me to Georgia," it was, "Oh, my God, they're shipping my baby down there." She says, "You go down there, you mind your own business, you hear me? If they say they don't want you in their places, don't go in their places. You're not in Detroit." "Okay, Mom. I hear you." But then I went down, and I didn't run into anything.

The baby was supposed to come around Christmas, so I took my leave then. I came home, but nothing happened. A few days after I got back to Georgia, Maxine called and told me, "I just had a boy." She said, "I named him after you." I said, "You don't have to," and she said, "No, I want to." So Charles, Jr., was born January 3, 1967. Maxine said, "Can you come home and see me?"

After I got off the phone, I go to the office and say, "Can I go home? My wife just had a kid." Well, orders is orders—"You had your turn."

I'm thinking, I should go AWOL to go home and see my kid. But I heard a rumor that they're shipping us out of here. So I sat around thinking and waiting and waiting. A whole month I'm sitting there. I could have been home and they never would have missed me. They had moved us from the barracks to tents to give the next group of students the room.

When I went overseas to Korea in February '67, I hadn't seen the kid yet. When I got to where I was going, I wrote and told my wife and she sent me a picture, and I had it pasted all over the place. When I first got in the army I told Maxine, "Maybe we should get our marriage annulled, because I don't feel right with you there and all those guys." And I was writing other chicks myself when I was in the service. I didn't think it was serious—just friends. But after the kid was born, I kind of mellowed down. I said, Man, you're married now. You're going to deal with it—no sense in acting silly.

In Korea I was a radio-teletype operator at headquarters on top of a mountain over there. I was in the Second Infantry Division, 122nd Signal Corps. I had a secret clearance because I used this machine. It was a highly sophisticated device that hadn't been decoded yet by none of our enemies. It was fun. I got up every morning to make sure I had everybody on frequency. Then, I'm switching over to teletype and everybody's going through their routine. I would do this every hour to make sure we got communication all over Korea.

Well, fighting the Cold War was better than a shooting war, and we lived pretty good over there. My stay in the service was real nice. The Koreans made you lazy. You didn't have to shine your boots; you didn't have to make your bed up; you didn't have to shine any brass. You'd pay houseboys three dollars and it's all done. All I did was lay around and eat and get fat. I'd smoke me some weed and I'd be eating up everything. Pork and beans and weenies was my favorite. I got up from 145 pounds to about 170 to 175.

One time it did get scary over there. I had been there over a year and I was getting ready to come home. I was asleep when the message came over. The guy that was up there couldn't get it because the weather was real bad. So he called down to the barracks and sent word for me to come up because he had an urgent message come over. So, hey, this is a little excitement. I got up there and it's "Handicap Red." I said, "Oh, wow, slide over, man; let me see if I can get it." I started zeroing in, and when I did get it, it came flashing across the teletype. The message was: "Handicap Red. U.S. Ship *Pueblo* has been seized by North Korea." I'm gone. I mean, I'm scared now. It was a joke at first, but now it's serious. Some hot stuff.

I took the message down to where the company commander was, and he orchestrated everything from there. It was my responsibility to get the message to the seven companies in our jurisdiction. We had to make sure they got that message. That was the really hairy part because of the weather. Then they had us load up and get in our combat gear and start moving. I hadn't seen my rifle, really, since I got out of basic, because where I was operating in Korea we had armed guards guarding us all the time, because of the machine I was using. As we was going down the hill back towards Seoul, we saw the infantry going in the opposite direction. I thought, I'm going the right way. The *Pueblo* incident caused me to spend two extra weeks over in Korea.

When I got back to the States, my wife, my mother-in-law and father-in-law and sister-in-law met me at the airport. I hadn't dealt with my wife in almost two years. She looked different. She'd had the baby. She had grown from a teenager to a woman. I'm looking at her, fascinated. I like what I'm looking at. We got home and I finally saw my son. He's fourteen months old. I said, "I'm going to put you under my wing, pal. It's going to be me and you."

We bought a small bungalow in Detroit and things started clicking off really nice. I was maybe the second black that moved onto that street. I was making good money working in the factories. Every month it seemed like there was a little raise. I bought me a '67 Buick LeSabre, made my car payments, my house payments. I never did have problems paying my bills, because I didn't get off into that drug scene.

After I came out of the service, the plant was different. They cranked up the line much faster. All the white people was gone. It's predominantly black now. I went back to the same department. I saw very few familiar faces. I can't relate to these new people. Before I went, there was no drugs. A joint was drugs. That was "dope." But now, hey, they're taking heroin. I mean, how can you function?

Then about '72, '73, they started hiring females. Oh, man, it was like *Peyton Place*. Everybody had a friend. You sit up there and see them chicks coming in, looking attractive—but working their butts off. I used to say, "Don't work like that. You make it look bad for *us.*"

I was always looking at the want ads, trying to find me a better job, because all we used to hear about was layoffs, layoffs. I look in the paper and I keep seeing, "Millwright, millwright," all over the want ads. I didn't know what a millwright did, but the millwrights in my area would be sitting there reading the paper all day. It turns out the millwright is supposed to be responsible for keeping the assembly line in operational form. Change motors, put in new additions. It's all blue-printed out. They had an apprenticeship course going, and they say, "You're getting a free education." I jump all over that. Quite a few black people did.

So starting in '72, I went to school part-time. I took a technical course to be a millwright at Henry Ford Community College in Dearborn. I did a lot of drafting, and learned how to read a blueprint. My first job as a millwright apprentice was at the assembly plant where I first started working down at Ford Motor Company. They was in the process of renovating the place and we had to tear out all that old stuff. I picked up on a piece of steel wrong and popped something in my back. I said to myself, What have I done? Here I have a good opportunity for an upgrade on my job, and I'm messing my back up.

I ruptured a muscle back there and the muscle was double the size. It was putting pressure on my kidney cord. They had to go in and operate and free it. I stayed off work for about three months. It seemed like after that my whole body started falling apart. I tore something in my knee and had a knee operation; I caught pneumonia—all these things. All the while I was on production, I didn't even catch a cold. As soon as I get an opportunity to make money, all these things happened and I had to take off from work. I went to school on crutches, and finished school on time. But I didn't finish the shop part, and never got past being an apprentice.

In '74 I met this young lady, and I think that was one mistake I shouldn't have made. I never have been in the habit of picking up people at bus stops or whatever. But this particular time my wife was out of town and I had to go to the bank to get some money to bring to Western Union to wire it to her. Coming out of the bank parking lot, this young lady was standing there and she said, "Hey, mister, which way are you going?" That turned into something that lasted for seven years.

It really got hairy. I told her, I take care of my own. I got a wife and kid, and I'm not going to party you. We could have a hell of a relationship going if that's understandable. She understood. I wasn't taking anything away from home, and the young lady had a little money that she didn't mind spending. It lasted for a long time, longer than I anticipated, longer than I wanted it to and more deeper.

I separated from my wife in June of '78. I never fought her. Words, yes. We came up with some mean words, but no physical stuff. After I left, I was off on medical leave. They sent me some papers to be filled out by my physician and sent back in: She didn't give it to me. She never mentioned about the mail, and I didn't know because I was still getting my benefits. When my leave was up and I went back to work, they told me, "We sent you some registered mail." And they terminated me. I thought it was a joke at first—me, with fourteen years' seniority. I said, "You've got to be kidding, man. You'll get fired before me."

I went to my union rep and told him what happened, and he was looking at me kind of funny. Later, putting it all together, this was something they had talked about. They found the forms—all those medical leaves of absence. If you've got a job, they want you to be there. It's just common sense. The union didn't fight for me. I had to wait thirteen weeks before I could get unemployment, and when I did get it, I only collected for five weeks. I guess they were penalizing me. I took the test for mail carrier and completely flunked it. I tried going back to school. I took three tests, and after the third flunk I just dropped out. I was wasting my time and their time, and somebody else could have my seat. My wife and I got back together for a while. She was working, but then it started getting to where I wouldn't accept nothing from her, and we got to arguing again.

The union kept me on hold for three years and the decision of my case finally came down against me in '82. During that time the economy had got real bad. Only places hiring was if you had something in computers. But I consider myself a common laborer and they weren't hiring nowhere. I just couldn't find a job. I haven't worked a steady job since 1979. I do a little mechanic work. I paneled a few basements. Put up displays at conventions, do some day labor. I have a stack of applications out, three-quarter-inch thick, but then they see on my résumé that I was terminated at Ford, even if it was after fourteen years. I did get one offer to maintain equipment at a chemical plant in Louisiana, but I turned it down because I didn't want to move down there.

I voted in the last election, but since I lost my job, I haven't had much incentive. I'm not a taxpayer anymore, so as far as they're concerned, I don't exist. I'm just a person occupying space.

In 1984 my parents divorced after being married for forty years. Last week I moved in with my mom. She can't drive because of her health, and she needs somebody there with her.

Sometimes I might not see my son for a couple of weeks, but I do call him. He lives with my sister because she lives in the school district he wants to go to. He's pretty level-headed. Last year in high school he won first place for solo singing, and last week he sang at a fashion show and the brochure had him announced as "Special Guest Star." We used to sit down and do his homework together, up until he got too heavy for me. I've had people tell me, "He's just like you. Every time you see him, he's with a different young lady." I only took a belt to him once, when he was in junior high and he wouldn't obey his mother and come straight home from school. His eyes got full and then there's both of us crying, and I said, "Just come home, man. When I hit you, that hurts me," because I imagine how that belt felt on his back. Mom put enough of them on mine.

I'll be glad when I get employed again. When I was at Ford, I didn't really try to climb the ladder. I was satisfied where I was. Now, I'm in a little different frame of mind. I'll get involved.

I guess I could have done a hell of a lot better than I've done, but don't let anyone tell you people like to be unemployed. It bothers me that I don't have the money to show a lady a proper time. I don't feel good about that. But at least I don't hang around the street corners, and I don't ride guys around in my car. And I still don't get out on those corners like some do, and build a fire in the trashcans to keep warm when the weather's bad. I've never gotten into that, and I'm glad. I just hope I get a job before it gets that bad.

THE BEATNIK:
Ramona Christopherson

Like blue jeans and basketball, the hippie movement began in the United States and spread around the world. Although it had many unique characteristics, it was actually a natural progression in the centuries-old tradition of counter-cultures. In fact, there are some ironic parallels between the hippies and the early Christians. The most important of these was the emphasis on peace and love, which was met by derision and hostility by those who felt that war and violence were justified and necessary.

Just as Jesus upset the tables of the money-lenders, the hippies mocked society's glorification of material values. And Jesus, like hippie men, wore long hair and a beard. Of course, Jesus and the early Christians never listened to rock music or took mind-altering drugs, but if you think that they weren't interested in experimenting with alternative forms of reality, try fasting in the desert sometime for forty days.

The most fragile aspects of the hippie culture, the caring and sharing with friends, neighbors, and strangers, were the first to disappear, overwhelmed by media attention and the realities of the non-hippie world. Simplicity in clothing gave way to "hippie fashion." Marijuana and LSD were driven off the streets by amphetamines, barbiturates, and heroin. The hippies themselves, those who desired to pursue their original ideals, retreated into communes and intentional communities, another aspect of the hippie culture that actually had a long tradition.

I consider it a stroke of luck that I happened to be living in San Francisco while the hippie movement was still alive and well. Brief though it was, it was an exciting time, full of challenges, surprises, and hope. At one point, I became aware of the Monday Night Class, a weekly spiritual lecture and discussion led by Stephen Gaskin, a former teaching assistant at San Francisco State College. One night, a roommate and I attended one of these classes at a ballroom by the beach. Hundreds of hippies wandered in and out, sat on the floor, and listened to Stephen's eclectic brand of psychedelic spirituality. Stephen was clearly the center of attention, but he was a far cry from the cult figures who would appear a few years later.

I have little memory of what was discussed that evening, but I do recall vividly, and with great pleasure, another event organized by Stephen Gaskin. Called the Holy Man Jam, it brought together spiritual teachers of great diversity who took turns at center stage leading meditations, giving sermons, and singing. The division between the wise and the phony was rapid and obvious.

In 1971, Stephen and his followers left San Francisco in a huge caravan of buses and headed east. Over the years, I followed their progress, as they settled in Tennessee, developed the largest commune in the United States, and called it the Farm. Through word of mouth and occasional encounters with Farm members, I learned that they had established various businesses, producing and marketing books, sorghum, and nondairy soy-based ice cream. They had also turned outward, creating a free ambulance service in the Bronx and an agricultural project in Guatemala.

Then, in 1983, came the intriguing news that the Farm had abandoned communalism and practically disbanded entirely. I was most curious to finally pay a visit to the remains of this semi-legendary social experiment.

As I drove south from Nashville through verdant Tennessee countryside, I felt a certain apprehension, and tried to analyze its source. I recalled that the Farm had developed a negative reputation for its anachronistic sex roles. Not only had the women's movement passed by the Farm, but Farm members had actually become more traditional, more reactionary, than the society around them. In addition, the Farm members whom I had met over the previous decade, all of them male, had been quite arrogant and self-righteous, traits I have found common among large groups who live their lives ideologically.

I stopped at the Gate House of the Farm and gained permission to enter. Immediately I realized that my apprehension had been unfounded. Every single person that I met was friendly, open, helpful. Either the arrogant men had all left or times had simply changed. I learned that communalism had, in fact, been abandoned, and that the Farm was now run on a cooperative basis, with each household paying its own way. The population had plummeted from a peak of about 2000 to barely 350. Past excesses were readily acknowledged. One woman told me that she had once been publicly criticized at a meeting for using the phrase "I averted my gaze" instead of saying "I looked the other way."

I was repeatedly told that I should have seen the Farm when it was packed with people and in full operation. However, I had seen plenty of communes in their heyday and found the present status of the Farm much more fascinating. Buildings that had once housed thirty, forty, fifty people were now occupied by single families, who felt absolutely blessed to be living in quiet woods and drinking pure, fresh water that tasted as water should. The disappearance of communal restrictions had allowed people to seek outside jobs and to acquire automobiles, satellite-TV dishes, and other goodies. The Farm had become a sort of hippie suburbia. Personally, I viewed this not as a sign of failure but as a natural, positive evolution. The Farm was a very pleasant place to be.

I spent the weekend at the home of Ramona Christopherson, whom I met as she came off the pitcher's mound at a women and children's softball game. Noticing that I was a bit worn out from my journey, Ramona served me a large bowl of soy yogurt with raisins. Soy yogurt is an unusual culinary creation that I had tried several times and never liked. But, made by the Farm dairy, it was not only palatable; it was delicious. I found myself eagerly awaiting dinner. In the evening, we were joined by her family, as she cooked up tempeh burgers. Tempeh, a soy product I first tried in Indonesia, is definitely an acquired taste, even for a confirmed vegetarian like myself. Yet, once again, skillfully prepared by the Farm dairy, it had me asking for seconds.

The night before I left the Farm, after everyone else had gone to bed, Ramona and I sat down at her kitchen table, and I began questioning her about her life.

My parents met when they were both in the service. My father was in the Air Force and my mother was in the Women's Air Corps, a WAC. She was one of those pretty girls of the '40s who wanted to leave their little hometowns and go out and work, to help in the war. I was born afterwards, while my father was stationed at Hamilton Air Force Base in Northern California. My sister, Donna, was born there too, a year later. She and I looked and dressed like twins.

I remember around '54 we moved to Utah, into a house that just had bunk beds, a table, and an ironing board. It was not the kind of house my parents usually had, and I often wonder if we might have been sent there during the atomic tests. A part of me doesn't want to know, but a part of me is curious.

After Utah, we moved to Oregon and then on to Spokane, Washington, where we lived with my grandmother. Then, while my father was in Korea, my mom and my sister and I lived in a farmhouse in Palouse, Washington, population 1036. That was my favorite place of all.

My Aunt Carmen and my grandmother did the ouija board, and they asked it where we would be going next. The ouija board said "South." Sure enough, in '58, we were transferred to Albany, Georgia. I remember one time walking down the street in Spokane with my grandmother and I saw a black person, and said, "Grandma, what's that?" She said, "That's a Negro, and don't ever call them niggers." Another time, I asked someone, "How come there's no Negroes here?" and he said, "Well, one came once and they would have killed him, but they wanted him to live so he could warn his friends not to come."

When I heard we were going to Georgia, I dreamed of palm trees, of having a black friend, and of everyone wearing long dresses. But when we got down there, it was mainly pine trees that had been planted six or seven years before, the black and white populations were separated into different and unequal areas, and everyone wore regular clothes.

When I was fourteen, my mother and my eighteen-year-old cousin, Karene, took me downtown to buy my first strapless formal—powder-blue net. We were in the Specialty Shop in downtown Albany, and all of a sudden we heard singing. It was soft and deep, a haunting melody, truly the most beautiful song I had ever heard. We looked out the window and there were thousands of black people marching down the street, quietly singing—"We shall overcome, we shall overcome"—softly and beautifully. My cousin and I wanted to go outside, but my mother wouldn't let us. There was an older black woman who sewed dresses there. She wanted to go out and join them, but the lady that owned the store said, "You can't go out!" So she and my cousin and I stood inside by the window and cried.

My cousin was also against racism, even then. Whenever we'd ride the bus, we'd sit in the back. We always drank out of the Colored fountains even though they were not cleaned as often. At the Dairy Queen they had a Colored window and a White window. They would serve all the white people; then, when they were through, they would serve the black people. So we'd stand in the Colored line. Most unfair of all were the public restrooms, which were marked "Men," "Women," and "Colored." Needless to say, they were rarely cleaned and seemed dangerous. We used the Women's room.

In the middle of the tenth grade, we moved to Charleston, South Carolina, and I went to East Dougherty High School. It was so square. I loved everybody in Albany, Georgia, but when I got to Charleston, I didn't like anyone. I read my way through school. I was particularly influenced by the Existentialists as well as by Thurber, Fitzgerald and Ring Lardner. I remember for one class, we read *Das Kapital*. I thought the capitalists were the bad guys and the communists were the good guys. "Communism" sounded like a pleasanter, nicer word than "capitalism." The teacher wrote on my report, "You have this all in reverse."

I just wanted to be a beatnik. I quit wearing pink and orange and always wore darker colors. I was one of the first people in Charleston to get dark stockings. I was in a shop once and a girl goes, "Look, Mommy, that lady has white arms with black legs."

I couldn't stand the lunchroom. I used to spend that time each day writing poems on toilet paper in the stalls for privacy and inspiration, or else I'd go to the library and read. I was sitting in the library and I saw this new girl, Verna, who had just moved in across the street from us. I said, "How come you're not in the lunchroom?" She said, "I'm not going in there with all those people." And I said, "I'm not either." And we became friends. She's the one who turned me on to Bob Dylan and Joan Baez, Judy Collins and Aretha Franklin.

We'd stay home from school some days and paint pictures. She liked to do beatniks and I liked to do people running through fields. We considered our whole graduation scene a joke. We thought people should want to do more with their lives than just be in the service. I couldn't stand girls who wanted to get married and have engagement rings. I knew I was different, and I was glad. And yet, in terms of being prepared for the world, I think I was overconfident.

I wanted to go to college, so I could become an artist and lead a collegiate life. My father thought I should work first. I talked my parents into sending me to a psychiatrist just once. He said I wasn't crazy, and that the problem with me was that not only did I not respect authority, but I didn't even know who or what authority was. My parents decided to let me go to college, anyway.

I was a very shy person, so I picked the most obscure college I could find: Campbell College, in Buies Creek, North Carolina. The brochure showed a beautiful, old-fashioned school with a brook running through it, and people on horses. When I got there, it was old-fashioned, but they were digging up the place, and instead of green grass in front of my dorm it had red clay. It was a Baptist school, and we had to go to chapel three times a week. And I was an atheist. Girls were not allowed to wear pants anywhere on campus, and we were only allowed to smoke in our rooms. Rebellion against that rule turned me into a frightful cigarette smoker.

I lost interest in my classes. I would read *The New Yorker* and *The Village Voice* and write poems about New York City and wish I was there. I was really in love with Allen Ginsberg. At the end of my second year, I just couldn't go to class at all. The dean called me in and told me, "You can't stay any longer. Give me one good reason why you should stay here."

I said, "Because I've already paid for my meals." She said, "That's not good enough." I said, "Well, don't tell my parents." She immediately called my parents. I went to my dorm and cried and sobbed. I told my dad I'd pay him back.

After Campbell I came back home to Charleston, and I got a job at the warehouse on the navy base doing inventories and putting little stickers on everything for minimum wage.

I still wanted to be a poet/artist. It seemed like anyone who was creative was an alcoholic, so I thought there was a definite connection between overdrinking and creativity. I decided to drink and be one of the boys. I lived a double life. I could outdrink anyone, but by the same token I was real sweet, and always went to the library.

I wanted to go to New York, so a friend decided he would drive me. This was the summer of '68. I told my parents I was going to go, and instead of saying okay, they flipped out. My dad goes, "There's people waiting in New York for someone like you: naive and inno-cent." My mother just says, "No, you may not go." That took me by surprise. So I waited until my mom went to work and my dad was sleeping, and I left.

We stayed at 14th Street and Seventh Ave. I was totally fearless. I went out at night a lot to go to foreign and/or avant-garde films. At the end of the summer my friend left to go to school in Florida, and I had to find a job. I kept putting it off because it had taken me so long to find one in Charleston. Finally, one day, I opened the *New York Times* and there were about six pages of "Female Wanted." There were limitless opportunities. I could have changed jobs every day of the week.

So I started out as a secretary for a small offset-printing company on 14th and Houston. I was there for three or four months. Then I got hired to work in the children's department of Lord and Taylor's for the Christmas season. I quit that and got a job at Avis Reservation Center on 65th and Broadway. By then I lived in the Hotel Ansonia at 72nd and Broadway and had a good roommate, Nancy, who worked on Wall Street. I was studying art with a tutor, who had an art school in Aspen, Colorado, and she wanted me to go there with her for the summer.

After nine months in New York, I went back to Charleston for a month. In New York I was just a regular person, but in Charleston it seemed like I was different. In Aspen I went to art school and moved into a big barn where our classes were held. I wanted to live like a hermit somewhere, just me and a dog. I noticed all these hippies would always be with a lot of people, and I found that kind of stupid. I didn't want to be a hippie because I thought they were anti-intellectual.

Our school was going through rebellion. The students discovered that the art teacher, who was charging them rent for their hotel, was also charging a little extra for herself. But it was also in line with the student unrest across the country at the same time. School ended and I decided to go to California with my teacher. She dropped me off in Santa Monica with my huge trunk. Why they call them "traveling trunks" I'll never know. Some people saw me getting off on the beach and offered to let me stay at their house in Venice.

We'd smoke grass. I wouldn't smoke at first because I didn't want to use up other people's stuff. I didn't understand about the grass culture—that everyone shared. So I bought some and then I would smoke. As a shy person, I loved grass. One thing about being introverted is you sit there and think, Oh, I wish I wasn't shy. But if you are high, you think, Oh, this is so nice sitting here.

Some of my friends came from Aspen and I stayed with them in a house in the suburbs, in Anaheim, with a color TV and a nice kitchen. The house of someone's uncle. We all moved in without asking. Eventually he asked us to leave and we lived for a while in a warehouse.

I loved the movie *The Graduate,* and wanted to go to Berkeley. I got a ride with a friend of a friend. The first night there we stopped a cop and asked him where we should sleep. He said, "Just drive out in the country, out in the woods somewhere." We picked up a young lady hitchhiking and she took us to stay out in a small place called Canyon—in a treehouse built over a ravine.

We stayed there for a while and then moved to a house in Berkeley. It was a bit of a dump, really. But everyone was nice, and I actually started to like it, and decided to stay. There were black folks living there, runaways, Hispanics, and middle-class hippies. Berkeley was really hot then. It was wall-to-wall people, right after People's Park. I became a street person. Every street was crowded. There were all these police, all these tourists; cars couldn't get through. You could hardly walk on the sidewalk, there were so many folks. There were people standing next to people waiting for them to get up so they could sit down and take their place.

But lots of people were into reds, downers. I walked into our house once and this girl was laying there with her face in a plate of Spam, like she was dead. She had these huge sores on her arms from running reds. I'd go to the ice-cream shop and the people who worked there had big sores all over *their* arms. I went to the Free Clinic, and they were all nice and sweet, but they had these big marks all over them, too. That was the point that if I was ever going to leave, it would have been then. To me, it was just horrible. But I already liked the folks in my house, the community, being close like a family.

Then the rents went up and I moved to another hippie house, actually three hippie houses in a row. We slept under tables, on top of tables, all over the place. I had a boyfriend named Lloyd. His vision was for us to be such a tight old man and old lady, always walking arm in arm and doing everything together, that if one of us wasn't there, everyone would ask where the other one was. And that really did happen. But eventually we split up.

We didn't need much money to live on. We lived on the streets. When one lady moved out and joined an ashram, we considered her a sell-out. That's how extreme we were. Mostly we paid our expenses by panhandling.

One time, my friend Lilly and I went to the airport to panhandle. It was New Year's weekend. An acquaintance came up to us and asked us if we wanted to go to a party. Yes, we'd like to party. He goes, "... in L.A." And we go, "Who'd want to go to a party in L.A.?"

He goes, "Well, where would you like to have a party?" And we went, "Hawaii." So he went back to the guy who's giving the party and told him about it. He had a $1300 check, which he couldn't cash because it was Sunday night, so he drove us home and told everyone in our house that they could go to Hawaii, about forty or fifty of these really scroungy people. Everyone's excited, but when he asks if he can spend the night, we all go, "No," because he was dressed nice and had a briefcase, and everyone thought that he might actually be a cop. So it was, "No, you can't spend the night, even though we'll let you take us to Hawaii."

The next morning we all figured, He's not really going to come. But, sure enough, he drives up with three cabs he'd hired. He bought cartons of cigarettes and passed them out to everybody. One woman, Jungle Jane, said, "You guys are crazy. You're all going to have to hitchhike back from the airport." But this guy, Richie, says, "Don't worry. Don't bring any clothes. I'll buy you all new ones when we get there. We're going to stay at the Hilton."

So he takes us to the airport—even picked up a guy hitchhiking the other way. We get to the airport and all the flights were booked. There's so many of us, and we're so ragtag. But we did all get on a flight and go to Hawaii. When we got there, Richie hired three cars and took us to a fancy, suburban house, where we all fall on the floor and go to sleep. Meanwhile, Richie asks to be taken to a mental institution. We talked to him on the telephone, but we never saw him again. We started living on the beach. By the way, there were twenty-one of us. We were the first big wave of street people in Honolulu.

I spent six months in Hawaii, but a lot happened while I was there. For one thing, I went to jail. Lilly and I were sleeping in a park and a guy said we could use his sleeping bag for the night if we watched his bag. He left behind a little baggie that had two teenie joints and some reds in it. I never even tried them, but these cops came on motorcycles, found the bag, and took me in.

I had no one to call, because everyone I knew was living on the beach. I was in jail for a week, but I got to be with real *Kanakas.* These ladies were young and pretty, and they were in there for six or nine months. I said, "How can you guys do that much time?" and one of them goes, "Oh, I've got six kids. This is a break for me, a vacation."

My friend Lilly was hitchhiking and a Hawaiian picked her up. She told him about me being in jail and he said I could use his name and address and family. So, out of the blue, I got out of jail.

Then I discovered I was pregnant. I lived on the beach again and in a treehouse for a while, and saved money until I had enough to fly back to Berkeley. The father actually wanted to come back to the mainland, and I really should have brought him. But Lilly didn't like him, and it was, like, him or her. I picked my girlfriend that I'd known for a long time over him, who I hadn't known for very long. When I got back, I wanted to write him a letter, but I couldn't find his address.

Berkeley was just impossible. Everyone there was on junk, and that depressed me. I searched around trying to find the right place to have my baby. Berkeley, San Francisco, a commune up north. I ended up in Colorado. The baby was born December 3, 1971. A little girl. I named her Ocean Oma Sattiva Saffron MeadowBloom Wine Christopherson. I put all that on the birth certificate. My grandmother said, "There's not one normal name in there."

My real name is Linda, but back then we all had different names. Lilly was really Christine. In 1972 I was nursing my baby and I drew a picture of a guy with the caption "Ramona, come weeth me." I showed people the picture and told them they could just call me Ramona. Most folks liked it better than Linda anyway, because it was more dramatic.

Lilly decided to go back to Traverse City, Michigan, where she was from. She wrote how nice it was, so I ended up going back there, too. I met this guy in Ann Arbor and it was love at first sight. He was a single father living with his little three-year-old boy. We started living together and tried to live by selling dope, which you can't do. You can keep yourself in smoke, but you can't pay your rent. We didn't know that then.

We decided to go to my hometown, to Charleston, but then I decided to split up from him. I went down to Gainesville, Florida, with just my child. I realized I was pregnant. So we got back together again and went to live in Atlanta. We tried living in West Virginia, but it was too poor and we were too poor so we went back down to Gainesville and had the baby there. Aaron was born September 13, 1973. I got pregnant again right after that, and we decided to move to where his parents were, so that we could get a little financial help. Erica was born September 9, 1974.

I finally separated from my old man at the end of 1975 and then lived in Madison, Wisconsin, for almost three years, working in offices, a day-care center and—my favorite job—insulating houses for low-income people. I loved Madison. I loved the life-style; I loved the food; I loved the people. But I was the only single mom with three kids. I needed more of a family environment. Everyone else had one or two children. In my opinion, having one kid is almost like not having any. It seems so easy, it doesn't even count.

I picked the Farm to move to because it was family-oriented, and I had a family. I had gone to the Monday Night Classes back in San Francisco, and I was there the night they left on the caravan. Through word of mouth I knew they had found a farm in Tennessee, and, in

Ann Arbor, I had read one of their books, *Hey Beatnik*. In fact, I had tried to move there once before, in the fall of '72. I got turned away, the first woman with child to be turned away at the gate. Someone at the gate suggested it was probably because I wouldn't drop my ego. I told him I liked my ego. It was what had kept me going that far.

When I came back again in the fall of '78, I wrote first and called. They said to come on by, but to bring enough money to get back home in case I decided not to stay. I arrived in a station wagon. My kids were four, five, and six. It was so crowded at the Farm that I had to stay at the Gate House with about forty other people because there was no room anywhere else. When I left Madison, my friends said, "How can you go to the Farm? It's so sexist. They call women 'ladies' instead of 'women.' " I said, "I'll cross that bridge when I come to it," but I really thought that was one thing I could never handle, because "ladies" is like a title, a hierarchy. But when I got down there, I got used to it. "Woman" sounded like a sex object, while "ladies" seemed nice and neutral. I actually started to prefer "ladies."

On Thanksgiving Day, they found us a house on the Farm. We went right away, that morning. It was incredibly stuffed with people, about thirty folks in a little house, with buses and vans parked around it, but they were all really good people. There were probably seventeen or twenty kids there. Actually, there was only room for us for one week while this one family went away for a while. Instead of having that empty space, they just filled it up with some more folks, because the important thing was "compassion." Folks wanted to be compassionate, to consider other people and help them out.

If I live in a house with thirty people, I get to know them really well, so we made thirty friends. By the end of the week we had found another place at Kissing Tree, a big house with about forty-five folks. After a month they wanted us to move out so a bigger family with six kids could move in instead.

So I went over and met the folks at Laughing Creek and they said we could live there. But they had already told a single mom with *four* kids that she could stay, so they finally decided that all nine of us could move into this house. I ended up living at Laughing Creek for five years, which is the longest I've lived anywhere in my whole life.

Being at the Farm was a lot of real work. I didn't think anything could be that hard, but it was so much fun because we all did it together. The first job I did was to chip bricks, because they were building the solar school. They had gotten the bricks by tearing down an old small-town theater that was being demolished. We had to chip the cement off, so it could be put back together. It was fun work, and the kids could run around and play while we did it.

Then I started helping Roberta do the school kitchen. She'd start at six o'clock in the morning after spending the night peeling potatoes. Then she'd get on six pots of beans to pressure-cook. By the time I got there at nine o'clock, the beans would be cooked and she'd be using the pots to boil big, huge pots of potatoes. Then we'd make twenty cakes that we'd mix up in buckets. At noon, three hundred kids would come through there, real fast, eat all the food, and be out by one. Then we'd spend about five hours cleaning up. I did this one day a week. Roberta did it every day.

I also did other cooking gigs: the bakery, crew snacks, woodshop breakfasts, as well as lifeguarding, the phones, and dispatching the ambulance. When the Farm started making money by doing tree-planting, I went out and did that a few times. Now I spend most of my time at the bakery. But I also help shingle mobile homes once a week. I like to work with my hands and I like to work harder than the guys. I used to try to smoke more dope, drop more tabs. Now I try to shingle harder and faster.

When the Farm began to fall apart and the big exodus started, some folks would say, "Did you hear So-and-so is leaving? Those traitors." I'd go, "We should be thanking these people for leaving," because it was way too top-heavy. A lot of people had been here a long time. They were sick of the overcrowding; they were sick of the climate, sick of outhouses, sick of this or that. I'd already lived in the city. When I got here, I was tired of variety. I wanted to try simplicity. A lot of folks had given up a lot to be here. They had disappointed their parents, been disinherited. I wasn't one of them. I actually regained my parents by coming here. My folks visited, and my mom thought it was so much fun to be in a houseful of ladies instead of sitting at home with just your husband and two grumpy kids.

You know the old saying "A woman needs a man like a fish needs a bicycle." That's how I believed. All the single people on the Farm were good friends. It was really fun. But it was hard raising kids alone and making all the decisions for three kids. I decided I wanted to have a husband, and I wanted him to be a Farm man who already knew all about kids, about being nice and not getting mad. I met Jeff and he was so nice. He loved my tempeh burgers. He used to buy four or five at a time. He was very organized, very neat, a perfectionist, a very good carpenter. He wanted to be with the kids on Sunday. I was so taken away by all of that; plus I was ready to share my life with someone. Two years earlier, no way. We wouldn't have gotten together because I thought it was weak to not stand on your own.

Having a father is nice for the kids. Having two people make decisions. Two inputs, two incomes. It makes the kids calmer, anchors the family and creates more warmth. The Farm believed that people should get married. At the time I didn't agree, but I never spoke up about it.

Jeff and I moved into our own house with the kids last year. Our bedroom is actually an old bus that's been shoved up against the house and a door built leading to it. However, this summer, we're replacing it with a solar addition. We've also put in electricity and now we have our own phones. The Farm used to have its own phone system and generate its own electricity, but it turned out to be cheaper and more efficient to hook up with the regular systems.

I thought my kids, or this new generation of kids, would be super-educated, super-scientific. I used to assume my kids would love to read, and they'd probably speak several languages. I thought, of course, they'd adopt our life-style. They are really natural, graceful, and athletic and love the outdoor life, but they are also your typical everyday kids, who like new store-bought things, pop tunes, and other teenagers. I gave up on them being super-educated. It's not their way. Now I just want them to have full consciousness of what they're doing, to assess situations and make judgments and decisions, be sweet, study hard, and do the best they can. I want them to live here on the Farm, but I want it to be on the condition of consciously choosing this place above anywhere else.

Then there's the matter of Ocean's name. I realize that it invades her privacy to have an unusual name. For example, if someone says "Mary did this" or "Kathy said this," you don't know which Mary or Kathy. But if someone refers to Ocean, well, there could only be one in the state of Tennessee. My grandmother's named Zula, and she said Ocean would hate me someday for giving her that name. But Ocean's really been pretty good about it. In fact this year, on her own, she changed it to a more conventional name.

I've learned a lot of lessons over the years. I learned never to try to panhandle from someone who wears a scarf around their head. I learned that if there's a sign saying MEN WORKING that means there's no men working. I've been told that generosity is a privilege of the

wealthy, but my experience is that poor people can be the most generous. I've learned compassion. I've learned that arrogance is contagious.
I've learned to read between the lines so you can't be fooled as often.
I've learned that youth *is* wasted on the young. I've learned not to
want only what I can't have. And I've learned that the indigenous people of the world are being picked off like flies.

As a person of '65, looking back twenty years later, I left school
wanting to be an artist or a poet. I tried to be a bohemian, gave it up to
become a hippie. Then I became a parent. As a parent, I joined a country "cult" and stayed in it even when it fell apart. I still love the city life,
but now I want to live a country life. I feel like I've made this home and
it's where I want to be. It's so beautiful here. I can hardly believe that I
could ever own a place somewhere else that's this beautiful.

THE BEAUTY:

Maryjane Johnson [*]

I was relieved that the skies were clear the day I drove to Maryjane Johnson's Hawaiian home, because I was sure the crude dirt road leading to her house would turn to mud with the slightest rain.

Maryjane's friendly manner exuded what I guessed was a lifetime of self-confidence. With her small daughter trailing along, she showed me the wide variety of fruit trees growing on her property. When we reached a clearing we stopped to watch three rainbows in a row actually pass overhead, accompanied by light rain. When I expressed concern about the road, she laughed and assured me that the rain would be of short duration, which it was. We returned to her sundeck to talk, breaking only to eat an occasional papaya or coconut served up by her daughter, curious to hear her mom's story.

My mother was a classic Nordic blond beauty from a prominent family who married a handsome corporate executive workaholic, also from a prominent family. My two brothers were both in their teens by the time I was born. My birth, I'm told, caused great rejoicing in my family. I was spoiled completely by both my parents, both my brothers, a nanny, a housekeeper, and assorted other relatives.

From the time I was very little, I was always referred to as "beautiful." "What a beautiful child!" "What a beautiful little girl!" "What a

*This is a pseudonym made necessary by the nature of Maryjane's most recent occupation.

beautiful girl." I don't recall ever being called "cute" or "pretty." It was always "beautiful." I always had a rather luxuriant head of blond hair, which, I later learned, required a blond gene from both parents, and sent my relatives scurrying up my father's side of the family tree to find the great-great-grandmother who was the culprit.

As I was growing up, my parents developed a routine: For most of the year, they would shuttle back and forth between a house outside the city where my father worked and a country estate in New England. In the summers we would always go to Europe.

When I was fourteen years old, I was sent off to Switzerland to a very posh girls' school, where we received instruction in three languages. I used to complain all the time about the harshness of the rules and the excessive amount of work, but it was actually quite a wonderful experience. I met girls from other countries, a couple of whom have become lifelong friends. And the quality of education was the best I would ever see. Also, my parents, to whom I was quite close, were never too far away for too long.

In 1963, just before the end of my second year in Switzerland, I was called into the headmistress's study and informed that terrible news had been received: My father had died suddenly of a heart attack. It was so unexpected that I couldn't accept it. I went back to my room and told my roommates. I was just numb. I couldn't cry. One of my brothers, who worked for a bank in England, came down and picked me up and we flew home together. The first moment I saw my brother was when I started to cry.

It was a devastating experience for me. Nothing bad had ever happened to me. I had always counted on my father being there and had taken his love for granted. People might expect that a rich man who was so involved with his work would be cold and emotionless, but my father was very demonstrative in his love for me. I still miss him, and I still think of him frequently.

It was decided that I shouldn't go back to Switzerland, that I should stay at home and live with my mother. We shared our grief.

I transferred to a public school in a very affluent suburban neighborhood. I'm sure it was nothing like the typical American public school, but it was a public school nonetheless, and it was a difficult transition for me to make. For one thing, the classwork was not in the least bit challenging. I was able to maintain excellent grades without even trying, even when I was promoted to advanced classes.

But the real shock was the transition from a small, elite girls' school to a huge coeducational institution. I was unprepared for the heavy doses of social pressure. Part of it, I suppose, was due to my appearance. I guess these kids had mostly gone to school together for years, and were tired of looking at each other. From the moment I stepped on campus, I was stared at constantly, and I was aware that people of both sexes were making judgments of me without ever having met me or exchanged a word with me. In a sense, I wished that I could have the anonymity that other new kids were trying to escape.

Because I had long blond hair and a tan, which I had acquired through annual visits to the French Riviera, I was nicknamed the California Girl, even though I had never been to California. I was also called Surfer Girl by loitering boys in the hallway, even though I didn't know what surfing was. I really hadn't been seriously interested in boys yet, and this school was not a good introduction. I considered the boys silly and immature, and even rude for treating me with such insensitivity. I suppose I could have curried favor with the elite group, who did, in fact, attempt to claim me as one of their own, but after the world I had been exposed to, their values seemed petty. I quickly gained a reputation as being aloof.

However, by senior year, the transparent foolishness of their snobbism made me examine my own snobbishness, and I did make some friends. Despite being at the school only two years, I actually won several slots on the class poll, including "Best Hair," "Best Body," and "Most Beautiful." For all my protestations, I was flattered, although it did disturb me to realize how many people must have been thinking about me, and what some of those thoughts must have been.

The real surprise was that I was also voted "Nicest" girl in the class. Here I had been thinking most of these people hated me, and yet they chose me as "Nicest" over girls that truly were "nice" to everybody. Such is the power of physical beauty in our society. I was vain enough to be pleased and honored by all this, but, in retrospect, it set me on a bad track.

I got so much praise and rewards and strokes just for looking good that I put even more attention into my appearance. The fact that I was an A student, and that I was a sensitive person, went virtually unnoticed and unrewarded, so I put less energy into developing those aspects of myself.

I had started to date in high school, but it had been mostly a result of social obligation and I really didn't enjoy it. I resisted all attempts at physical intimacy. And yet, when I applied to colleges, I made sure that they were all coeducational. I was hooked on the easy popularity.

I was accepted at a very good university. But by this time, the high quality of education which I had previously desired was now wasted on me. I was no longer interested, and my grades suffered, not badly enough to really cause trouble but enough to no longer be anywhere near the top of my class.

When I first got to college, I visited all the sororities, but was embarrassed by the attention I received. I remember walking into one house for the first time, and the mere sight of me caused several sorority members to walk away from a new girl in mid-sentence to come over and greet me. Everyone wanted me. I had my pick of the lot. Foolishly, I overlooked the houses with the nicest girls, and instead joined the most prestigious, most snobbish sorority.

Throughout my college years, I was treated the same way by any group I joined or showed an interest in. When I showed up for a meeting of the French Club, they were all stumbly around me, as if I were a celebrity. When I tried to join a service organization that tutored ghetto kids, they were so proud to have me that they flaunted my membership, like they had scored a coup over this other organization. I felt dehumanized and quit.

Meanwhile, it was becoming increasingly difficult for me to preserve my virginity. It wasn't that I had taken some vow to remain a virgin until I married, or anything like that. I'm not sure what it was. I think I was just suspicious of boys and their sincerity. As more and more of my friends finally "went all the way," they would come back with horror stories, not only of physical pain instead of pleasure but of being rejected once the boys got what they wanted. Since my own sex drive was minimal, it just didn't seem like an attractive experience.

And yet, because skirts were getting shorter, and because I was still trying to look my best, the pressure started to get quite intense. I would go out on dates with the most desirable men on campus, and they would get very angry at me when I resisted their advances. The word went around the fraternities that I was "frigid." I was hurt by this and confused. In addition to all this, I had to contend with a group of freshmen boys who used to follow me around campus between classes.

My mother and I continued to go to Europe each summer after my father died, but in 1968 I was allowed to go instead with a sorority sister who was my closest friend. We managed to take our exams early and we flew directly to Paris. When we arrived, the city was in chaos. There was fighting in the streets, barricades, the whole bit. We met some students who tried to explain to us what was going on, but I didn't really understand. I knew the same sort of thing was happening in the United States, but I hadn't paid any attention. In Paris, we went out one afternoon to go shopping, ended up in the wrong neighborhood, and were chased down the street by policemen with billy clubs and shields. We decided to leave Paris immediately.

Coincidentally, our next stop was Prague, because my friend had relatives in Czechoslovakia. Well, the mood there was much different. The people were throwing off the shackles of Communist authority and tasting freedom. You could feel it in the air. It was thrilling. People were on the streets talking all the time, discussing new ideas and possibilities. It was something brand new to me. It was like waking up out of a dream for the first time in my life.

My friend and I had planned to meet up with my mother in Cannes. On the train there I was filled with excitement and anticipation. I couldn't wait to see my mother and tell her all that we had seen and experienced. I was exhilarated. When we arrived at the hotel, the concierge, whom I had known for years, was solemn, and cold in his greeting. He rushed off and returned with the manager, who led us into a private lounge. He informed us that the previous evening my mother had been a passenger in a car that had missed a turn on a mountain road and fallen off a cliff. She had been killed instantly.

This time, with my good friend right beside me, I began crying immediately. In fact, I couldn't stop crying. I totally surrendered my self-control and sobbed and sobbed until I was physically exhausted. Once again, my brother came down to pick me up and, this time, to make arrangements for the transfer of the body. It was like a *déjà vu* nightmare.

Back home, I went through the funeral and the condolences in a mechanical state, as if I were following a script. However, it was a script I was glad to follow. At some point, my brothers and I were told that our mother's will provided that the family fortune be split three ways. This made me quite wealthy, but I was so grief-stricken that I paid no attention, and didn't realize the financial implications of what had happened for quite some time. All I knew was that a lawyer would cover my living expenses, just as my parents had until then.

I decided to go back to school and try to go on with normal life. My girlfriend, the one who had been in Europe with me, she and I had planned to get our own apartment for the year, so we went ahead and did that. I remember walking to school one day—I think it was registration day—and I passed by a newspaper-vending machine. I hadn't read a newspaper since my mother died, but the headline was so big that it caught my attention: "Russians Invade Czechoslovakia."

It was like being kicked when you're already down. The one thing that was giving me hope for the future was gone. I hid behind a tree and sat down and cried again. The reasons for my sorrow got all mixed together.

That semester I made a point of enrolling in classes that had some meaning beyond just fulfilling requirements. But it didn't work. I just couldn't concentrate. I lost interest in my sorority, too, and dropped out of any activities I was still involved in. I also gradually stopped dating. I felt a need to talk to someone, but I didn't know who, and I didn't even know what it was I wanted to say. It was definitely a confused period for me—searching for whatever it was I wanted to search for.

The one bright spot in all this was the group of underclassmen who used to follow me around. I don't know if they had just matured over the summer or if they sensed that something was wrong with me. They were much gentler to me. They had formed a club in honor of me and had taken in new members. One of these new guys was a gangly, pimple-faced kid with glasses. Today he'd be called a nerd. But, boy, was he funny. They would accompany me from class to class, like bodyguards, and he would stand behind me and make teasing comments about the way I walked or what I was wearing. It was this guy that finally caused me to drop the barrier and finally talk to them.

One day I stopped in my tracks and I said, "Listen, you guys complain if I have one hair out of place or if my bra strap is showing. Well, how about you? Look at you guys. You're slobs." I went right down the line—and I berated them individually. I told each one what I didn't like about the way he combed his hair or the clothes he wore. They were shocked, speechless.

The next day they all showed up at school wearing rented tuxedos. I laughed so hard I thought I would cry. In fact, tears did appear. When I realized that they were the first happy tears I had had in a long time, I became emotional. And I told them what had happened to me, about my parents dying, and the tremendous loss I felt. They were all so concerned about me. All these years later, it makes me emotional just to talk about it.

It would have been like Snow White and the Seven Dwarfs, except they were all taller than me. I think it disturbed one or two of them to realize that I was a real person instead of a goddess. But the rest of them became very protective of me. They carried my books; they listened to me vent my frustrations; they demanded daily reports on my mental health. In a way, they really saved me. They were so sweet.

My twenty-first birthday came right before Christmas vacation, and I got it in my head that the time had come to lose my virginity. The big question was, Who should be the lucky guy to have the honor? My girlfriend and I spent several nights going through the long list of boys who had tried in the past. We rejected all of them. It was fun. We considered holding an auction or a raffle. I thought of choosing someone from my club, but I didn't want to ruin the relationship we had, and I certainly didn't want to bring them all in on it.

But then I decided that it should be the funny guy, the one with pimples. From earlier conversations I knew that he had a late-afternoon class on Fridays and that none of the other club members would be there. So I went home after my own last class and got myself ready. I pulled out my shortest miniskirt and my most form-fitting blouse, and put it on without a bra. All I wore underneath were tiny, frilly bikini panties that I had bought specially for the occasion. I was lucky I didn't get raped walking from my apartment to the campus. And, mind you, this was December!

I caught the boy—his name was Billy—as he left the class building. Unfortunately, I hadn't planned what I would do next. I tried to look sexy, and waited for him to take over. But he just stood there. So I took his hand and led him to a quiet spot. Still nothing. Then I said, "Billy, I feel like being touched." I thought he was going to faint. All he could say was, "Touched? By me?" I took him by the hand again and said, "Why don't we go back to my apartment?"

My God, we were both so scared. What a pair! My roommate had already left for the weekend, so we had the place to ourselves. While he stood there awkwardly, I did all the things I thought you were supposed to do. I put on a pile of romantic records; I poured some wine. Then I leaned back on the couch and tried to be seductive. I squirmed and wiggled and pouted and thrust my chest forward and rotated my hips. All this stuff I had seen in movies. I must have looked ridiculous. I mean, after all, the films I had seen all this in were all comedies!

Finally, Billy sat down beside me and began touching me. But his mood was more one of awe and reverence than lust, and it soon became clear that this wasn't going to work. Nothing was happening inside his pants. We began talking, and it turned out that he was a virgin, too, and that he was terribly embarrassed, ashamed, about his acne. Eventually, we hugged and then kissed good-bye and he left. It had turned into a lovely communication, but I was really quite depressed. When you've been told all your life that you're beautiful, and you do everything you know how to be sexy, and you can't get one of your biggest fans excited, well, I lost a lot of my self-confidence.

The next evening, just before sunset, Billy showed up at my door. He seemed emboldened, better prepared. We began necking, then he excused himself and went to the bathroom. When he returned, he had an erection. So, we did it. It took less time than cooking a soft-boiled egg. Fortunately, he stuck around for the evening, so we were able to relax a bit and try it again. By morning, we had learned quite a lot.

My brothers and I gathered at home for Christmas. It was comforting to be reminded that I had a family, but really they already had families of their own that meant more to them. When they left to go back to their homes, I stayed behind. I never returned to school. I never finished my senior year. I never graduated. I never saw Billy or the other boys again. Never even knew their last names.

I spent a few months doing nothing. Just sleeping a lot, thinking, eating, reading. I didn't have the pressures other people had. I didn't have to worry about making a living or being drafted. I had no responsibilities. But I also had no purpose or passion.

Then along came my next savior. Her name was Denise, and she had been my roommate in Switzerland. I hadn't seen her in six years. She suddenly showed up at my door, talking to me like nothing had happened, like she had just gone out for a walk and come back, and the six years had never happened.

Denise was French. She was very outgoing and earthy and full of adventure. It was her first trip to the United States. Friends of hers who had been over had given her a list of places to go—about forty of them. She planned to visit them all, and she had marked them all on a big map she had. It was like playing follow the dots. It was a crazy list—a mixture of natural-beauty spots with weird things. You know, the largest gas station in the world, a restaurant shaped like a hot dog—things that her French friends felt captured the true spirit of America.

Denise asked me to join her on her pilgrimage and I accepted. It turned out to be one of the better decisions of my life. Denise was a great companion. She wouldn't tolerate depression or angst. And the fact was that I had never been west of Washington, D.C., myself. It was a real eye-opener for me. I was overwhelmed by how much I *didn't* know about my own country.

We ate lunch at a café in the poorest town in Mississippi. We hiked down into the Grand Canyon to visit an Indian reservation. We went to Yellowstone and Yosemite and the redwoods. All along the way we stayed with friends of friends of Denise. It seemed to be the hippie circuit, which was certainly a new world to me. We were always treated well, even though we were complete strangers. Communes, ashrams, political demonstrations, we saw it all. I could see that something of the mood I had seen in Prague also existed in America.

We were two attractive women, so, as usual, people were glad to have us around for a while to brighten up their environment. Drugs and sexual relationships were available. I was selective, but I was also more relaxed about experimenting. But I was still restless. I came across a little booklet about Hinduism called "Who Am I?" I kept asking myself that question. I still needed a purpose. Out west, it seemed like everybody had one to offer. "Join the revolution." "Devote your life to God." "Help retarded children." "Be my wife." A few months earlier I couldn't think of anything to do with my life. Now I was overwhelmed with all the possibilities.

In California I met this boy, this young man, who was about to leave for India. His name was Mark. Mark invited me to come with him, but I declined. I looked at him as yet another person offering me a *raison d'être,* a purpose. Just before he left, he gave me a hand-carved wooden box containing an assortment of consciousness-altering drugs: marijuana, LSD, hashish, psilocybin mushrooms—I don't remember what else. He told me that something in that box was bound to help me answer the question "Who am I?" When Denise returned to France and I went back to New England, I took the box with me.

I went up to our country home and started taking these drugs. I would smoke marijuana or hashish six days a week, take psychedelics about twice a week, and then fast on Sundays. It was a pretty groggy period, and I wouldn't recommend it for my own children. On the other hand, I did find a satisfactory answer to my question.

I concluded that I was a sometimes conscious mass of cells, and that what is called death is just a tiny transformation in the way the cells of the universe are aligned. I decided my purpose was to follow the various happy and nervous feelings in my body, and to do my best to replace negative energy with positive. And yet I felt no compulsion to dedicate my life to some cause. I wasn't ready for that.

I decided that I was too attached to my appearance, to being beautiful, and especially to my long hair. So I cut it. Just as I took the first snip, I realized that cutting it was a greater sign of attachment than not cutting it. But I went ahead and finished the job. I also began dressing down, wearing clothes that hid my figure rather than accentuated it. I was making a desperate attempt to be anonymous. I did a fairly good job of it and I enjoyed walking around the city without being stared at.

Then it came to me that I, too, should go to India—or a least to head, by myself, in that direction. It was a voyage of discovery. I learned that I could take care of myself, even in the most adverse conditions. I started to gain a lot of respect for myself.

I did make it to India. I was sitting in the train station in Benares when I thought I saw Mark. I went up to him, and it turned out I was wrong. But I did strike up a conversation with this guy. He was a very, very peaceful person, with a calm and calming nature. He had just spent two years at a Buddhist monastery in Sri Lanka and another year at a Buddhist monastery in Burma. He was on his way home to visit his parents in Chicago, who thought he was crazy. I thought he was wonderful. I had a lot of men try to convince me how spiritual they were, but this guy—his name was Rick—he convinced me without trying.

I asked if I could accompany him back to the United States and he said yes. In fact, with my newly found competence and self-assurance, I made all our arrangements and generally took over the daily organization and maintenance of our lives. We traveled overland to London and flew to New York with money saved from my trust fund.

It was very difficult for me to convince Rick to make love to me. He was totally out of practice and he was purposely reducing his protein intake so as not to "awaken" his "lust." I was all turned on because he had met me at my homeliest and liked me anyway. I hadn't tried to seduce anyone since my first time in college. I was pretty sure that squirming and wriggling wasn't going to do it with Rick. So I spent weeks lecturing him on the spiritual aspects of sex, tantric yoga, and all that.

One day I walked into the room where we were staying in London, and Rick, who was a vegetarian, was eating a cheese-and-tofu sandwich with nuts. I knew we were in for a big evening. That night we engaged in sex in a much more relaxed manner than I had been exposed to. I liked it. But we parted in New York. I got a letter from him a few months later saying that he had entered another Buddhist monastery—this time in California.

When we had been in London, I had visited my brother and noticed that he was living much better off than he had been. I was so into Rick and the spiritual world that I didn't ask my brother about it. But when I got home, it hit me that he must have been using his inheritance.

I contacted the lawyer in charge of my trust fund and learned that my share of the inheritance had grown to three million dollars! It wasn't all due to me until I was older, but I was floored anyway. I went back to the country house and made lists of all the things I could do with the money. Splurge things, philanthropic things, businesses I could start. Finally I became so exasperated by the whole thing that I decided to forget about it and continue living on my trust-fund allowance.

In fact, I decided to get a job. I had a premonition that someday I would use my money to become a corporate executive, so I thought it would be useful if I "disguised" myself and entered a corporation from the bottom. I began by going to secretarial school and then got a job as a typist with a very large corporation.

By this time I was back into looking my best. The corporate world rewards good looks. Appearance is very important. There was a great deal of jealousy and competition and bitchiness among the secretarial pool. But I had complete confidence in my skills, as well as my image. Sure enough, I was noticed by an executive, and one of the big ones at that, and took over as his personal secretary.

I kept the job for a number of years, learning all I could and not letting on that I was a soon-to-be millionairess. In 1976 I adopted a baby boy. I'm a bit ashamed to admit it, but money and connections allowed me to overcome the usual red tape.

I also began having an affair with my boss. It's a trite, standard story. The usual married executive and secretary affair. Lots of business trips together to exotic places. When I adopted the baby, it put a strain on my romantic life. It was in the midst of this turmoil that I received a letter from Rick the Buddhist. He had given up the monastic life because he got tired of the discipline, and because he wanted to smoke marijuana again after eight years of abstinence.

In fact, he wanted to grow it—which was exactly what he was doing. He asked me to join him on his "farm" in Hawaii. I considered the alternatives for about half an hour, then quit my job and my affair, packed up my boy, and headed to Hawaii.

Rick had bought some acreage near a national forest, and was camped out growing his crop. Over the next few years, with his hard work and my business skills, we built up a pretty good business and even constructed a very nice house. It was an almost idyllic existence. My boy loved it in the jungle there, and in 1980 I adopted a baby girl. I am a strong believer in adoption because there are so many unwanted children in the world that there is no need to bring in new ones.

When I first moved to Hawaii, marijuana-growing was more like a cottage industry than a big business. Each grower had a few plants here and there and all selling was done to friends. It was friendly. The police made token raids—just enough to justify asking for a bigger budget each year. I'm convinced that the police would sell much of what they confiscated, because no self-respecting grower would harvest his crop before it matured and put it on the market a month or two early, which someone always did, every year.

After a while, an ugly element entered the scene. People looking for big bucks moved onto the islands and planted huge crops. They brought with them rifles and paranoia, not to mention sophisticated chemical fertilizers. They also attracted poachers and greater government surveillance, and made it difficult for the rest of us. Where we are it's never been as bad as it has been in Northern California, with helicopters chasing women through the woods and federal agents shooting people's dogs, but it has gotten bad enough that we decided to quit the business in 1984.

Rick and I talked about it and came to the conclusion that we shouldn't hesitate to start living modestly off my inheritance. We have done quite well without using even half of the interest earned each year. It was easy for us to quit growing because we had an outside source of income. But I know for a fact that growers who are being harassed in California and Hawaii are simply moving to other states.

Rick has gone back to meditating and reading more, and I take care of the kids and garden. I'm not saying we won't move on to something new in the near future, but right now it's a pleasure to know that our lives are completely legal.

I will say this, though: I feel very strongly that marijuana should be legalized. Instead of wasting the taxpayers' money by fighting the growers, they should tax it and create revenue. With legalization, the price would go down, the real criminals would leave, and the paranoia would go away. People could grow on their own land and not disrupt national forests. Jobs would be created. I really think it's hypocritical for people who go to cocktail parties and bars to declare that marijuana is bad for your health and should be against the law.

The marijuana business, at present, is a rare example of true free-market capitalism. But I'd rather they taxed it than sent in the helicopters.

I still feel that the time will come when I take control of my inheritance and put it to good use, but I'm just not ready yet. If I were to rush into it, the money would control me instead of vice-versa. I am confident that I will just know when the right project arises.

Just before I was about to leave Hawaii, I received a call from Maryjane suggesting that I might want to delay my departure a couple days in order to attend an unusual gathering: the annual Marijuana Growers' Convention. Attendance was restricted to growers, but Rick wasn't interested in going, so Maryjane invited me to take his place as her guest. In the interest of scholarly research, I accepted.

At the appointed time, we drove to a prearranged spot where we and several others were put in the back of vans with blacked-out windows and a wooden partition blocking any view of the front seat. After about twenty minutes on a very bumpy road, we were blindfolded. We then linked hands outside the van and were led up a pathway. When our blindfolds were removed, we found ourselves in front of a magnificent three-story house that commanded a spectacular view of the ocean. A sign reading "This Bud's for You" hung above the front door.

I had fully expected the convention to be dominated by discussions of tax shelters and fertilizers, but it actually was more of a contest—like a county fair. A dedicated crew of judges had weeded through no fewer than eighty-six entrants and come up with twenty finalists.

These finalists were displayed in shoeboxes on tables arranged in a semicircle. Each finalist's shoebox contained a "show bud" chosen strictly for appearance, a mason jar filled with several "smoking buds," scissors, a small pipe, cigarette papers, and a lighter. In the next room was a micro-scope and slides with samples of each finalist.

Each of the sixty growers and guests was considered a judge and given a scorecard so that each entrant could be judged according to ap-pearance, fragrance, taste, tightness, and effect. There was also a special "sticky fingers" award for the most resinous brand. A judges' guide was posted as a reminder to watch out for such factors as bouquet (jar smell), aroma (crushed smell), character, clarity, and strength (come-on, dura-tion, and hammer).

The first half-hour was spent studying the twenty finalists without anyone lighting up. Show buds were sniffed, eyeballed, squeezed. Joints were rolled up and "dry toked"—sucked on without being lit—to test for taste. I was impressed by the restraint of the participants. Then, one fel-low, as if sensing my thoughts, turned to me and said, "I think this has gone on long enough." He opened one of the mason jars, pulled out a smoking bud, clipped off enough marijuana to roll a joint, and lit it up. Within two minutes, the room was filled with smoke.

After studying the situation, I reckoned that if I took one puff of one brand every fifteen minutes, I might be able to reasonably pick a winner in the "effect" category. Fifteen minutes after my first puff, my judgment was so distorted by a single sample of Hawaii's finest that I gave up my plan and smoked whatever was passed to me.

The basic satiric mood of the gathering became apparent. I doubt if anyone could properly judge the effects of twenty brands of top-quality marijuana in three days, much less in the three hours which were allotted. Yet I also became aware that for the growers themselves, this was a seri-ous affair. Winning the Grand Prize, aside from providing pride and pres-tige, was also good advertising, and allowed the champion grower to raise his prices significantly for the coming year. Although each finalist was identified only by number, most growers recognized their own product. Several of them stood next to their shoeboxes, loudly proclaiming the merits of "number eight" or "number fourteen," pretending to be neutral observers but fooling no one.

I was particularly intrigued by one fellow who spent most of his time with the microscope. At one point, he called out to a friend, "Joe, come take a look at this!" (Everyone at the gathering was referred to only as "Joe" or "Jane.") When "Joe" peered into the viewer, the first fellow said, "Now if that isn't an example of a pine forest with too much rain, I don't know what is." It developed that this gentleman was not actually a grower, as such, but a breeder, who made his living selling seeds and seed-lings of exotic origin.

After the scorecards were turned in, waitresses circulated among the crowd, which consisted almost entirely of males aged twenty-five to forty-five, and distributed hors d'oeuvres. Meanwhile, the scores were being tabulated by computer. As the prolonged wait continued, I could sense a genuine nervousness throughout the room.

Finally, a man who looked more like an accountant than an outlaw appeared in front of the crowd bearing a handful of envelopes. The room immediately turned quiet. The first envelope was opened: "Fragrance: The winner is number three!" A young longhair jumped for joy, pushed to the front, received his victor's plaque, and gave an acceptance speech in which he thanked several associates, all named Joe. When the "sticky fingers" plaque was claimed by two women, this surprise development caused much talk around the room. The smug winner of the "tightest bud" competition had also won the same prize the previous two years—a noteworthy achievement that had the other growers shaking their heads in admiration.

Before the announcement of the final award, the Grand Prize trophy was pulled out and displayed to the crowd. Engraved on it were the names of the winning farms for the previous nine years. Then there was a hush; the envelope was ripped open and the grand champion declared: number seventeen. Two large men, one Hawaiian and one haole, *rushed to the front amid much cheering and whooping. They were obviously a popular pair.*

On the way home, Maryjane and I joked and fantasized about what these conventions might be like if marijuana were legalized. Regional contests, professional judges, week-long judging periods, separate categories for Cannabis sativa *and* Cannabis indica, *special awards for contemplative strains as opposed to brands that just make you laugh.*

There seems no doubt that smoking marijuana is harmful to the lungs. However, as I said good-bye to Maryjane, I thought about how illogical it really was that alcohol drinkers could buy their drug anywhere and could gather in public places to drink it, often acting in an offensive manner, while marijuana smokers were forced to go underground to obtain their recreational drug of preference and to smoke it in hiding. It does not appear, though, that marijuana will be legalized in the near future. The nonsmoking public, often confusing marijuana with harder drugs, opposes legislation, and the people whose occupations are marijuana-related—growers, dealers, smugglers, and law-enforcement officers—would all lose a fortune if it were legalized. Still, I could not help but recall Maryjane's words when I opened the newspaper one morning back at home and came upon a photograph of President Reagan of the United States and President de la Madrid of Mexico celebrating the signing of a new anti-drug agreement—by toasting with glasses of champagne.

THE UNWANTED:

Barbara Palmer

Maryjane Johnson came from a background that offered her seemingly limitless possibilities. But there are others whose personal progress has been stymied not so much by poverty as by a lack of exposure to options.

It was bitterly cold when I went to visit Barbara Palmer at the home she and her children shared with a friend in Pleasant Ridge, Michigan. I found Barbara taping her favorite soap opera on a VCR, which seemed, initially, to be an unexpected luxury considering the hard times she had been facing.

If I ever wrote a book about my life, I would name it *The Unwanted from Day One.*

I have two brothers and two half-sisters. My mother was married twice. In the first marriage there were two boys and myself. I was the baby. Then she got married again and had two girls. But before that she left my brothers and myself on the street. The way I was told, we were left on Wall Street in Newburgh, New York, when I was two years old. My father says he was away in the service when she did this. Welfare picked us up and these people took us, this family. Actually, how it all came about, legal-wise, I don't know, and I don't know how they were chosen. My foster dad looks a lot like my dad, but according to my foster family, they're not relatives. There was two foster brothers and one foster sister.

My one brother ended up going to juvenile home, but my young-

332

est brother stayed with me and we grew up together. My two foster brothers were already married and my foster sister was about fifteen or twenty years older than I am. The town I grew up in was Rifton, New York. Rifton is a very small town, probably five hundred people in the whole town. You got one store, one bar, and one gas station. You blink your eye and you're through it; that's how small Rifton is.

My foster mother, she was a dream. She passed away when I was seventeen, and then the welfare came out and wanted to put me in a home till I was 18, because I didn't have two parents. That's when my foster sister signed for me to keep me from going in a home for a year. My brother had already gone into the navy and my other brother I very seldom ever seen.

The real shocker was much later, many, many years later, after my foster dad died and I was living in New York. My dad married my foster sister. I mean that took me time to accept and get over. I used to pace my floor trying to figure this mess out.

I went to Kingston High School in Kingston. I was quiet and shy. I always got pretty good grades, B's and C's. I just went to school, did my work, came home, did my homework, done my housecleaning, and went to school. I worked in Montgomery Ward's in the catalogue department after school, five to nine. Then when they used to have a tent sale in the parking lot, I used to work the concession stand there, hot dogs and stuff.

I was always a good girl in high school. When I got to senior year, I said, well, I'll get in trouble. My big thing was slipping out of school and going down and getting submarine sandwiches. That was the only time I got sent down to the principal. And the principal was my neighbor. I lived a sheltered life all that time. I did win an essay contest, writing a composition on the old covered bridge in Rifton. It's the oldest bridge in the United States and I won a book on the Hudson River and won ten dollars. So that was outstanding, but that was about it. The only date I was allowed to go on was the senior prom and then I had to go with my foster parents' best friends' son.

I remember graduation was a proud time. I was proud and happy because me and my brother Bud were the only Palmers that ever graduated from high school. I remember I was sad and cried, too. Even though I was quiet, I had friends in school, and you know you're not going to see none of your friends afterwards. Everybody goes their own way and everything.

After graduation I worked at a clothes store for quite a while. Then I met this guy, he was from Canada. And, believe it or not, he drove every weekend from Canada down to Kingston, New York, and that's a long way. I ended up getting in trouble over it. I got pregnant. And my foster people, they didn't want me to keep the baby. My foster father was a cop.

So they sent me away to a home for pregnant women, unwed women. Me, I had to be the brave one of them all. Every time one of the girls would fall apart over having their child and giving it off for adoption, good old strong me stood right there and helped them through it. But then when it came my turn, it was rough. But my foster daddy told me, "If you don't give him up, you can't come back here." Well, I didn't know at the time that welfare would help you or get you a place or anything like that. So I was scared. Because I figured if I had kept the kid I'm in a world all alone, nobody to help me. So I said, I guess that's the only choice I do have.

He was gorgeous, handsome. I put him in a brand-new yellow outfit and the father come down to see him, but my foster parents had it down on paper that they didn't want him nowheres near me, which I didn't know at the time. He was willing to marry me, and he sent me a black-onyx diamond ring. They made me send that back and they wouldn't let me marry him.

I nursed my baby until he was about nine days old. I breast-fed. I was always told that it makes your child closer to you. So I figured if I done that, maybe someday he'd look for me and I'll find him. He was born October the 8th, 1966, and I named him Michael Andrew. The social worker told me the people that adopted him kept his name Michael Andrew because they thought it was pretty and it went together good. So maybe someday he'll come and find me, because it wasn't something that I wanted to do. I didn't do it willingly. When I went to give him up, my foster dad came and I said, "Do you want to see the baby before I give him up?" He goes, "No." So I got mad at him and hollered at him. When they went to come and get the baby, they had to give me shots and everything because I screamed and hollered and tried to bust the door down.

Afterwards, I moved to Ellenville, New York, and I worked in an antenna place that makes antennas for television, radios. I met my husband because he worked in the same shop. He felt like I married him for an escape. It could have been. If you really love somebody, it takes a lot more than a little bit of nothing to cause a divorce. I only stayed with him a year and then I split. I said I would never marry again and so far I haven't.

I met this other guy and then I got pregnant again. Angie was born in 1969. The father didn't want to believe it was his. When I got ready to end up having her, that's when he showed up at the hospital. But he wouldn't give her his name. So I raised her myself. It wasn't easy. For a while I ate bean sandwiches for every meal so I could afford formula for Angie.

Her godparents owned a boardinghouse for young people that would come over from Puerto Rico, so her godmother took care of her so I could go back to work. I was back to work after a month. I worked making antennas five nights a week, then two nights a week in a bar as a waitress.

After about two or three years her godmother's son went to New York City and I decided to go there too. I was on ADC, Aid to Dependent Children, and I had an apartment on Hoe Street in the lower Bronx. I became pretty tight with a lady named Maria and that's how I met the guy who's the father of my other two kids. Denise was born in '72 and Raymond in '73. This guy and I got a place together and we were together for quite a while, but he was into drugs. Heroin. I got him on the methadone program, but it took quite a while. He was brutal to Angie, but when I had the other two, he kind of mellowed out, kind of.

I had Mafia people come to my house and knock down my door looking for him because of the money he owed. I told the leader of this group, "You'd better fix my door because if you don't, I'm going to blow your damn head off. If you want to kick the crap out of him out on the street, be my guest, but it has nothing to do with me, my house, my family, so you leave my door alone!" It was a scary situation. They hit him in the head with a gun and tied him up. They told me not to untie him before they left or they would shoot us all. But you believe it or not, that guy came back and fixed my door himself. This was before the two little ones were born.

When Raymond was about eight months old he had viral mono and he had enlarged kidney, liver, and spleen, and he almost died on me. When I brought him home from the hospital, he developed pneumonia, so he was in pretty bad shape. I prayed to the Lord to keep him to me, don't take him away, because I lost one son and I didn't want to lose my second one. Every week for a year I had to bring him in to a doctor and have him check his stomach out to make sure it wasn't hard and he wasn't bleeding internally. So I would keep him in his playpen most of the time. I was a nervous wreck. And his father wouldn't straighten out.

One day I got a phone call and it was one of my brothers. God only knows how he found me. He tracked down the whole family after all those years. My dad and my oldest brother came and got me and I packed up the kids, and they brought me to my ma's in New Jersey. I stayed at my mother's house for a year or two, but that turned out to be a total disaster. She was married to a very sweet, lovable person, but I just couldn't get along with my mom. I had a gall-bladder operation when I was living out there in New Jersey. After that I called my brother that lived out in Michigan and I told him the problems I was having.

So I came out here and stayed at my brother's while I looked for a job. When I came out here all we owned was a garbage bag full of clothes between us. My brother took me down to Social Service for food stamps and some help. I got a job in a motel part-time and I started putting money away to get our own place. I started hitting rummages and in less than a year I rented a place and had it completely furnished. I had also gotten me a car. I was like thirty-one, thirty-two years old before I ever got a driver's license. But it got so expensive, it was hard for me to pay gas and water and phone, so we moved out to Lafayette and Royal Oak. I started working in machine shops. I can run a screw machine; I can run a lathe; I can run a press; I can run a bender; I can run just about any machine you can put me on. When the depression hit Detroit, I got laid off and the shop moved away. I had gotten up to six dollars an hour. I collected unemployment for a year and then I worked in phone-sales work until I found this job I've got now.

It doesn't pay the best, but it's better than not working at all. Right now my job's real easy because this shop is simple. They make parts for Fords. They're little tiny presses and they're very simple to run. You stick a part in, push the two buttons, take the part out, and throw it in a bag. I work the night shift because I don't like getting up early in the morning. I make four dollars an hour. Six days a week, forty-six hours, sometimes more. I've been so tired that on Sunday once I got up and got in my car and started for work. I was working so many hours, I was on automatic. I had to turn around and start back home.

A couple years ago my kids used to go to the Y all the time, swimming. And Raymond met this man named Bill Riley, who took him roller-skating. Raymond asked him if next time he could bring a friend and he said sure, so next time Raymond brought Denise. Then they asked if they could bring another friend next time and he said okay, and they brought Angie. Well, by this time I was starting to get suspicious, so I told the kids I wanted to meet this guy. I asked my brother to be there when he came over in case he saw something differently than I would.

Well, Bill seemed pretty nice. He was older and he was no dummy. He's a college graduate, and been a teacher and a psychologist, and he's a writer. He makes good money writing books for the army. He just loved my kids. He's really a super good guy. He's not my type of guy, but he is really a nice guy. I never in my life have ever had a man do for us and care for us, without wanting something in return, sleeping with them or something. I never would have believed it with all I've been through.

The kids asked him one day if we could move to his house because he has this great big house all to himself. They hated living in the neighborhood we were in. Bill thought about it and he come back like two days later and he said, "I've thought about it and it's fine." I said, "If I move in I want to have an understanding that you don't make no play." He agreed and we moved in. We've lived here two and a half years and it's been fine ever since we moved in. It's been a platonic relationship, which my brothers just can't believe. Sometimes I want to move, though, because I get tired of living under somebody's roof. I mean, if I meet a guy and bring him here for dinner and he sees Bill sitting there, what is he going to think?

The main thing that keeps me going now is my kids. You gotta have love to give love, and I've got love, but only for the children. Right now I think I pinpoint a lot more on Angie. It's just that right now she's at the age where she needs guidance. She's going to be sixteen and she's on the borderline of hanging with bad people. I'm not saying it's all her friends, but she's gotten to where she'll lie, she'll sneak, she'll do things that she's never done.

Some of the things that she's seen is probably not good for a child to see, but at the same time it kind of taught her and woke her up to the way life is. One time she was going out with this one boy and I guess they got in an argument and he smacked her in the face. She brought back her fist and punched him. And she says, "There ain't no man ever gonna hit me the way my ma's been hit." He tried to make up with her, but she wouldn't do it.

With me working the hours that I do, the children are getting totally way out of hand. They're becoming totally disrespectful. But who wants to stay on welfare just to stay home and take care of them? My girlfriend's ex–old man, he's sitting home on welfare, collecting, drinking up a storm, don't work, and having himself a ball. Me? I got three kids, can't get help, and I got to work for four dollars an hour and I got to neglect the kids just to keep the job. Is that fair?

At least my kids come to me. Like my youngest girl come home one day: "Ma, if I take an aspirin, would I ever get pregnant?" Good thing she asked. I said, "Don't ever believe that one. Believe me, I pop a lot of aspirins and I get pregnant. You've got to take birth control, and you've got to take them at least a month before they're effective."

I told my oldest girl, "If you ever feel like there's a time where you'll be weak—and believe me, that time will come—you come to me. Talk to me. And I'll take you to get something so you don't end up having a child before you're ready to have one." I wished when I was a kid I had someone I could go talk to and discuss things, but the subject was taboo.

I want my children to grow up and be something. I want them to have a chance in life to make it. If Angie wants to be a model, that's what I want. If Denise wants to be a lawyer, that's what I want. If Raymond wants to be a soccer player, that's the way I want it. But I have no way to send them to college and I have no way to get them out of here and into a better financial situation. I don't have the money to make a portfolio for Angie and I don't know how to find an agency that you can trust. It's something that I don't know anything about, but this is what her dream is. So that means her dream won't be fulfilled because I don't have the knowledge or the money to back her. When I was her age, I was just as thin as she is and I always wanted to be a model. But I didn't know how to go about it, nor had the money.

All I ask for is a break in life to where I don't have to work so dang hard. I'm not asking to be a millionaire. I know I ain't never gonna be rich. But I would like to make enough to where we could get our own place and we could live comfortable, where I don't have to go from week to week and let two or three bills go to pay for other ones, or you gotta let them all go to get your car running.

I had a business once, a couple years ago, a tree business. But I didn't have the money to get it going right, and I lost my shirt. What I always wanted to do in life, if I had the money to do it, was to start a place where children can go and have a place to hang out, like I had when I was a kid. You'd go and have pop, chips, hot dogs, and you can dance and get off the streets and get away from drugs. But I don't know anyone with the knowledge to help me, and I don't have the money to sit there and learn from my mistakes.

MOST ARTISTIC:
Paul Glover

I first met Paul Glover in Miami Beach during the summer of 1972. Both of us had gone there to demonstrate against the Democrats and Republicans at their respective party conventions. I didn't see him again until several years later, when, like so many New Yorkers, he moved to California. However, Paul's journey west, like his journey through life, was most unusual and most creative.

When we got together, once again, for an interview, it was at the Venice, California, home that Paul shared with a retired German boatbuilder.

I was born in Canandaigua, New York, the fourth of five children. My father was a salesman on the road, selling heating and air-conditioning units. Then one of the dealers of this equipment invited Dad to be a partner in his business, so the whole family moved to Ithaca.

Ithaca's a village city. It has a village feeling. It's surrounded on three sides with high hills, and that has kept the city stable and isolated, in some ways. We didn't suffer the upheaval of urban sprawl. There were three major streams passing through town on their way to a big lake. So we had dramatic hills and miles of cascades and lots of parks and ponds, all within walking distance. It was a paradise for kids.

When I was eleven, we left the city for the suburbs. I was disappointed because I lost the ready availability of lots of playmates. It was a rough transition. But then I made friends with the trees. By my parents' example, I developed a very deep love of nature. I now find greater enjoyment in a blade of grass bending in the breeze than in anything else our culture provides—movies, television, sports. I think a blade of grass is electronically far more complex than a video game.

My family was not an academic bunch, but we loved learning. Reading encyclopedias, doing crafts, playing instruments, collecting things, trying new sports, kept us lively. Ithaca High School was very stimulating—rated among the top ten in the nation at one point. But I couldn't confine my interest to the things that I was being taught in school, and I never got very good grades.

My romantic life in high school was absolutely zero. I was covered with pimples and had thick-framed glasses and felt like a toad. I was extremely shy, painfully shy. If I had known years ago about junk food, I probably wouldn't have suffered through the acne that made me so ashamed to look at others, because I knew if I looked at them, they would look back at me.

I *was* voted "Most Artistic" in my high-school graduating class. I used to draw little cartoons for the school paper, mocking school life. I left cartoons on all the desks that I sat at and was always being told to erase them. I did nothing but doodle. All I wanted to do was play chess and draw pictures.

The main thing that I remember about graduation was that a real nice girl smiled at me, and I felt good about that. I probably went home and sat in my treehouse. I had built a treehouse, and even though I was old enough to do more sophisticated things, I would sit in my treehouse and read *Mad* magazine and study the drawing styles.

That summer I turned eighteen and was expected to sign up for the draft. I took church very seriously and was taught that Jesus was the example that people should follow. I couldn't imagine Jesus walking around with a helmet and a machine gun. So I said, "No, I don't intend to sign up." For three days, family and friends argued at me about why it was my duty. They tried to reason with me, and when that didn't work, I was accused of being a Communist and a coward. Finally they said I could get a student deferment, and I went along with that and signed up. That was the beginning of my disillusionment— that we weren't supposed to live by what was right, that we weren't really supposed to follow Jesus's example. We were supposed to worship him instead.

I was accepted into a two-year advertising course at Mohawk Valley College in Utica, and immediately my repressed rebelliousness came out. I drew political cartoons and became editor of the college paper. I organized seniors successfully to keep the right to live off campus. The most important lesson for me was that advertising is bullshit. I don't suppose many people would disagree, but some people think that it's a valuable kind of bullshit to run society with.

I was being taught to lie to people. I was being taught to teach people that there was value in a product that did not have any value, except what value you told them it had. We were taught to sell items, not in terms of any intrinsic value these things might have, or the function they were intended to serve, but for the association that would be attached to them, such as sex, the need to belong, the need to be accepted, the need to have status.

We were being taught to create commercial substitutes for these basic human needs, rather than to promote forms of society which would directly satisfy these human needs. I managed to graduate and get a degree in advertising, even though I was disgusted by it. I became a rebel against the advertising morality. The main authority for what is real and valuable for many people is the advertisement. Having raised some generations that way, we now sell politicians with style rather than substance. Nineteen sixty-nine was the last year I watched television. Having done summer work in advertising, I was offered a job as art director of an advertising agency, right after graduation.

But I decided that I wanted wisdom. I had a craving for wisdom. So I went to Harpur College, in Binghamton, New York, to study philosophy. Recently I calculated that I could have earned over a million dollars by now had I pursued the advertising career. Since then, however, I have steered my life instead by the values which are most basically important to me, few of which are rewarded by money.

So I studied philosophy, and found out that was even worse bullshit than advertising. We were being taught to reformulate musty paragraphs from long-dead heavyweight thinkers. We were not being encouraged to do original thinking.

I realized that I was being protected in this college while people who did not have middle-class backgrounds were being killed in Vietnam. I gave up my student deferment voluntarily and applied to become a conscientious objector. I felt a deep inner satisfaction for having done what I thought was right. I felt a deep acceptance of myself. The CO status that I was eventually given was to me a higher rank than general.

As soon as I gave up my student deferment, I met the most wonderful person, and the best friend I ever had. A person who, in retrospect, was ideally suited as a life's companion. Her name was Monica. We lived in the same dorm at college. She was studying Spanish and campaigning for Nixon. She was a member of the Conservative Club. She had written articles saying how we needed to kill Communists and despise the hippies. I talked to her about what the New Testament would have us do as alternatives to war. The example of Christ was an example of nonviolence. Within two weeks, she had changed her mind, and we started going in the same direction.

I remember one night coming back from a film about the horrors of Nazi Germany. For some reason this sparked something between her and me. We were jumping up and down on her bed, ecstatic with the determination that we were going to change the world, that we were going to do whatever we could to make the world as good a place as it could be. We were less wed, at that point, to career and college than to each other and to the world. It was, for both of us, a moment of liberation, or release, from whatever had bound us, or kept us from being adults. It was an intense moment, and it set a direction for both of us for years.

As a conscientious objector, I was assigned to Auburn Memorial Hospital, northeast of Ithaca. I was assigned to the emergency-resuscitation squad. I was learning, on the job, how to retrieve people from the edge of death. I had been a protected middle-class kid. It was a rude shock to discover that people smelled bad, had fragile bones, suffered horrible, crippling diseases, and died. I was supposed to pump air into their lungs with my own mouth, and pump blood through their heart with my hands.

Auburn is an industrial, working-class community. They had little sympathy for hippies who were against war. I was finally fired from that job because I refused to remove a peace symbol from my uniform, refused to cut my hair, and refused to quit speaking with patients about such matters of concern as war.

They later reassigned me to another hospital, but I decided to cooperate no further with the draft, and went to Washington, D.C. I worked on the Student Mobilization Committee as a staff cartoonist. All I got was a place to live, but I was very proud. It was a very exciting place to be. That was the time of the major mass demonstrations of hundreds of thousands of people. I wandered around just soaking it up. The varieties of people, the varieties of perspectives, the piles of literature, the great sense of significance of events. I never affiliated with the violent groups in the antiwar movement, but I did get tear-gassed for the first time, anyway.

I went back home and Monica and I got married. We had a big peace symbol on the wedding cake. Some said they didn't believe it was a real marriage because we wrote our own vows: "That in a world of too little faith, I will be faithful." In front of sixty people, I said that I would stay with her always.

My parents loved Monica as much as me. Monica was the all-American girl, with a great sense of humor. She was a fashion model, and was a respected reporter for the daily newspaper in Ithaca. She was just a gorgeous human being, and she was loved by pretty much everybody. *Her* parents thought the marriage was a mistake. They wanted for her a conventional ceremony to a conventional man.

On our wedding night, it hit me that I had done something irrevocable. Now I was expected to live with her forever. It scared me. I think I should have spoken about it with Monica, because she may have felt the same way. We took off riding across the United States on our honeymoon. Monica and I had slept together before we were married, but never had sex. She wanted to wait until we were married. She was such a good friend that I didn't care.

On the ninth day of our marriage, she injured her back lifting our canoe. She felt increasing pain as we were driving across the country. We checked five doctors en route. Two said her pain was caused by lovemaking; another said it was birth-control pills. The fifth doctor told us she had a slipped disc, and we believed him. She flew to Ithaca and entered a hospital while I drove home. The doctors wanted to keep her in the hospital, but I said no. My folks took us in, and we waited on her day and night until her back healed.

I had a vasectomy. We had talked about this and decided that there were enough kids in the world, and if we were going to have any, we were going to adopt them.

While Monica was convalescing, we applied to the Brethren Volunteer Service, because we wanted to give our lives to service for social justice. After a training period in Maryland, we were assigned to Lafayette, Louisiana, and began to do public relations for a black-owned co-op called the Southern Consumers' Cooperative. They had a black bakery and a black insurance company, and they were giving loans to black businesses. We had never lived with black people before. We had never known black people as friends. All of a sudden, all our neighbors were black people and all our friends and acquaintances were black people.

I can't say that we did much good for the public relations of this co-op. We were trying to be intermediaries to a white community from which we were also ostracized for our strange New York ways. But we did make friends and connections. We left the co-op, though, because we realized that we weren't so devoted to black capitalism as to economic democracy.

We started a community newspaper which dealt with issues that the daily newspaper did not consider, like murders by police. We were often threatened with violence. Finally our house was broken into by off-duty police and two of the people were taken for a ride and slapped around.

A short time after that, FBI men tapped me on the shoulder and said that my refusal to cooperate with the draft was making me liable to trial. I didn't know at the time that you didn't have to talk to the FBI. I did go in and talk to them. I said that I was doing what I thought was service to my country. We'd gotten exhausted by the paper at that time anyhow, and decided to take off.

We came back to New York and I talked to the U.S. attorney for the region which was handling my case, and told him that I didn't intend to cooperate with the draft. Talked with him earnestly. Then we went underground. We changed our names. I changed mine to Paul Simon, taking a friend's last name. I knew so little about popular culture that it didn't occur to me that this was not a good way to become anonymous.

We worked on a community paper in Jacksonville, Florida. Then we found out the U.S. attorney had decided to drop our case because prosecuting draft resisters was not as popular in 1972 as it had formerly been.

I felt the need to take a little while on my own, so Monica and I separated for a month. I hitchhiked around the country and visited other underground newspapers, and she worked on a Hutterite farm in North Dakota. Then we met up and went to the first Rainbow Family Gathering in Colorado. We chanted "Om" in a big mountain field in a circle of thousands of naked nature lovers.

Then we went back to Louisiana, said hello to the people we used to work with, and then went to Miami Beach, because we heard that the Democratic and Republican conventions were going to be there. We connected with the Miami Conventions Coalition and were given a room in a fancy hotel in exchange for being cultural workers for "Exposé 72," which was a presentation of counter-cultures, both American and Vietnamese. Monica made a display of conditions in South Africa under apartheid.

However, I started to get the impression then that Monica was less enthusiastic about chasing all over the country, encouraging rebellion against the war. I was interested in street demonstrations, and in the push and pull of contending forces, police and demonstrators. I was never interested in the violent aspect of it, but found the rest of it exciting. Monica had always kept to her religious beliefs, and didn't feel this was her style.

We went back to Ithaca. I started to look for work, and she located a beautiful apartment on Main Street for a very small amount of money. She was no longer interested in being a radical. She wanted to domesticate. She wanted to settle down. She wanted to have the family over. Various of our friends lived with us, and we had lots of good times. But I was still foremost devoted to political concerns. I was still living on my savings from having worked in the hospital and from selling my coin collection for $1500.

I issued this newspaper called *Treetop,* a small journal of liberation and education. Education was a major issue in Ithaca. I offered this to the community and had a lot of fun with it. I was still resisting growing up, finding a job, and being a husband to my wife.

I got tired of *Treetop* after six issues, and decided to run for city council as an anarchist. I was going to be a city councilperson who would, as I emphasized throughout my campaign, rely on people to initiate political reforms and to make sure the government was kept off their backs.

I issued campaign literature, knocked on 1800 doors, talked with hundreds of people, and was endorsed by the Liberal Party. I also had good conversations with working-class conservatives, who supported me because I was opposed to big government. Dr. Spock came to town to speak for me. I received 22 percent of the vote and finished in second place. I beat the Democrat.

At the conclusion of the campaign, I moved out of the apartment and became the sexton of the Unitarian church. In exchange for locking the doors at night, taking out the trash, and setting up chairs for meetings, I was given an apartment free, next to the church. I had access to all the facilities of the church, so we had lots of fun, my friends and I. Showed movies, ran around naked, put on plays.

Monica had become a Jehovah's Witness. As our relationship un-raveled, she had turned to a new source of certainty. She told me later that I had been for her a source of certainty because I knew exactly what was right and wrong, and was firm about acting on it. I guess she liked that. But as U.S. involvement in the Vietnam War wound down, I wasn't so certain anymore about what was going on in the world.

I went to some of the Jehovah's Witness meetings with Monica. I found them to be good people who had genuine good feeling with each other. They are probably the world's largest pacifist organization. I do respect them, though I have large disagreements with some things they embrace, like the end of the world, for example.

Monica found another apartment and was back reporting for the newspaper. I was working on yet another little newspaper, and then, with some friends, started a Vocations for Social Change office, coun-seling people on alternatives to conventional careers. This, as with everything else I had done before, paid me nothing. One of the projects we undertook was to issue a People's Yellow Pages—sixty pages of alternative-life-style resources in Ithaca. After that, I decided I wanted to issue a Tompkins County almanac—a comprehensive collection of history, culture, environment, politics, economics, and education in that county.

My younger brother, Stephen, had been diagnosed by psychia-trists and educators as being brain-damaged, and he became convinced that he couldn't add two plus two. Finally he got away from the pressure of the school system, which had no place for him, and was taken in hand by some Christians in a community in Switzerland. In no time at all, he was reading good literature and making speeches and making friends as he had never done before.

He came back home for a visit. He was twenty-three years old, and was feeling happy one day. He asked me if I'd take him walking. But I was too busy writing the outline of my almanac, so he went on the walk himself. That evening I was visiting my folks, and my mother said, "I just have this terrible feeling." She said, "Why don't you go look for Stephen?" My father and I went down into the creek because she said that's where he'd gone. It was getting dark. We walked all the way down the creek, several miles. Then we went to the police station to ask if they'd heard anything.

The cop took me aside and showed me Stephen's picture. He had gone swimming and didn't know how. And he sank. I embraced my dad. I was afraid he was going to have a heart attack, so I was massaging him. He was immediately thinking of my mother and how she would take it. The police drove us home, and my father said to her, "We've lost our son."

Then we just sat in that living room for ... it must have been weeks. Time warps. You lose track. Visitors came. People sat with us. We were all just quiet there together.

I tried to continue my life, and tried to be happy with my friends. I managed pretty well. But I was keeping something inside. I was sitting on something. Early in 1975, I took a lover, and told Monica, and the divorce was under way.

I always thought that drugs were a substitute for dealing with real situations, and diminished the integrity of the mind, and had never taken any. I felt the same way about liquor and smoking, and, in fact, have never even had a cup of coffee. My father said that was un-American. But I never took drugs until I separated from Monica. Then I wanted to do what I thought drugs did, which was to avoid facing certain things. I was devoted to avoiding facing responsibility for having put Monica aside, and whatever responsibility I felt for my brother's death, because I hadn't gone walking with him. So I started to take drugs. I took LSD probably half a dozen times. Extraordinary experiences. Never had a bad experience. But I stopped taking drugs because it became difficult to comprehend everyday life. LSD was like being in Disneyland all the time. And it was ever harder to go home.

My divorce with Monica was finalized June 6, 1975. I feel like if I had a second chance with someone like her, I would plant some roots. But I had started a relationship with this other woman, which became like death by a thousand cuts. It was showing me what I had done to Monica. I had felt restrained about sex, but with this woman I became a galloping animal. I let my penis go to my head, and I lost perspective on the other things that were important to me—family and friends, even social and political concerns. I became dependent on her as Monica had been dependent on me. She ran hot and cold, and I felt I was only worthwhile if she accepted me. She doubted me, this woman did, and, little by little, I began to doubt myself. I was walking around town staring at trees and waterfalls—without drugs. I was completely baffled by everything. I was left sitting on the floor babbling. Then the family and friends I had neglected came and picked me up.

After two years, this woman finally became the only person I have ever hit in anger. I was put through a wringer that I needed to go through in order to face a part of me that I had not understood—the

part that was warlike, the part that was unloving, the part that was unfair, the part that was the opposite of what I said people should do.

During this two-year fling, I did manage to do other things. My
Tompkins County Almanac became an illustrated calendar of local history and sold faster than I could get them printed. It was very popular,
and I was respected in the community for it. I thought publishing was
my way to go. So I reprinted an old book of scenic views of Ithaca,
edited, with my introduction. I sold these things at low prices, like a
Christmas present to Ithaca. I felt I was setting an example—that if everyone in a community acted foremost in the interest of the community, then lots of grand things would be available to everybody. That's
how I felt an economic system should operate.

In 1976 I found out planners intended to put an elevated super-
highway through the middle of Ithaca, which would completely destroy everything that I loved about this small community. It would
have made Ithaca into a truck stop. So I got the government documents
on the highway project, including memos from government agencies,
and in one week put together a powerful 3000-word review of everything written about the road. It remains the thing about my time in
Ithaca of which I'm most proud. I took that review from group to group
and stirred up a popular movement against the road, where there had
been absolutely none before. The road has still not been built.

In 1977 they wanted to build a huge shopping center on the outskirts of town, which would eventually deflate the downtown district
and draw the commerce away to their own shopping center. The
developers sought to make Ithaca grow and progress profitably toward
decay. We did whatever we could to communicate our concerns to the
community. Even though Ithacans were against the shopping center,
the people who were building the thing had enough legal right and
enough friends in the courts.

So we said we would trespass on this land to stop the construction,
because these people were trespassers in our county. Our actions cul-
minated in a five-mile march to the construction site, in which I led
about a hundred people and talked with each person on the way.

When we got there, I handed out seedlings to everyone and we
planted trees on the site. We linked hands in a circle, laid a curse on the
site, and sang "America the Beautiful." We stopped construction for a
day. The place has since been built.

There grew a terrible momentum in building such places without
regard to their effects on the balance of commerce, the health of small

businesses, the added load on fire, police, water, and other municipal services, without regard to the balance of the community with nature, and our increasing urban dependence on distant supplies of food and fuel and metals. We were seeing piecemeal destruction of a way of life we loved.

After doing these things for years, I felt less and less leverage. I was exhausted with merely kicking back. I decided I wanted to figure out what kind of society could be offered by those of us who valued nature and ecology and more intimate-scale communities. We started to make drawings of what it could look like.

My imagination was being filled with bold urban designs. I was seeing shadows of things yet to be. I was describing ways of supplying food and fuel and water, and of metropolitan transit and governance, that were so different than what we understood as normal that even people who usually agreed with me felt I was not being realistic. Yet I could not shake loose of these ideas. To rebuild our housing so that our houses held midday heat at night and shielded us from heat at noon. To produce a lot more food in the city, grown without dependence on pesticides. To produce most of our energy with sun and wind and falling water. To move without cars.

I felt I was losing any capability to affect the course of events in Ithaca, and that Ithaca was on its way to becoming yet another gray place. I could not stand to see this happen, so I decided to leave.

My first attempt at leaving was with a couple of buddies. We got in a Volkswagen bus, and we rode around the United States visiting solar-energy innovators, people who had new ideas, who had built new models, and who were trying to live different ways. In Arizona, I decided to return and do the great American riding of rails. I talked to some hoboes and they told me how to board a train. Rolling through the night, I found myself the next morning several hundred miles east.

I was looking around in the train yard for another train to get on when one of them hit me from behind. It plowed me into the ground beside the track. It was slow, but heavy. I lay there with blood rolling out of my mouth, waiting to be dead. I was hauled into the local hospital. I had no severe injury, and after about two hours I was on my way hitchhiking back home. It was no big deal, but it gave me a dramatic scar, and I had a great story to tell when I arrived.

The feelings I had just before I was hit were that I'm completely loose in the world, unconnected to anything, and no one cares about me. Then I got hit. There's a certain psychic guard which keeps us safe. I had let mine drop.

I was only in Ithaca for maybe another month. I took off to Boston with a few dollars in my pocket. A young woman took me into her home and took care of me and let me off at Boston. This was a time when, for some reason, women found me instantly attractive, wanted to sleep with me. I was quite proud of how I took hold in Boston for the short while I was there. I got a job washing dishes at a posh restaurant in Cambridge and had all the cheesecake I could eat for free. I got a grant from the Cambridge Arts Council to teach sidewalk art. At the same time, I got paid part-time by Boston Urban Gardeners (BUG), promoting urban agriculture. I led a varied and vigorous life there, commuting by running.

I wasn't sure what I wanted to do next. For some time, the idea of walking across the United States had intrigued me. Since I had just become disconnected from wife and lovers and business, and disconnected too from my family and my hometown of Ithaca, it seemed like it was the right time to hike. I was tired of knowing about the world secondhand through books and the media, and what other people told me. I wanted to see reality directly.

So, on June 9, 1978, with twenty dollars in my pocket, I started walking. I took a trolley to the Atlantic Ocean, put some sand in my pack, and headed inland toward the other ocean. The first day, I'd gone maybe fifteen miles when a fellow pulled up and said, "Where are you going?" I said, "I'm going to Oregon." And he said, "Well, I'm an airline pilot and I'm flying to Oregon tomorrow. Would you like a free ride?" I said, "No thanks, I'm out for a walk," and he went on.

It started to rain and another fellow stopped and offered me a place for the night. I said, "I'll go on walking. Thanks, anyhow." I found my way to the woods and put up a little tent. I had gone about twenty miles.

I headed southwest, through Massachusetts, Connecticut, New York, New Jersey, Pennsylvania. I kept to the rural routes, staggering through the sun. A farmer stopped me and gave me a hat. He put it on my head, and I wore that hat all the way to the Pacific Ocean. A woman stopped me and asked me where I was going. She was back an hour later with a Boy Scout troop. I gave them a talk about the environment. Other women would stop and bring me cookies and things.

As I went further and got more oriented to the lay of the land, I would find myself more on dirt roads and in the woods. I would take a state map and draw a pencil line straight across it. Then, for counties I would cross, I'd write ahead to get county road maps and ask they be sent to me general delivery. With those county road maps, I could follow the labyrinth of tiny dirt roads, or just cut between these roads and go through the woods. I got better and better at that, and developed instincts about crossing untracked country.

Across the Appalachians I met lots of fine, fine people. People who had lived their lives quietly at the end of dirt roads, in homes that their parents and their parents' parents and their parents' parents' parents had all lived in.

Along the way, if I came to a construction site or a highway being built, I would do what I could to unhinge that distorted idea of progress. They lay out location markers and you just pull them up. Or in the middle of the woods, you'd see where they have parceled off the land, and you just remove those stakes, and they have to resurvey. Or there's a piece of equipment that is used to knock down trees and plow foundations. You render those inoperable. Property and tools can be used in violent ways, and I felt that I could in good conscience destroy those tools.

Near Rabbit Hash, Kentucky, I met a family that had recently lost its farm to the bank. They had ten kids. They housed me, protected me from the mosquitoes one night. In the morning, they sat me down to breakfast and served up pancakes. All the kids waited until I was done before eating. I finally sent them some money when I got out to the West Coast.

I had to cross rivers where there were no bridges. I crossed the Ohio twice, as I like to phrase it: the former on a ladder, and the latter on a dormer. That is to say, the first time I crossed the Ohio, I found an old ladder by the shore, strapped my pack to it, reinforced it with more boards, and swam across, pushing it.

The latter time, the second time, I crossed on a dormer—a window frame that I found on the beach. Some big cargo boat was crossing midriver, and the last thing I heard was this woman on the shore saying, as I pushed off, "You're a fixin' to get killed!"

The wake of the boat nearly did upset me. I climbed out of the water and felt scummy and terrible. I walked way up into the hills and found an abandoned barn. A huge downpour split through the sky, and I stood lightning naked out in that storm, and just exalted in getting clean that way.

In the Ozarks, when I wanted to cross from one place to another through dense thickets, I asked a forester how to get to this village a number of miles away. He said, "Don't go. A man doesn't belong in those woods without a map. I still get so lost I don't believe my compass."

I said, "Well, I'm crossing the United States, and this is the way I'm going."

He said, "Go yonder and you'll find a little path. Go down that and you'll be in Bee Hollow."

I started down through Bee Hollow, and the most violent rainstorm I had ever experienced opens up. Like it's trying to pound me down and make me part of the mud. I get deep in Bee Hollow, and it's just a blur of water and green. I'm sloshing along in what appears to be a leftover pathway, and it's twisting and rising and falling, as if to escape the monotony of its own isolation out there in the middle of nowhere. It disappears, and I'm walking through grass, and then it reappears, and the storm is full of fury, and I just keep walking, just follow my instincts. Just as the light is completely gone, I come out to exactly where I intended to go. That was a triumph.

In many cases, my determination to walk across the country on foot had to override all kinds of common sense. I would come to cliffs or rivers or wild animals. I accidentally started stampedes. I was constantly lucky, but felt a certain invincibility and power. At one point, with full pack, I had to jump from one side of a stream, probably seven feet wide and nine feet down. Without hesitation, I jumped, and kept right on going.

Once, I was so discouraged I decided to give up. I spent a whole day crossing through woods near Black, Missouri, and found that I'd only gone five miles because I got so lost. I knocked on a farmhouse door that night, and the people drew me maps, and were so caring and so helpful, so encouraging.

After using up money sent to me from prior publishing, my cash ran out in Missouri, and I started to look for work. I worked in an apple orchard, picking apples, and earned good money. Met people who claim themselves to be the poorest people in PeePee Township. Salt of the earth hillbillies. I heard the music sung by these people, that we usually hear only on old-time records. Songs that reconcile misery and love.

Gradually, as the summer got hotter, I found myself out in Oklahoma, having crossed through hundreds of miles of corn and mosquitoes and pig shit and flies and swamp and hill and forest.

Just south of Muskogee, I stepped up to a fence and asked this guy where I was and he pulled a pistol on me. I got his wife laughing, but he took it pretty seriously. The sheriff's department came and handcuffed me, and put me in the car and jailed me. There had been some murders in this small town that weren't solved. The next morning they let me out and left me further back than I had been.

The other time I was so discouraged I almost gave up was when I sat down to rest in a Laundromat in a little town in Oklahoma, and they kicked me out. I felt bad about this and I talked with the deputy about it. The last thing he said was, "Y'all come back." Cops were usually helpful.

In that same state, a man ran after me for a mile to invite me for dinner. He said his wife had seen me go by. She was a Cherokee Indian. People were so helpful.

Across Oklahoma and Texas it was a month of a hundred degrees plus. But it soon got cooler and colder. I realized that had I gone toward Oregon—by this time I was in the Western states—the winter would cover me with snow, so I kept going southwest instead. As it got colder, I would just pile on more and more clothes, and I smelled awful.

If I wanted company for the night, I would knock on a farmhouse door and ask if I could sleep in the barn or the shed. They would usually invite me in for dinner and treat me like a member of the family. But they'd also invite me to put my clothes in the washing machine. There was tremendous hospitality offered to me all the way across that made the episode in Oklahoma insignificant by comparison.

Over and over again, people would say, "You watch out; there are mean people up ahead. They'll knock you down and take your things." I'd get up ahead and they'd be regular, decent people, and they'd say, "How'd you get past those people back there? They'll knock you down and take your things." Over and over again.

A couple of times I found myself face to face with a bull. I realized if I ran away I would get stabbed from behind. If I did something hostile, I was liable to be horned in the gut. So I just walked by easy, like, "People are always walking through here, aren't they?" and was allowed to pass.

Early in the walk I lay down to sleep in the woods. I was dreaming that there was an animal saying, "People must get out of the way of animals!" I woke up immediately and heard the grunting of a woodchuck. When I rose up next morning, I realized I had lain down in the middle of an animal trail. They had to go out of their way that night to get around me. Their attitude had penetrated my dream. When we cut loose from the normal, rational procedures by which we get information, we get it intuitively.

Once, walking on the desert, I was really thirsty and out of water, and thinking how desperate I was for it. Just over the next turn, behind the next cactus, was a gallon jug of water. Or I would be thinking, These pack straps hurt like hell; I wish I had some foam padding for them. I would go no more than fifty paces and there on the ground would be a length of foam padding exactly the width of my pack straps.

By the time I got to the desert, it was cold weather. The only time I ever got snowed on was west of Tucson, Arizona. I woke up with icicles on my feet. I became very animal. Dampness and cold were just a part of me. If there was dirt and mud, mosquitoes, whatever surrounded me, that's what I was. In the desert I stayed closer to roads, for the most part. But I did get lost out there on one occasion, and wondered if I'd find my way. But I kept on and thought, If I'm going to die, I'm going to die. I think that the willingness to accept death was a part of what protected me. I was able to set the fear aside and continue.

I crossed into Mexico, carrying a little pocket Spanish dictionary. About 120 miles from the coast, my shin gave me such torment that I could scarcely drag my foot. I began to walk, in agony, only five miles a day. The night before I crossed into California, I stayed in Mexicali, sleeping on the steps of a church with orphans who covered themselves, in this cold night, with cardboard boxes. I had two sleeping bags, and I offered a sleeping bag to one of them. He laughed at me. "How can you keep warm in that?" I bought them bananas, and the next day I crossed into the United States.

It began then to dawn on me that I was accomplishing something, that I'd gotten to California. It's a long way on foot. Finally I called a chiropractor in a little town and described my symptoms, and he said, "You probably have a slipped disc. You have to get off your feet and lie down for as long as it takes to heal." This was only sixty miles from the coast. As soon as I hung up the phone, the pain was gone. Which reinforces the idea that a lot of pain and illness comes from emotional causes, and there was some stress he relieved by stating what I had feared.

The main coherence in my life was that I was walking across the

United States. And part of the reason I did it was because I didn't have much other coherence in my life. I had dignified my vagabondage and my incoherence by undertaking this project.

The last night of the walk, I camped probably eighteen miles from the coast, and I could see the lights of San Diego. On the whole trip, 199 days, I had spent only $503. Probably a month of that time was staying with people or working various jobs, rather than walking, so I averaged about 20 miles a day for 3500 miles.

In the morning I walked down the hills towards the city. I saw more and more houses, and more and more cars, and noise, noise, noise. I got angry at all this. I saw a little girl run across the street, trying to avoid being hit by a car, and an old lady trying to negotiate the street. And I did something to a bulldozer on my way.

A few blocks from Imperial Beach, I heard the waves and I started to laugh and cry. I did it! It's real. You can actually walk from one ocean to the other. It became a reality to me. Before that, it was theoretical. Through my head went the images and sensations of the women I had known. I was laughing at myself: Here you are. You did it. So what? And crying because there was the ocean. I went down to it and stepped in. It was real cold. The whole scene was a luminous white mist. I remember the hissing of the water coming up the beach. I stepped back and I sat down and just stared at the water.

After a little while, I walked over to a store to make a phone call home and find out where my cousin lived in San Diego. But it was December 24th, and I couldn't get through because it was a busy evening for telephoning. A young guy comes up to me and invites me over to his house, where they were having a Christmas party.

On Christmas Day I called home. Later that day my cousin came with her family and picked me up and took me home and put my clothes in the laundry. I ate them out of house and home for a few weeks and entertained the local media. I couldn't adjust to sleeping indoors, so I slept outdoors.

I was introduced to the University of California at San Diego. They have a beautiful library, and woods nearby. I worked as a dishwasher, wrote and broadcast news for the campus radio station, helped out at the food co-op, slept in a eucalyptus grove, and spent nine months reading in the library, trying to figure what I wanted to do next.

I kept feeling this pull to go to San Francisco, and did so. Sure enough, when I got there, situations were open to me. Through the Ecology Center, I organized a symposium on waste-treatment alternatives for the city of San Francisco. Brought together the state, federal, and local officials with ecologists for a day-long symposium on alternatives to their proposed crosstown waste channel, which would dump the city's excreta into the ocean.

I ran out of money, and within a few days was hired by a publisher to do a history calendar of San Francisco. Then in May of '80 I came down to Los Angeles because they were about to celebrate their bicentennial. I got there and walked around City Hall and thought, This is the place where there's a lot for me to do. I thought it would be a great idea to do a local history calendar for the bicentennial. I knocked on a few doors, looking for publishers. And, after having not eaten for a few days, I found myself with a large check to get started on the project.

The Ithaca calendar had been the culmination of a life of knowing Ithaca. San Francisco is a very exciting, compact, dynamic city. L.A. was more of a challenge than a pleasure. I didn't know the territory. It's so big and diverse that it took me months just to do enough background reading to get started. I was fighting the place. It didn't make any sense. Why would people want to live here? Why didn't people rise up in revolt against the pollution? I was scared of the place, but determined to get right into the middle of the grit of it. I figured if ideas of appropriate technology and environmental balance had real capability to improve the world, then they had to be applied in the worst places. And L.A. was one of the world's best challenges.

I think I did a good job with the calendar. It was bilingual and was the first history of Los Angeles ever issued in the Spanish language. We printed up 15,000 copies, but it didn't sell. I couldn't get them distributed. I was actually using piles of them as a bed and sleeping on top of them. My friend Norma helped me to take the remaining 14,500 copies and distribute them free to schools in East Los Angeles.

I took a student loan from CitiCorp at that time, and didn't know that they were the largest American banking investor in South Africa. When I found that out, I decided that I would repay them at the rate that they divested their holdings in South Africa. I went to International College and got a degree in city management with a specialization in metropolitan-appropriate technology.

I lived with a Norwegian lady, and learned her language. She had a jewel-box smile. I had written a little book called *Los Angeles: A History of the Future,* showing how, gradually, over several decades, urban neighborhoods could change to near-total self-reliance in the production of energy, fuel, food, and water. A lot of the present area used for housing and streets could be released for gardens and orchards by the creation of solar co-op community houses that I called "ecolonies." Another idea was gradual change in the transportation system, combining revival of the trolley system in Los Angeles, which used to be the largest in the world, with a bicycle-path system, to replace the street grid.

The next woman I lived with encouraged me to start an organization based on the ideas I was writing about. I presented these kinds of images in public places and people responded far better than expected. I had thought everybody in L.A. was too busy making money to care about where their food and water and metals and fuels came from. Instead, I found hundreds of people who cared, and paid to join us.

We called the organization Citizen Planners. We're the Bring Back the Land Movement. Instead of escaping from horrible cities and creating the same problems out in rural areas, we would take the places where we already were and make them good to live in, by bringing the best of country life to the city. Depave parking lots and put up a paradise.

So, it's under way, and it's a very gradual process. We are seeking donors for the construction of a sample urban eco-village. We want to show how good the future could be. We aim to encourage people to think about better possibilities, and to take first steps, house by house, neighborhood by neighborhood, city by city, to create a world in balance with nature.

Along the way I married an Australian teacher. We were good pals and neither of us took the marriage dead seriously, and continued to see others, but when she moved in with another guy, and the Swiss woman I was with left the country, I felt left behind. After eighteen years of intimacy with women, I haven't settled into love, even though my parents, Elson and Julia, have set a fine example, being married fifty years.

After twenty years of devoting my life to political and social concerns rather than a career, I find myself without much money, without any domestic stability at all, and still trying to sort out how I can satisfy my inclination to be stable and share life with a woman. Right now I work two days a week selling food in a co-op food store, in which 130 member families are the bosses, where I'm an owner and a member and an employee. That's the kind of business I like to work in. I also give historical, botanical, and architectural walking tours of Venice, and do consulting work.

Today I'm feeling like I have my understanding of the world fairly well ordered. There's a lot that I don't know, and at any given time, like all of us, I'm wrong about some things. But there's a lot that I feel fairly sure of. I feel that people are basically good, that peace is more inevitable than war, and that if we can put people safely on the moon, we can put people safely on the earth.

My way of life in Los Angeles pivots on my bicycle. I feel that cars, especially, to the extent that we've become dependent on them, are a major drain on our natural resources. I think it's the height of patriotism to ride a bike, because the metal and fuel resources of America that we put into automobiles will run out much sooner than those of Russia, which has its own strategic metals, twice our petroleum reserves, and four times our natural-gas reserves. One of the main things by which future generations will measure patriotism will be use of bikes. I think the bicycle is the American equivalent of Gandhi's spinning wheel.

To the extent that we rely on unstable nations to supply our essential industrial metals and fuel, we will become a weak and dependent nation, desperate to control other nations. We can no longer be proud to be affluent, because we have an affluence which is wasteful. We cannot be patriotic and wasteful of resources at the same time. The American way of life has become anti-American. An essential part of keeping America strong is to rebuild our cities toward peace with nature and nations, to satisfy our physical and emotional needs within neighborhoods and recycle everything. This is the example we should set for the world. These are good uses for our machines. I think we stand before the most exciting future any people has ever faced.

After the conclusion of our discussion, Paul took me outside and led me on a mini-tour of his neighborhood. Besides explaining to me the formal history of Venice and showing me the remnants of its failed attempt to recreate the landscape of Venice, Italy, Paul also told me personal anecdotes about the people who lived in the houses we passed. By the time we had returned to his home, Paul had successfully brought to life for me a part of Los Angeles that I had driven by many times without noticing.

There were two "sights" in the tour that made a particular impression on me. In the midst of the world's most famous automobile-oriented city were several "walk streets," constructed during the 1920s so that the houses faced footpaths rather than roadways and parking places. The result was a considerably more relaxed and comfortable environment. Paul also pointed out to me a house on his block in which dwelled a couple who had converted their small suburban lawn into a rich, weedless vegetable garden by covering it with rugs to keep down the weeds, adding mulch on top, and planting.

    Both the walk streets and the weedless food lawn were clearly present-day examples of Paul's vision of the future, a vision for which I find myself rooting.

THE LINGUIST:

Claudine Schneider

By the time a generation has reached its late thirties, a few of its members have started to enter positions of power and influence. There are not enough of them yet to seriously affect the policy of the nation, but this vanguard can give a hint as to which directions the generation may be headed in.

Claudine Schneider was the busiest person I met. One would expect nothing less of someone in her profession. Her schedule was so tight that it took two sessions to find enough time for her to answer all my questions.

My hometown is a small town outside of Pittsburgh called Clairton, Pennsylvania. It's very much a blue-collar, middle-income, working-class community where there's a large population of Slovaks, which I am, and also Italians. The economy has been primarily dependent upon the cokeworks, U.S. Steel, and Bethlehem Steel. Unfortunately, the steel industry is for the most part closed down in Clairton, and now, as a result, the town is in sad disarray.

My father ran a men's clothing store. He owned it and ran it, as did my mother. They worked side by side, six days out of the week, and that was primarily their life. The main reason that they worked so hard was because neither of them had had the opportunity to get the education that they had hoped for. They both come from very large families and they decided to limit their family to two, my younger brother and myself.

My father's father came to America and set up his own tailor shop.

Then came the era of the dry-goods shops, so he did both tailoring and sold dry goods. Then the lot fell to my father to take over the business, and at that point he turned it into a very successful men's clothing store, and then, with the assistance of my mother, into a men's clothing store that also had a women's boutique. The whole family was involved in the clothing business. I have an aunt who had run a children's clothing store, and yet another aunt who owned a women's clothing store. My parents met in Belgium during the Second World War and my mother came to this country right after the war. My father passed away in 1982, and my mother is still living in Clairton.

I went to a Catholic grade school, one through eight, and at the time the nuns, and also my parents, taught me that you should not hurt others and that if and when you do damage somebody's property or you hurt someone by saying something mean, something will come back and hurt you, too. But if you're kind to other people, others will be kind to you. My parents got along very well with all kinds of people, and they detested class structure. Yet if it would have helped me to be better equipped to deal in the world to associate with a high-class group of students, that's what they wanted for me.

So they sent me to a private high school, Winchester-Thurston, in Pittsburgh. This was a very significant move for my parents, because they felt it would be helpful for me to attend a college-preparatory school in order to be well equipped for college. This was something that had been ingrained in me, that this was my goal, my parents' goal or my goal, whatever—to become well educated and take advantage of all lessons offered me. It was an all-girls school, and I started there in the ninth grade. It was a boarding school, so I stayed in a dormitory for three out of four years. It was a forty-five-minute drive from home, so I went home every weekend and had telephone communication with my family regularly. My father would pick me up every Friday afternoon. I always looked forward to him coming and just talking about what was going on while we drove home. I remember perfectly the day that President Kennedy was assassinated. I walked out of the school building and my father was sitting there in our car. He had the radio on. He was somber-faced and he had a little tear in his eye.

I hugged him and I said, "Daddy, who would have done this?" And he said, "I don't know. What a terrible thing." We both sat in the car for a while, just very sad and listening to the news. It was a very moving moment, but I was glad that I was there to share it with my father.

I guess whatever I do, I really go all out, and when I studied, I would really study hard. Part of it, initially, in high school, was because I was doing it for my parents. They so much wanted me to do well, and they had sacrificed so much, and obviously were trying to realize their dreams, through me, of being well educated and reaping the benefits of a good education. So I did study very conscientiously and was very serious about my studies. But then, on the other hand, when it came time to party, I would dance until three in the morning and have a terrific time. I say that now, but in high school I did not really do that much partying around. Of course, we girls had our little parties in the dormitory, but I only had two dates the entire time I was in high school. They were each for the proms, the junior prom and the senior prom, and it was with the same guy, who was the brother of my best friend.

I was about as boy-crazy as any other girl at that time. One of the courses that I thought was terrific was a speech class because the teacher was the only male teacher that we had in the school! Every girl was in love with him. I also enjoyed languages. I studied Latin and French and was the first to organize a French club in our class. I also speak Spanish, which I studied later in college, and after college I took an adult course in Chinese, and in my spare time, just for fun, I started learning Swahili. To me, languages are like puzzles that need to be unraveled, and once you unravel them, they are almost a road to happiness because they enable you to talk to people from different cultures. A true delight!

I remember high-school graduation—I remember the picture of all the girls coming out of this regal church where they held the ceremony. We were wearing our white long gowns and carrying flowers. Our eyes were so red and tears were coming down. None of us wanted to leave one another, and we really weren't ready to move on to college. We just wanted to stick together.

That summer I went to Europe with my parents, brother, and girlfriend. We had a grand time. It was fabulous. I had sent out a whole slew of college applications. I had applied to mostly coeducational schools because I worked hard, was conscientious, and, you know, I thought that it would be fun and exciting to go to a coed school. But in the end I chose Rosemont College, a Catholic women's college! My interview was the best, the warmest, the friendliest. And the campus was beautiful and it was also close to my family. Plus, close to *lots* of boys' schools, not just one! Villanova, St. Joseph's, and Haverford, and

Swarthmore and the University of Pennsylvania. I figured I could have my pick of the lot.

When I was in high school, I had one roommate whose father was a surgeon. On Saturday mornings I used to go with him to the operating room and watch the whole process, and I thought, I really like this; maybe I'd like to be a surgeon. However, my mother and father said, "Well, I don't know about that," and I said, "Well, either that or a dancer." And they said, "I don't know about that either!" So my mother said, "Why don't you become a French major, because then you can always be a French teacher, and you'll always have employment, and it's a good job for a *woman*"! So I thought, Oh, all right, Mom, I will.

I started off and we were only permitted four courses as freshmen. I had a French-grammar course and I had a French-literature course and then I had, because it was a Catholic school, two courses that were oriented toward religion. So I had "Early Church Teachings" and the other one was "Philosophy and Logic."

Then, after my sophomore year, I was pretty good in French, so I switched over to Spanish. I still had to take more of those religion courses. I was getting very frustrated because I really wanted to study psychology. I wanted to study anatomy. I wanted to study art history, a variety of things. And I felt so confined. At that point I was frustrated that I was not being exposed to the variety of things I'd always dreamed I would learn in college. I decided to transfer.

I chose to go to Windham College, which is in Putney, Vermont, primarily because of the foreign-exchange program that they had. I had the opportunity to study for six months at the University of Barcelona. This was 1968. I was still pretty apolitical and it was not until I got there that I became sensitized to the fact that it really was a repressive government. I found it brave for the students to be rioting like that.

I remember sitting in a coffeeshop, talking to a couple of Spanish students, and I was asking them questions about the government. They said, "We shouldn't be talking about this here. We could get in serious trouble." And I just thought, What a terrible way to have to live. You can't even sit down and talk about what's going on in your own country.

By the time I got to Windham College, I was feeling much more comfortable and self-assured that I knew how to study. I knew how to get the job done. At that time I ran for student government. In my senior year I was vice-president of the student government, and then something happened to the president of the student government, so I took over his position.

One of the more serious things that we did in student government was a community-outreach program. We identified children within the community with learning disabilities, and we identified students who wanted to do some tutoring, and we matched them. We also had a program around Thanksgiving and Christmas where we collected food from the community and we put it all in the Student Union. Then a group of us went out and distributed it to various needy households.

Graduation from college was a different feeling than graduation from high school. Everybody was just like a bursting balloon—couldn't wait to get out of there. All I wanted was my diploma, and I got it in the mail. The prevailing attitude was "Let me out of here. I'm ready for the real world now! Look out, here we come!"

Well, I was very excited to go to Washington, D.C., because it was one of the more cosmopolitan parts of the United States. I was anxious to use my skills, my languages, and also to learn about other cultures. I thought I'd like to get involved in international government or international business, but I thought preferably international government. The lure of working with an embassy was pretty exciting, to be stationed in one exotic spot or another for a while and then come back here and work.

So I came to Washington, circulated a number of résumés, primarily to government agencies and the State Department, and waited for a response. I figured, Well, I've got to bring home the bacon in the interim. I thought I should do something fun for a change, because I'm sure that once I start working, it's going to be grind, grind, all over again. As I said before, I really was pretty conscientious in school, so I was looking for some frivolity.

I thought, What would be the most different, fun thing I'd like to do? Since I'm interested in fashion, having grown up in a household of clothiers, I considered doing something with fashion. Well, I was reading a magazine one day and a woman was describing her career as a fashion photographer, and I thought, Wouldn't that be fascinating? It would be a wonderful interim source of income until I hear from my other jobs. Fashion photography was the first idea, but then I very quickly learned that Washington is not one of the great fashion capitals of the East. So I thought, Well, what *is* Washington noted for?

The way I found my employer was unique. I looked in the Yellow Pages for the largest ad for a photography studio. I thought, Those people ought to be able to afford me, if they have that enormous ad in the Yellow Pages. I walked in the door and there were two older gentlemen in their sixties. I said, "I've got a proposal for you. I think you ought to hire me to do your public-relations work." I said, "I'll tell you what I can do. I will go out to the different embassies and to the Congress, to the House and to the Senate, and I'll make appointments for these people to come in and have their portraits taken."

They thought out loud: "What's this cute young thing doing here?" They got such a charge out of seeing this young girl coming in off the street and making that proposal, they said, almost instantaneously, "You're hired; we'll take you!" I was stationed at the front desk, much like a receptionist, nothing more, *but* they gave me a fancy card with my name on it, plus a title: "executive public relations."

It was really a fun experience. I met King Faisal, Senator Tunney, Senator Mansfield, and a whole series of very exciting people. One woman that walked in the door to have her portrait taken unfortunately had a long wait. The photographer was behind schedule. However, it was very fortunate for me. She said that she was part of an environmental consumer group that was doing research into different pollutants and their connections with human health. There was something about the woman's manner, or sensitivity, that really attracted me to her. She said I could contact her group if I wanted to do volunteer work.

I thought, Well, I'm new in town. I've got time on my hands. I'll do volunteer work in my spare time. As it turned out, I started pulling together research data and consolidating information for public circulation. The group was called Concern, Inc. It's a national group that's still in existence. The founders of the group were quite intelligent, dedicated women who were married to intelligent, dedicated men. It was heartening to work with these women, who could have easily been sitting home having their fingernails filed. Instead, they were selflessly dedicated to taking care of the earth. They were seeking neither fame nor fortune. Instead they were giving of their time, energy, and intelligence to improve the quality of life for all people. I was most impressed.

After working at Concern for a while as a volunteer, I started thinking, This is truly very exciting. Perhaps what I ought to do is offer to work for them full-time and tell them that I'll not only raise my own salary but I'll be a fund raiser for the organization. It was, of course, incidental that I had never raised money before in my life. I made the proposal, and they agreed.

During that time period, my social life was such that I was dating lots of guys, a variety of fellows. My father had always ingrained in my mind "Make sure that you date many different men." I'm sure he was thinking, This poor kid hasn't had much exposure to men, so she'd better check out the field. So what happened was that while I was working for the photography studio, I got a call from a friend of a friend who invited me out on a date—a blind date! I thought, Sure, why not? He sounded nice on the telephone, and I'd heard he was a good guy.

We had dinner, and that blind date turned out to be my husband, Eric. I think the thing that was most appealing to me about him was that he was a diversified person. That meant that he was, and still is, a scientist, an oceanographer, and he had interests in everything from mountain-climbing to dancing to going to museums—to just about everything. I felt we were a good match. Prior to that, I would date one fellow who was a dance-a-holic, and that was great, but he didn't like to do much else. Another guy belonged to the American Film Institute. Every date we had, we would go to the movies. As a movie buff, he was a genius on actors and films, but after a while that can get mundane. Eric was not only knowledgeable about a variety of topics but he also enjoyed doing a number of different things. That was extremely appealing to me.

I can remember in college sitting around with roommates, talking about "The Man you'll someday marry," and I was really uptight about participating in those conversations because I didn't know. I think the one thing that I had made up in my own mind was that, more important than any other characteristic, my husband would be intelligent. I felt that if he were smart and on the ball—not just brilliant, Ph.D. brilliant, but a person who had street smarts too—then we could overcome any obstacles that might come along. That he would be smart enough to help us get out of one situation or another. And, sure enough, that's what I chose.

Eric had been working at the Environmental Protection Agency since 1970, when it was first founded. In 1973 he was offered a job either in San Francisco or in Rhode Island. So we went out to San Francisco to check out the job there and we went to Rhode Island. We concluded that Rhode Island was where we wanted to be. It was a beautiful environment, it was near the water, the people were very friendly. It was New England, you know, full of tradition and calm.

Eric had decided to go to Rhode Island to start his job. He felt badly because my job with Concern was so special to me. And being very sensitive, he was not anxious to pull me away from a group of people that I became very close with. Also I was just beginning to blossom in self-confidence and learning and being able to do different things.

At any rate, though, Concern said to me, "Maybe you should go up to Boston and see if we should set up a branch office." Boston being a whole lot closer than Washington to Rhode Island, the proposal had an immediate appeal. I set off for Boston and started doing some groundwork, checking out the kinds of environmental groups they had up there already. Eric and I were planning on getting married within several months.

While we were still in Washington, Eric had discovered a little bump on my neck. By the time I moved up to Boston, I had been to five different doctors. Everybody said, "Are you accustomed to sore throats?" And I said, "Yes, I had them all the time." And they said, "Not to worry; you've got swollen lymph glands." Then I discovered another node, and I called Eric and said, "Would you please find me a cancer doctor?" He was a little perturbed, and he kept saying, "Why do you want to keep seeing doctors?" But intuitively I felt something was wrong. I said, "I think we've been skirting around this thing, and I believe we ought to see a cancer doctor." This was right around my twenty-fifth birthday. Some present!

Eric found the best of all doctors for me in Rhode Island. I came down from Boston and met with him on Thursday and he said, "I'd like to operate on you tomorrow morning."

I said, "Well, if you think that that's what we should do, I trust your judgment." I was depending on my intuition. The other doctors who told me nothing was wrong, somehow, didn't have my confidence. This doctor, I felt, knew what he was talking about. The rest of this story is a foggy whirlwind.

I was operated on on Friday. I was an out-patient, so I went home for the weekend. It was a horrible weekend. I was supposed to return to the doctor on Tuesday for the results of the biopsy. Instead I called up on Monday and I said, "Doctor, I'm getting real impatient—I'm tough. I can take it." And I said, "Why don't you just tell me over the phone?"

And there was this long silence, and the phone began to slip from my hand. I felt I was about to faint. The room was spinning around.

He said, "You have Hodgkin's disease." And I said, "What does that mean?" I said, "Is that cancer?" And he said, "It's a form of cancer." So the rest of the conversation I hardly remember, except I remember he was very kind. He said, "You must come in and we'll talk about it, and we'll talk about what we'll do."

Well, at that point we were on the fast track. I went to see him Tuesday and pleaded, "Let's get going with whatever treatment you recommend." We immediately started radiation therapy.

That weekend and those next couple of days were the toughest ever. Eric and I spent so much time reminiscing about our past, when suddenly we got very shook up with the realization that we were subliminally suggesting that we would have no future. We should be focusing on the future! I'm going to survive! And Eric said, "If we have a fifty-fifty chance, you're going to be that one person that makes it over to fifty-one." I mean, we didn't conclude that right away—we were scared to death at first.

My parents were completely disheartened. The only people they ever knew who had cancer died. They said, "Come home to Pittsburgh; we'll take care of you." They did not like the idea of my staying in Rhode Island with a man I hadn't married yet—if you can believe that, given the crisis situation. That was very upsetting to them. But I decided to stay with Eric because I saw our future together and I was much more self-confident that we could beat this thing *together*.

One of the best signals I got from my father and mother was when they came to visit us for the first time after I had told them I had cancer. My father gave me a tennis dress. That really said it: You're going to be up and around and you're going to be playing tennis. That was great!

One of the things I always loved to do was to travel. So when Eric had a business trip to Portugal and Greece, I said, "I've never been to Greece. That's great." My radiation treatment continued until the summer. He had to travel in the summer, so he said, "Let's go." I told my parents, "I don't know how long I'm going to be around, but the one thing I'd like to be able to have done, if I do die, is to at least see some more of this wonderful world." So they said, "Go with our blessing." We did—knowing in advance that I had to come back in September to have my spleen removed. That was to thoroughly check to make sure that the cancer had not spread.

The radiation therapy was *awful.* I was radiated from the top of my ears down. Part of my brain was temporarily put on hold. I was like a vegetable! I was horrified. They told me I'd lose my hair, and I did lose that, but they didn't warn me that I would lose my memory, too, and that was the most frightening. But I figured, Well, other people will help me remember, and it hopefully will come back. But I was scared to death. Somebody would call me in the morning, and in the evening I couldn't tell you who had called me or what the conversation had been about. That's how zapped I was. I just wondered, Am I dying? Am I going now? Have they maybe radiated too much? Or has the cancer gone too far, or what? So I was frightened. But then I felt, Fear is the wrong emotion. I've got to think positively. I've got to get fear out of me. Fear is a negative; hope is a positive. I was sort of visualizing myself with positive energy. I was trying to make myself strong and optimistic.

Traveling with Eric in Europe was glorious. Words cannot describe how happy I was. There was some sort of uneasiness in my stomach—you know, nervous tension. Combined with that, there was a hope and trust that everything would be all right. I tried to brainwash myself by saying, You're going to make it. You're too young to die. You've got too many things you've got to do on this earth. I kept thinking, I'm not going to die, go to heaven, and meet God, who will say, "What've you done?" and I'll say, "Gee, God, not a whole lot." And I thought, I've got to stick around here a bit longer. So even though I had fears about the operation in September, I somehow felt that it was going to be okay. I would say I was 90 percent optimistic during that time period, despite my lethargy, and hair and memory loss.

I came back and had the surgery. They told me that I'd probably be in the hospital for two weeks or more. Around the eighth day I was starting to get restless—I'm ready to go; let's get on with this. I became very impatient. So I was only there about ten days.

Shortly thereafter, October 6th, Eric and I got married in Rhode Island under an apple tree in the yard of the house that we were renting. It was a very small ceremony because it was a very difficult time. Eric's parents couldn't quite understand why he wanted to marry somebody with cancer. My parents didn't know what end was up or down. All Eric and I knew was that we just wanted to be alone.

Later that month Eric had the opportunity to go to the Soviet Union. Richard Nixon appointed him chairman of a delegation on ocean pollution. The idea of the Soviet Union as our honeymoon site was not terribly appealing. I suggested we go somewhere a bit more romantic—like Morocco, the Marrakesh Express. So from the USSR we took a side trip to the land of intrigue and fantasy.

It took about a year to get myself physically back in shape, to get my energy level up, to retrieve my memory, to be a person again, so that I could take care of my husband and be an equal partner and wife. It was a real challenge.

I think that the technical elements of my treatment, the radiation, the surgery, were necessary. I would never have made it without them. But how large of a role they played in my recovery is questionable, especially when you compare it with the confidence that I had in God, that He wanted me around a bit longer, the confidence I had in the doctor, that he was going to make me better, the confidence that I had in Eric, that he would hold my hand through this whole process and stick with me, and the confidence that I had in myself, which was directed very graphically toward removing those diseased cells from my body.

I read in an encyclopedia where the lymph system was. I was shown the X-rays, and shown exactly where the cancer cells were. I don't know how I came up with the idea, but I just decided that I would mentally focus on where they are and I would put all of my energy into dissolving and eliminating them.

I thought about the possible causes of the cancer and I do see a connection between the Hodgkin's disease and growing up in Clairton, even though I didn't have any tangible evidence. It's more intuitive. I remember as a child that one of my daily chores was to dust the house. I thought that *every* little child across the country dusted the house every day. I also recall that oftentimes the water would taste funny, and in the evenings there was always a foul smell in the air, and that's when the furnaces would open up and release their pollutants. But I didn't know that at the time.

When the cancer was first discovered, my mother prayed, and said, "Oh, God, if you save my daughter, I'll spend the next ten years working in a hospital and doing volunteer work." She's been doing that for the last twelve years. I wasn't as specific as she was, but I did say, "I really don't want to die, and if I am fortunate enough to live, let me know, and help me understand why I'm living and how I can best spend this life." I prayed and meditated: "Please show me. Help me figure out what it is you want me to do." I didn't really know where I was supposed to go, or what I was to do on this earth. But I figured, Stay tuned in and He'll let me know sooner or later.

Eric was married before. He had two sons, and one of his sons came to live with us after we got married. I thought, Well, maybe my job is to help his son straighten out. Perhaps I should focus my energies on him. I immediately became an instant wife and instant mother. At least I was keeping myself occupied.

One of the early things in my marriage was that the state and utility company wanted to build a nuclear power plant not far from where we lived, and I thought, My God, that's interesting. Even though I worked for an environmental group, we hadn't really gotten into nuclear power. What was more upsetting was the fact that the government had proposed building the facility, and they hadn't asked any of the citizens. And I thought, How dare the government be so insensitive to the people that are living there? This is supposed to be a democracy, a government of the people—and they had not let the town council know. It was the federal government attempting to bypass procedures—sell beachfront property to a utility company for half the price.

Well, when I found out, I got real mad, and look out when I get mad. So Eric said, "Well, you guys ought to organize. They're breaking federal law." So, with his support, I got together with some other citizens and we formed a little citizens' group. We did some investigations through the Freedom of Information Act. I drove up to Boston with another woman, and she and I went through all the files and we found out that they were intentionally avoiding the law. Then I went to one of Ralph Nader's Critical Mass conferences looking for a lawyer who knew something about nuclear power and the federal laws. And I happened upon a lawyer, so, sure enough, we got him, and killed that nuclear power plant. It took years of work, was practically a full-time occupation for me. It seemed like forever, especially since they were pulling every fast move you could possibly think of. It was a matter of one-upmanship—for every dirty move they would make, we'd try to keep a step ahead of them. They finally gave up after about four years. I thought, Well, maybe Eric and I are supposed to be team members and protect the environment and people's health.

Eric and I had consistently been turned off by the politics in Rhode Island, while at the same time we were becoming increasingly in love with the people and with the environment. We felt that we ought to contribute to help it realize its potential.

I had been registered as a Democrat because my parents had been

Democrats, and I hadn't really thought about political philosophy much beyond that. The Democratic Party in Rhode Island was the party of the good old boys in the back room who had neglected women, who had neglected blacks, who had neglected public participation and ran a very closed-door government. And that represented everything contrary to what I believed in. So I thought, Well, if these guys are Democrats, I want to be the exact opposite. Besides, those few people in the state that were Republicans were people that I admired and respected. So it was easy for me to change and register as a Republican.

In 1978 the Republican candidate for governor was suddenly exposed in a terrible scandal. That left the Republican Party in a very embarrassing situation, and also high and dry without a candidate with very short notice. I think it was May or June. So Senator Chafee approached my husband and the request was made of him to run for governor. Unfortunately, there was not enough of a Republican organization to finance a successful campaign. He thought about it and recognized that the fellow he would be taking on had so much money and was practically an institution in the state, the chances of Eric winning were limited, and if he lost, it would mean that the only real source of income for our family would be gone. So he decided that he would continue being the director of the Environmental Protection Agency and doing his environmental research.

Then he turned and looked at me, and said, "I think *you* ought to run." I was still very much cloaked, I guess, in the traditional mindset of women which said, "I'll be the support system for the man." But because he had the confidence in me, and the liberated spirit to encourage me to run, I thought, Sure, why not. So I declared for governor, and a few days thereafter the party leaders said to me, "We found somebody else we like better. But how would you like to run for Congress?"

It was not as if I were their dream candidate, or that I would be their ideal of a congressman. The Republican Party was desperate. They were merely filling a slot with me—that was all.

I said, "Congress? Well, now, that is something more up my alley because I have more of a national and global perspective, and I have worked in Washington as a lobbyist on environmental issues, and am knowledgeable about how the system works." I thought that could be very exciting, but once again, more realistically, the situation was such that because the registration was fifteen to one, Democrat to Republican, the likelihood of my succeeding was very slim.

At best, I had my own personal agenda, which was even if I did not win, I would accomplish two goals. One goal was to stir up some of the apathy that existed among people of our generation. My husband and I were overwhelmed by the fact that many of our friends, who were very well educated and caring people, did not vote anymore in Rhode Island because their attitude was "All those politicians are all alike; they're all self-interested." Well, Eric and I had always felt that unless you're part of the solution, you're part of the problem. So what I wanted to do was to stir up those who had given up on good government.

My second goal was to articulate some of the issues. In Rhode Island, as in many states, historically, political campaigns are based on personal mud-slinging. What I wanted to do was to have a campaign that would focus on the issues. Talk about the pollution, talk about the excess of government spending that was digging our country deeper into debt, and just speak common sense. And try to hype people's awareness as to the importance of involvement in making things right.

So all along, as I ran, I kept thinking, I will do the best job I possibly can, to the end of the campaign, despite the fact that all the people I'd meet in the streets were saying, "You gotta be kidding, Claudine! Your opponent has an 80 percent approval rating; you've got no name recognition; you've got no money; you've got nothing—so good luck, sister." Well, I went off and did it anyway.

My opponent, Edward Beard, was, or is, very much, let me politely say, an unenlightened individual who is more talk than action. Once, our paths crossed on the campaign trail, and he turned to me and said, "Why are you working so hard, Claudine? Pretty soon you'll be back in the kitchen scrubbing floors and washing dishes anyway." I think that pretty much exemplifies his attitude toward women!

I think that what I was doing in this campaign was showing other people who felt the same way that you can't judge a book by its cover. That if you give me a chance, I will show you that I will represent you better than anybody you've ever been represented by before. So it's a matter of breaking down those barriers and walls of prejudice, whether they be against Republicans or against women in politics, or whether it's being against environmentalists, who, in many Rhode Islanders' minds, embodied anti-growth, which meant no jobs—and jobs have always been the theme of political campaigns. So I was mostly trying to connect with my potential constituents on a level where they viewed me as a person they could trust, as a person that would use my best judgment not based on who twisted my arm last but rather on what I thought was best for them and for the country.

In the end, at the end of the 1978 campaign, I was able to look over my shoulder and say that I believed that I did everything that I could possibly do. I went to every factory; I spoke on every issue; I did everything that I felt was appropriate. So I have no regrets, even though I lost. And to me that's real important—to live a life with as few regrets as possible.

Well, the election night really gave me a very clear message, because when I went out to give my concession speech, the place was going berserk. People were screaming, shouting, carrying on, cheering. It was as though I had won. To have got almost 48 percent of the vote and to have spent only fifty thousand dollars was nothing short of a miracle. That woke up a lot of people. And everyone started saying, "Don't worry about it next time, kid. You'll make it next time." That impressed me. Eric and I discussed this and we concluded, yes, we ought to give it one more shot. Because talk is cheap, and in the '78 campaign I was able to talk about the things I would like to do, but what really counts are the actions. And if I were put in that situation of power and responsibility, then I would have the opportunity to bring about the change.

So I laid down my game plan. I got a list of every Rotary Club in the state. I got a list of every church group in the state. All the different entities of people that would pool together on an evening or luncheon meeting or whatever. I got those lists and I started calling them. I felt the more people I would be able to touch, the more receptive they might be to me politically. I also decided, What better way to accomplish this goal of getting elected than to use the media? So I approached the three TV stations in Rhode Island and said, "Would you like me to do a public-affairs program on issues of interest to Rhode Island?" I thought a TV show should enable me to show a little bit of my knowledge and let me at least be in a position where I could ask a guest on the program the right questions. Because sometimes questions are as important as the answers.

Just about that time, the NBC affiliate was calling me, so we immediately connected and I had my own public-affairs program, which was on once a week at eleven o'clock for half an hour, right before *Meet the Press*. I was paid fifty dollars a week. I did this for about six to eight months. It was a very exciting project, very challenging. And it increased my visibility.

By the time of the 1980 election I think Mr. Beard was still very confident, but I think he was also frightened. He had seen the writing on the wall. We had one televised debate and that was very important because many people said that that really turned them around. There was no Senate or governor's race that year, so ours was *the* race of the year. There was enormous media hype.

They were even calling the whole debate as to whether or not my opponent would debate me "The Claudine and Eddie Show." Because Eddie would say, "No, I'm not going to debate." And then Claudine would say, "Well, it's in the historic tradition to have debates. Remember, Lincoln versus Douglas." And then my opponent would say blah, blah, blah, and it was going back and forth.

We finally had our debate. There was a great deal of attention paid to it. Many people told me that that debate showed them that I had what it takes to discuss the issues. And I think that's what everybody was looking for. So I won the election. In the 1980 race I believe more people voted *against* Eddie Beard than voted *for* Claudine Schneider. But I think in '82 and '84, more people were voting *for* Claudine Schneider.

Prior to my election, I had never been inside the House of Representatives. So when I first got there, it was very exciting. It was like starting a new school. Meeting all the new friends, saying hello, being very outgoing, and making new contacts. In fact, I did go to classes, in a way. It was really fun. I started off by going to a session at the Kennedy School of Government, where they had brought in freshmen, Democrats and Republicans, who had chosen to go there for an indoctrination into what is the budget process—how does the budget work in Congress? We had briefings on such issues as tax policy, foreign policy, and domestic issues. We learned basically how the system works.

We were also briefed on the administrative workings of Congress by the Republican Congressional Committee. They had set up courses for Republican freshmen, and advised us on a variety of things, such as "Don't bring all of your staff from your district; hire some people with Washington experience." They explained that members of Congress are either legislators or constituent servants. Of course, that didn't sit well with me, because I wanted to be both. But the National Congressional Committee *was* very helpful with the mechanics of hiring staff, of getting resources, even on where to find a place to live.

We were allowed a total of eighteen employees. If we chose to pay some people more, we could hire only fifteen people. That's for both my Washington and my Rhode Island office.

Right at the beginning of my first term, I was granted a meeting with President Reagan and George Bush. It was over the budget, specifically to discuss where the cuts were coming from. I was not intimidated. I was prepared to present my case, and I just went in as though I were going to talk to almost anybody. They are both very congenial personalities, and so they put me at ease immediately. They were not difficult to talk to. I was not overwhelmed by their positions, and I felt their equal—which is a heady thing to say, but it strictly points out that I didn't stand in awe. I looked upon them as team members, as people that I need to be working with to do what we had to do. So we had a nice conversation. I tried to share with them the need that I saw to shift some of the cuts in different areas, that the proposals for cuts in human services were unbalanced in comparison to the defense budget.

Unfortunately, I felt that their minds were already made up, and it was more of a courtesy visit. They did not heed my words, but I guess time is the best teacher, and maybe this year they will have seen that it *is* more appropriate to make that kind of balance. I respect their position of authority and I respect their ideas, but I don't necessarily go along with them. And it's important that they hear that.

In the end, I concluded that I was not able to vote for the president's budget. The president was elected with a mandate, and many of my colleagues felt that they were elected on his coattails. I knew that in my case only 37 percent of the people in Rhode Island voted for Ronald Reagan. They wanted Jimmy Carter to win. So I didn't have any mandate. And I knew from my own conscience that I couldn't support the budget. So I told the leadership, because I felt it would be appropriate for me to let them know, that I was not going to be with them. And this was pretty gutsy.

Then, when we were on the floor for the vote, the president called me on the telephone in the cloakroom. I went in and talked to him. I told him, "I'm sorry, but I really cannot do it." I hadn't told the press; I hadn't told anybody else what I was going to do because I had a feeling I was going to be the only Republican not to vote for the president's budget.

I voted against the budget and found out that another fellow, Charlie Dougherty, from Philadelphia, had done the same. So there were two of us. So then I'm there sitting on the floor of the House, and after all the cheering and commotion and everything, a member of the leadership comes up to me and says, "Well, Claudine, you've got to offer the motion to recommit."

I said, "Well, wait a minute. What *is* the motion to recommit?" And they said, "It's the motion that you have to offer because there were only two of you that voted against the president's budget, and it must be offered by someone who voted no on the previous question."

I said, "Well, why don't you have the other guy do it, because he's been around longer? He's more senior and he knows what he's doing." And they said, "Well, he skipped out." He knew something I didn't, obviously! So then I stood up and in rather halting and embarrassing terms attempted to offer the motion to recommit, which I understood that according to the laws I had to do. Later, after I learned parliamentary procedure, I found out that it was not mandatory that I do that. If I didn't do it, some Democrat could have done it. But at the time I was not aware of that.

You know, there's nothing wrong with learning on your feet, but there were some things I didn't learn in time, and that was one of them. So that was very embarrassing to me, to say the least. I felt like I had no choice and I could not say no. Now I know that I can say no at any time.

Only once, fortunately, have I voted against my conscience. And I do not intend to have it ever happen to me again, if I can help it. It was a situation where I could see the arguments on both sides of the issue, and made a decision that better reflected what my constituents wanted, but what I knew, gut-wise, should have been the other way. I did not have the benefit of time to educate my constituents as to why it should be otherwise. The way I deal with controversial issues now is that I attempt to inform my constituents through newsletters and through town meetings and forums. It's important to me not only for people to know *how* I voted but also *why* I voted that way. I am confident that if they had the benefit of all the information I have, they would agree with me.

Prior to politics I'd always believed that women should be treated fairly and equally. I'd always felt that women in the U.S. had few, if any, barriers legally against them. I knew that in my own case, if I wanted to go to a certain school or if I wanted a certain job or whatever, I had a pretty smooth route in achieving those things. I never felt discrimination personally. My mother and aunts were all businesswomen. None of them, to my knowledge, had ever felt discrimination. So I thought things were fair and equal.

But after getting elected, I had a woman who was seventy-three years old come to me. She started crying and said, "Claudine, I've never come to visit my congress*man* before, but since you are a woman, I thought you would understand." And then I practically started crying, because she was crying, and I asked, "What's the problem?"

She said, "My husband and I planned that if he would pass away before I did, I would be able to live on his pension. Well, he passed away, and now I find out that I am penniless. I do not have one dime that I am going to get out of his pension because he died prior to blah, blah, blah, blah, blah."

Short of asking the lady to come and live with me in my home in Rhode Island, I didn't know what to say. So I went to Washington that week and checked it out. Sure enough, there was some legislation that had already been introduced, but didn't go anywhere. It didn't move. It was Geraldine Ferraro's bill. She'd introduced it two years prior to my getting here. So I cosponsored it and that was the top, number-one issue when we Republican women went to the White House. Pension reform was the first thing we discussed. And we got it through.

Another young woman came to me in a similar situation, saying, "Isn't there anything that can be done about day care? My husband works two jobs, I work one, and we've got two kids." And she showed me all her bills and receipts, and I could see it. I could touch it. I could feel her pain, and it made it easier for me to get excited about solving the problem. So I came back here and moved on day care. We recommended expanding tax credits for day care. That was accepted by the president, but it was not enacted into law because of the Democratic leadership in the House. And unfortunately, the administration didn't push hard enough, so it didn't happen.

There *is* discrimination in the laws as they are written now. The more I know, the more I am inclined to get angry, but then I think, Don't get angry, Claudine. Keep in mind that many of these laws were written twenty or thirty years ago, when society was different. And right now we are going through this transitional phase of transcending some of those inequalities that were accepted by society in the past.

I think it's important for there to be more of a balance within the Republican Party and also to let the country know that this is not the Conservative Party. It's the Republican Party. Over the last four years, granted, it would be easy to generalize and say that my voting record looks more like that of a Democrat than of a Republican, but if you look at it in a more comprehensive view, you would see that my voting record would probably be similar to Abraham Lincoln's voting record, or maybe Theodore Roosevelt's voting record. I think that I'm reflecting historic Republicanism as opposed to 1986 Republicanism. I think what you're reading and seeing in the national press and with Ronald Reagan is the Conservative Party, not the Republican Party.

I am very solidly convinced, having met people from all different backgrounds and all geographic areas, that the majority of the American people are moderate Republicans. I think that most people believe in fiscal constraint. They don't believe in a lot of taxes. But they do believe in adequate funding for environmental protection. They do believe in adequate funding for those people who are genuinely in need. And we recognize that there are some people who just cannot help themselves no matter what kind of system you may structure—some folks just need a little extra help.

So I think that that's really a definition of the moderate Republican: one who is a combination of being fiscally responsible and humanly responsible.

I am not setting myself up as a symbol, but because I am a congresswoman, and because we are rare, I am in a position of being a role model to young girls and other women. Just as I am a woman who has fought off cancer, I am a role model that many people who have cancer can look at and decide that they too can fight and win this battle. What I seek to do is empower people by looking at their potential and actualizing it—I guess through my own dedication to solving problems and my urging others not to leave our problems to the government or others. We're responsible for solving them ourselves. I tell people, "I'm a member of the government and I need your help. We need to work together." We can only bring about fairness in tax or budget or foreign policy if we work together. We can only bring about peace on earth if we can agree that it *is* our higher goal. It's in our mutual best interest to work collectively to improve the quality of life for all people. We each must do our share.

THE MAVERICK:
David Hinkley

I am not a joiner. I have not been an active *member of a single organization, of any kind, since I was part of a neighborhood food-buying co-op in 1973. However, there are numerous organizations whose efforts I heartily support. One such organization is Amnesty International, the human-rights group that was awarded the Nobel Peace Prize in 1977.*

I find it distressing that so few Americans have ever heard of Amnesty International. They are more likely to know the film that won the Academy Award for 1977 (Annie Hall), or the song that was number one for the year ("You Light Up My Life"), or who won the World Series (the New York Yankees) than they are to know who won the Nobel Peace Prize.

I met David Hinkley at the Amnesty International office in Los Angeles. Before we began discussing his life, I told him of an Amnesty International–related experience I had had in China in 1979. The night before the fortieth anniversary of the liberation—the only day of the year when almost everyone takes off from work—I happened to be in Guilin, a city where students often approach Americans and others to practice their English. After dinner I plunged into the streets, which were packed with promenading Chinese.

Almost immediately, I was hailed by a French member of our tour group. "I think you'd better handle this one, David," he said, directing my attention to a wise-looking fellow of about my age. "He wants to know how to join Amnesty International."

I explained to the man that Amnesty International wasn't the sort of organization that he could join, but that it did do good work around the world. I asked him how he had learned of Amnesty and he replied, "Newsweek."

I then said to him, "What a coincidence that you should mention Amnesty International. Just recently they released two reports, one about the United States and one about China. The first one was critical of police brutality in my country and the second one dealt with the suppression of political dissent in your country."

By this time a large crowd had gathered around us, as so often happens when a foreigner stands still in China. The young man placed a smile across his face and said, "One never knows who is listening. Perhaps we should speak of other things." We discussed the firecrackers being exploded nearby and then parted.

A couple days later, I chanced to look out the window of the bus that was taking us to the train depot, just in time to see the same young man riding by on a bicycle. As our eyes met, he gave me a knowing look, smiled broadly, and gave a short wave good-bye.

I was born in Cherokee, Iowa, on November 29, 1946. Both my parents were natives of Iowa. I'm one of three—the other two are girls. I'm the middle. I had a very happy boyhood in Iowa—summer on the farm, a little town. My mother was a schoolteacher before she got married. My father, when I was born, worked in a clothing-store chain which his father was a partner in. Later he opened his own store in Palo Alto, California, and that's why we moved to California in 1953.

When I was a younger child, I was completely ignorant as to what was going on with my parents. I had an idyllic view of their relationship, of them as individuals. My memory is of a tremendously happy early childhood. I thought very well of myself, and thought all people in my family were wonderful and life was full of possibilities. When we moved to California, it was like, God, there's a world out there.

The revelations about my father came in waves, the first revelation being that he was an alcoholic. At the age of eleven, I was exposed to him in a stupor. At the time, I worshiped and admired him and loved him. I had never seen him drunk before. At least, if I had, I didn't know it. But each of us, my two sisters and I, were trotted out to the car to see this. It was a walk that I will never forget. It was like a major trauma. I suppose the kind of thing that one never really gets over. You deal with it, and eventually don't think about it any longer, but the effect is clear. That was a turning point in my life, to be sure. Thereafter, I took a totally different view of my place in the family, of my life, my concept of truth—everything changed.

I personally don't have a strong judgment to make about alcoholism. I view it as a pity to see, but I don't really hold it against a person. It's like something that once it's on you, it's very hard to shake, and many of the reasons that lead you to it in the first place inhibit you from being able to recover from it.

My father's business was doing quite well until he gambled and spent the money and caused its collapse. We went bankrupt, and our home, where we had lived for ten years, was auctioned. My mother had gone back to teaching to supplement the family income. They were divorced in 1964.

Going to Catholic grammar school from second grade until eighth grade, and with my mother's leadership being the strong element in the family, I had been thinking that I would become a priest. This was my thought up until eighth grade. But with the onset of puberty, I found some flaws in this plan. I had really only taken an interest in two high schools: the seminary and a Catholic school run by the Benedictine order. I ended up sort of compromising with myself and going to a Catholic school, but a Jesuit school, which was seen as the more scholastic approach to education, as opposed to the religious, doctrinal approach which the Benedictines were famous for. In retrospect, it doesn't seem to have been a compromise at all because there were no girls. I might as well have been in the seminary, in some respects, socially at least.

So I went to high school at Bellarmine College Preparatory School in San Jose, California, the oldest private school in the Western United States. It was named after Saint Robert Bellarmine, who was the persecutor of Galileo. Bellarmine was all boys, four years, no electives. I had four years of math, four years of science, four years of history, four years of Latin, and two years of Greek. It was a very competitive meritocracy. You did have one choice, and that was which language to take as a sophomore. You were only given this choice if your grade-point average was at a certain level. The preferred choice was Greek. If you got into the Greek class, you were considered to be amongst the intellectual elite in the school. Below that was French, and Spanish was tertiary. It really was the kind of place that encouraged intellectual snobbism and competitive behavior and style.

I was the best in Greek. I was gifted in Greek and Latin. It was esoteric enough to keep my interest, and I found it very charming. My overall image was a maverick, an oddball, a pain in the ass, a nonconformist. I didn't misbehave, but I would challenge a teacher. If I didn't like a teacher, or didn't respect a teacher, I would go after him. I had a lot of ego, big head, really sure that I was pretty hot shit. My mother always encouraged that self-image, and I took her word over anybody else's. The football players and other jocks would moan whenever I asked a question because it would be an intellectually pompous question, usually designed to reveal how much I knew.

I had a two-year war with one English professor that made my reputation as a crazy. This guy really was a weirdo, and he persecuted people. Once I established his image in my mind, I just went to war with him, and fought him constantly. I questioned everything he did. I mocked his analysis of different books. I was really more obnoxious with him than all the others combined, and really polarized the class. Some people who also hated him loved to see that somebody would get up there and confront him and say the things they would never even bother to say. Other people thought, Oh, Christ, do we have to listen to this again? Can't we just read the book and write the report? They thought there was far too much emotion.

I also had a tendency to get in a lot of fights. There were so many of us, all boys, and a lot of competition, and it resulted in fights. Just fistfights, but I found myself in more than my share of them. So I had a reputation for being a little tough. I think a lot of the anger that I was suppressing at home was coming out. I didn't start fights, but I was really violent if anybody started anything. Not particularly effective, just violent. So I had a reputation of being a little unpredictable.

There was one day in high school that I remember vividly. That was the day that some American advisers were killed in a tent in Vietnam. There was a bombing or something and it was announced at the school. We'd already been through being told by the Selective Service System that we had to register within five days of our eighteenth birthday, so I had already done that. But this was different. This was like an air raid. Suddenly the boys who were eighteen in the school, of which there were only a couple of dozen, were singled out.

We were sent down to the basement of the physics lab and we were told, "You'd better get ready, because you're going to Vietnam. This is going to be war. They asked for it, and your country needs you, and you'd better prepare yourself because you're going to be in the first wave that goes over." There was discussion about 2-S deferments and how to postpone your entry into the military until you could enter at officer's rank, that we should see ourselves as leaders, and move in at that level.

Well, I mean, there was no sense of paranoia or whimsicality about this at all. This brought up pictures of Tyrone Power and people going off to World War II. Talking about all our older brothers and uncles that went to Korea, and fathers who went to the Philippines in World War II, and now it's my turn. That's what I thought. I thought, Well, here we go again, another war in Asia. Who knows what it's all about, but we're in it now, and they can't kill our soldiers. That was the scariest day. That day was even more vivid to me than the day that Kennedy was shot. And I came out of that older than when I went in. I came out of that thinking I was a man, whereas before I was still thinking of myself as a boy. I thought, If I'm going to go over and get killed or kill somebody, I'm a man, and I want to be treated like one at this school from here on in. It really did affect my attitude. Not consistently, but from then on, every once in a while I would remember that day and I would think, Wait a minute, in a few months I may be going off in a troop carrier. I don't have to listen to this crap.

The summer after graduation I worked at a Girl Scout camp in the Santa Cruz Mountains as a maintenance man. I had worked with a partner of mine, Michael, my best friend, from about the age of fifteen or sixteen. We put out handbills in the neighborhood and hired out to wash cars, wash windows, mow lawns, dirty jobs, ovens, floors, anything. We basically both needed money and were too young to get work permits, so we went out and hired ourselves out.

We developed a nice little income from this partnership and it led to other jobs, including this one. So we went to this camp as maintenance men and that is where I met the woman I married. Her name's Tina. She was a counselor. It was a very romantic setting. There were five males there and about thirty females and two hundred little girls. So the males really had it sweet. You were there seven days a week, so you really got to know each other fast. And it was very romantic—the beautiful redwood trees, mountain streams, moonlight, no supervision. We got really close fast. Tina was twenty and I was almost nineteen. She was in college, going to San Jose State.

I had a state scholarship because of high marks on the college exams, SAT's, so basically any university I could get into I could get a scholarship for. I was interested in Berkeley, Stanford, and Santa Clara University. Stanford, at that time, had a policy of requiring freshmen to live on campus, which was beyond my means since it wouldn't have been covered by the scholarship. So that ruled out Stanford. Berkeley, I don't know. I suppose it was some of that same snobbism that came over from the Bellarmine days. Santa Clara was a private school, Jesuit. I felt comfortable there; I felt secure, no risks. They offered me an additional scholarship with the state scholarship, which I thought was attractive. They wanted me. So I said, Sure. It was basically the same area, just a continuation.

I had no idea when I went to Santa Clara that it was mandatory for freshman males to enroll in Reserve Officers' Training Corps. I had no idea of it. It was not in the literature. But it was the case. Actually, it's funny how I ended up in ROTC. If I had accepted the possibility of going into the honors program, that got you out of ROTC. But I looked at the honors program and saw they were a bunch of snobs, although a different kind of snobbism from my own. I didn't want anything to do with them. I was basically not the type who wanted to hang around these people and discuss Carlton Kuhn. I wanted to have a more normal life than I'd had in the last four years. So out of that, I ended up in ROTC.

So there I was on the drill field and my first reaction to it was this vast comic amusement. I thought it was the silliest, most absurd stuff. I mean, ROTC gives you this ancient equipment. They give you these shoes that were World War II issue—round, shiny clown shoes, and brass buckles that you have to shine just so with Brasso, and pins that are made differently from any normal accoutrements of clothing. It's almost like Cub Scouts. All these initiation things, and I thought it was comical. It was so ritualistic, and so fundamentally absurd, that I couldn't take it seriously. I couldn't.

I basically thought, Well, the war will end before I get into the regular army, and I'll just have to put in my time and that's it. I really thought the war would end. But it escalated through '65 to '66 pretty rapidly. You could see where it was going. You didn't have to be astute. And then my view changed. You are only obligated to stay in for, I think, one year, and then you had the option of dropping out. But my attitude was, Why go into the enlisted grade if I'm going to be drafted? I might as well be an officer. I don't want some jerk telling *me* to go someplace. I'd rather be the jerk telling other people.

So the second year was the first time that I made a deliberate commitment. I stayed with it. At that point I was still saying, "Hey, this is my country, and I still get tears in my eyes when I hear 'America the

Beautiful'—and I'm going over there." It wasn't quite "My country right or wrong," but it was pretty close to it. And I was from the heartland. I really came from the heartland and I felt that. I was a strong, red-blooded American guy. So I thought, I'll get in there and I'll have an effect on it.

My politics were still unformed at that time. I really got my political education from Tina. The first discussions we had, to be sure, were not political discussions. But it came out as I got to know her. She was also a bohemian, so she would go to coffeehouses and hang out listening to Lightning Hopkins and whatever the latest poet was. I loved her bohemianism. I found that fascinating, but slightly threatening. She exposed me to Allen Ginsberg at a time when I was reading only Keats and Shelley and Coleridge. The argument in my high school and college was, Had literature died in the seventeenth century or the nineteenth century? That was the argument. It was, Was nothing decent written after Milton, or was nothing decent written after Tennyson? And the liberal position was the latter, which I took. I had no idea that there was any such person as Gregory Corso or William Carlos Williams. And all of a sudden I realized, My God, it is still alive!

I loved the stuff even though I also maintained a posture of criticism. I was using classical criticism to attack this stuff, which didn't work at all. And I knew it and she knew it, but it made for some interesting conversation. She would just say, "What you have to do is listen to the record. Listen to him read it. Listen to it all." So then I'd have to slog through it. It's enchanting. It's a different approach. And it made me think and it made me feel. So she had this many-leveled attack on my sterile analysis, or lack of. And it worked. Gradually one would work.

I would see a great deal of Tina, especially on the weekends. We would take trips to the wine country, Valley of the Moon, and out to Yosemite. We had a great courtship, wonderful romance. But meanwhile, every once in a while, something would come up. She would have gone to a demonstration or a sit-in or something, and she would tell me about it, and I would tense up. I was for the war and she was against the war. I didn't like her politics at all.

She didn't try to persuade me much, but she made it clear that she wasn't at all sympathetic to *my* arguments. Because I would try to persuade her. I mean, "How can you see yourself aligned with these guys that hate this country, these Communists? They're doctrinaire; they're Marxist-Leninist." I just trotted it out. I made it up as I went along. I didn't start out to be pro-capitalist, and I had no concept of the unity between the economic structure of this country and the politics of it. I really thought that the politics flowed out of the Constitution and the Declaration of Independence and all this. It's amazing when I think back on it.

I would try to sell that to her, and she would say, "Look, you're wrong. What we're talking about here is people being killed by U.S. soldiers in a foreign land where we have no business. It's a civil war," etc., etc. Then she would feed me stuff. She would feed me an article that she knew had enough intellectual content that I couldn't dismiss it—because she herself wasn't particularly adept at presenting intellectual arguments. She was more appealing to the gut, to the heart, and saying, "It isn't like you to be defending atrocities." Trying to make me realize that this was an intellectually indefensible posture that I was taking, and I didn't have to take it. Having taken it, I didn't have to stay with it.

She was subversive. That was her style. She was trying to subvert the foundation of my position. And, brilliantly, she did. She's an anarchist by political stand rather than a Marxist-Leninist. I have to admit that I had a sneaking admiration for her defiant posture because she was in Students for a Democratic Society, and she was willing to take the heat that people were getting for being in SDS in those days, which was a lot of heat. People don't remember, but you were really under suspicion if you took that stand in 1965 or 1966. The stunning independence of her attitude, given the time, attracted me enormously.

In 1967 I decided to leave Santa Clara. There were two reasons. I thought I'd gone as far as I could go in the direction I was going in then. I was seen the same way I'd been seen in high school: a maverick, somebody who was difficult, who was independent, who was spoiled, who wouldn't go to classes, didn't find the lectures interesting, but would end up with A's because he wrote a really good paper. I was still performing the same intellectual shenanigans that I had been performing in high school, only more ruthlessly so, because my real interest was now in my girlfriend and not at all in school. I was doing it with my left hand. And the arrogance of that was clear to me.

The other reason was that I couldn't bear living at home anymore. I'm really fond of my mother, and I like being with her, but I was twenty years old, and at this point I just couldn't be telling people where I was going to be, or having her worry about me if I didn't call at a certain time.

I transferred to UCLA because my best friend, Michael, was transferring to L.A. State. He and I had hitchhiked around a lot. We were buddies, partners, and I thought we could live together easily in L.A. We'd get away from it all and it would be a new adventure. The other reason, besides wanting to be with him, and wanting to change like he was changing, was that I felt I was headed for a marriage and I was pretty sure that I didn't want to go in that direction. I felt like Tina and I were getting more and more involved, and it was inevitable, if it kept on like it was, that before I got out of college I was going to be married and probably have kids. By this time, we had made love. Once you've had sex, you don't go back to making out. I didn't realize that that was the case. I thought you could just do it once and then go back to what you were doing before. I was wrong.

So I thought, If I go to Los Angeles I'll be far enough away to live a separate life. Well, that was a delusion. All I did was spend all of my money on telephone calls and trips back and forth from L.A. to Berkeley. Tina had transferred to Berkeley and consolidated her political analysis and become a visible radical. Not a leader, but a known active radical.

Meanwhile, I joined the ROTC program at UCLA, which I didn't have to do. And by so doing I was enlisted. I was now in the army. I could not leave voluntarily. I'd signed on the dotted line, committed myself to four years' active duty. My plan was to become a pilot. I wanted to fly jets.

ROTC was Mickey Mouse army. But it became more and more army while staying Mickey Mouse throughout. And my friend Michael began to raise questions about the war. He was just like me—and here I had just signed up for four years. So I was finding myself pretty alienated.

During my ROTC career, I was always asking these inappropriate questions. At UCLA, we had a military-tactics class. I asked, "Why are we using napalm?" We were talking about hearts and minds. We were talking about winning the propaganda war. And I said, "How can you reconcile the propaganda war with the use of napalm?" This was just a logical question. And the answer was, "I'll see you after class." The gist of that answer was, "It's too complicated to explain and I'm not sure there's others who are interested in it."

But the effect was, I was brought before a tribunal and questioned about my loyalty, questioned about why I had failed certain courses and so on. These guys were all dummies. If you get close enough to the military world you find out that they're mostly pretty ignorant guys. Once in a while you find a smart one who just has certain blind spots, in my view, but most of them are really dumb, even at officer level. In fact, *especially* at officer level. That's a cliché, but it's actually true. The NCOs are much more a level-headed bunch of guys. When you get up to major level, you're dealing with some real brain-dead individuals, especially the ones that are given charge of ROTC units. You can imagine that this is not a high-prestige position, and they really send their bums into it. I was interviewed by three bums. I made a mockery of what they were doing. Eventually, I reiterated my question. I said, "I still haven't received an answer to my question, and I think it's a legitimate question to ask for somebody who's going to be in a tactical position. I mean, if I'm going to be in for four years, I don't expect to be a second lieutenant when I leave. By the time I do my tour, I think I'm going to be expected to answer some of these questions, at least in my own mind." What could they say to that? It's a legitimate question from a military point of view.

Meanwhile, I had a very good field record. I did well on the tests and I had a good record on the superficial level, and it was harder for them to get rid of me.

I transferred to Berkeley after only one quarter at UCLA. That fall of '67, I decided, Hey, this is ridiculous. I'm obviously going to marry this woman, so let's get it over with. I moved to Berkeley and we got married January of '68. My friend Michael moved to San Francisco State from L.A. State.

The Berkeley period was the sort of penultimate stage in my radicalization. I was exposed not only to Tina but to Telegraph Avenue. I had to walk with my closely cropped hair and my uniform down Telegraph Avenue to get to drill on Thursday. And it was excruciating. Everybody from the bikers to the radicals would give me either cold-eyed glances or out-and-out abuse. The fervor there was getting to a fever pitch by 1968, and friends of mine who had come from the same background that I had were already attending demonstrations and sit-ins at the Oakland induction center, and so on—including Michael. Although Michael managed to keep that from me for about as long as he could. I basically had total confidence in his morality and his honesty and his loyalty. If he could question it, then it *must* be wrong.

Anyway, the main thing was, the military itself revealed itself to me as I got closer and closer to it. And I thought, I'm defending this? There was a week's block of time in which I went down to Fort Ord with all the other guys in ROTC. You were supposed to get your first taste of regular army life.

I had always been a good marksman. I don't know why—I never learned how to shoot guns when I was a kid. But I really scored very well. I was probably the best or second best in each of the schools that I was in ROTC at. Part of my superficially good record. When I went to Fort Ord, we went out on the firing range and I did very well when shooting at a little piece of white paper. Then we moved to a firing range that had targets shaped like men. And I couldn't hit them. I could not hit them. I tried to hit them. I aimed at them. They were big. They were much easier to hit than these little pieces of white paper. You could fire in front of them, anything within two or three feet, you were going to knock them down. You didn't have to be close. I didn't hit one. I must have fired forty rounds at these big targets, and they weren't flashing up and down—they were right there.

I thought there was something wrong with my rifle. They checked the rifle and I tried again. Nothing. They gave me special preference because I was known as a good marksman. I was supposed to be a showcase for the program. They were looking for me to distinguish myself, and I didn't hit one. I was humiliated. I was shamefaced. I went away from there just apologizing.

It dawned on me that night: I can't shoot men. I'm not going to be able to look at a man and shoot him—and it's going to get me killed. That's what I was thinking. Not a wonderful moral statement, but I'm going to be killed. I'm going to be a dead man. If they weren't shaped like men, if they were blocks, I'm sure I would have done really well. But I couldn't do it. It kept coming to me—there's something wrong here. Something in my nature rebels against this. It's rebelled against it from the start, and I've refused to listen to that voice within myself. Tina's been trying to tell me that that's there, and she's been right. And I have to face it.

The second incident that happened that week at Fort Ord really turned me against them morally. I had seen pictures of U.S. atrocities, torture, heard stories of people being thrown out of helicopters. I rejected them. I actually believed that they were trumped-up photographs. But then I got the proof.

There was an exercise at Fort Ord called "Survival, Escape, and Evasion." They show you supposedly what'll happen to you if you get caught by the VC. First they show you all this irrelevant stuff about how to survive in case you get separated from your unit. They kill a rabbit and show you how to strip it. I mean, how many rabbits were there out in the rice paddies and the jungle? I don't know. Anyway, we were all accustomed from sitting in classes to know that there was a high bullshit factor in this whole training. We knew it, and we didn't care. But this one turned ugly—really ugly.

We were taken out on a road and we were told that when we heard shots over our heads, we should run and try to escape, and basically head east to the safe area across the chaparral. And that maximum points would be given for reaching the safe area before the whistle blew. Second best would be to evade capture until the whistle blew, and then come in. Minimum points would be for being caught. This sounded like it could be fun. We went out there and marched down the road and boom, boom, boom, boom, boom! First they fired a volley of shots over our heads, probably blanks. Then we broke and ran. Then they fired tear-gas canisters in the direction we were headed, to round us up.

I was with two guys who had been my buddies—in the army you make buddies. It's inevitable and one of the nicer things about it. So we ran for it. And all hell broke loose. The regular army guys had their one shot at the officers who would later be telling them what to do. So they were really going to give it to us while they had their chance. They really came down; they really did. They were beating guys, shoving them down on the ground, hitting with the butt of a rifle between the shoulder blades—just to really make you feel like you were in the war. I thought, What is the matter with these guys? Don't they know this is an exercise? I saw guys being dragged by the hair across the ground, facedown. Literally dragging them by the fatigues and kicking them in the butt and yelling at them. There was gas everywhere, and it was horrible. It was just awful. This is at night and it was dark. You couldn't see much of anything.

I figured that one place they're not going to go after me is right in the cloud of tear gas. So the three of us put our heads down, waited for an opening, and ran for it. But one of my buddies, Ray, broke. He couldn't go in the gas. He was choking, and he broke and ran and he got caught. So the other buddy, Jim, and I got through the gas. We got away.

When I came back to the safe area after the whistle blew, the trucks were bringing in guys who had been caught and had been in the stockade. This was hours later. I came up to Ray and said, "Jesus, what happened?" He couldn't talk to me. He was crying. He had broken. He had given information under torture. It wasn't all-out torture, but it wasn't mock torture either. They had put these guys in a chair, strapped their wrists down, and applied electrodes to their wrists, and then they had poured water on them, and given them up to a hundred volts. It wasn't dangerous to anybody that had a sound heart, but it scares hell out of you. And they're taking their field caps and dipping them in water and slapping you with them. This was supposed to be how you would be treated if you were a captive. Plus they'd been made to crawl the entire two miles or whatever back to the stockade. This was a different situation than we'd ever seen in ROTC before.

I thought this was just outrageous, absolutely outrageous. I mean, to take your own men and subject them to this in the name of preparing you for some hypothetical situation in a way that was really designed to break down people that they didn't think were macho enough to do this stuff. The thing that appalled me about it was their attitude towards their own men; the way that they humiliated Ray in front of his peers and his friends.

I thought, It's true. If they'll do this to cadets, of course they'll do it to the Vietcong. Why should I doubt it any longer? I've seen it up close. They think they can justify putting a man in an electric chair who's on our side.

Well, I told our CO, "That's outrageous. One of these days somebody's going to write an article, and it's going to expose this, and you're going to be very embarrassed." All he said was, "Well, it better not be you." So they *knew* that this was totally wrong. It's sick. And it's as sick as it was when being described to me, but I had to see it for myself. And having seen it for myself, I was finished with the army forever. I was more radicalized than I could have ever been by having been educated from outside.

So from then on, I had only one purpose, and that was to get out. I came home and I agonized about how I was going to do it. Shall I make myself a cause and go to jail and stand up with the other people who are refusing to participate? Or shall I take the easy way out and go live in the mountains someplace in Canada or Mexico?

So I called the Coordinating Center for Conscientious Objectors in San Francisco. They are the ones who told me about this loophole. Because I had never applied for a 2-S, a student deferment, I qualified for a 3-A, a hardship deferment, because by this time my wife was pregnant. I went to my commanding officer, who was Colonel Brandt at Berkeley. He was a tough guy, but not a particularly political one.

He was just a regular army grunt who'd become a colonel. I said, "My wife's pregnant. I'm the sole source of support for the family. I have major reservations about my participation, and I'm not going." I was very polite. I wasn't defiant.

He said, "I believe you're making the wrong decision. I think I can talk you out of it." And I said, "You can't. I've made up my mind."

So he says, "Well, I don't want anybody in my unit who doesn't want to be here. You have to write me a letter saying that you don't have the leadership abilities to be an officer in the U.S. Army. And I'm betting that your integrity won't permit you to write that letter." I said, "See you tomorrow, Colonel."

I went home and I wrote the letter. I wrote, "The nature of the leadership abilities with which I am gifted are not those that would inspire me into leading men into combat." I stuck to the letter, but not the spirit, of what he had asked for. I bet that he was going to take it rather than have a messy hassle on his hands. And it worked. He gave me an honorable discharge. I could never be drafted. I think what really was at work was that he respected my decision even though he disagreed with it. I'll always be grateful, because I could have suffered major consequences and, as it was, I slid through.

Immediately I recognized the value of conscientious-objection organizing and draft-resistance organizing, because I had just experienced tremendous rescue from this. So I made up my mind I was going to volunteer to help these guys who needed to get out. So I went right from ROTC into the draft-resistance movement.

I also transferred from Berkeley to San Francisco State. Berkeley was very demanding. Their literature department stressed bibliography, research, classical criticism. I was bored. I was offended by it. I wanted a more progressive approach, because by now everything seemed possible to me. And my friend Michael was at San Francisco State and I thought, Wouldn't it be fun? So I transferred, and I was never happier about a decision. But then, bam! The strike hit.

Michael and I opposed the strike. We still had some residue of just wanting to get on with our lives, and the strike was presented to us as a really marginal issue, the firing of a black teacher. It really didn't seem to us worthy of shutting down the college. We didn't actually know all the issues at the time. We were in the same English class together and the teacher let the Third World Liberation Front and the other guys come in and make a pitch to us. And Michael and I were booing them.

Well, a few days later the police rioted. I was working in the library and Michael came running into the library and said, "They've drawn their guns!" I said, "Well, fuck this. They can't do that." And I quit my job. Boom—like that. I went to my supervisor and I said, "I'm leaving. There's too much going on outside, and you ought to shut this library down immediately."

So then I left, and I was shocked at what I saw. It was like a war zone. I couldn't believe it. From then on, I was right there with them in the picket lines. We were chased up and down the streets by the police. Michael was run down by a mounted cop. We got hit with billy clubs. We were there every day for like the next five months. There were six hundred police there every day. The goddamn tactical squad, the highway patrol, mounted police, park police. And they had all those jerky guys that went around in blazers and carried high-school history books and pretended to be part of the student body.

There were a lot of humorous things about it, like when they tried to clamp down on the language at the rallies. People would say fuck this and fuck that, and there'd be a police announcement: "By the power vested in me by the people of the state of California, I order you to desist, and you are not to use this language in public." And everybody would turn around on cue and yell, *"Fuck you!"*

But it did get pretty serious, too. The confrontations were bloody, they were frequent, they were frightening. One time all the furniture was dragged out of the cafeteria and piled into barricades and burned. And one guy threw a tray towards the police and it hit a reporter in the forehead. I thought he was dead. I thought, This is it. Now it's lethal violence, and from our side. And the police had those pepper-fog machines staring down our throats. I thought, This could go any distance. There's no end to how violent this can get.

There were some powerful moments and there were awful scenes. I remember the time that some guy brought two dogs on campus, a Saint Bernard and a Doberman, and the cops maced the dogs. And I thought, Boy, that says a lot. You know, the cops got pretty snarly, pretty surly, and pretty nasty. They would take people into those black marias and they would just beat the shit out of them, and you could hear them yelling. A lot of students suffered brain damage, loss of vision. A lot of people really paid the price.

I was lucky. I was never busted. But there were hundreds of arrests. People would be arrested if they threw an acorn. They'd be arrested for attempt to commit murder, and willful assault on an officer, and resisting arrest. You asked a cop for his badge number as a defiant gesture and boom, you were busted for resisting arrest. And then they'd hit you, and then they'd have to arrest you. It was an ugly, dangerous scene. It was really making my life pretty miserable, but I also was proud of it and it was such a contrast to be in that kind of war posture from what I'd been in for years and was never comfortable with, really.

In those days, to me, it was, in a sense, a nonviolent war. My policy was, I won't throw rocks; I won't do anything indiscriminate. I guess I had the same reaction I had about shooting somebody. I didn't want to really hit anybody in the face with a rock. I thought the key was for me to put my body there, be there. That was *my* statement. And if they tried to hit me, I was going to run. And if I couldn't run, I was going to fight. I wasn't going to allow myself to be hit. But I did *not* want to go to jail. I did *not* want to get into those black marias.

It's funny—I got a lot of political education over those several months, a lot. More than I've ever had in a similar period of time since. I felt, this shows me what kind of a society I really live in. This is what they'll do if you really step out of line. As long as you just argue in class, they'll just argue back at you. But you step outside and say, "We're going to shut this institution down," you attack any institution funded by public monies, they will do whatever they want. They will send any amount of violence that's necessary, and this is just more of the war. It's come home. There was a growing number of us polarized by police violence primarily, and secondarily by our politics, our growing distance from U.S. mainstream politics. We were not going to put up with this. We weren't going to just go back to our books or our jobs.

There were some nice moments in the whole thing, like when the American Federation of Teachers finally came around and joined the strike, and you had the feeling we could win. But eventually the strike fell apart, and I didn't like that. That left me worried about my hopes for the movement. Michael and I were utterly shocked at registration time when the student body made the political decision that they had to register. That was, to us, a tremendous sell-out. But when everybody did it, we did it too, because what was the point? There was no movement left.

I continued to get involved with other political actions, but I also held three jobs for a while. I got my job back at the San Francisco State library, I worked in a B. Dalton bookstore near the school, and I worked in the reserved-book room at the University of California library in Berkeley. We lived in married-student housing at San Francisco State and Tina was taking in kids to babysit. We had no financial support from our parents.

It was my job at Berkeley that got me involved in the People's Park demonstrations. Once again, it was not the issue itself that moved me. I felt that the whole program, to turn university-owned land into a park, was quixotic. It was a spiritual confrontation between a mindset that said "This is a piece of private property" and a mindset that said "We live here; we use this; this is ours." It was basically the anarchists rather than the Marxist-Leninists, and I found myself in great sympathy with them spiritually—but I knew that it was hopeless. I just didn't know how bad it would get. But I was there the day that James Rector was shot, killed, and Alan Blanchard was blinded that same day.

Eventually I walked off the job at Berkeley, because when the National Guard came out, I maintained that the University of California should be shut down. I was an assistant supervisor at the reserved-book room and I said to my supervisor, who was also a student and a radical, "Have you been outside? They pointed bayonets at me when I came up here. I'm not going to take that. If we close the reserved-book room, they'll have to close the library, and if they close the library, they might close the university. We're in a pivotal position."

She refused, of course, so I walked. After I walked, they were really embarrassed, and a bunch of the people who were political on the staff decided to go with it. They shut down the reserved-book room, and they shut down the library, and they shut down the university all in that day. I thought we could tip the scales, and I think we had an effect. Maybe not the main reason, but I think it was an important one.

Kent State, to me, marked the end of the movement. Kent State and Jackson State. I mean, I would have thought that when those things happened, there'd have been major national demonstrations hitting the streets. There weren't. I think Kent State frightened people. It was the first indication for a lot of people that they would shoot and shoot to kill. Here we had the killing of U.S. college students on two campuses, and somehow, even though there was a big upheaval, I thought there'd be a bigger one. I thought that would be the moment when, if there was ever going to be a revolution, that would be it. Well, it was a far cry from that, of course. I was still naive. I was still the boy from Iowa who liked to see things in black and white.

I was demoralized in 1970, partly by the fact that my life wasn't going anywhere. I knew that my college education was coming to an end and I really didn't know what I was doing with my college degree. My second son was born that year, my first one having been born in 1968. There were a lot of demands on me, but I had no direction. I couldn't go on supporting myself with nickels and dimes, but I didn't care. I mean, I was so angry. I was so angry at the society that I couldn't see myself just taking a job and going to work every day and pretending that nothing had happened. I finished up at San Francisco State in 1971 and then I decided to drop out for a while, write a book, and really distance myself from society as a kind of gesture, and also as a way of avoiding a decision. My wife was all for this. She was sick of the losses and the lack of progress, and we'd had a lot of friends hurt and arrested.

I'd become violent with Tina, and with my kids. I would get in fights in the street. As a grown man, this is dangerous business. People would demand money or something and I'd start hitting them.

So, in January of '72, we moved to the country, to Navarro, in Mendocino County. I took a job with a guy just setting up TV antennas, cable-TV antennas, and fixing people's irrigation systems in their vineyards. Whatever work needed to be done. I'd always done menial work, manual labor, and I just went back to it and dropped out. Of course, you couldn't really drop out. If my heart was really for dropping out, I wouldn't have gone to Mendocino County, where there was a war going on between the rednecks, the loggers, and the hippies, who were pouring sand into people's Caterpillars and were getting clubbed and raped by the locals. And I was in the middle.

My wife, by the way, was happy. She had found nirvana. She loved it there. We had a garden; the children were happy. And it was gorgeous. Redwood groves, blue skies, sun—the simple life. My being home every day, me writing a book. It was all very romantic. It was a beautiful old redwood house, a drop-in center for all the dropouts and characters. So she was in bohemia. She was happy. I wasn't. I was filled with guilt for having dropped out. We were broke; we were on welfare; the book was a joke. I was embarrassed by it. I wanted to get involved in the McGovern campaign. So I went back. I went to work as a canvasser, a really low-level volunteer for McGovern, and got inspired by the guy. I started seeing my friends again and got back into whatever politics there were available.

But mainly I was teaching school and working at a bookstore and trying to get on my feet. Through the good offices of my mother, who was still teaching in the Catholic schools, I got a job teaching seventh and eighth grade in a largely Chicano area in East San Jose. I wasn't a bad teacher. I really liked the kids. I wasn't afraid of them. At junior-high-school level, kids are just seen as pariahs. Nobody likes them. They lose their cuteness, they become defiant, and they make enemies of their parents or vice versa. So they're desperate for a positive adult model, and I gave it to them. They loved me. It was a very high-pitched, emotional year. I got fired from my first teaching job after two years, because of differences in philosophy with the new principal who came in. The progressive nun who hired me was replaced by a conservative nun, and I was fired.

Then I went to work at another Catholic school in Sunnyvale, and worked there for two years. After four years of teaching, I worked my way up to a salary offer of nine thousand dollars, and basically said, No, I can't do this anymore. The biggest reason why I quit was that I wanted to move out of the Bay Area. I couldn't handle it anymore. I decided to move to Seattle, to follow Michael again. Arrived there intent upon teaching school, and found that there was a teachers' strike on, and I couldn't cross the picket lines. So I went to work for the YMCA, day care and recreation.

By this time I was becoming more and more active in Amnesty International, which works for the release of prisoners of conscience around the world. I'd heard about the organization for the first time in May or June of '73 on a radio interview with Joan Baez. The idea of Amnesty, which is fundamentally a nonviolent, nonconfrontational organization, appealed to me as far as what effect it would have on my personal life. I saw it as a way of channeling my outrage in a constructive and organized way. What convinced me that it was useful was that it did have some effect on individuals. I didn't think it would have a broad impact on policies of government, but I thought if you put enough pressure on governments, they'd probably rather release somebody from jail than have to deal with the pressure. Even though it's nonconfrontational in technique, it's confrontational in stance. It says, "You can't do this," and I liked that. I felt there was a hard edge to its absolutism on the principles, and I admire that.

I had to make certain concessions to style, but at that time I was ready for that. I mean, I really had doubts about letter-writing. Letter-writing is a long way from the barricades, a long way. But it's been good for me to have some way to express my anger and my outrage and compassion and all the things I feel.

When I joined Amnesty in 1973, it was fairly well known around Europe but was really unheard of in the United States. I started a local chapter in Los Gatos, which was group twenty-six in the whole country. Now there's over four hundred groups. Our budget was like $50,000 a year and now it's $6,000,000. I founded our publication and was the first editor. I began to work a lot on Indonesia, which was a country that was unknown in the United States. It was a classic case. Thousands upon thousands of political prisoners, a huge atrocity that had gone virtually unnoticed in America. It had strategic importance to the U.S. government and, as a major producer of low-sulfate oil, it was economically important to the country. But nobody in the United States knew where it was. I mean, it's the fifth-largest country in the world. It was stunning to me that I was so ignorant about it, and that everybody was.

So I started a group that would coordinate activities on Indonesia, and I studied. I read everything in the library about the country—everything. There was so little, it was easy to do. I really did become an expert, in an academic sense. I didn't have the language. I had never been there. But I knew an awful lot about the circumstances surrounding political imprisonment and torture and killings. Much more than the press, for example.

In June of '74 I was invited to the national meeting of Amnesty in New York. It was my first time to represent the West, and I liked it. I found myself very comfortable in a leadership position. I was able to get this section to declare a national campaign, a year of concern about Indonesia, and on that basis I was sent all over the country—editorial boards, radio, television, university lectures. I just did everything to get the word "Indonesia" in front of people's eyes. And it was not easy. It was really impossible.

The State Department was acting in their usual capacity of apologist for their ally, denying what we were saying, criticizing us, challenging our basis for information, criticizing me personally. But we had all the facts and they didn't. So their reaction helped a lot. It got more press interest, got a few editorials. There were demonstrations. We organized a corporate strategy where we found out all the corporations that had field offices in Indonesia and gave them all the data, and then copied those letters to the Indonesian Embassy. We let the government of Indonesia know that we were really agitating for the whole U.S. society to pay attention to this.

Meanwhile, I was elected a member of the board in December of

'75. I had never really been in a leadership position before, not with an organization behind me. I'd never even joined an organization in my life. So it was different for me, but I liked it. I felt I didn't have to say anything that I didn't believe in. And people listened; and they formed groups. It caught on, and it caught on quite rapidly. So it became the most fulfilling work in my life, much more so than teaching. I ended up working twenty, thirty, forty hours a week in my spare time.

In 1977, a lucky thing happened. In October of '77 we were scheduled to have hearings on Indonesia that we'd worked on for a long, long time. They'd finally given us hearings at the Human Rights Committee in the House of Representatives, and we had a press conference scheduled. But we'd done one in the year before when I'd done that tour. That year, Voice of America had shown up, university papers and such. This time, we were scheduled for the press conference on October 17th. And on October 10th or 11th, they announced the Nobel Peace Prize for Amnesty International, and all of a sudden we were news.

Well, on October 17th I appeared as a speaker at the press conference in New York, and ABC, CBS, NBC were there. The *Washington Post*. Everybody but the *New York Times* was there. I was astonished. I'd never seen microphones in my face, not like this. I thought, Wow, the Indonesians are *not* going to like this, because the heading in the *Washington Post* was "Nobel Prize–Winning Organization Assails Indonesia." And it put a different cast on the hearings, which were the 18th of October. It got to a head-to-head kind of thing between Amnesty and the Indonesians and the State Department.

So I was stunned when the Indonesians announced that they were going to release all 35,000 of their B-category prisoners, the prisoners whom they had no intention of putting on trial because they admitted they didn't have any evidence of wrongdoing. I know that, in my own view, the primary reason for the release program was the Indonesian army's invasion of East Timor. The Indonesians didn't feel they could carry two major liabilities. They were being condemned at the UN for the occupation of East Timor and now they were getting heat on their political-prisoner situation and they had to make a choice. They chose to keep their occupation army in place and to release the prisoners.

In other words, I'm not taking credit for the release of those 35,000 prisoners, but I feel that we played a role. We helped to tip the balance. So that was a sea-change in my attitude toward the organization. Because when the Indonesians announced it, I didn't think they'd do it, but when they actually did start releasing people by the thousands, I was astonished. I really was. Because I was acting in good faith. I was doing what I felt you should do to try to make this happen, but in my heart of hearts ... So when I saw that it was possible to play a role, then my attitude toward the organization and to the human-rights movement really changed. I saw it as one of the most interesting reformist movements around.

Again, it's not a revolutionary organization. It's not even a radical organization. It avoids political analysis very, very carefully. But, still, it's human beings against repressive state policies, and I'm comfortable with that. It's human beings saying, first of all, "We're all a human family, and don't tell me it's not my business. You're putting somebody in jail and torturing him, and that's my business. And I'm saying that to you openly. And furthermore, the international laws don't accept that, and you signed them. Right away, see, I'm on a high moral ground and you're not. And I'm going to keep you reminded of that constantly." Every once in a while, accidents of history and chance will play in such a way that you *can* have an impact, a major impact.

I moved to New York in 1978 when I was elected chairman of the board of Amnesty in the United States. I was chairman for two years. I knew that New York would be far too expensive to live in to support myself on a salary of a community-service organization, so I had to get a job. I couldn't get a job as a schoolteacher because of the certification requirements. So I looked for jobs where I could get a kind of executive salary within a nonprofit environment.

I worked first for Clergy and Laity Concerned, this social-justice group. I was supposed to revamp their membership system. All my ideas were rejected, and it was a totally unsatisfactory situation. Besides which, I was working forty hours a week as chairman of Amnesty and my employers were a little frustrated—understandably so. The same thing happened to me in my next job, which was with a tribal-rights organization called Survival International. I was their first executive director in the States. They fired me because I wasn't raising enough money. I basically went from one job to another, doing more Amnesty than anything else, and incurring the resentment of my professional employers, who eventually had to let me go.

Eventually I went to work as a partner in a new outfit that was set up by a friend of mine, Carl Rogers. He wanted to set up a technical-assistance outfit that would help nonprofit organizations get access to celebrities. The idea was to match the dignitary to the cause, the issue. I'd seen it over and over again in my work that groups that needed to raise money and were not well known, not very visible, needed some identification with some public figure. We struggled along for two years and eventually I dropped out. But Carl influenced me a lot on the issue of using dignitaries, and I've made maximum use out of that for Amnesty. So I profited a great deal from the association, even though in the long run I went broke again.

You can only have three consecutive terms on the board of Amnesty, so I ran out of terms. And I moved back west again. I moved to Seattle in 1981. Looked for work, couldn't find it. I was struggling. Our third son had been born in New York. I was substitute-teaching in Seattle. I tried for a job in a prison as a teacher, and couldn't get that because of civil-service requirements. I spent a month picking apples in central Washington. Tina was working selling puppets at Pike Place Market, and taking in kids. We were back to square one.

I had applied for the job of executive director of Amnesty, but was not selected. However, in 1982, the guy who was the choice hired me. He set up my current job as director of the Western Region. And I have loved this job. It's been the easiest job I ever had to do because I know the stuff. I'm a good speaker and I deal with the media, I think, effectively. I've never had a job that basically gave me a chance to do what I wanted to do and get paid for it, and where the check came every two weeks and I didn't have to go out and raise the money. So I feel very, very fortunate. I mean, really privileged and lucky at this point in my life. I'm also chairman of the International Council Meeting, which is the international assembly of Amnesty. That's the leadership of the whole international movement. It's just a task, not a position. I chair the biennial meeting. It's a great privilege and a real exciting experience because you see people from more than forty countries, all with their own agendas.

I am deadly serious about this work. I really want us to continue to be a frustration to the efforts of governments to keep these things secret. Amnesty has provided me not only with a way to work and do what I want but also some wonderful side benefits like traveling and meeting very kind people, many of whom were former prisoners themselves.

Tina and I now have five children, four boys and a baby girl. I have found myself so much more comfortable in the role of father with these last three than I was with the first two. It wouldn't even cross my mind to be violent with these kids. Where with the first ones I'd pick them up and shake them, I would never do that with one of the little ones today. I'm more the kind of a father that I would want than I was then.

So many people have said that the youth today are different than we were. And it's true: The students and the young are a very conservative bloc at the moment, but so were we until the draft and the war. I think that there aren't very many circumstances that would polarize the country like it was in 1968. Anything short of a draft *and* a military intervention *together* would not do it, in my view.

A lot of people also like to talk about members of our generation "selling out." But really most people who were involved had complex motivations that moved their lives, and some of those other motivations became predominant in their lives and eclipsed their political conscience. But that isn't the same as a sell-out to me. What that means is that there are a lot of people out there who, given either the right issue or the right degree of outrage over something, would undergo another shift in what motivates them back to what motivated them in 1968.

Then there are those of us who have been so heavily polarized that we could never really return. We can accommodate to the way things are, but we're not at peace with it. We find our ways to make war with it, even if it's within a much more respectable "framework." But some of us became citizens of the world. We became human beings, and our politics became the politics of a human being rather than of a citizen of a fallible government and nation and economic structure. Some of us detached ourselves from an immoral political and economic framework in such a way that we were liberated to pursue our own destinies and to pursue our own political will. It's certainly a small number, as far as I can see, in relative terms to the nation as a whole. It's not a mainstream thing, but there are a lot of us; there are not a few of us.

I think that's created a sector of society which is going to strengthen the whole by agitation, by criticism and self-criticism, by intellectual honesty and determination. It has taken a lot to stay with that politics even though, in fact, for me and for a lot of other people, there's no choice. You can't sell out. It isn't even a choice that's available to you. You couldn't do it because it would be like taking on an acting job.

I look back on that period of upheaval with a mixture of feelings, not just with a sense of defeat. We won in a way; we lost in a way. On the whole, it's a story without an end. We haven't heard the last of them, and they haven't heard the last of us.

When I first sat down with David Hinkley, I knew nothing of his background. So it came as quite a surprise to learn that our paths had crossed. Like David, I was a student at San Francisco State College during the student-teacher strike of 1968–1969. In fact, we were able to pinpoint a moment when we were both surrounded by police while standing on the steps of the school library.

I would have passed off this coincidence as just another example of how small the world really is, except that the period we shared turned out to be a major turning point in my life. Like David Hinkley, I learned more about politics during those six months than during any equivalent period in my life.

My conversation with David stirred my own memories of San Francisco State. I, too, had taken little interest when the strike started. Early on, members of the Black Students' Union had committed acts of violence, of which I disapproved. Then one day I emerged from a meeting to discover that police had arrived on campus to make arrests and to bully people. Confronted with violence on both sides, I was forced to deal with the actual issues that had provoked the strike.

I was given a splendid opportunity a week later when classes were suspended (except in the science departments) so that a convocation could be held to air the demands of the black and other minority students and to hear the responses of the administration. It took a few hours to work through the enormous egos of the student leaders and the haughtiness of the administrators. But when they finally got around to discussing the concept of creating black- and ethnic-studies departments, I was fascinated.

I still remember clearly the impassioned and thoughtful speeches by the representatives of the Asian Students' Union. Their descriptions of life behind the facade of Chinatown were revelations to me. I had been unaware of the poverty and overcrowding that existed behind the fancy and colorful shops. One speaker pointed out that although the college carried courses in Mandarin Chinese, there were none in Cantonese, the language of 98 percent of the immigrants to Chinatown. I began to see the logic in creating ethnic-studies departments.

One of the more revealing moments of the convocation came when one of the black students turned to the administration panelists and asked them what had become of the money that had been willed to the college by a local black woman with instructions that it be used to set up a scholar-

ship fund for black students. The administrators were speechless. They had obviously never heard of the bequest. After fumbling around, they agreed to look into it. A lunch break was conveniently called. When the panelists returned, the administration acknowledged that the fund had been overlooked and that it would be implemented as soon as possible. Seeing that the black students had "done their homework" better than the people who ran the college gave me more respect for their position. After an evening of discussing with my roommates the idea of ethnic studies, I became a supporter of the strike.

I was never a big fan of the strike leaders, though. Most of them were egotistical and dogmatic, haranguing people to adhere to the "correct line." But I endured these guys because I believed in the issues. Besides, the leaders on the other side were at least as bad. The number one man leading the battle against the students was the governor of California, a fellow named Ronald Reagan. His assistant was named Edwin Meese. And it was a battle. Each day Reagan would send in six hundred police from all over the state. He would have sent in the National Guard if Mayor Alioto of San Francisco hadn't objected.

The police first appeared as plainclothesmen. Dressed in lettermen jackets and sporting crew cuts, they looked completely different from real 1968 college students in San Francisco. For a couple of days it was funny, but the humor evaporated when the police put their uniforms back on and armed themselves with guns, batons, and tear gas. In the months that followed, I saw more beatings and saw more blood flow than I hope to see ever again. For a year afterward I would dream of rows upon rows of blue-uniformed police marching toward me, gas masks on and bayonets drawn.

Considering that ethnic-studies departments are now so widespread that their legitimacy isn't even questioned, you have to wonder why Ronald Reagan and his handlers thought that opposing the strike at San Francisco State was so important that it was worth cracking skulls and spines and spilling blood. I can't believe that they found the concept of ethnic studies so objectionable, though one never knows. I think that Reagan just liked a good fight, and saw a chance to exploit the situation to enhance his image and advance his career.

There was one Ronald Reagan incident from that period that made a great impression on me. One morning it was revealed in the newspapers that in the midst of a speech to a private club, Governor Reagan had told a story about how violent college students really were. A certain director of admissions, Reagan said, at a certain California state college, had been forced at knifepoint to enroll unqualified minority students. It was a shocking story that must have impressed the audience with the seriousness of the campus threat.

When the story leaked to the media, reporters immediately pressed Reagan to share the details of the incident and to tell from whom he had heard the story. Reagan refused to talk about it. At his next press conference, he was questioned again. This time he revealed that the incident had occurred at San Francisco State and that he had learned of it from Robert Smith, the president of the college, during a meeting of the State College Board of Trustees. Reporters rushed off to interview those involved.

The director of admissions denied that the incident had occurred. President Smith denied having told the story. The rest of the board of trustees (save one) individually denied that the story had come up at a meeting. Reagan had evidently made the whole thing up. As a man who had spent years making his living as an after-dinner speaker, he knew the value of a good anecdote. Whether or not it was true was irrelevant.

At the time, I was so politically naive that when it became clear that Reagan had lied, I was sure that the press would spread the story near and far, that the public would be outraged to have a public official telling such inflammatory lies, and that Ronald Reagan's career would be ruined. The next morning I raced out to buy the local newspapers. There was nothing. No follow-up, no editorials, not even a "clarification" from the governor's office. The story was finished, stopped cold. It was never mentioned again.

I was very confused by this. The system had not worked the way I thought it did. In the next couple years, I would see pepper-fog machines dispersing huge demonstrations, reluctant National Guardsmen enforcing curfews, downtown areas shut down by antiwar protestors, and even, once, police aiming their rifles in my direction and shooting. But there was something about that little event with Ronald Reagan and San Francisco State that haunted me, that wouldn't let me go. I became convinced that Ronald Reagan was a dangerous man and feared that he might someday become president.

Twelve years later, I followed the speeches and statements of President Ronald Reagan, as he first outlined his economic program to the nation. His plan was to cut the tax rate and to increase military spending more than he would decrease domestic spending. The result was supposed to be a reduced deficit and a more balanced budget. It was so ridiculous, I couldn't believe he had the nerve to say such things. You didn't have to know much about economics to know that decreasing income and increasing spending created the opposite of a balanced budget. It was "voo-

doo economics," just as George Bush, Reagan's vice-president, had said it would be.

After one of Reagan's speeches, which I had watched on television at the home of some well-educated friends, I turned around to share the absurdity of Reagan's proposal with the others in the room. But each of them was expressionless, passively watching the TV screen. None of them had noticed. They were hypnotized—back in the fourth grade being lectured to by a kindly old man using a pointer and very simple charts. Instead of hearing what Reagan had said they had been transfixed by the way he had said it. It was a chilling moment. I knew then that it would be a long four years—at best.

MIDTERM REPORT

"The people of the world respect a nation that can see beyond its own image."
PRESIDENT JOHN F. KENNEDY

After much consideration, I decided that the best format for evaluating the class of '65 as a generation halfway through life would be that traditional American institution: the midterm report. Looking back on my own high-school years, I recall all too clearly the ten-week report card. It didn't really go on your record, but it could get you in trouble just the same. It had the effect of a warning: This is how poorly you might do if you don't shape up during the second half of the semester.

In applying the concept of a midterm report to a generation, I asked myself which criteria should be used for judgment. Basically, I believe there is only one criterion for judging a generation: Did they leave the world in a better condition than they found it? I have divided this one measure of success into seven categories: Progress Toward Peace and Security; Improved Standard of Living and Quality of Life; Technological Advancements; Cultural Contributions; Maintenance of the Environment; Furthering Education and the Spread of Knowledge; and Progress Toward Freedom and the Advancement of Human Rights.

With full awareness that others may disagree, I give the class of '65 the following midterm marks:

MIDTERM REPORT

CLASS: 1965
NATION: USA
DATES OF BIRTH: 1946–1948

PEACE AND SECURITY	B
STANDARD OF LIVING	C
TECHNOLOGY	A
CULTURE	C
ENVIRONMENT	A
EDUCATION	B
FREEDOM	B

REMARKS: I give the generation a high midterm grade in Peace and Security for the role it played in stopping the Vietnam War, and for forcing the nation to reevaluate its willingness to send U.S. combat troops all over the world just because the president and his advisers think it would be a good idea. For example, when Ronald Reagan first became president, one of his goals was the sending of troops to El Salvador. Public opinion was so overwhelmingly opposed to this prospect that Reagan dropped it like a hot potato, and Alexander Haig took the blame for the idea. Later, Reagan went to tremendous lengths to whip up a war hysteria against Nicaragua. Despite a major, prolonged propaganda effort, U.S. citizens just wouldn't bite, and the Reagan Administration was forced to accept the fact that a war with Nicaragua would have to be fought without U.S. troops.

I give an average grade in Standard of Living because the generation has done nothing outstanding in the field. The nation has seen improvements, but no more than in any other period.

Technology, an A. The '60s generation has been very active in the computer field, in medical technology, in space technology, and in developing all sorts of goodies that make our lives easier and more enjoyable.

Culture, an average grade again. The generation has certainly been active and prolific, particularly in the fields of music and cinema, but it remains to be seen whether this quantity will translate into a legacy of quality.

Environment, another A. The generation has distinguished itself early, helping build a large and sometimes effective movement where none existed before. When the '60s generation was growing up, no one thought about pollution, pesticides, topsoil erosion, or alternative sources of energy. Now there is a national awareness that quality of life is as important as standard of living, that it is necessary to live in harmony with the earth, rather than to see it merely as a source of exploitation.

Education, a B. The class of '65 are now teachers and parents. The twenty-eight people in this book now have thirty-eight children. I was impressed by the concern that I heard expressed about the importance of educating children. I see this field as a source of great potential for the generation.

As a generation that served as foot soldiers not only in the Vietnam War but also in the civil-rights movement and the antiwar movement, the class of '65 became involved early on with issues of freedom and human rights. It was a concern for freedom that motivated many class members to risk their lives by fighting a war in Southeast Asia. It was also a concern for freedom that motivated many of them to oppose that war, including some of the veterans themselves.

For this sense of commitment alone, I would give the class an A, were it not for the fact that that commitment has lain dormant for a number of years. An A generation would have continued to actively oppose the suppression of human rights in Southeast Asia despite the end of the war, and would have extended that concern to the rest of the world.

So I give the class a B. This should be an interesting subject to watch, especially around the turn of the century, when the generation gets its chance to put its values into practice.

I am sure that many people might disagree with the grades I have assigned. I certainly disagreed with many grades that I received. I suggest taking a look at a similar midterm report for a different generation: the class of 1935. This generation, the parents of the '60s generation, would have received their midterm report in 1955.

MIDTERM REPORT

CLASS: 1935
NATION: USA
DATES OF BIRTH: 1916–1918

PEACE AND SECURITY	A
STANDARD OF LIVING	A
TECHNOLOGY	A
CULTURE	C
ENVIRONMENT	B
EDUCATION	B
FREEDOM	A

REMARKS: Judged in 1955, the '30s generation would have earned very high marks. They fought and won a war against tyrants, saving the world from Nazism, fascism, and Japanese imperialism. They worked hard and turned a depressed economy into a booming one. They developed new machines and processes that could not have been imagined while they were growing up. I give a B in Environment because there was little sense of a problem even existing. Culture, a C, for the same reason the class of '65 gets a C.

What I find fascinating is the opportunity to reevaluate the '30s generation three decades later. I hesitate to call it a final report, since that would be a bit premature, but the generation *is* at the stage of completing everything but their term paper and final exam.

LATE-TERM REPORT

CLASS: 1935
NATION: USA
BIRTHDATES: 1916–1918

	MIDTERM	*LATE-TERM*
PEACE AND SECURITY	A	B
STANDARD OF LIVING	A	B
TECHNOLOGY	A	A
CULTURE	C	B
ENVIRONMENT	B	D
EDUCATION	B	A
FREEDOM	A	B

REMARKS: The class of 1935 has faced unexpected challenges during the second half of its life. Post–World War II feelings of peace and security were soon replaced by a discomforting Cold War and a growing fear of Communism. The continued growth and spread of nuclear weapons have forced us to live with the threat of sudden annihilation. Life is not as secure as it was in the glory days after the war. I would drop Peace and Security to a C, but the generation's fine work during the first half of the term ensured the higher grade.

Standard of Living also dropped a notch, despite increased wealth, because of the unexpected, unchecked threat to the *quality* of life that eventually accompanied the increase in *quantity*. Along with the conveniences and luxuries of modern life have come new fears and worries: plane crashes, car crashes, pollution, stress-related illnesses, and a far worse crime rate.

It is in the field of Maintenance of the Environment that I feel the class of 1935 has performed most disappointingly. For all the individual voices that have been raised by members of the generation, in general the problem seems to have caught the '30s generation by surprise. The situation has become a lot worse, very quickly.

The pleasant surprise for the class of '35 has been its accomplishments in education. The curriculum was broadened; continuing education was made available to more people; a wide range of experimental programs were instituted. I have many objections to the public-school education I received, but I give the generation who taught us a high mark for giving it their best shot.

After fighting for the cause of freedom in World War II, the class of '35 turned inward. The Korean War didn't provoke the same sense of urgency and purpose as did World War II. The civil-rights movement was a slow, arduous struggle that required great perseverance. The class of '35 played a major role in bringing minority rights in America as far as they have come. And yet there is something slightly amiss with the record of the class of '35 on freedom and human rights. The high standards of individual rights that are respected in the United States have been violated abroad by a wide range of odious dictators, supported by the U.S. government, despite being unpopular and morally reprehensible.

The class of '35 is a generation that saw their children rebel against authority beyond that of the family. They, too, faced questions of conscience that split the class. It is also a generation that, at the peak of its voting power, elected Richard Nixon president of the United States—twice. Freedom and human rights? Still a good grade, but no longer an A.

It is clear, then, in looking at the class of 1935 at midterm and late-term, that to judge a generation in their late thirties is premature. In school, the midterm report is a useful indication of progress, but the real basis for a final grade comes in the second half of the semester, with numerous tests, a term paper, and a final exam. As I recall, up to 75 percent of one's grade could be determined by work completed in the second half of the term. I believe that it works the same way with generations.

The class of '65 and the rest of the '60s generation received a lot of attention early. But this early attention obscures the fact that most generations don't really start to make their mark on society until they reach their late forties or early fifties. So, in reality, the class of '65 is still waiting in the wings, impatiently working its way up the hierarchy until that time in the late 1990s when it begins to dominate not only the economy but the political structure as well.

After talking with people all over the country, I see no certain vision of what will happen when that day comes. The future, I believe, is up for grabs.

The '60s generation, like all American generations, has on its side my three favorite attributes of the United States: a population of tremendous diversity; spectacular natural beauty, highlighted by awe-inspiring wilderness areas; and the Bill of Rights, which has established a level of freedom that is the envy and dream of people all over the world.

However, the class of '65 will also inherit from previous generations a wide range of unsolved problems. Barring a sudden outbreak of effective solutions, it is possible to predict what some of those problems will be. And members of the generation might as well start thinking about those problems now, examining alternative futures, so that they will not be caught unprepared, as other generations have been.

The first problem, which makes all other problems seem irrelevant, is the threat of nuclear war. Previous generations have let the stockpiles of nuclear weapons grow larger and larger. I think it should be a goal of the '60s generation, and all other generations as well, to leave to future generations a world with *fewer* weapons instead of more.

Another unfortunate legacy of previous generations is a huge national debt, which was allowed by President Reagan to get completely out of hand. Reagan, essentially, mortgaged the country to cover the cost of his failed economic program. Now the baby-boom generation and its children will be stuck paying off his debt, and dealing with annual budgets distorted by massive interest payments.

It is not a pleasant fact to face, but the class of '65 approaches its period of power at a time when anti-Americanism is on the rise. People respect the United States for its domestic freedom and affluence, but despise the U.S. government for supporting dictators who suppress the very freedom and democracy that we cherish in our own country. The United States "lost" Iran and Nicaragua because it insisted on supporting very unpopular dictators rather than the democratic opposition. When those dictators were finally overthrown, the U.S. was out in the cold, and so was the democratic opposition. Because the high standard of living to which the United States has become accustomed is dependent on materials, goods, and markets provided by other nations, it seems certain that the future will bring further involvements with countries torn by uprisings against unpopular governments. South Africa, South Korea, Chile, and Guatemala are only a few of the more obvious examples. I hope that when the '60s generation comes to power, it will be able to plan strategy with allied nations to encourage the spread of democracy, instead of just anti-Communism, while ensuring the flow of goods that the nation now requires.

Another challenge which the generation has a decade or so to prepare for is the creation of new sources of energy. The class of '65 could probably muddle through with existing reserves of oil and coal as well as that Edsel of the energy field, nuclear power. However, I believe we owe it to our grandchildren to drastically increase research and experimentation on renewable energy sources: solar, wind, methane, recycling, etc. Previous generations have allowed the energy field to be controlled by large self-interested corporations, looking to the future in no more than the four-year increments that coincide with presidential elections. It would be a great accomplishment if the class of '65 and the rest of the baby boomers could tackle this unsexy issue and set into motion a process the rewards of which would be reaped by future generations.

It is possible, of course, that the class of '65 will prove to be nothing out of the ordinary. Perhaps the generation will follow the post–World War II tradition of being befuddled by world affairs, continuing to build up its nuclear stockpile, continuing to support any dictator who calls himself an anti-Communist, losing respect around the world while insisting to ourselves that we are "standing tall." Perhaps the class of '65 will simply pass on to future generations such difficult issues as energy and the deficit, satisfied to treat any crack in the economy with a patch or Band-Aid. I hope that this is not the case. But I have to admit that my journeys across the United States have led me to the inescapable conclusion that Americans, on the whole, are frighteningly ill-informed, and especially so about foreign countries, about which most Americans are not only painfully ignorant but also needlessly paranoid. As someone who tries to maintain a global perspective, I have found this to be the most disheartening discovery of my study.

Over and over again, I heard Americans of all generations complain that we need better leaders. My response that competent leaders will appear only if the public is well informed was generally met with blank stares. The class of '65 can expect to inherit drastically lowered standards for its leaders. In 1958, it was revealed that presidential assistant Sherman Adams, in exchange for making a few phone calls, had received as gifts from an old friend a $2400 rug, two suits, a vicuña coat, and $3000 worth of hotel bills paid. This indiscretion was considered so heinous that he was forced to resign.

Twenty-six years later, in 1984, it was revealed that several people who had done financial favors for presidential counsel Edwin Meese were subsequently appointed to government jobs. For example, a man who extended to Meese a $60,000 unsecured loan, with no payments made for 26 months, was appointed to the U.S. Postal Service Board of Governors. The chairman of a bank that lent Meese more than $400,000 was appointed alternate U.S. delegate to the United Nations. A senior vice-president of the same bank became chairman of the Federal Home Loan Bank Board. Another man who gave Mrs. Meese a $15,000 interest-free loan was appointed regional director of the General Services Administration in San Francisco. The man's wife and son also received federal jobs.

Ed Meese's actions were far more outrageous than those of Sherman Adams, yet not only was Meese not forced to resign; he was actually appointed to the post of attorney-general, the highest law-enforcement position in the United States! I think we are talking here about a serious erosion of values.

Unfortunately, these reduced standards apply not only to Cabinet members but to the president of the United States as well. I do not mean my criticism of Ronald Reagan to suggest an endorsement of the Democratic Party or any of its members—far from it. But I do believe that Ronald Reagan's reelection and continual popularity indicate a real "dumbing" of America. It's bad enough that the president of the United States believes that hotels and restaurants in South Africa are integrated, or that Trident missiles are recallable, or that all of the oil off the shoreline of California should be removed so that an earthquake won't cause it to spill into the ocean. But what really bothers me is that so few people care that the president believes these things. And isn't it just a bit repulsive to realize that the president of the United States considered Ferdinand Marcos, a corrupt dictator who tortured and murdered his opponents, to be a close personal friend worthy of embracing in public?

The American people, by choosing to be ill-informed about issues, have allowed the political system to get away from them. Our present method of campaigning, with its emphasis on image instead of substance, has evolved into a system that produces first-rate candidates instead of first-rate presidents.

I found it absorbing, in 1984, to follow Gary Hart's campaign for president. His repeated calls for "new ideas" provoked an excited response from the baby-boom generation. Unfortunately, as the campaign progressed, it became clear that Gary Hart didn't actually have any new ideas. The generation, as usual, was left without a candidate. Ronald Reagan's 1984 "landslide" reelection really meant that only one out of three voting-age Americans voted for him. Almost half of the class of '65 did not vote. I found these people to be not so much apathetic as cynical or unimpressed. What some consider to be vast differences between Democrats and Republicans are viewed by others as negligible.

If the class of '65 expects to enjoy better leaders, they will have to pay more attention to the actions of politicians and less attention to their words and images. Otherwise, if and when better leaders do appear, the generation won't be able to recognize them.

On the personal level, I found the class of '65 to be friendly, open, concerned. A number of people made a special point of mentioning to me the importance of friendship in their lives. Ten years ago, when I interviewed members of the class of '65, I found them, for the most part, to be in a state of flux. This time, in their late thirties instead of their late twenties, I found them to be more settled, not only in their work but in their emotional development. People had had time to reflect and to gain insights, a stage that will, I hope, be the first step on the road to wisdom.

A couple of people mentioned experiencing a midlife crisis, but on the whole that appeared to be a stage not yet reached. Yet according to lectures I have received from people in their forties, a slew of midlife crises would seem to be just around the corner.

Parenthood is now a major part of the lives of most members of the class of '65. In my travels, I even came across a few class-of-'65 grandparents. Although male involvement in child-rearing is increasing, parenting is still primarily the responsibility of women.

It is much too early to evaluate the children of the class of '65. With few exceptions, they are not old enough to vote or join the armed services, or even to show up in public-opinion polls.

I retain high hopes for the class of '65. Most of us have spent the last decade quietly building our lives. But a social conscience and a desire for "new ideas" remain just below the surface. I believe the generation would respond with great enthusiasm to a "leader" who advocates—and delivers—economic growth, a cleaner environment, emphasis on renewable energy sources, expanded national forests, traditional Tom Sawyer small-town values altered by respect for lifestyle diversity and ever-improved technology, greater peace in the world, a more active role in promoting human rights around the world, and a pride in the United States, not because it has a big army and big weapons but because it supports democracy instead of dictators and because it sets an example that others want to follow.

The class of '65 has done some wild and weird things as it has struggled through the first half of its life, but now it is on track and preparing for power. I repeat that I don't believe the class of '65 is any better or worse than any other generation, and that the book is far from being closed on the story of its journey. Ours was definitely a difficult period in which to have grown up, but I wouldn't have missed it for anything.

Despite all the excitement of the first half, I still see the second half of life as being more interesting, richer, and more full of challenges. The second half is the one in which we gain greater control over our lives and over the world around us. The second half is the one in which we might gain more understanding and more peace of mind. I have no doubt that our future will include many new problems, many disappointments, many frustrations. Nevertheless, I have seen enough good in people to have developed a nostalgia for the future, an eagerness to find out what comes next.